BOOKS BY RICHARD B. WRIGHT

Clara Callan
The Age of Longing
Sunset Manor
Tourists
The Teacher's Daughter
Final Things
Farthing's Fortunes
In the Middle of a Life
The Weekend Man

The Teacher's Daughter

The Teacher's Daughter

Richard B. Wright

A Phyllis Bruce Book
Harper*Perennial*Canada
HarperCollins*Publishers*Ltd

The Teacher's Daughter
© 1982 by Richard B. Wright.
© 2002 by R.B.W. Books Inc. All rights reserved.

A Phyllis Bruce Book, published by Harper-*Perennial*Canada, an imprint of HarperCollins Publishers Ltd

No part of this book may be used or reproduced in any manner whatsoever without the prior written permission of HarperCollins Publishers Ltd, except in the case of brief quotations embodied in reviews.

First published in hardcover by The Macmillan Company of Canada, Ltd, 1982. First paperback edition published by McClelland and Stewart–Bantam 1984. This paperback edition 2004.

HarperCollins books may be purchased for educational, business, or sales promotional use through our Special Markets Department.

HarperCollins Publishers Ltd
2 Bloor Street East, 20th Floor
Toronto, Ontario, Canada
M4W 1A8

www.harpercanada.com

National Library of Canada Cataloguing in Publication

Wright, Richard B., 1937–
The teacher's daughter / Richard B. Wright.

"A Phyllis Bruce book".
ISBN 0-00-639270-9

I. Title.

PS8595.R6T43 2004   C813'.54
C2003-905660-0

RRD   9 8 7 6 5 4 3 2 1

Printed and bound in the United States
Set in Sabon

TO PHYLLIS, CHRIS, AND ANDREW

The Teacher's Daughter

Part One

One

I

And now a word to the dear departed. While she fixes herself a salad plate for supper. It's too damn hot to cook anything, and besides, her sinuses ache. Outside, the heavy, warm air is laden with pollen. Standing at the kitchen counter she slices a tomato and composes a note to Travers.

> Dear Bastard:
> How are you? I am not so fine though the odds are on survival. Meantime, please drop dead. If you can't manage that, can you come back for an hour?
> Harper

Through her kitchen window she can look up and see beyond a hedge into the Bonners' backyard. Little puffs of blue smoke and now and then Bob Bonner's greying head emerge as he gets up from a chair to tend to the hamburgers. Barbecue night in the suburbs! And in a basement apartment you often see only part of your neighbours. Now, for instance, she can see only Bob's head and the top half of his cooking apron with the words "Turkey Power" across the chest. She can hear but not see Betty and the children, who are playing some kind of game. Betty Bonner is very big on playing games with the kids. And if Jan were outside they would almost certainly invite her over for a beer and one of Bob's hamburgers. Which she would have to eat with half a box of Kleenex. Goddamn this hayfever season!

Overhead, Mother's footsteps move from the bedroom to the bathroom. The floorboards creak. But living underground you get used to various noises: wood yielding to the pressure of a footstep, the muffled roar of a vacuum cleaner, a toilet draining and refilling. And now Mother is in the bathroom standing before the mirror. Tilting her birdy little head to one side and giving her stiff grey curls a final pat. At sixty-two she's a regular ball of fire. As they used to say. It wears you out to go shopping with her. Now she's on her way to the Friday Nite Club at the church. In a few minutes she'll stand at the top of the basement stairs and call down to me. She'll say, "Goodbye, dear. I'm off now." And how I wish that sometimes she would vary these farewells. Just for a blessed change. Maybe "Au revoir, kid." Or "Adios down there." Something! Anything! On the radio a lady announces a Beethoven piano sonata with Mr. Ashkenazy at the keyboard. Very nice too and I am going to have a glass of wine with this little meal.

Sitting on a stool at the kitchen counter, she wonders what it would be like to have the lady announcer's job. Sitting in a little booth listening to Beethoven and Mozart for a living. No more yakking about Prince Hamlet, or the uses of the apostrophe. No more illiterate essays on "My Favourite Movie" or "Why We Should Bring Back the Death Penalty." And speaking of essays, there are a hundred and twenty-five of the damn things arranged in four neat piles on the sofa in the living room. Murray's brainstorm, damn his eyes. "Let's get them writing something the first week so we can isolate the trouble spots and see just what we're up against." And at the departmental meeting on Thursday Jan had said, "I can tell you what we're up against, Murray. What we're up against are nine hundred illiterates who will be sitting on their butts all week waiting for Friday afternoon. That's what we're up against." There were disapproving looks from all, and Murray offered a sour smile. "Now Janice, my love, it's too early in the year for that kind of cynicism." And maybe so she now thinks, but one hundred and twenty-five times five hundred? How many words is that? And he wants them graded by next Wednesday! The term is only one week old and she feels worn out. However, this music is very nice. Well done, Ludwig! And I think I'm going to have another glass of plonk with these meager greens.

The wine is left over from Maxine's visit. Just a week ago Jan drove through the holiday traffic to the airport to pick up Max. The place was thronged with travellers and visitors, but there finally was Max, elbowing her way past people, heedless of the dirty looks that followed her. And hard to ignore at five feet ten and in a pantsuit the colour of tangerines. On her head was a kind of yellow ribbed turban. The old Carmen Miranda look! Also large gold hoop earrings. The whole get-up was outrageous and only Max could get away with it. Always had. Even in high school she wore crazy outfits. No angora sweaters and tartan skirts for Max. It had to be something outlandish. In those days she even wore pleated trousers and a shirt and tie. Twenty years ahead of everyone else. There were often great strings of beads or seashells around her neck. It was hard not to feel like a plain old starling beside this spectacular tropical bird.

In the airport Max set down her Gucci travelling case and a wicker basket filled with bottles while the old friends embraced. Then Max held Jan at arm's length and said loudly, "My God, Slim! How are you? Truth to tell, you look a bit washed-out."

"I am, old friend," said Jan, pressing Max's arms. "Pining away for love, I'm afraid." In fact, she was dying to tell Max about Travers. So, minutes later, stopped in heavy traffic on the Macdonald-Cartier Freeway, Jan spilled the beans. "It'll be three weeks this Sunday since he delivered the funeral oration. Quote. 'I'm going back, Harper. She wants me to come back. And I really miss the girls. I'm sorry.' End of quote." Maxine was fanning herself with an advertising flier that someone had thrown into the front seat at the airport. The late-afternoon air was foul with engine exhaust and Max seemed suddenly irritable. Jan wasn't sure her friend was even listening. Though the windows were open, the Honda was like an oven and Max was perspiring. Jan was about to say something when Max stuck her turbaned head out the window and screamed at the stalled traffic: "Get the fuck going, why don't you?" People stared. Here and there a smile or two appeared. Then Max looked across at Jan. "And what did you say to all that?" So she had been listening after all. "Oh, the usual thing," said Jan. "C'est la vie, my friend. Thanks for the memories. It was just one of those things. You can't beat those old songs when you want to come up with a cliché."

"And then, after he left, you bawled your eyes out for a couple of days. Right?"

"Something like that, yes."

Maxine fired up a long Menthol cigarette. "Well, what I say is fuck him, my dear. You're better off without him. Married men are poison. It's strictly a no-win situation for a woman. Actually, Slim, I thought you had more sense." She looked fed up. "Jesus Christ, this traffic is worse than Montreal's."

In the next lane a tractor trailer inched forward. The driver, a bearded character in his late twenties, grinned down at the two women. Behind his high cab the diesel stack smoked and vibrated. He looked amused by events and he called down to them, "Are you getting much, ladies?" Maxine looked up and said, "Why don't you go fuck your right hand, Earl?" It broke the guy up. He leaned his head on the steering wheel. Shoulders shaking with laughter. Beside himself with the mirth of it all. And, smiling, Jan thought, "Max, Max. You always did give the guys a hard time." In high school she was known as the flame-thrower. It had something to do with her red hair, but there was something sexual in it too. The boys had an ugly word for it. And Max was still at it. She referred to her divorced husband, now remarried and a successful advertising type out in Vancouver, as "my late husband." But Max was company when you've just been ditched by a great-looking guy who just happens also to be intelligent and funny. The son of a bitch!

When they finally reached the apartment, Maxine stepped from her clothes and, standing in Jan's small kitchen in bikini underwear, made a pitcher of martinis. They also drank a bottle of champagne with dinner and got a little bombed. No harm done. Jan hadn't seen her friend in months and longed to tell her more about Travers and their summer together. But Max was having none of it. "Spare me, child. I don't want to hear about yet another creep, however *wonderful* he was in the sack." About this she was serious, and when Jan thought more about it, she remembered. In high school Max was never interested in hearing about what boy was currently breaking your heart by ignoring your existence. As far as Max was concerned, it all interfered with basketball. So Jan shut up about Travers. Instead she asked Max about Montreal and her job. Outside in the warm dusk Betty Bonner called to her children. And sitting on the sofa Indian-fashion in a loosely flowing silk robe, Max frowned. She was a little drunk by then.

7

"Slim. It defeats me why you live out here in the sticks. I suppose all this suburban stuff is okay if you've got hubby and the two little ones down in the rec room. But God, it would drive me crazy living *alone* out here. I mean, I know your mom is upstairs and all that. But Christ!" She shook her head and sipped some wine. Looking at her, Jan felt a pang of annoyance. Why she lived the way she did was her own business. True, when her father was alive it made more sense. There were always books to talk about and notes to compare on school life. Each day he drove down to the city to the old collegiate in his stiff little Plymouth, while she headed for the suburban high school. Two or three evenings a week they had coffee together and talked about students and teachers and the imbeciles in the Ministry of Education.

After his death she often wondered about finding another place. But the thought of her mother's reaction always left her numb with apprehension. Could she bear the persistent whining that would inevitably accompany such a move? Maybe yes, maybe no. In any case, if Max thought it was dull, then too bad.

When Jan turned on a table lamp, she thought her friend looked old for thirty-six. At her age she shouldn't stay in the sunlight so long. By the end of the summer her skin had the leathery look of an old golf pro. But then Jan rebuked herself for being unkind. Max was, after all, her best friend.

The next morning they went shopping at the A&P with Mrs. Harper. Max looked sensational in a peasant blouse and dirndl skirt with sandals. On her slender brown throat lay a string of wooden beads. From Mexico. Big as ducks' eggs. She also wore hoop earrings and her hair was in a bandana. With the sunglasses, she looked like some movie tycoon's wife. In their jeans and shorts the suburban housewives stopped pushing their carts to stare at this exotic creature. Max was in excellent form too; she kept Jan's mother in hysterics. In the old days Mrs. Harper had disapproved of Maxine Ross. Max was too loud. Too flashy. Too forward. A favourite word at the time. "That one will have serious man trouble down the line," Mrs. Harper used to say. "You mark my words." But now, twenty years later, in the air-conditioned aisles of the A&P, she was tickled by Max's jokes. Flattered by the attention. Jan guessed it was Max's success that did it. Mrs. Harper is an old-fashioned Ontario Protestant. Such people can forgive you almost anything if you make it in business. And Max has made it. As a head buyer in one of Montreal's largest department stores, she is doing very well indeed. A big salary and glamorous trips to New York and London and Paris. Mrs. Harper often speculated on just what Max's salary might be; she even asked Jan from time to time. But Jan had no idea and guessed only that it was large. Certainly, for Mrs. Harper, Maxine Ross had turned out to be the most successful of "The Three Stooges" as she used to call them when they went to high school.

Later Max chilled a couple of bottles of Chablis; her wicker basket seemed endless. With the wine, she and Jan ate pears and Camembert. Talked about the old days at Eastview Collegiate. Over the years they kept returning to this territory. Still it was fun. Max and Jan were the two tallest girls in the school, with Ruth Dunlop a close third. The three of them were the heart of the Eastview Spartans who worked their magic on the high-school basketball courts of Toronto between 1959 and 1963. So, shamelessly nostalgic and mellow with the wine, they talked about those times. And about Ruth Dunlop. "Is she still married to that American?" asked Max. "The draft-dodger?"

"Seth?"

"That's the one. A biologist or something, isn't he? He always gave me the creeps."

"Well, yes she is," said Jan. Max could be heartless in her judgments. You couldn't exactly call Seth creepy; perhaps vague or absent would be more accurate. From time to time Jan visits the Calders. Their old brick home on Huron Street is worth a fortune. Yet they complain constantly about money. Seth, a large, shambling man, bearded like a Mormon and invariably dressed in sweaters and baggy cords, is striving to finish his doctorate in something or other. Jan can never remember just what; only that it has something to do with recycling waste material. And that it has been going on for years. Seth's parents come from upstate New York and are wealthy. Undoubtedly they have bought the old brick house near the university. Ruth harps all the time about the mortgage payments.

The Calders are big on jogging and natural foods. It's worth your life to ask for an ashtray. Oddly enough there is often illness in the family. The two children, a boy of six and a girl of eight, look pale and languid much of the time. The entire house has a peculiar farty smell to it. After five minutes you long to open a window. Ruth, a blocky, myopic girl in high school, is now even heavier in the shoulders. But what a guard she had been! In her kitchen twenty years later, wearing faded bib overalls, cross-strapped at the back over an old sweater, she boils water for Red Zinger tea and talks about the Women's Distress Clinic where she helps out two nights a week. Looking after battered women and runaway teenagers. Listening to her, Seth nods behind his whiskers, his soft brown eyes unfocussed. He always looks mildly bewildered. Thinking probably of his thesis. Jan sees him as a large, gentle

American child. At thirty-three years of age Seth has yet to hold a steady job.

One July evening Jan took Travers to the Calders' for dinner. Not a good idea! Travers and Seth were uneasy in each other's company; there was nothing to say, and while Ruth was preparing dinner, Jan tried frantically to fill in the silences. She felt she was babbling like an idiot. Ruth served them some vegetable concoction that tasted like straw; Seth's homemade wine left a film on your teeth. Jan checked this out later in the bathroom. Grinning fiercely into the mirror she saw her purple teeth. Like some kid who has just finished a grape Popsicle. Later Travers told her the Calders were bores and how the hell did she think he would enjoy such an evening. Jan admitted it was a mistake and suggested they go for hamburgers at Burger King. As Jan told this story, Max smiled. There was malice in her cold green eyes. She loves to hear such tales. There is something inherently nasty in Max. *Schadenfreude* is right up her alley.

The Sunday before Labor Day Jan drove Max back to the airport. Both of them were talked out and a little hung over. But in the airport they embraced again and spoke about another visit soon. Jan mentioned Christmas, but Max confided that she was thinking of a trip some place warm. With her lover! Out at last. Mentioned for the first time near the Air Canada ticket counter. And offered with Max's sly little smile that always announced mischief. Jan remembered her smiling like this after she spiked the punch with vodka at their Grade Twelve class party. "She's a wonderful little person, Slim," said Max grinning. "You'd like her. I know it. We've got to get together soon. The three of us I mean." Jan smiled. When they called Max's flight she kissed Jan's cheek and headed quickly for the first-class gate. She looked wonderfully happy, tall and slim in an ochre-coloured dress with a wide-brimmed straw hat on her head. She turned to wave a final time. And why shouldn't she be happy, thought Jan at the time. She's returning to someone she loves.

Now, sipping her wine, Jan wonders why she never saw Max that way before. Because when you think about it, well it fits. Her aloofness around boys in high school, her disastrous six-month marriage to the advertising man. But so what! To each his own. Better make that *her* own, Harper. Now she hears her mother's footsteps at the top of the basement stairs. "Goodbye, dear. I'm off now."

"All right, Mom," Jan calls. She shuts her eyes. Has to shout through her door. "Have a nice time." Jan listens as the side door opens and closes. A moment later she hears the ten-year-old Plymouth start up with a roar. And watch it, Mother, please, as you back down the driveway. Last week she nearly wiped out the Dicky Dee vendor as he pedaled his wagon past the house.

After her mother leaves, Jan rinses her few dishes and leaves them in the sink. Do the damn things tomorrow after breakfast. It's Friday night in the workhouse, as Dad used to say. Another good man gone from her life. And standing for a moment, listening to the music, she wonders if she shouldn't have gone out with Bruce tonight. After all, it is the first week of school, and following the excitement of opening day, the first week is a bummer. Sitting down on the sofa she absently rubs her calves. I'm just not used to being on my feet all day, and anyway, damn it, I'm out of shape. I should go to exercise class or take up kung fu or something this fall. Judy Barowski is forever after me to take up jogging. But all that running day after day; it's so boring. Speaking of which, there is Bruce Horton, who asked me to go to the movies tonight. Apparently the Film Society is offering a double bill. A couple of Second World War movies. *Flags Over Guadalcanal* or something. Van Johnson is in it. Van Johnson is one of Bruce's favorite actors. According to Bruce, Van has been neglected by the critics. Ye gods, Van Johnson! Poor Bruce. With his old movies and his antique cars and his comic-book collection and his mom, whom I first saw in the rear of a 1929 Packard touring car. Bruce was at the wheel as they pulled into the school parking lot two years ago last Sunday. I was preparing notes in my classroom and looking down; I couldn't believe my eyes. There was this ancient open automobile with a middle-aged man at the wheel. And in the back, a large, matronly woman in light-brown trousers and a beige field-jacket. A birdwatcher's outfit. On her head a fedora. The Packard looked like an old German staff car, and Mrs. Horton might have been a field marshal in the Wehrmacht. Were they acting out some World War II fantasy, I wondered? In fact, it was all very innocent. Bruce had been transferred from another school and was just showing his mother around. It was only a Sunday drive. Bruce! Bruce! Permanently locked into some summer afternoon at the movies in 1944. Weird when you think about it. Still, Bruce is the only bachelor over thirty on the staff, except for Ernie Perkins, who is exactly one year older than my mother. And Murray, of course. And Bruce is harmless enough. Someone to go to the Christmas party with. Or the Film Society meetings. Once he took me for a spin in his 1938 Nash. Just around the block, mind you, and on a Sunday morning when the traffic was light because, according to Bruce, you can't be too careful. Some old fool could run into you from behind. And replacing the tail light on a 1938 Nash is not easy. Bruce is a careful man. In the glove compartment of his everyday Toyota is a pair of scissors. Just in case he has an accident and the seat belt is jammed. Bruce is the kind of man who would never go to bed without putting shoe trees in his large, pebbled brogues. Bruce is very boring. But at least he is not a groper. No, I can't see Bruce Horton ever groping, though from time to time I've wondered why the man never tried to "feel me up" as we used to say in the locker room at Eastview Collegiate. Do kids still use that expression, I wonder? Probably not. These days everybody is going "all the way." Another one from the old locker room. Ye gods, there must have been ten girls who left school pregnant last year. But old Bruce has never even gone for a grab, God bless him. He just doesn't seem to have a sexual tremor in him. Now Travers! A different sort altogether. When we weren't in bed, we were laughing. We laughed an awful lot. He told me more than once that his wife has no sense of humor. Once he said, "I like you, Harper. You're funny and you're good company." Not exactly a resounding testament of eternal affection, but at least he didn't give me a lot of folderol about love. A forthright man, Travers. Now back with the Everlasting Bitch. Well, chum, you've made your bed, so lie in it. Though, damn it, I wish you were in mine tonight.

    The Bonner family has now gone in for an evening of television, and Jan wonders if there is anything worth watching. It's still mostly reruns, and anyway she should get started on those essays. She knows she'll feel better tomorrow if she can get a few of the damn things out of the way tonight. But first a glance at the paper. And out of habit the Companions Wanted section. Toronto seems to be filled with people looking for companions. *European gentleman in late forties. Non-smoker. Enjoys the outdoors. Looking for athletic lady in her thirties with similar interests. Please include snapshot.* A hearty type no doubt. Jan sees a burly Teuton, heavy-thighed in lederhosen. Good for at least ten miles before his Gatorade and granola. Such a type would move his barbells right into your bedroom. Scowl while you sip your Bloody Mary at Sunday brunch. And nein with the cigarettes. Probably grind them underfoot with his hiking boots. Auf wiedersehen, Heinrich.

And here is a woman who advertises herself as *a single attractive lady in her mid-thirties. Interested in books, theater, and quiet intimate times.* Quiet intimate times? Ye gods. Why not just say "Calling all sex maniacs!" But then, probably most of the women advertising are hookers. And most of the men are probably married and looking for a strange tumble. A new pasture to graze in.

Before starting the essays Jan goes to the kitchen and sticks her head in the freezer. The cold, smoking air helps clear her sinuses. Afterwards she swallows a couple of Sinutabs and in her old terrycloth robe settles down to work at the desk in her bedroom. When the telephone rings she guesses it's Murray Ford, who is still monkeying with the timetable and may have bad news for her. Like an extra five kids in each class.

The voice at the other end is male. Pleasant enough. A little hesitant. "Is that Miss Janice Harper?" And pray God he's not some weirdo who wants her to listen to him masturbate. This town is full of kooks. "Yes, this is Jan Harper." She affects her best no-nonsense schoolmarm voice.

"My name is James Hicks," says the voice. "We met last Monday night. At the Waggoners'. Diane Waggoner is my aunt. You probably don't remember me." Well, no pervert, thank God. And she does remember him. Young. Well, late twenties, maybe thirty. Very good-looking. Dark-haired. Lean and muscular. A blue-collar tough-guy look to him. He didn't have much to say and seemed lost among all the schoolteachers at Harry's party. He just stood there in the shadows near the patio, sipping beer. She can't even remember what they talked about. Or can she? Yes, they talked about jobs. At the moment he's out of work. That's it. "Yes, I remember," says

Jan. "We talked about jobs, didn't we? You were helping Harry finish his basement, weren't you?"

"That's it. Yes." He sounds pleased that she remembered. A long silence and then the man seems to be asking for a date. It's hard to tell because his words are jammed into a hurried mumble. "Wondering if you'd like to go out for a coffee? Or maybe a pizza? I don't know. Whatever you like." Jan is careful not to laugh, but the guy sounds like a fifteen-year-old asking for his first date.

"Well, I don't know," she says. What in Heaven's name would they talk about over a coffee? At the party he had so little to say and seemed so uncomfortable that she felt sorry for him. And why is he interested in her anyway? A good-looking man like him must know plenty of women. It's all very strange. "What don't you know?" he asks. He seems to be in a phone booth; Jan can hear traffic noises in the background.

"I mean about having coffee," she says. "Don't take offence but I don't really know you."

"Well, that's the idea of having a coffee with me, isn't it? Then you could get to know me."

Presumptuous, aren't you, thinks Jan. "Why would I want to do that?" she asks sharply.

"Do what?"

"Get to know you."

A long pause, and maybe that was a little sharp, Harper. After all, the guy asked you out for a coffee. You needn't sound so snooty.

"I'd like to get to know *you* better," says James Hicks. "Just a cup of coffee. We could go to Mister Donut. Or any place you like."

"Why do you want to know *me*, Mr. Hicks?" asks Jan.

"I like you."

"You don't even know me." They both suddenly laugh. "I

guess we're talking in circles," says Jan. But they hadn't talked more than five minutes at Harry's party! And then he disappeared. Said he was going for a beer or something and never returned. At the time she was certain she'd bored him.

"I thought I frightened you off last Monday night," Jan says.

"That's definitely not true," says Hicks. "You didn't frighten me off at all. I left because I didn't want you to think that I was going to take up all your time. The other people there . . . I had trouble talking to them, eh? I mean you're all schoolteachers . . ." He leaves it at that, and Jan feels herself agreeing with him. There *were* a lot of stuffed shirts at that party. Put a group of teachers together and they can make someone else feel very uncomfortable. "Well, maybe tomorrow then," she says.

"What?"

"Maybe tomorrow we could have coffee."

"Great. But I was thinking of tonight."

"That's absolutely out of the question. I'm busy."

"You got a date?"

"I don't really think that's any of your business, Mr. Hicks."

"Sorry. You're right. Call me James, eh? But not Jim. Or Jimmy. I really dislike the name Jimmy."

"All right," says Jan dryly, "we'll call you James. No use getting off on the wrong foot, is there?"

"What do you mean?"

"Nothing, James. Nothing at all."

Jan is suddenly tired of talking to James Hicks; she even feels a passing regret for having agreed to meet him for coffee. "What time tomorrow?" asks Hicks.

"Well, the morning is out," says Jan. "On Saturday mornings I go shopping with my mother." She doesn't know why she offers this information; it's really none of his business what she does on Saturday mornings. But he says nothing about it.

"What about three o'clock at Mister Donut? It's handy for both of us."

"How do you know where I live?" asks Jan.

"I asked my aunt."

"I see."

"Is Mister Donut okay with you?"

"I suppose so, yes."

"If you want to go to another place, you name it."

"No, Mister Donut is fine."

"What about three o'clock? Is that all right?"

"Yes. Three o'clock. Mister Donut."

"You got it."

"Fine, James."

"See you."

"Yes. Goodbye."

Jan hangs up the phone feeling vaguely uneasy. Wondering in fact why she agreed to all that. She should have gone to *Flags Over Guadalcanal* with old Bruce. Much less complicated. Perhaps tomorrow morning she could give Diane Waggoner a call and ask a discreet question or two about her nephew. But she knows she won't. Too damn awkward. Naturally Diane would want to know why I want to know about James Hicks. And then, face it, Harper, you don't really like Diane Waggoner and she doesn't like you. A person can sense these things. Maybe I'm jealous of her good looks. She's a terrifically handsome woman and she must be nearly fifty. And when I think about it, I can see the resemblance between her and her nephew.

Jan stares at the essay, but her mind is elsewhere. Her life seems suddenly and needlessly cluttered. And what is it with this year in my life anyway? 1980. The year of the Queen Bee. First there was Travers and now there is James Hicks. As unlike as night and day, except that they're both good-looking. Perhaps I'm emitting some special ray.

She is watching TV when she hears the Plymouth in the driveway. A moment later her mother calls down to her. "I'm home now, dear."

"Fine, Mother," shouts Jan.

"Would you like to come up for a cup of Sanka and watch the news with me?"

"No thanks, Mother. Not tonight." Jan's words seem to reverberate off the walls before traveling under the door and up the stairs."

"As you wish, dear," calls Mrs. Harper. "Goodnight."

"Goodnight, Mother."

On the screen they are still harping about the hostages in Iran. But Jan thinks only of James Hicks. What is it about her that he likes? It certainly can't be her looks. And she can't remember saying anything particularly witty to him. And if it comes to that, he doesn't seem the sort to appreciate much wit anyway. Or is she judging him too hastily? It all seems suddenly and unnecessarily complicated. "I should have gone to *Flags Over Guadalcanal*," she says aloud to the man reading the news on television.

2

When Hicks steps from the phone booth, he is elated. It wasn't all that difficult. You just have to set your mind to do something and then do it. The shopping plaza is filled with Friday-night business: husbands and wives are tucking grocery bags into the trunks of their cars; there is a heavy stream of customers over at Sears and Canadian Tire; all the hamburger places are busy. Standing by the phone booth, Hicks sniffs the warm, malodorous air. He likes the shopping plaza. Feels at home here and, though he has never told anyone, has even driven around the place on Sunday mornings when it's abandoned.

Now that he's asked her out for a coffee, Hicks feels he's entitled to a beer. He thinks of going to the bar at the Jade Gardens. It's nice there, but the beer is twenty cents more than most places. Still, it has more class than the Puss 'n' Boots Club where he usually does his drinking. But tonight the Puss 'n' Boots will be too crowded. Too smoky. So, instead, Hicks walks to his car feeling pretty good about things in general. Who needs beer anyway? It feels good just to be walking across the shopping-plaza parking lot on this warm September evening. Looking at the lighted stores. Watching the people. The only problem, as Hicks sees it, is the teenagers. To begin with, the plaza is filled with them on Friday nights. And then, sometimes, if they feel like it, the sons of bitches will run a key or a nail along the side of your car. Just for the hell of it. And that will cost you a hundred, a hundred and fifty, to fix. When he thinks about this Hicks's mood darkens. In fact he can see several teenagers standing around the front of Burger King. Hicks knows if he ever catches one of them pulling that stuff on his car, he'll kick his head in. Totally justified, too. Everybody's got a right to protect his own property. Even so, it makes no sense to park too close to those fast-food places, because even if you do kick the crap out of some guy, there's still the paint job to deal with. You're still looking at a hundred and fifty going out the window. So Hicks always parks his Trans Am a good distance from Harvey's and the Colonel's and places like that. Now he's back near the Color

Your World paint store. Right in line with all the family-type wagons and sedans.

Inside the Trans Am Hicks turns on the radio and listens to Merle Haggard singing "Misery and Gin." He listens to the song and thinks about Janice Harper and what he will say to her tomorrow afternoon at Mister Donut. And that is the problem as he sees it. Conversation! Worrisome, because of course she's a schoolteacher and knows a lot about different things. Not that all schoolteachers are that smart. For instance, Hicks is not so impressed with his Uncle Harry. His uncle teaches mathematics at the high school, but he doesn't necessarily talk like an educated man. Even Hicks can tell that his uncle doesn't know that much about proper grammar and things like that. Also, when they were laying tiles in the basement, Hicks had to show him a number of simple things. And in other ways he is not so sharp either. He cannot see, for example, that his wife is stepping out on him. Hicks only stayed in their house a few days and he could figure that one out. The phone calls she'd get and the look on her face when she said she was going to the Stop 'n' Shop for milk and stuff. Bullshit! You can tell when a woman is stepping out like that. His Aunt Diane is still a sexy woman for her age, and probably Harry isn't giving her enough. Hicks read in a magazine at the library that most men lose interest in sex after forty. That gives him only ten more years.

Thinking about Janice Harper, he has to admit that she doesn't appeal to him in the line of sex. She is no looker, that's for sure. In fact, she is very plain. Not ugly certainly. She has a pleasant enough face. But plain. Hicks guesses that very few men ask her out. She's still unmarried and she has to be somewhere in her thirties. That alone speaks for itself. But she's very intelligent. You can tell that after talking to her for five minutes. And she has a great sense of humor. In Hicks' opinion not many women have a sense of humor. He's known plenty of women who will laugh at a dirty story. But that's not the same as having a sense of humor.

Sitting there, Hicks listens to the radio and watches the people leaving the plaza. It's nearly dark, but to the west behind Sears the sky is still light and Hicks can see a single star. Very nice. On the radio Emmylou Harris sings "Blue Kentucky Girl." Hicks doubts whether Janice Harper would like Emmylou Harris. Probably she likes classical music. But that's all right; he can listen to some of that now and then. The really big obstacle tomorrow is going to be the conversation. You've got to have something in common to talk about or what's the use. Again Hicks wonders whether he should go for a beer. He wouldn't mind, but the money situation is tight too. On Monday he gets his unemployment insurance check, but until then he has maybe thirty dollars. Ridiculous! What can you do with thirty fucking dollars? Nevertheless he thinks that maybe if he squeezed it, he could take her to a movie tomorrow night. Or maybe Chinese food at the Jade Gardens if she preferred. A dinner for two is, he thinks, about twelve dollars. With a couple of beers and tip he might get out under twenty. Still, it would be tight. He'll need gas before Monday, and he has to eat over the weekend. He tried to remember what there is to eat in the apartment. A couple of frozen ravioli dinners. Some bread and eggs. Milk. Jesus Christ. The whole situation has got to be improved.

Thinking about tomorrow, Hicks decides to forget about the movie or dinner. It can't be worked out in the money line. Instead he could buy her something. A little present. It would be a way to start the conversational ball rolling. He could, for instance, buy her a book. After all, she's an English teacher, so she must like reading. He could buy her a paperback book of poems tomorrow at Browse 'n' Buy. Poems, thinks Hicks, would be perfect. A very good idea! Starting up the Trans Am, he gives the gas pedal a few extra taps. Listens, pleased, as the dual pipes throb. The big velour dice sway from the rearview mirror and Hicks cranks up the radio for a better listen to Dolly Parton singing "Old Flames Can't Hold a Candle to You." Without knowing why, Hicks likes other people, total strangers, to know what he's listening to on his car radio. So now Dolly is booming out through the open windows and across the parking lot. Near Burger King, Hicks burns a little rubber as he gears down and then swings hard to the right and accelerates. The Trans Am shoots diagonally across the parking lot like a lighted arrow. The teenagers standing around the hamburger place watch it go.

Driving south on Crown Hall Road, Hicks considers topics for conversation with Janice Harper. For a start there will be books and movies. He will make a list. Inspired by the idea, he pulls out and guns the Trans Am past a poky old Impala. At Iroquois Avenue he runs the orange, thinking maybe he'll hit the sack early. Work out for fifteen minutes and then bed. He'll do some set-ups and some high kicks. A half-dozen sets of ten reps. As far as Hicks is concerned, staying in shape is absolutely vital.

Two

I

On Saturdays, after shopping, Jan and her mother eat lunch together in Mrs. Harper's kitchen. As they eat, Mrs. Harper glances through the *National Enquirer*, which she buys each week at the A&P check-out. Mrs. Harper enjoys reading about other people's troubles and the possibility of major disasters. Thus, celestial interference in human affairs and the blemishes of the show-biz famous are meat and drink to her. She is always on the alert for new information on geological faults in the earth's crust, fresh UFO sightings, miracle cures for the body's ailments, and scandal in high places.

Today, as they eat their tuna-fish sandwiches, she reads aloud from an article on prostate cancer. "Listen to this, dear. It says that this clinic near Phoenix, Arizona, reports a ninety-perfect recovery rate. Now isn't that amazing!" She stops reading and light reflects off her glasses as she stares away, her mind fastened on the injustice of life in general. "If only they'd had something like that when your dad was alive." The death of her husband nearly three years ago remains a perpetual mystery to Lillian Harper, a cosmic impropriety that can never be excused. Death, it seems, is something that should happen in other people's households. And so she feels forever put upon when she thinks of her husband's death. But, listening to her, Jan reflects that Lorne Harper would have scoffed at anything in the *National Enquirer*. He was too skeptical and intelligent to swallow any of that guff. And looking across at her mother, Jan again wonders how her father ever put up with this nice bird-brained little woman for thirty-six years. But he loved her. Oh yes, he did. She exasperated him nearly every day of his life, and he retreated into his study of history. But for all that, he loved her. Mysterious!

From her mother's kitchen window she can see Bob Bonner washing his Pontiac. He stands on tiptoe to take long swipes at the roof with his chamois. A waste of time too, thinks Jan, because it's bound to rain before long. The warm, grey afternoon air seems oppressive. Perhaps a thunderstorm will lighten the pressure. The pollen count today must be astronomical, because her nose feels like a raw wound and both eyes are swollen. Giving me a decidedly odd, simian look. And, Mr. James Hicks, you sure ain't going to see me at my best today. Not that my best is anything to write home about. But these eyes of mine aren't going to help one bit. Perhaps I should wear shades. Sunglasses in a rainstorm. That would look very sharp, Harper. And again she wonders why she agreed to have coffee with this guy. Who is he anyway, besides Harry Waggoner's nephew? Maybe she should just forget about it. A no-show. But I know I can't do that, because the truth is I am hopelessly old-fashioned and believe in keeping my word. I blame my father for this failing. For Brutus was an honorable man. Which reminds me that I must take another look at old Julius C. some time over the weekend. I'll start 10A Monday morning with the tapes. Meantime there are those essays. This morning she had looked at the A&P cashier with envy. Tonight *she* can put her feet up and watch *B.J. and the Bear*.

Mrs. Harper is again reading from the *Enquirer*, and as she reads she shakes her head of tight grey curls. This piece is on a TV talk-show host who, it seems, is overly fond of teenage girls. Young teenage girls. Say, about thirteen. To Jan's mother these show-biz types are a constant source of bewilderment. "I would never have believed that of him," she says. "Why, the man has a family!" Jan finishes her tea and looks out at Bob Bonner, who waves to her. Long ago she gave up trying to talk to her mother about the perils of believing tabloid gossip. As far as Mrs. Harper is concerned, if it's in print, it must be true. Or mostly true. Where there's smoke, there's fire, etc., etc. So, these Saturday lunches can be a trial. Thank God for her little apartment downstairs.

It was not always so. For a while, after graduation, she lived upstairs with her parents. But it didn't work out, and after a few months she moved in with Max and Ruth downtown. Ye gods, that was the fall of 1968. And they welcomed her with open arms. Already, after only a few weeks, they were getting on one another's nerves. They were looking for a referee. But the apartment was terrific. A new building with a view southward to Lake Ontario. They were on the top floor and below them were the dockyards and the rail lines and waterfront warehouses of Toronto. You could pass hours watching the toy trains chug along the tracks or the ferries crossing to Centre Island. The rent was crazy, but so what. They were "making it" as Max said, striding around the place barefoot, in jeans with a poncho over her shoulders. Even indoors she wore a big floppy hat. Sometimes an old fox fur. They had no furniture to speak of and so sat cross-legged on cushions and drank Chianti. Coughed their way through their first joints. Three chicks from Eastview Collegiate. On their own at last.

On the night Jan moved in, Max bought a bottle of champagne. "We've got it made, guys." She was writing catalogue copy for Eaton's, while Ruth worked in a medical lab at Toronto East General. Jan's first teaching job was only minutes away at a downtown school. At night they sat around listening to Peter, Paul, and Mary. Pete Seeger. Bob Dylan. On Sundays they attended peace rallies at Nathan Phillips Square and marched on the American Embassy to protest the war in Viet Nam. But the following spring Max moved to a better job in Montreal and then Ruth met Seth Calder and that was that. Two or three other friends from university were already married. So Jan moved back to the suburbs and a job at Scarborough Secondary.

When she came back it was only on condition that she have her own place. Her father agreed. "It's only sensible," he said. "You're entitled to live your own life. Have some privacy. Your mother and I understand that." But her mother didn't understand at all. She failed to see why Jan couldn't live upstairs. She could even use Bobby's old room as a study. Why waste money on a basement apartment? And the mess! But all that summer, workmen sawed and hammered and tore up the plumbing of the new house Lorne Harper had moved into only three years before. After a lifetime on Beech Avenue in east Toronto. For years his wife had pestered him about a move from that old, dark city house to the suburbs. So here they were at last. In a ranch-style bungalow being violated by Italians wielding hammers and saws. Watching the workmen chop a new door into the side of the house by the carport, Lorne Harper said only, "Well, in the long run it will probably improve the value of the house." But his eyes looked worried and unconvinced. And his wife thought she would lose her mind trying to keep ahead of things in the cleaning department. Brick dust filled the air and sifted through windows and doors to coat everything. It was tracked into the bedrooms and the living room, where Mrs. Harper ran the vacuum cleaner virtually all the time. But though he looked worried in the midst of all this chaos (for he hated disorder of any kind), Lorne Harper was happy. His daughter was back! And so there would be somebody to do crosswords with and talk to about his beloved history. Which he'd been teaching since 1934.

And Harper you still miss him, damn it! Still remember the night three years ago when she awakened to hear him crying out in anguish. Terrifying to hear your father so afflicted. A man who never once in his life complained of anything physical. Not so much as a headache. But rushing upstairs she found him—the proud and aloof history teacher—on his hands and knees. Weeping on the bathroom floor with his pyjamas still around his ankles. Saw for the first time her father's pale, thin buttocks. Saw in his face beyond the pain to his terrible humiliation. And in the toilet bowl the bloodied urine. Evidence of the vile disease. Her mother was literally wringing her hands and crying while she paced back and forth in her floral-cotton housecoat. And then ambulance sounds and big uniformed men moving him out of the house on a stretcher. A ghastly night.

She visited him every day. He was working through a long and difficult book on the debasement of Roman currency and the subsequent fall of the Empire. Also, he was looking at *Grimm's Fairy Tales* and rereading, for perhaps the hundredth time, *Huckleberry Finn*. Very tired most of the time and he often fell asleep in the middle of a conversation. Jan guessed it was the drugs. Still there were jokes between them right to the end. He died the first week of January and they took him to the cemetery on a cold, sunlit day, passing, as they went, the trucks that were gathering old Christmas trees from in front of house. Jan still feels certain that would have amused him.

• • •

Now, looking across at her mother who is reading, Jan wonders what they saw in one another. How can you ever understand the mysteries of the heart? She remembers seeing an old snapshot taken shortly after her parents' marriage in 1942. Her mother was in a kind of tennis outfit. A full skirt and jumper. White socks and sneakers. Blonde ringlets. A pretty little thing who looked saucy. Full of ginger. And her father, thin and tall and serious in baggy trousers and dress shirt, the sleeves rolled past the elbows. The thirty-year-old history teacher, squinting into the sun of a summer's day. Now Lillian Harper looks up from her paper.

"And what are your plans for today, dear?"

"Well, Mom, I have to go out to Plaza Drugs. I'm out of antihistamines. I forgot to pick some up this morning."

"Well, you certainly do look stuffed up. I wish you'd go and see Dr. Han and get those shots. Norma Henderson had those shots and she's never had any trouble since." They've been through all this many times before.

"I hate needles, Mom. You know that. Maybe this weather will break soon."

"Well, I certainly hope so. I hate to see you stuffed up like that. It is awfully muggy." She looks away. "But then I hope we don't have frost too soon. The winters are so long." She is preparing, thinks Jan, to complain about loneliness. Instead she asks about Sunday dinner with Bobby.

"He's coming over to pick me up at three. Why don't you come along?"

"I don't think so, Mom. You know Bobby and I always get into some senseless argument. Who needs the aggravation?"

Mrs. Harper looks sorrowful. "How I wish you two didn't carry on so! I often wonder how a brother and sister can be so different!" She pauses to consider this anomaly. "I used to ask your father about that. He was supposed to be the smart one in the family." There's a hint of reproach in her voice. Now she says, "I don't think Bobby and Marjorie are getting on. There's a strain in that household. You can feel it when you walk in the door. You can see it in the children." All this is true, but Mrs. Harper conveys the information as though it were fresh. In fact it has been going on for years. Jan is certain that no reasonable person could live with her brother for very long. And Marjorie is not the most reasonable person in the world. It's to her credit, however, that she's stuck it out this long. But then they both seem to be staying together for the sake of the children. Jan is tired of hearing about Bobby and Marjorie and her two nieces, who, sad to report, she doesn't like very much. They really are spoiled and disagreeable little girls. Thinking about her brother and his wife and their two children, Jan finds herself growing mildly annoyed. However, her mother won't quit. "You should really come along, Janice. Bobby is always asking about you. You haven't eaten Sunday dinner with them in months." Five months to be exact. Easter Sunday. And a disaster. She and Bobby got into the usual nonsensical argument. About what? Politics? Religion? The economy for God sakes? She can't even remember, and it doesn't matter anyway.

"I'll see how I feel tomorrow, Mom. Okay?"

"I wish you would, dear. It would be so nice if we all sat down to a family dinner again. I know your father would have wanted that."

Jan feels sorry for her mother when she talks like this. Her mother has organized her entire life around a family that has always been quarrelsome. Jan and Bobby were always fighting in the old house on Beech Avenue. Or Bobby and his father. Or Jan and her mother. Sometimes both parents. Everyone except Jan and her father, who usually sided with each other. But those awful wars! Followed by slammed bedroom doors and long, ominous silences that sometimes stretched into days. Even weeks. God bless our happy home. Yet Mother could never figure out why everyone couldn't get along. Even though she herself is as stubborn and argumentative as they come. On the other hand, she gets most of her ideas about family life from *The Waltons* and *Little House on the Prairie*.

Mrs. Harper now gets up to clear away the lunch dishes. "Do you want me to help you with these, Mom?" asks Jan.

"No, no, dear. You run along. I'll be just fine." There's a slight whine in her voice. A suggestion of sacrifice and painful duty. But then, Saturdays are her worst days. After the morning shopping there is little to do. No church, and no soap operas on the tube.

So Jan escapes to her apartment. And in her own living room feels again oppressed by the heavy, brooding afternoon. Even indoors the grey, heated air seems to press against her skin. Or is it simply that I must now prepare to meet a man, when in fact I'd prefer to just stay home with my feet up and crack some of these essays.

But in the shower, feeling the warm water rinse away the days' grime, she admonishes herself. Harper, this is exactly what happens to middle-aged broads like you. You can't be bothered to put on a face and go out. It's so much easier just to stick around the apartment and putter away a Saturday. And then first thing you know, bingo! You've puttered all your Saturdays away and you're not thirty-six, you're fifty-six. An aging spinster with dry palms. An old, dry maid. Un-made. Like Norma Kirstead. With heavy walking shoes and good stout ashplant for the Sunday birding. Where's your sense of adventure, woman? A cup of coffee with a good-looking guy? And that may be a problem. He's too damn good-looking and that's always trouble. Not that I've had that much experience with good-looking men. But I've heard there's nearly always something wrong with them. A fatal flaw! Not tragic, just annoying. Calculating? Vain? Of course. A sex fiend? Well, come on, Harper, he can't rape you by the coffee urn in Mister Donut. Or am I just having an old maid's fantasy?

Under the pouring water she examines her pale skin, her freckled arms and shoulders. How she hated those freckles when she was young! Now they no longer seem that important. You'll have to take me as I am, James Hicks. Swollen eyes, red nose, and a freckle here and there. And I'm going to give you my down-home country look. I'll wear denims and that blue-and-white-checked shirt. Hell, it's only a coffee. As the water drums along her spine she remembers other showers when she was preparing herself for Travers. Ah, Travers! Well, I just hope that bitch is giving you the business now for not cleaning out the garage. Or something. But what a funny man he was! Is? And how easy it was to talk to him! Thinking about this, she again wonders what on earth she can talk about with James Hicks.

2

The weather is really weird, thinks Hicks, as he looks out his window at the parking lot. The afternoon is now heavy and dark. All the cars along Shaver Road have their lights on, and in the bathroom Hicks has to switch on his light to see. The bathroom walls are covered in posters of Bruce Lee kicking and chopping away. Surrounded by these menacing pictures, Hicks checks himself out in the mirror. He hasn't had a haircut for three weeks, but it doesn't look too bad. Besides, his thick black hair always looks better when it's a little on the long side. But he's shaved carefully and clipped the hairs in his nose. Tapped on a little Aqua Velva. Not too much. The last thing you want is to smell like one of those fucking Wops who turn up Friday nights at the Puss 'n' Boots Club. Dirt still under their fingernails. Fucking dummies don't know any better.

Hicks is wearing a pair of grey slacks. Only slightly flared. Plus a dark-green shirt, short-sleeved and open at the throat. A dark-grey sports jacket. Basically he sees it as a conservative look. Not too dressy, but not too casual either. This outfit he bought off the rack at Tip Top three weeks ago. Just before Manpower sent him across town to Vertical Knitwear, who advertised an opening in their shipping department. However, when he got there, nothing doing. They kept him waiting a half-hour, and then this old bitch in the personnel department told him he didn't have enough experience in the shipping line. She went on about Manpower sending out the wrong people and wasting everybody's time. As if that was his fault!

Later in the parking lot he brooded he brooded on the fact that he still owed Tip Top a hundred and seventy-five for the clothes. Sitting there and thinking about this plus the wasted morning and the gas used, he felt like burning down the fucking factory with the old bitch in it. However, when he got back to the apartment he calmed down. Drank a few beers and thought about it. There's no percentage in burning down places like Vertical Knitwear. No matter how strongly you feel about things.

Dressed to go, Hicks now walks around his apartment in the darkening afternoon, cracking his knuckles. He hates waiting for anything and it's only twenty minutes to three. He knows he can make Mister Donut in seven minutes without pushing it. Also he feels a restless and intense dislike for this cluttered little apartment where he has to pull out the sofa to make a bed. Sleeping in the living room! Fucking ridiculous. The place needs cleaning too. You couldn't bring a decent woman into this place and expect her to be impressed. Pacing around the apartment he resolves to get at this cleaning one day soon. At the window he watches, dismayed, as the late-summer storm erupts. Over the plaza to the north, a great jagged fork of lightning pierces the sky. Moments later Hicks listens to his windows vibrate from the thunder. The windows are now also streaked with rain, and soon it's coming down harder, so that leaning against the window he can see the rain beating hard on the pavement of the parking lot. A downpour! And this morning he took the Trans Am over to the auto wash on Industrial Road. Wash and hot wax! Four-fifty! Now it's going to piss all over it! What kind of fucking luck do you call that?

After the car wash Hicks went over to the plaza and bought a paperback book of poems in Browse 'n' Buy. He didn't know what kind of poems she might like and he spent a lot of time looking around the poetry section. Most of it you couldn't understand. He remembered from his English teacher in Grade Ten that a lot of poetry was just symbols and stuff. Something meaning something else. Confusing. Still, he liked English in Grade Ten and even now he doesn't mind a little poetry, providing that you can understand what's going on. Most of it is probably written by faggots, but so what? Some of it is still okay. In the end a saleslady helped him out by suggesting that his friend might like something by some guy named Rod McKuen. She said he was very popular with women. So Hicks bought a copy of a book called *Celebrations of the Heart* and for the rest of the morning he glanced through it. And he had to admit that the saleslady had been right. Some of the guy's stuff wasn't bad at all. Hicks especially liked one called "August Rainbow" and he read it over several times.

> *And after every summer rain*
> *an August rainbow*

> *sunlight in the good green wood*
> *laughter in the town*
> *shelter in the noontime shadows*
> *or here inside each other's arms*
>
> *No one can kill our rainbows*
> *though sometimes the world*
> *seems bent on trying.*

Nice! And true enough, too, thought Hicks when he read it over. It's not hard to see what the guy is getting at. How two people in love have to appreciate the beautiful things in life because most of the rest of the world doesn't. The poem made a lot of sense to Hicks.

On his way out of the apartment he slips the book of poems into his jacket pocket. But it makes a bad bulge and spoils the shape of the garment. Still, he doesn't feel like being seen holding a book of poetry. And he doesn't own a raincoat. Never had any use for one. In the lobby, however, he gets a break. The heavy rain slackens for a few moments and Hicks sprints to his car through a light drizzle. But the storm is not over, and another flash of lightning is followed by a tremendous clap of thunder. A close fucker, thinks Hicks, starting up the car. The truth is he's never liked storms. All that lightning and banging around makes him edgy. When he was a kid, a bad thunderstorm could scare the shit out of him. And still, though he doesn't like to admit it, he feels some fear. Now he watches as the rain comes down again with immense force. Somewhere a siren starts up.

It's a bitch driving in this rain, but Hicks has the road nearly all to himself. Most drivers have pulled off into service-station lots or gone up side streets to wait things out. Along the street the gutters are running fast and deep with the overflow. Only a few cars with their lights on crawl northbound along Crown Hall Road. When he reaches the plaza, he can see that the parking lot is half empty. Just a few people here and there running for cover. He watches a woman holding a cellophane thing against her head as she runs toward her car. It's exactly five minutes to three when he pulls up in front of Mister Donut. No one else is around, so he stays put. No use getting soaked; then you have to sit there wiping your face and hair with paper napkins. It doesn't look good. So he sits in the car, listening to the static on the radio and waiting for the rain to ease a little. And again, like a tap being turned off and on, the rain does let up. Hicks takes advantage of it and runs for the doughnut place.

Inside there is only one customer, an older guy who sits at a corner table reading the *Sun*. Behind the counter is a young chick, maybe eighteen, who stands there looking out at the storm. When she sees Hicks, she smiles.

"That's coming down hard out there," she says.

"Yeh. Really." Hicks orders a black coffee with double cream and a plain doughnut. With the fancy kind you can get sugar and crumbs all over the corners of your mouth. Looks like hell unless you can remember to keep wiping your mouth with a paper napkin. Once he saw a guy on a date with this good-looking chick. They were in a restaurant, and this guy was eating cream pie. And a chuck of the stuff stayed in the corner of his mouth throughout the entire conversation. It really looked fucking stupid, and the guy didn't have enough brains to wipe his mouth. And you could tell that the girl was disgusted but didn't want to say anything.

Hicks figures the little blonde with the ponytail expects him to sit down at the counter and talk to her. Instead he takes his coffee and doughnut to a table at the front, where he sits by the window. Here he can look out through the streaked glass at the wet, abandoned parking lot. There's another fantastic crack of thunder and the counter-girl jumps a little. Even the guy in the corner looks up from his *Sun*. "That was close," says the girl to Hicks. They listen to more siren sounds. Hicks nods and looks away through the wet glass. Normally he would chat up the little blonde. He's picked up a few chicks this way and she's not bad looking. But she's too young and probably dumb. Or why would she be serving coffee and doughnuts? Hicks is tired of women like her. Besides, he's a bit on the nervous side, though careful not to show it. Maybe, after all, Janice Harper won't show up. It's a rotten day and, when he thinks about it, she didn't sound all that enthusiastic on the phone last night. Hicks hates the thought of being stood up. He can't remember it ever happening to him, though there's always a first time. Thinking about this, he stares glumly out the window at the rain. He knows the blonde is studying him in an approving way, and it feels good to be stared at like that. It goes to show you how important it is to take care of yourself physically. As far as the physical side of things goes, Hicks figures he's way ahead of most guys his age. So, if Janice Harper doesn't show up, maybe he'll talk to the little blonde. To pass the time. You never can tell what will happen. Yet he knows it won't be the same. And when he dwells on it he feels vaguely depressed. In his jacket pocket the book of poems lies like a dead weight.

3

Southbound traffic is stopped at Crown Hall Road and Belmont. The light is green but things are held up by fire trucks hurrying eastward along Belmont, their bells and sirens rending the air. The voices of catastrophe, thinks Jan. Drowning out even the thunder that is rumbling around Scarborough skies this afternoon. After the trucks pass, traffic moves cautiously forward. The storm is traveling around to the south over the city and the lake. Already the sky overhead is brightening, but behind the plaza, to the south, it is dark as night, and now and then shards of lightning break forth. A great electrical show if you don't get zapped by one of those bolts, thinks Jan inside her Honda.

Her mother thought she was crazy to go out in this weather. As the storm approached, Mrs. Harper was busy preparing for the worst. Shutting windows. Pulling out all the electrical plugs. *And please don't anyone stand by the piano!* No explanation was ever offered to support this eccentric advice, but it was always uttered in the house on Beech Avenue in the midst of lightning and thunder. As a child Jan would look wonderingly into the parlour at the old Heintzman, half terrified yet half hopeful that she would be vouchsafed the spectacle of this grand old instrument being demolished by lightning. The old, dark wood splintered and smoking. All those piano wires unsprung. A mess of metallic spaghetti. Something to tell her friends. In those times, if a thunderstorm appeared in the night, Mrs. Harper always awakened her children and made them get dressed. She could never, however, persuade her husband to leave his bed. But with all the racket going on and his family hurrying half-dressed to the front hall, he could not sleep. And so, calmly, he read through it all, turning on his bedside lamp to squint at a few pages of Marcus Aurelius. An elegant paragraph or two by Gibbon. As far as he was concerned, being struck by a heavenly bolt was not such a bad way to go. Vastly amused by his wife's fussy precautions, he would bellow between the rolls of thunder, "Repent, ye sinners, for the end is near." And still, twenty-five years later, Mrs. Harper gets up in the night during a thunderstorm and sits in the living room in her plastic raincoat. So, today, when she heard Jan's car starting up, she hurried around to the side door and peered through the screen at her daughter. Fat raindrops were already splattering the driveway. "What on earth are you going out now for, Janice? There's going to be a terrible storm. Look at that sky!" Jan had rolled down the window and waved. "It's all right, Mom. I'll be fine. A car is supposed to be the safest place in a storm." Was that true? She thought she'd read it somewhere. One of those pieces of information that you're vaguely aware of having accepted as the truth. However, she didn't understand the physics of it; it must have something to do with being on rubber.

The shopping plaza is half filled with cars as most people sit tight and wait for the storm to pass. The only other car in front of Mister Donut is a preposterous-looking black job. Does that thing belong to him? She thinks she can now remember seeing it parked in Harry Waggoner's driveway last Monday night. What is it anyway? A Trans Am. She can see the name now across the back. As she pulls alongside she can also see that on the hood there is some sort of red design. It looks a bit like an eagle with wings outspread. And what's all that in aid of, I wonder? Symbolic, I suppose. Masculine power. Virility. Ho hum. And ye gods, are those actually velour dice hanging from the rearview mirror? And a fake leopard-skin interior. Wonderful! She sits for a moment and listens to the thunder rolling away to the south. The rain, too, is letting up, and the plaza is coming back to life as people leave stores and start up their cars. She waits another moment and takes a deep breath before getting out of the Honda.

Inside he is seated at a table near the windows, and he watches unsmiling as she approaches. Behind the glass case of doughnuts the little blonde with the ponytail looks puzzled as Jan walks over to Hicks's table. Before sitting down she takes off her raincoat and shakes the water from it. And thank God for this short, straight hair of mine because a few raindrops mean nothing to these poor strands. "Hi," she says, hanging up her coat. Hicks has stood up. "Hi." Still unsmiling and serious as a young priest, though in that get-up he could be working for the mob. And there's something bulging in his jacket pocket. A gun, perhaps? As she sits down Hicks asks, "How do you like your coffee?"

"One milk, please," says Jan.

"You want anything to eat?"

"No thanks."

"You sure?" he asks, frowning.

"Quite sure, thanks."

He is still frowning as he walks across to Blondie, who is, as they say, agog. And no wonder! He is a terrific-looking man. He may dress like a hood, but no question about it, Harper, he's a doll. And little Blondie can hardly keep her eyes off him; she has trouble pouring my coffee. No doubt she is wondering what this good-looking guy is doing with the flat-chested Plain Jane in the denims and check shirt. And I think I remember that little number from a couple of years ago. I didn't teach her but she was in Grade Ten. Dropped out in the middle of the year. Maybe she even remembers me as one of those old-maid schoolteachers. Well, up yours too, Blondie! Still, Harper, you can't blame the child for wondering.

Hicks carries her coffee like an offering. There's an old-fashioned courtliness in the way he places it before her. Oddly touching. As he sits down, Jan studies his face. Extraordinary brown eyes, but his skin is a little sallow. Perhaps diet! He looks like a man who eats on the run. Under the Chinese lanterns at Harry's party I didn't really get a good look at his guy. But now I can see Diane Waggoner in him. Diane is a looker. Always driving the men crazy at staff parties. And an ugly rumor has it that she's stepping out on Harry. And, Mr. Hicks, one of us had better start talking! I feel as if I'm back in one of those gumwood booths at Waller's Drug and Variety on Danforth Avenue. 1959. I'm fifteen years old and having my first Coke with Herman Kaplinsky. Who, as I recall, said not ten words, but just stared around as though expecting to be either arrested or assaulted. And now James Hicks sits there staring out the window while I look at him. Behind the doughnut case Blondie looks at both of us. This is ridiculous, Harper. Say something to the man. But then he asks her if she's sure she wouldn't like something to eat. Jan again says she's not hungry.

"You're sure now?" he asks.

"No food, thanks," says Jan, reaching into her bag for a Kleenex.

The storm has cleared the air but her nose is still stuffed. Watching her, Hicks looks concerned. "You got a cold?"

"No," says Jan, blowing hard. "Allergies. Ragweed. It's the season for it."

"That's too bad," says Hicks softly.

"It's a nuisance once a year," she says.

The door opens and a family enters. A man, a woman, three little kids, all wet and noisy. They are charged up by the storm and, excited and talkative, they gather in front of the doughnut case. Jan watches them for a moment and then turns back to Hicks, who has placed a book on the table. "I bought you a little present," he says. "A book of poems. I figured you'd probably like poetry." Jan picks up the book and wordlessly leafs through it. *Celebrations of the Heart*. By that bearded California beachboy. An old hipster who probably knocks off these little verses as he walks barefoot along the seashore. With Jonathan Livingston Seagull perched on his head. But Harper, be nice! The man has just given you a gift.

"Thank you very much," she says. "But why would you buy me a book of verse, Mr. Hicks?"

"Call me James," says Hicks.

"All right then, James. Now why did you buy this book for me, James? I mean, you don't even know me. It seems rather unusual."

"Well, I want to know you," says Hicks, looking again out the window.

"Why?" asks Jan.

Hicks looks back at her and frowns. "Why what? Why do I want to get to know you? What kind of a question is that? Are you fishing for a compliment or something?"

Jan smiles and raises her coffee cup in a mock toast. "Touché." Hicks still looks stern. Does he ever smile she wonders?

"Why does anybody want to get to know anybody else?" he asks. "I like you. I enjoyed talking to you at Harry's party the other night. I thought we might become friends." He looks away. "I'd like to take you out on a real date. You know, maybe dinner and a movie. Something like that."

And this is really incredible. Are my stars in conjunction this year or what? First there was Travers and now there is James Hicks. Both handsome devils. But Travers! At least we had something in common. We could talk about his sample case full of textbooks. And we did until there were other more interesting things to do. But Mr. Hicks with his muscle car. Another type altogether. "I don't know what to say, James," she says.

"You don't sound very enthusiastic." He sounds offended. A touchy type, she decides.

"Maybe it's because I'm not a schoolteacher or a lawyer or something. Is that it?" His eyes are now fixed directly on her. In fact, he looks ready for a bit of a fight.

"No, of course not," she says, lighting a cigarette. She notices his mildly disapproving look.

"Well, what's the problem then?" he asks.

"There isn't any problem," she says, thinking of at least a dozen. Starting with what do we have in common? And ending with what do we have in common? And in between the suspicion that he might just possibly be carrying a spring knife in his pants. Not to mention that he's got a few years on you, Harper. You're not exactly robbing the cradle, but I'll bet my thesaurus he's not yet celebrated his thirtieth birthday. Still, is it not fashionable to go out with younger men? Don't you read about this kind of thing in the Sunday papers? Can it just possibly be that you're worried about how things will look? Your mother's daughter after all! *What will the neighbors think?* How many times had she heard that in her lifetime?

The place is starting to fill up and they both watch the customers coming and going. Then Hicks says quickly, "I think you're a very nice person. Very intelligent. A good person." As he says all this, he looks so severe that Jan feels like laughing.

"Thank you, James."

"Well," he asks, "what do you say? How about tonight we see a movie. You name it."

"Well no," says Jan. "I'm afraid I can't manage tonight. Tonight I'm busy." She's not, but it doesn't do to appear too available. She is beginning to feel a little trapped by things.

"I guess," says Hicks, "you're kind of busy through the week. So why don't we say next Friday night?" Breathing room anyway. She could ask Harry Waggoner some questions about him. Discreet of course. Jan hesitates.

"All right. Friday night sounds fine."

Hicks finally smiles, and the truth is that he's really a beautiful young man. "That's fantastic," he says. "Tell you what. Why don't we have dinner over at the Jade Gardens? That is, if you like Chinese food. We could go after the movie." Jan hates the Jade Gardens with its little toy bridge and its goldfish pond. Also the food is lousy. Bobby and Marjorie took Jan and her mother there on Mother's Day. Every lady got a yellow plastic rose. Compliments of the management. Still, Hicks looks so enthusiastic about the idea that she can't disappoint him.

"That sounds fine."

"Great." He drums his fingers on the top of the table. He has beautiful, lean hands. She finds herself staring at them.

"So what kind of movie do you like anyways?" he asks. And you'll have to start taking the "s" off anyway, Mr. Hicks, if you want to stick around this fussy old English teacher. But time enough for that, I suppose.

"Oh, I don't know," she says. "Anything. It doesn't really matter. I'm not much for the gore. No disembowelments or axes in the throat please. On the other hand, I find something like *The Sound of Music* a bit thick." Hicks doesn't appear to be listening and Jan wonders if the man has ever heard of *The Sound of Music*. He grins at her.

"We'll see something nice," he says. "Don't worry."

Outside the air seems cleansed. They stand on the sidewalk in front of Mister Donut and watch the great shredding clouds boom southward toward Lake Ontario. Already it feels cooler and more like autumn.

"How does seven o'clock on Friday sound?" asks Hicks.

"That's fine," says Jan, walking over to her Honda and getting in. She rolls down the window and watches him come over and put his hands on the door. Leaning in he looks around. She can smell something faintly sweet on him. Shaving lotion? Cologne? A few dark hairs sprout from his open-throated shirt.

"You like this little thing?" he asks.

"It does the job," she says dryly. He grins down at her. He

takes care of his teeth. The goddam man could probably make it in the movies. Or model clothes or something. He straightens up and gives her a little wave.

"See you on Friday, Janice."

"Okay." She starts up the Honda and quickly backs out. When she pulls away, she can see in her rearview mirror that he's still standing there with his hands in his pockets watching her. She's almost home before she remembers the hayfever pills.

4

On the sofa Hicks leans forward with his elbows on his knees. Sips some beer. Barefoot and wearing only jeans, he is watching a movie called *Bring Me the Head of Alfredo Garcia*. The movie is set in Mexico. Some day Hicks wouldn't mind visiting Mexico, especially during the winter months. Normally, on a Saturday night, Hicks goes to the Puss 'n' Boots Club for a few beers. There he meets a chick and afterwards takes her for Chinese food at the Jade Gardens or maybe over to Crock & Block. Then they come back to his place and he fucks her. Sometimes the chick will stay all night, but mostly he drives her home before morning. That way you don't have to deal with her next day. Making coffee and toast and all that. Hicks has always enjoyed good luck in this regard. In fact, earlier this evening, one of these chicks, a Vicky Pruit, phoned and invited him to a party over in the Shelburne Manor near the Parkway. One of those bring-your-own-bottle affairs. However, Hicks declined. The truth is he's tired of those kinds of parties. And he believes, too, that maybe he's finished with chicks like Vicky Pruit. *Vicky!* What kind of fucking name is that for a grown woman?

As he watches the movie, Hicks enjoys a little reverie in which he sees himself settling down with Janice Harper. They could first go on a honeymoon in Mexico. It's true she's no beauty, but everyone knows that in time looks fade. What counts is that she's a very nice person with manners and feelings and intelligence. And those are the things on the bottom line when you are looking for someone to share a life with. Hicks gets up and goes to the kitchen for another beer. The kitchen is only big enough for cupboards and gas stove and small refrigerator, a tiny table and two chairs. Hicks hates the cramped feeling he always gets in the room, but what can you do? The finances are too tight for a move right now. Opening the beer, he decides he'll ignore the rent for this month. They can't kick you out until you're three months behind. That's the law; somebody told him that, and it's probably true. Also, he'll wait another month to pay something on the clothes. He'll put fifty on the car. To keep them quiet. The furniture can wait.

Hicks's furniture is mostly junk. He brought it along from an apartment he shared with a guy named Brian Latimer. They knew each other in Guelph Reformatory years ago, and then they met again at Ace Insulation. So, they decided to share this apartment over in Bramalea, and for a while it worked. One day they went to this warehouse on Dixie Road and bought furniture for three rooms. Everything! From a waterbed right down to a set of Melmac dinnerware. All for one price! After a few weeks, though, Latimer's girlfriend, a chunky brunette with big tits, begins spending a lot of time there. She cooked a little, mostly chops and hamburgers and stuff like that. But most of the time she sat around smoking and watching TV. Next thing she started sleeping over, and Hicks had to pull out the sofa bed in the living room. Also, she wasn't forking out any cash for food and rent, though by then she more or less lived there. Hicks used to lie awake on the sofa bed and think of moving out and sticking Latimer with the lease and the furniture payments. Latimer, however, beat him to the punch by doing that very thing. One day he booked off sick, and when Hicks got back to the apartment, he found this note saying they'd gone out to Alberta to look for better things. So, Hicks was left with the lease and the furniture and a sink filled with dirty dishes. They didn't even make the waterbed, and there were gum spots all over the sheets. No class!

So Hicks moved. Had no choice. He couldn't keep up the payments on that place. He rented a pick-up and he and a guy from the insulation company moved everything out at two o'clock in the morning. The only good thing from that whole arrangement was the colour TV. Probably Latimer would have taken it, but he couldn't get it into his girlfriend's Volkswagen. So he left this twenty-six-inch Zenith. A beautiful machine, and he and Latimer got a deal on it. They bought it from a guy at work for two hundred. This guy had ten of them in his basement. His brother-in-law worked for a trucking company or something. Anyway, that at least was a bargain. As Hicks sees it, the Zenith is the only thing in the apartment worth more than ten fucking cents.

By eleven o'clock Hicks is a little drunk. He's finished all the beer, and that's bad because tomorrow's Sunday and that's always a long day. Sometimes on Sundays he drives sixty miles north to Barrie to visit his mother and his son. But that's out for tomorrow. Not enough gas for the round trip. Hungry now, he heats a ravioli dinner in the oven and toasts a few slices of Kream Loaf. Taking the food into the living room, he sits down to watch the news. Same old crap. Oil shortages. Inflation. The hostages in Iran. That hostage business is totally ridiculous, thinks Hicks, watching some film footage of this old bearded man addressing thousands of Iranians. If Hicks

47

were in charge of things he'd get those hostages out of there and fast too. Drop an atom bomb right on that old Arab cocksucker. It's stupid to put up with that kind of shit when you've got all those bombs. Same with the oil. There's lots of fucking oil over there. So say to the Russians, for instance, all right, you take half and we'll take half. And let the fuckers eat sand. Holding up the rest of the world like that. A bunch of fucking barbarians. Most of them still live in tents for Christ sakes.

As he watches the TV news, Hicks feels himself growing angry at what seems like the vast confusion and insecurity of things in general. Nobody is fucking straightening anything out. Everything is going down the fucking pipe. Disgusted, he turns off the TV and pulls out the sofa bed. Lying there, he listens to his transistor radio. Eddie Rabbit sings "Gone Too Far." He could still phone Vicky Pruit and ask her to jump in a cab and come over. He knows she'd do it. But he rejects the idea. He's tired of chicks like that. They never have anything to say; they just want to fuck and watch TV. Instead he'll get a good night's sleep. Tomorrow he'll do his exercises and spend some time reading from a book he got at the library called *The Dynamics of Power Personality*. Written by some psychologist in the States. While reading this book the other day, Hicks was so impressed by one sentence that he wrote it out on a piece of paper and Scotch-taped it to the refrigerator door. The sentence reads, "In every person lies the capacity to realize his/her potential." There are many other items in the book that Hicks considers worthwhile. A person has to learn how to improve himself in various directions. That's what the man means by realizing your potential.

Lying there, Hicks listens to the radio and the traffic moving below him along Shaver Road. He thinks of Janice Harper and what a good companion she would be. A really nice woman and he'll show her a good time next Friday night. Perhaps he'll take along another little present. Some chocolates maybe. Or flowers. All women like flowers. He wonders if maybe he should have told her about his wife and son. But then she didn't ask him if he was married, so it isn't like he's exactly misleading her. Besides, he'll tell her all about that when he's ready. Also about the time he spent in the bucket.

He falls asleep listening to an old Hank Williams song called "Kaw-Liga." His father used to sing that on Saturday nights when there'd be a party at the trailer court. But Hicks can hardly remember those times now.

Three

1

Sitting in the Calders' living room, Jan carries on a conversation with Ruth Calder, who is in the kitchen preparing dinner. The questions and answers are ceremonial. A kind of litany. How is school? Did you have a nice summer? Did you go to Glen Falls? How is Seth's thesis coming along? How are the kids? Jan is talking around doors out of consideration for Ruth, who likes to be alone when she mixes and chops up things. It was the same when they lived in the apartment. If Ruth was making dinner, she wanted the kitchen to herself. Max, of course, would come in from work and lean against the refrigerator talking about her day while Ruth quietly fumed. But this present arrangement suits Jan because, sadly, there seems less and less to talk about each time they meet. However, she's grateful to be here; Ruth's phone call this morning saved her from Sunday dinner at Bobby's. And in her own way Ruth has always been a good friend.

"Mom sends her love," calls Jan.

"How is she anyway?"

"She's fine, but you can't really tell with Mom. She's always complaining about something. It's her nature." Ruth says nothing to this, and Jan gets up holding a glass of low-calorie beer. And how she wishes it were a large Scotch. But Seth and Ruth disapprove of spirits. Ruth doesn't drink at all and Seth very little. Their besetting sin is gluttony. Both are compulsive eaters who will reach for anything edible. So, despite the jogging and the crunchy household diet, they both have weight problems.

Jan stands at the front window overlooking Huron Street. A breezy late-summer evening and the leaves on the big maples are flowing in the wind. A nice part of the city, and most of these old brick houses are being remodeled by developers and sold at scandalous prices. The Calders are sitting on a gold mine. Yet they are always going on about how tough things are. Since Seth is a graduate student with no salary, they see themselves as members of the working poor. In the last election they canvassed like slaves for the local NDP candidate. Seth in his baggy cords and Ruth in her cotton granny dresses. Refugees from the sixties. Complaining about the mortgage, which I'll bet is looked after by Papa Calder.

Jan finishes her beer and wanders into the hallway leading to the kitchen. For a moment she leans unnoticed against the doorway. Ruth's back is to her. Busy at the chopping board, punishing mushrooms with a murderous-looking cleaver. She is barefoot and wears a rough cotton smock. Her coarse black hair is knotted in a single braid which hangs like a rope down her back. She could be an Ojibway squaw. With the birth of the children her hips have broadened, but in many ways she is unchanged from the days at Eastview Collegiate. Ruth Dunlop in that smelly old gymnasium with its high, narrow windows covered by wire mesh. Heavy-thighed in Eastview green, her weak eyes hidden behind Coke-bottle glasses secured to her by a string. A sturdy, reliable guard, whom you couldn't move from under the basket. While Max, her long legs blotched pink from running, dribbled up the court. Passing, shifting, feinting, her long red hair held in place by a headband. Feeding the ball to Jan, and bingo. Through the hoop without touching the rim. The lovely swishing sound of netting as the ball drops through. And the applause. The sweaty hugs. *Way to go, Slim.*

As she looks at her old friend, Jan smiles at the memory. Ruth is busy sprinkling something over the chopped mushrooms. And this kitchen is something else! Remodelled and outfitted like a *Good Housekeeping* advertisement. Julia Child would not look out of place in this room. Along one wall hang several copper-bottomed pots and pans. Hand-hammered steel woks of various sizes. A row of knives. Another wall is lined with cupboards, and along the counter are large glass jars holding twelve-grain cereals and dried apricots and God alone knows what else. There is also a huge dark-brown refrigerator and stove.

From time to time the shouts of the children can be heard from the narrow backyard. They are playing in a kind of maze cunningly fashioned from old rubber tires. It must have taken Seth an age to do it. But perhaps it took his mind off bacteria.

"Hey, Ruthie," says Jan finally. "Can I have another beer?"

Ruth turns slowly from the chopping board and regards Jan. It is very hard to surprise Ruth. She still wears glasses, but they are not as thick as in the old days. Yet her round face is still as earnest and impassive as ever. "Gosh, Harp, I'm sorry. Sure, help yourself." She is chopping celery into the biggest salad bowl in the world. Jan takes a beer from the fridge and says, "Did I tell you that Max stayed with me last weekend?" Without looking up, Ruth says, "Is that so? And how is she?" It's not difficult to detect the mild condescension in Ruth's voice. She's never really approved of Max or her style. How they ever imagined they could live together will remain an eternal mystery. But Jan finds Ruth's patronizing tone irritating. Always has. Ruth is a dear, sweet creature in her own way, but she can also be infuriatingly smug. Convinced she's on the right side of every question. Or *issue*, to use one of her favorite words. Her children are enrolled in the only *worthwhile* reading program available. Seth's research is environmentally *crucial*. The Distress Clinic is *vital* to the security of women in Toronto. *Everyone* should start the day with All-Bran.

"Max looks wonderful," says Jan. "Years younger than when I last saw her." A lie, but never mind. She feels a sudden and fierce loyalty toward Max. "She has a new lover and it's working out marvellously for her."

"That's nice," says Ruth, carrying the immense salad bowl into the dining room. Jan feels like giving her a good shaking. Can't she at least take an interest in an old friend? "It's a woman," Jan says a little loudly. Ruth returns to the kitchen to collect plates and cutlery. "Do you mean," she says, "that Maxine is having a lesbian relationship?"

"It looks that way, yes," says Jan triumphantly. And why am I so eager to press all this on poor old Ruth? But Ruth is already back in the dining room setting out the knives and forks. "Isn't that interesting?" she says. When she returns to the kitchen the subject seems closed.

"I wonder what's keeping Seth?" asks Ruth. Jan finishes her beer. Ruth! Ruth! Orbiting in your own little solar system. Forever going on about how she and Seth divide the household chores between them. If Seth cleans the bathtub, she takes out the garbage. If she makes dinner, Seth vacuums one of the bedrooms. On a corkboard near the refrigerator is a list of duties under His and Hers. It's all based on fair play and the equal roles of men and women in a satisfactory relationship in today's society blah blah blah. Yet, when it comes down to the old nitty-gritty, Seth is the sun in this little solar system and

53

Ruth and the kids are only tiny moons that revolve around him. Most of Ruth's conversations have to do with Seth. "Seth is having such a hard time getting ready for his orals. The tension is incredible, Harp. It's hard working at home with two small children. That's why he spends nearly all weekend down at the university. It's so quiet." Or "Seth worries so much about money. The mortgage comes up for renewal next year. And with these high interest rates! And the cost of things when you have a family! The price of things is outrageous. Seth says we are all being manipulated by the giant food corporations." Good old sweet old Seth! No doubt he's a wonderful husband and daddy and useful and concerned citizen. But it's very easy to grow sick of him before he even walks in the door. And of course Ruth never asks if there's a man in my life. So, after the opening ritualistic questions, everything is focussed on the Calder household.

She asks Ruth if she can help, but Ruth declines assistance. Food preparation and serving is one of her "things," and so Jan leans against the fridge door, holding her empty beer glass, and wondering if she dare ask for another without appearing to be an incipient alcoholic. There is, after all, nothing in these ridiculous light beers to give you even a mild buzz. She is thinking about this when Seth comes in. The front door opens and Seth wheels his ten-speed bicycle into the long hallway, propping it against the wall.

"Hi, everybody," he calls, "I'm home."

"Hi, hon," calls Ruth, and Jan raises her glass in greeting. From the kitchen she can see Seth stooping to take off his bicycle clips. Dressed in the same old baggy cords and an old roll-neck sweater. Another day peering into microscopes and examining slides. Ruth has explained a dozen times what Seth is studying, but Jan has trouble making any sense of it. All she knows is that for the last five years Seth has spent most of his time studying lumps of shit. No doubt it's all ecologically worthwhile and he will some day help to save the earth from turning into a planetary garbage pail. Now he walks down the hallway in his old sneakers, a big, whiskered, bear-like man with soft brown eyes. "Hi, Seth," says Jan. "How goes it in the bacterial world? Is it the same dirty business we have to deal with? Is it a microbe-eat-microbe world out there? In there? Wherever?" But she should know by now that Seth does not enjoy jokes about his work.

"Hi, Jan," he says. "It goes." He sounds a bit depleted. But soon he is standing in the kitchen nuzzling Ruth's neck like a TV husband. Jan watches them. Two big endomorphs at affectionate play. Seth waves out the back window at the children, and they yell for him to join them. But opening the window a crack he shouts, "No can do. We're going to eat pretty soon. You better come in and get washed." As he talks, his hand gropes for a piece of raw cauliflower. Absently he dips it into a dish of mayonnaise. "This all looks so good, Ruthie." He is already helping her carry bowls of food into the dining room and suddenly Jan feels like a third wheel. It's as though they've temporarily forgotten she's there.

"Want a beer before dinner, hon?" asks Ruth.

"No, I don't think so," says Seth. "I think I'll open a bottle of wine. After all, it's a special occasion. We don't see Jan all that often." Now he stops and looks over at Jan, intent on providing a good-natured scolding. "You should come and see us more often, Jan. Ruthie is always talking about you. You're family. You know that."

Jan is thinking of something to say to all this when the back door bursts open and the children come in: the boy pale and peevish-looking with Seth's matted brown hair; the girl, a serious eight-year-old with glasses and braids, who is already reading beyond her age level. According to Ruth. Seth sweeps them both into an enormous bear hug, lifting them off the floor. "And how are my two angels today? Did you have fun?"

The two children are shy in the presence of a guest. The boy does not remember Jan and frowns at her over his father's shoulder. The girl does remember and offers a bashful smile. Seth puts them down and addresses his son. "You remember Jan, don't you, Timothy?" And that's another thing Miss Grundy Harper! When did parents stop using adults' surnames when introducing guests to children? Jan tries to remember the girl's name. Something outlandish. She was named after one of Seth's aunts, who will no doubt leave the child five million dollars. Morgana! That's it, Morgana! On Jan's last visit Morgana read several stories to her while poor Travers, thinking no doubt of his own kids, sat staring at the burlap-covered walls. Like a man waiting for something unspeakably tiresome to end. Another nail in that evening's coffin. Now Seth sets down the children. "Okay. Now wash up, you two. Time to put on the feed-bag. I'm going down to the cellar and get a bottle of wine."

"Can I have some too?" asks Timothy. He looks about ready to kick up a fuss.

"We'll see, Mister Tim," says Seth. "Maybe a little for dinner."

And ye gods, the children are not going to eat with us are they? Why can't they feed their children first? It's so much easier on everyone. But charity, Harper. Charity suffereth long and is kind. So I've read.

In fact, however, the dinner is not a success. Timothy won't touch his spinach omelette or any of the bean stuff in the grey stone pot. For some reason he also takes an immediate dislike to Jan. "I don't like her," he announces flatly. Ah well! And I'm not too crazy about you either, you little bastard. Nor are matters helped by Morgana, who seems determined to impress Jan by displaying her new reader, which she is already halfway through after only a week of school. Throughout this turmoil Seth maintains a calm dignity. Too busy eating to be bothered by distractions. But Ruth finally admits defeat and sends both children to a small room, where they eat organic peanut-butter sandwiches and watch *Disney's Wonderful World*.

After dinner Jan listens to Ruth talk about her Tuesday and Thursday evenings at the Women's Distress Clinic. The things men do to women! Jan should just see some of the poor wretches who turn up at the Clinic. Listening, Seth nods his head. As he sees it, the problem is lack of government funding. To provide more counselling services. Introduce more programs in the schools. Family management of interpersonal relationships. Stuff like that. Jan remarks that there certainly are a lot of nut cases walking around these days. Seth frowns at the word "nut," but lets it pass. And listening to them Jan wonders what a man like James Hicks would make of the Calders. Would he ever begin to understand them? Would they understand him? I'll bet they'd like to think they could. But I wonder. He seems such a strange and off-beat character. How odd and touching was that silly little book of verse. A terribly funny and gauche thing to do. One of those things you just don't bother telling anyone about. But nevertheless touching.

She leaves at ten-thirty. Unlocking her car door in the cool, fresh September night, she feels suddenly very happy. Perhaps it's only because she's escaped from the oppressively earnest atmosphere of the Calder household. But perhaps, too, it's because of who knows? Enjoy, Harper. Enjoy!

2

On Sunday Hicks gets up at ten o'clock and does a half-hour of exercises. Mostly stretches and kicks from a book called *Essential Karate*. Then he eats a bowl of cornflakes in front of the TV. Some preacher with a drawl is talking about Jesus, and Hicks watches this even though he doesn't buy the Heaven and Hell stuff. He does not, however, discount the possibility that God exists. In fact, Hicks once defended the proposition that God exists. This happened in the Puss 'n' Boots Club, where this guy was yakking away about God. "Where is God?" the guy kept saying. "Show Him to me. Is He up in the clouds sitting on a thunderbolt?" A fucking smart aleck, and the guy was getting numerous laughs carrying on like this. His whole attitude annoyed Hicks, who finally said to this guy, "Do you believe there is such a thing as an atom bomb?" And the guy said, "Sure. Everybody knows that for fuck sakes."

"And what's in an atom bomb?" asked Hicks.

"How the fuck should I know?" said the guy. "And anyways, we're talking about God here, not fucking atom bombs."

"Well, just listen for a fucking minute," said Hicks, "and I'll tell you what's in an atom bomb." He knew he had the guy by the balls. A real fucking know-it-all. So Hicks said to him, "An atom bomb is made of fucking atoms. Right?"

"So fucking what?" the guy said.

"So," said Hicks, "you can't see a fucking atom. It's impossible. Too fucking small to see with the naked eye or even the most powerful telescope. Yet it is a scientific fact that atoms exist. Or you wouldn't have a fucking atom bomb. Same thing with God. Just because you can't see Him doesn't mean He isn't there." That shut the fucker up. In fact, one guy listening to all this was so impressed with Hicks's argument that he bought him a drink. But this guy on TV is something else. He's peddling pamphlets and inviting people to send in money to save themselves from eternal damnation. A fucking hustler, Hicks decides, turning off the television.

After this he starts to read from *The Dynamics of Power Personality*. In this book are several ideas on how to develop a more attractive and positive personality. It amounts to this. If you want to get ahead in life, you have to impress people. Hicks can understand that. After all, it only makes sense. People enjoy being around friendly types. But this has always been a problem for Hicks. It's not that he wouldn't like to be liked. It's just that he finds it very hard to appear friendly. His mother used to say he had a chip on his shoulder. And reading the book Hicks wonders if maybe it is possible for him to change his basic outlook and become a more friendly type of person. As the book says, "If you want people to like you, you have to radiate confidence and cheerfulness." Instead of which Hicks always looks like he's disgusted with everything and everybody. He supposes he gives off bad vibrations. Once he had this job helping a guy sell vinyl siding door to door. But he only lasted three days and the guy fired him. "No hard feelings," he said to Hicks, "but you're scaring customers with that scowl of yours." However, he paid Hicks for the full week. Some people, of course, don't care what the fuck you look like. The people at Ace Insulation, for instance. But the guy who wrote this book is right. Most people are put off by a serious, unsmiling type. Yet Hicks looks at it this way. How the fuck can you look friendly if you don't feel friendly? A major problem, and reading along Hicks wonders if it's solvable.

At noon he puts down the book and, while frying two eggs, decides he'll go for a little drive. He finds driving relaxes him, though you have to be careful when you drive a car like this because the cops pick on you. They'll stop you just to bug your ass. Check your lights and brakes and ask for your insurance card. And Hicks can't afford any tickets.

So, on the freeway, he's careful to stay within the limits. When he was eighteen, nineteen, he drove like a maniac most of the time. Wrecked two cars. Total write-offs. He collected speeding tickets by the handful. Even lost his licence once. Now, driving along the freeway through the Sunday afternoon traffic, Hicks shakes his head at the memory of those years. What a punk he was then! An absolute jerk. In the westbound collector lane he moves in behind a Ford station wagon loaded with kids, the dog, Mom and Dad, the whole fucking family scene. Hicks figures if the cops pull him over, they'll also have to pull over Mr. Suburban Bungalow up ahead. And he's moving it along pretty briskly.

The odd thing about these Sunday drives is that they always take Hicks to the same places. If he's visiting his mother and Dale, he takes the freeway to the 400 exit and then north to Barrie. Other times, like today, almost without realizing it, he continues west to Dixie Road and then north a few miles past the warehouses and factories to Bramalea. The airport is nearby, and the air is filled with the sound of the big jets taking off and landing. Hicks has never been in an airplane and he feels vaguely ashamed that, at the age of thirty, this should be a fact in his life. It's not something he'd ever tell anyone.

In Bramalea Hicks parks at a Gulf station across the street from the apartment building where his wife lives with her boyfriend, a man named Ed Dunkley. Hicks met Dunkley at Cross-Canada Transport. Actually introduced the man to Gail at a party. Hicks doesn't particularly care for Gail anymore. She's a part of his life that's finished. Still, several times a year he will drive here and sit in the car at the Gulf station, which is closed on Sundays. Sometimes he catches a glimpse of them coming up the ramp from the underground garage in Dunkley's LTD. Dunkley is a truck driver and makes a good dollar. Also they have no kids, so expenses are low, though Dunkley is a bit of a boozer. Every year they take Florida vacations, and the thought of his wife taking winter holidays is a sore spot with Hicks. It's like she doesn't deserve such luxuries.

Hicks hasn't lived with Gail now for over two years, and he really doesn't know why he drives over here some Sunday afternoons. Unless it could be that by looking at his wife, even catching a glimpse of her in the LTD, he might find a clue as to why he married her. She was a good-looking woman, and still is for that matter. She used to wear her blonde hair in a kind of beehive hairstyle, which looked sharp. With that hairstyle and in a party dress and wearing strapless, high-heeled shoes, she could turn a head. Now she wears her hair long and straight down her back. Hicks saw her once get out of the car and go into a milk store. She looked to have put on a few pounds, but is still quite attractive, even though Hicks no longer thinks of her in a sexual way.

When she walked out on Hicks and Dale two years ago, Hick's pride was hurt. Things had been going downhill for some time, and in a way he didn't mind her leaving. But he had trouble with the idea that she was getting it from another guy. Worse, they had apparently been screwing at Hicks's place. He was working nights then at the transport warehouse on Rexdale Road. So, they were fucking in Hicks's bed while he was working and his son was asleep. At first Hicks couldn't believe this, but one night he got it out of Gail. Hicks was really sickened by their behaviour. What, he argued, if the kid woke up and saw this guy in his mother's bed? That kind of thing could seriously affect him later on. Maybe screw him up psychologically with women? Gail had no answer to that. Wasn't even interested in talking about it. She was ashamed of the whole thing and just got mad at Hicks. As if it was all his fault! They had a big fight over it and Hicks hit her pretty hard. For a moment he thought he might have broken her jaw. She was on the floor a long time, and Dale was crying. A terrible night! One of the worst of his life in fact. That night Gail packed a bag and moved in with Dunkley. Took a taxi over to his apartment.

After she left, Hicks bundled his son into a snowsuit and drove up to Barrie, where he left him with his grandmother. As Hicks was leaving, his mother and stepfather warned him not to get rough and do anything foolish. The way they looked at it was that these things happen, so ride it out. Cool off. Sleep on it. You're better off without her and all that. But driving back to the city Hicks could only think violent thoughts. He felt capable of killing them both. Dunkley was a big bastard with maybe four inches and thirty pounds on Hicks, and this was before Hicks took up karate. So, when he arrived at the apartment-building parking lot, Hicks stuck a tire-iron down the front of his pants and buttoned his jacket. By then it was three o'clock in the morning.

Hicks was not exactly certain what he was going to do when he got to them, but he knew he could not leave things hanging the way they were. So, in the apartment-building lobby, he buzzed Dunkley's number and when he identified himself, Dunkley opened up. And he was waiting for Hicks, too, standing by his open door in a pair of light slacks and a blue shirt with tropical birds painted all over it. At the time it struck Hicks as ridiculous to wear that kind of shirt in the middle of winter. Even indoors. Dunkley had had a few drinks but was far from loaded. The first thing he said to Hicks was, "You want to come in and talk about this?" So Hicks followed him into the apartment, which was nicely laid out with basket chairs and shag rugs and a stereo-TV console. Gail was sitting on a sofa, drinking and having a cigarette. To Hicks it looked as though they'd been sitting around all night talking things over and making plans.

Gail's face was badly swollen. He'd really dropped one on her, and he could tell she'd been crying a lot too. She avoided his eyes, and nobody said anything for a bit. Hicks could feel the cold tire-iron next to his skin. He'd expected Dunkley to be a little more belligerent, particularly because of Gail's face. But after a while Hicks decided that while Dunkley could probably handle himself, he wasn't basically a violent type. Instead, Dunkley asked him if he wanted a drink, and Hicks said he wouldn't mind. Dunkley had a little bar in the corner of his living room and he went behind the bar and mixed Hicks a rum and Coke. Standing there in his painted shirt, Dunkley looked like a bartender in some holiday resort. Dunkley made himself another drink, too, and then surprised Hicks by saying that if Hicks wanted to go outside and settle all this in the parking lot, Dunkley would go along with that. However, he wasn't sure that would solve anything and maybe it would involve the cops and who needed trouble from them. Still, he was would accommodate Hicks if that's what he came for. It was strictly up to Hicks. Hicks sipped his rum and Coke and thought about this, listening as Dunkley went on to say that Gail was finished with Hicks and wanted him out of her life. As far as Dunkley was concerned, he had nothing personal against Hicks, but just wanted him to stay away and not bother Gail, because he and Gail were very much in love and wanted to build a new life together.

Hicks listened to all this leaning against a wall. Gail still wouldn't look at him but stared ahead, smoking one cigarette after another. Hicks accepted another drink from Dunkley. He wasn't going to be pushed out in a hurry, so he stayed leaning against the wall. The rum was giving him a little boost, and he began to think that if Dunkley wanted her, he could have her. She was not worth fighting over. Hicks just felt blank toward his wife. So finally he said, "I'm keeping Dale. My mother's going to look after him." Dunkley said that he and Gail had discussed all that and there was no problem there. So Hicks left feeling mildly vindicated. A week later, while he was at work, Gail came by and got the rest of her clothes.

3

Hicks lives in one of several red-brick apartment buildings off Shaver Road in Scarborough. The whole thing is called Terrace Court Gardens, which has always struck Hicks as ridiculous because there is no terrace and no court and no gardens. Just these six brick buildings grouped around a parking lot and filled with people who don't make much money. In recent years a number of black families have moved into Terrace Court Gardens, and this does not sit well with Hicks, who will admit that he feels uncomfortable around them. The place is only fifteen years old, but it has a desolate air to it. The superintendents don't seem to care about anything except collecting the rent. For instance, there was once a nice little playground with swings and slides and monkey-bars. Now that's all gone. Maybe somebody kept smashing it up and the owners got tired of replacing things. Anyway, only the steel frame for the swings is left, and sometimes kids will shinny up one side and go hand-over-hand across the top bar to the other side. But today the whole place is deserted and a kind of Sunday-afternoon sadness hangs in the air. There aren't even any kids playing road-hockey in the parking lot.

As Hicks walks along the hall, he can smell meat roasting and hear the televisions. Sunday-afternoon football. That's all people do anymore, thinks Hicks. Watch fucking TV. In his apartment he sheds his clothes and steps into the shower. And standing there under the warm, streaming water, soaping his genitals, he is stricken by lust. So, leaning a hand against the wall he quickly masturbates, his jissom spurting forth against the warm tile. And then, legs apart like a man being searched, he leans forward to wash his seed off the wall, directing the water with his hands.

After the shower he puts on fresh underwear and jeans. Checks himself out in the bathroom mirror. Combing his damp hair he tries to shake off the corrosive loneliness of the afternoon. At this time of the day it would be good to sit down and talk with a nice woman like Janice Harper. Just sit and enjoy a beer or a rum and Coke. And talk about anything that comes to mind. Then they could go for a bite. The woman has a very warm personality and she's funny. Hicks is certain that Janice Harper could make him laugh or feel better when he's a little on the low side.

He decides to give her a call. Probably she's eating her supper now, but maybe not. Maybe she'd feel like a couple of char-broils over at Harvey's. Hicks dials her number but feels a little nervous about things. Asking a woman out for a hamburger at supper time on Sunday! She might see that as ridiculous. Childish. He has half a mind to hang up, but he lets it ring through. It rings a half-dozen times before Hicks hangs up. In a way he's relieved she's not there. In another way, he's not.

Four

I

Before the nine o'clock bell the staffroom is like a madhouse, with people rushing about carrying books and papers and talking. Talking, talking, talking. Ye gods but teachers talk a lot, thinks Jan, sipping her coffee and lighting her third cigarette of the day. No more till after lunch. Most of the men are talking about yesterday's NFL games. But not Murray Ford, who loathes sports. This morning Murray is wearing a black pinstripe suit, with pink shirt and white tie. He looks like a character out of *Guys and Dolls*. Murray affects the most outlandish attire, and the kids have a field day wondering what Fairy Ford will turn up in next. They talk about him all the time, particularly the Grades Nine and Ten students, who find Murray a very exotic creature indeed. But if the ridicule bothers him, he certainly doesn't let on. Now and then, if he is particularly overwrought, his eczema will flare along his brow and neck. Most of the time, however, he carries about him an air of admirable insouciance. This may come from knowing he's the best teacher in the school. Murray knows his stuff, and senior kids line up to get into his classes. Small and delicate and graceful, he now makes his way past people toward Jan. He is smiling wickedly.

"And did you have a nice weekend with the essays, my dear?"

"Go to hell, Murray."

He laughs. "And do you by any chance have a set of *Caesar* tapes?"

"Yes I do, Murray," says Jan, holding up the cassettes. "And you're not getting your hands on these for the next two weeks."

Murray makes a face. "Hell! And Kirstead has the other one. Ah well, not to worry. I suppose I could *read* the play to the poor dears. See you later, love." And he's quickly gone and soon talking to Norma Kirstead, who shakes her head. Murray throws up his hands in mock helplessness, and watching him, Jan smiles. Beside her, in his gym suit and sneakers, is Mark Beamish. With Harry Waggoner, Mark is going over a list of players for the football team. Harry is an assistant coach. Looking at him, Jan thinks of James Hicks; some time this week she must ask Harry a discreet question or two about Mr. Hicks.

Sitting in a chair, oblivious to the confusion surrounding him, is John Trimble. Looking worried as he works on the *Globe and Mail* crossword. His wife is in the hospital for some kind of operating. Is it gallstones or kidney stones? Jan feels ashamed not to know. She should ask. But John is such a prickly character, especially at this time of day. She'll ask him later.

On her way out she is stopped by Bob Lipscombe, who wants to know if she can help with the casting for *Oliver*. Is Wednesday at four all right? And always it is like this. People asking you to make up your mind on the spot. She should be used to it by now but somehow isn't. But yes, Wednesday at four sounds fine, and Bob is grateful. He gives her arm a firm squeeze. "Thanks, Jan, you've saved my life." Then Bruce Horton almost knocks her down as he comes in the room.

"Hi there," says Bruce, working himself out of his topcoat. "Did you have a nice weekend?"

"Very nice, Bruce, thanks. Quiet."

"Uh-huh." Bruce's large, heavy face is creased by a frown. "Can I talk to you later?" he asks quietly.

"Yes, I suppose so. I have to go now."

"Sure thing," says Bruce. "See you later then."

In the hallway she encounters the old familiar smells of floor polish and body odour. And noise! Always this incredible noise of the young in a hurry. Another thing I should be used to by now. With her sweater across her shoulders she makes her way through the students who are on the move toward classrooms or stand by their lockers banging shut the doors. And is this really my twelfth year of dodging past young people in these crowded hallways? Taking the stairs and watching carefully for those coming down who are talking and paying no attention to the traffic. Twelfth year! And another twelve would make me nearly fifty years old! Ye gods, Harper. Monday morning is no time for such gruesome reflections. Just get on with the ruddy job. And 10A is a fairly good-humoured lot. It's a little early in the year, but three or four actually show some promise.

Near her classroom door a girl says, "Good morning, Miss Harper. Have you read my essay yet?"

Jan tries to place the girl. Ah yes, Laura Keyes. A pale, unhealthy-looking girl in 12D. Plain as a field mouse. But she tries! Lord how she tries! Unfortunately she hasn't much to work with, poor kid.

"No I haven't, Laura, I'm afraid." As she walks away the girl looks cast down, her bitter little mouth stopped. Poor Laura! Always trying to ingratiate herself with the teachers. Always angling for marks and favours. She'll try out again for the cheerleading squad, though she hasn't a prayer. She'll turn up on Wednesday at four determined to try for the role of Nancy in *Oliver*. What can you do for people like that? Meantime the class awaits. Sitting in there yawning and opening books. Jan walks into the classroom thinking, I'll do my best for you, Willy, but I ain't promising anything.

2

Three or four afternoons a week Hicks spends an hour or so at the Public Library on Transit Road. The library is a large white building with tall windows. In the afternoon the sunlight floods through these windows and makes it a nice place to read and think. Here sit the old men from Fairfield Park, a senior citizens' home nearby. They like to doze in the big orange chairs or maybe go along the reading tables and glance at the newspapers. It's a restful place, and Hicks figures these old guys like to get out of their rooms whenever they can. That's understandable. Sometimes they will talk about politics or religion, so that it's a kind of club for them. There are also a number of weird types around. Real characters, who look like they've spent some time in a mental institution.

One guy, for instance, is about thirty. Very angry-looking. In fact, he looks as though he'd like to kill everybody in the world. He wears old army fatigues and is always reading books about Hitler. He seems hung up on the subject as he sits at the reading table poring over these books on Germany way back when. From time to time he'll look up and glare at anybody in sight. Another guy is called Big John. He is exceptionally strange. A huge man with a shaven head and this fantastic body. Hicks figures the guy must work out with weights because he looks like a fucking wrestler. In the summer he wears jeans and snug tee shirts and sometimes a little beret. In the winter he favors a lumber jacket and toque. And running shoes, for Christ sakes! In the middle of winter he wears these sneakers.

Big John is always looking through books on philosophy or economics or psychology, and sometimes he'll discuss these subjects with one or two of the old men. They seem to get a kick out of him, though he can be moody some days and not talk to anyone. Just wander through the stacks by himself. Hicks often watches him out of the corner of his eye, and sometimes he will see the big man making crazy faces or whispering angrily about something or other. At such times he looks like he's involved in some incredible discussion, trying to convince some invisible opponent. Hicks is careful not to catch his eye because, while Hicks does not see himself as a coward, he would not like to tangle with someone who looks that strong and who is obviously working with loose hinges. A guy like that could probably strangle you in thirty seconds.

Mostly Hicks catches up on the news, often reading items that make him reflect on the terrible things that can happen to people. Today, for instance, he reads about this tanker truck that goes out of control and crosses the median on some interstate in California. Smashes into three or four cars and kills eleven people. After reading this, Hicks tries to imagine what it would be like to see this huge rig crossing the median and bearing down on him at seventy miles an hour. The sound of all that grinding metal. But maybe there would be just a helluva big bang and then nothing. Total silence! Everything done with. Thinking about this gives Hicks a little tingle in the small of his back. He also reads about this woman and her common-law husband who beat her three-year-old son to death. They told the cops the kid had cried a lot and wet the bed and it all got on their nerves. So they took turns beating him and finally this guy picked up the kid by the legs and smashed his head against the wall. They'd been drinking, too. Reading this leaves Hicks sickened and outraged, and thinking about Dale. If anyone so much as laid a finger on his son, Hicks knows he'd kill the son of a bitch. He'd bead his head in with a baseball bat. Or maybe kick him to death. Hanging is too good for people like that. Never mind twenty years in the fucking bin where you can get used to things if you really set your mind to it.

Sometimes Hicks takes out a book or two. He used to have a library card, but he kept forgetting to bring the books back. Either that or he would get so interested in a particular book that he didn't want to return it. Then the library would keep sending him overdue notices. But there was no way he was going to pay six or seven dollars for a library book. So now when he sees a book that might be interesting or educational, say something like *The Dynamics of Power Personality,* he just slips it under his arm and buttons his shirt. He can't see the library worrying all that much about a book now and again.

At the library Hicks sometimes looks over at the women, but most of them do not interest him. Usually they are housewives with little kids. Or old ladies poking around. Now and then some high-school girls working on a project. But as far as Hicks is concerned, that's all right. You don't go to the library to pick up women.

3

Jan is standing by her car in the school parking lot when she sees Bruce Horton waving at her. And ye gods, she'd completely forgotten about Bruce. Now he moves toward her between the cars. For a big man, Bruce moves quickly. On the field next to the parking lot the football team is busy with stride jumps. From the open windows of the gymnasium comes the voice of Judy Barowski, urging her girls through the school cheers. Looking down, Jan reads the bumper sticker on Mark Beamish's Pacer. *Rugby Players Have Leather Balls.* Right, Mark! And leather heads, too!

Now Bruce arrives, panting a little, some sweat along his upper lip where this summer he wore a big, droopy moustache. Jan saw him once at the shopping plaza, where he was helping his mother get out of the car. She remembers thinking at the time that the moustache just didn't work for Bruce. It didn't sit well on his big, friendly face, which usually looks as innocent as an apple. The moustache made him look a bit dubious. Like a hotel detective or a security guard. She's glad he's shaved it off. "I thought you were going to wait for me," says Bruce. He's easily bruised, so Jan apologizes as she listens to Judy Barowski scold the girls for a little droop at the end of the "Choo-choo Train." Then Jan listens to Bruce invite her to dinner on Friday night. "I know you probably get a little tired of those Film Society things," he says. "I can understand that. But anyhow, they're playing some Buster Keaton films this week, and he's not for me. I've never been able to see any humour in that man. So I thought maybe we could go downtown to some place nice. You know what things get like once the term gets under way. I'm starting the History Club next week, and I'm going to be helping Murray with the debaters. He wants me to explain parliamentary procedures, and stuff like that." As Jan listens to Bruce describe his busy life, she looks across at the football players, who are now on their backs, their legs fiercely pedalling the air.

"I can't, Bruce. I'm sorry, but I'm busy Friday night."

"You've got a date?" asks Bruce. He sounds surprised, and Jan feels herself growing annoyed with Bruce Horton. Why the hell shouldn't she have a date?

"Yes I have, Bruce," she says. Bruce frowns at her.

"Are you still seeing that book salesman? I thought that was all finished."

"No Bruce," says Jan. "I'm not going with Bill Travers anymore."

"You've got a new boyfriend?" He sounds incredulous, and Jan feels like saying, And what do you think I've got for God sakes, three heads? But keep the peace, Harper. "I'm going out on a date, Bruce. He's not exactly a boyfriend. It's no big deal."

"A schoolteacher?"

Jan waves to Norma Kirstead, who glides down the sidewalk on her black Raleigh Traveler, the wicker basket crammed with papers weighted down by a stone. "No," says Jan. For a moment they stand in a clumsy silence, and then Bruce says, "Well, okay then. Maybe another time. I'll see you tomorrow, I guess." He sounds hurt, and he'll pout a little over the next few days.

As Jan drives away she watches Bruce as he walks slowly toward the football field, his hands jammed into the pockets of his baggy grey flannels. Let him sulk, damn it. Does he think I'm just some old convenience that's always there to be used any time he feels like it? She's surprised at how angry she feels. But it's a lovely late-summer afternoon and to hell with Bruce Horton anyway. Along the street the students are drifting homeward or over to McDonald's at the shopping plaza. A small army of young people in blue jeans. And in another few weeks the young trees along these streets will lose their leaves. In the mornings there'll be hoar frost on these lawns. Autumn! What a lovely word! She remembers how she used to love sitting on the verandah steps of the old brick house on Beech Avenue. An October afternoon and the leaves falling from the big trees. Across the street Ruth Dunlop staring out from her front window. Probably they had argued again on the way home from school. In those days they were always fighting. Ruth was such a little brat. I suppose I was, too. And then her father would turn the corner and come down the street, a tall, lean man with a little sandy moustache. Usually he wore a sweater under his suit coat, and always he carried a briefcase filled with tests and essays. Stopping in front of her he would say something like "Do you know, Janice, that one hundred and seventy-seven years ago this very day General Burgoyne surrendered. It was the end of the Saratoga campaign and a turning point in the American Revolution. It changed the course of history on this continent. And not one person in my senior history class gives a hoot." All this to his ten-year-old daughter. And was it moments like those that made me want to be a teacher? Who knows?

When Jan pulls into the driveway she can see her mother standing at the front window. She looks as though she's been waiting for her daughter. As Jan gets out of the car Mrs. Harper has already opened the screen door at the side of the house. She smiles at Jan. "How did it go today, dear?" "Fine, Mom," says Jan, reaching into the back seat for her briefcase and her sweater. And what on earth is bothering Mother? She looks so flushed and excited. However, it is warm now. "How are things with you, Mom?"

"Oh, not too bad, dear, thank you. About the same." Jan straightens up. The woolen skirt clings to her and she can smell herself. She should have worn that linen suit today. She throws the cardigan over her shoulder and hefts the briefcase in her other hand. Another day for the working girl and wouldn't a cold beer taste good now? And why the hell don't they make beer commercials in which the hard-working girl comes home and cracks a cold one? Instead of those dumb little broads roasting wienies for the boys at the beach parties. And what, dear Mother, is on your mind?

Mrs. Harper holds open the door and allows Jan to pass. "Did you have a nice evening at Ruth's?" she asks.

"Yes. Fine, Mom, thanks. Ruth sends her love."

"That's nice," says Mrs. Harper. They stand poised for a moment inside the door. And here, by custom, they should part company. Jan down the steps to her own door. And Mrs. Harper up five steps to her kitchen. But Mrs. Harper says, "There's a present here for you."

"A present?" says Jan. "From whom, pray?"

"Oh I wouldn't know that, dear. I certainly wouldn't open anything addressed to you," Mrs. Harper says proudly. "But I know they're flowers. The delivery man brought them around two. I was watching my program when I heard the side doorbell, so I got up and came around. The man was going to leave the box between the doors but I thought what a shame. On a warm day like this they could wilt before you even got home. So I just took the box and put it in my fridge."

"Well, thanks, Mom," says Jan, following her mother up to the kitchen, where Mrs. Harper opens the refrigerator door and takes out a long grey cardboard box. Behind the steel-framed glasses her eyes are alive with excited interest.

"Flowers on a Monday afternoon," she says. "What a nice idea!" She's consumed with curiosity, and Jan has to decide whether to take them down to her apartment or open them here in her mother's kitchen. But surely, to deny her would be cruel and unusual punishment, Harper.

"Is Bruce Horton playing Romeo again?" asks Mrs. Harper. And ye gods, is that actually a twinkle in her eye? "Bruce? Send flowers?" says Jan, running a thumbnail underneath the Scotch tape. "You must be kidding, Mom." Jan has already guessed who sent them, but for a wild moment she hopes they might be from Travers. He's left the bitch again and is inviting me to a weekend in New York. Fat chance, kid. Anyway, flowers aren't Travers's style. Too corny. Once, while they were out walking, he picked her some dandelions. "For your hay fever," he said.

And there on top of the dozen long-stemmed red beauties is the plain white card. *From James.* "Roses!" cries Mrs. Harper. "My, aren't they lovely!" And Harper, let's get this over with, because sooner or later she's going to have to know. "They're from a fellow I met at Harry Waggoner's party last week. As a matter of fact, we're going out on Friday night." She taps the card against her teeth while Mrs. Harper examines the roses.

"Well, you certainly must have made an impression, dear. Is he a schoolteacher too?"

"No, Mom, he's not."

Mrs. Harper is fussing with some green stuff in the box. She also holds up a little package of something or other. "Don't forget to put this in the water. They'll last twice as long."

"Right."

"What *does* he do, dear?" asks Mrs. Harper. Jan gathers up the box. Time to be going, Harper. "To tell you the truth, Mom, I don't know."

"I see," says Mrs. Harper, looking only mildly appalled. She has difficulty sorting anyone out until she knows what a person does for a living. Now she looks as though she doesn't quite believe her own daughter. "Do you have a vase big enough for those? I could let you have the green one in the living room. They'd look nice in that."

"No thanks," says Jan. "It's all right. I'll find something." She starts down the stairs holding sweater, briefcase, and flowers, carefully stepping sideways. No use breaking your neck with roses in your arms. From the top of the stairs her mother calls, "What's your friend's name, dear?"

"Hicks," calls Jan over her shoulder. "James Hicks."

"That's nice," says Mrs. Harper, meaning, Jan supposes, that at least he's Anglo-Saxon.

She fits the key into her lock and once inside the apartment lays the flowers on the kitchen counter and opens a beer. She wonders where she can put the roses and finally arranges them in two old pickle jars.

"You could never make your living in a flower shop, Harper," she says aloud. "No artistic touch at all. Now if Max were here, she'd doll these things up. Probably walk around naked with one in her teeth." Jan places one jar on the dresser in her bedroom and the other near the TV in the living room. It was nice of him all right, but why is he doing these things? It seems somehow inappropriate. A book of verse and now roses. He's actually giving me the rush.

She sits on the sofa and puts her feet up on the coffee table. As she sips her beer and smokes a cigarette, she looks at the roses near the TV. She supposes she'll have to phone the man and thank him. It was nice of him, yes, and no one is ungrateful. But all the same, she wishes he hadn't bothered.

4

When the telephone rings Hicks is sleeping. His unlighted apartment lies in the shadows of evening. He awakens to the sound of the ringing telephone and for a moment he can't even remember having fallen asleep on the sofa. Then he remembers having had a few beers at the Puss 'n' Boots Club and driving home. By his head the radio is softly playing. Barbara Mandrell singing "Years."

The telephone hangs on the kitchen wall, and Hicks, yawning, leans against the wall. He wishes he could remember how many beers he had. It seems somehow important. When he picks up the phone, someone is saying hello but Hicks can't place the voice. "Who is this?" he asks. It could be a wrong number.

"It's Jan Harper," says the voice. Hicks is mortified.

"Remember?" says the voice. "The woman in the doughnut shop on Saturday? The one you gave the book of Rod McKuen's verse to?"

"Well sure," says Hicks. He could fall through the floor. "You don't have to go through all that. I know who you are. I was sleeping, see . . ."

"Why did you send me those roses, James?"

"Why?" asks Hicks. "What's the matter with them?"

"There's nothing the matter with them and, as they say, you shouldn't have. But I just wondered, you know. It's a certain kind of gesture . . . oh, never mind. I don't really know what I'm trying to say. They must have cost you a fortune."

Listening, Hicks feels obscurely threatened. Somehow he has blundered, and he must be careful. Perhaps she doesn't like roses. But fuck, every woman likes roses.

"The money was nothing," he says. "Don't worry about the money."

"I'm not worrying about it, James."

"That's good. I just want you to enjoy them, that's all." He hesitates. "I just felt like giving you flowers today. What's wrong with that?"

"Did I say anything was wrong with it? Look, please don't get me wrong. The roses are lovely. Thank you."

"That's all right," says Hicks. "I was glad to do it." He waits, and listening to nothing, feels a surge of panic. "Are you sure there isn't any particular movie you'd like to see on Friday night? I mean, anything is okay by me."

78

"No, you decide. I don't really care. But as I said on Saturday, just so long as it isn't filled with blood and gore."

"I'll get a paper and check them out."

"Right."

Hicks's mind has gone to numb. "How's school?" he asks desperately. He feels like a fucking fifteen-year-old.

"Well, right now school is a little hectic. The kids haven't really settled down to the idea that it's school-time again. A lot of them still think it's summer. The weather doesn't help. When it gets cooler, they'll settle down."

Hicks has nothing to say to that, but it's all right because she is telling him that she has to go. "I have a lot of work to do, so I'd better get at it. But I did want to thank you for the flowers."

"Well, that's all right. I was glad to do it. I wanted to buy you something. It felt good buying you those flowers. And I'll pick you up Friday night at seven. Right?"

"Right."

"Okay. I'll be there."

"Fine, James. Goodnight."

"Yeh, goodnight. See you Friday. Take care of yourself." But she has already rung off and missed the bit about taking care of herself.

Standing by the phone in the darkening kitchen, Hicks feels a bit let down. Fucking stupid not to have recognized her voice. And what the fuck is he going to talk about on Friday night anyway? She probably knows all about books and movies and plays. And what if the movie he chooses is really stupid? He should have stayed in school longer. Education is important, and he neglected that part of his life. What an asshole he was at seventeen! Still, it's maybe not too late. In *The Dynamics of Power Personality* there is an entire chapter on people who change the direction of their lives while in their thirties and forties. Some even in their fifties. Hicks isn't sure he believes any of this. On the other hand, he figures that's because he never met anyone like that. You never know. It's all worth thinking about.

Five

1

A quarter to seven and her mother is still upstairs moving from room to room. Usually she's gone by now. As secretary of the Friday Nite Club she has to be on time. To take the minutes. Or whatever the hell it is that secretaries do at meetings. But not tonight. Still up there fussing about, and no doubt hoping for a gander at Mr. Hicks. Jan sits on the sofa finishing her second vodka and tonic and thinking that if her mother doesn't soon get the show on the road, she is indeed going to catch an eyeful of James Hicks and his Trans Am. And won't that make for an interesting question-and-answer period tomorrow after our adventures at the A&P? Jan raises her glass. To James Hicks, sender of bad poetry and red roses and owner of one muscle car which any moment will be barooming down this quiet suburban street. Because, unless I miss my guess, Mr. Hicks is a compulsive type who likes to be on time. And I wonder if this dress is too dressy, damn it. She is wearing a dark mauve dress she bought last May. A date with Travers, and he liked it. But that was Travers. And oh, these men in my life! Right now, for instance, instead of sitting here fretting, I could be downtown in, say, Noodles, plugging home some pasta with good old Bruce, who has given me the silent treatment all week. Along with all those hurt looks. Poor old thing. And why don't you just go fly a kite, Bruce? And if Mother dear is going to insist on blowing her punctuality record for a glimpse at her daughter's date, then I'm going to have another noggin of Smirnoff. It'll calm me down because, after talking with Harry Waggoner today, I feel I'm being perhaps a touch rash going out with this good-looking dude Hicks. But not to worry, Harper. We'll go see a movie. Have a little meal and then bye-bye James Hicks. And the best of British luck to you and yours.

She goes into the kitchen and pours another vodka and tonic. But go easy, kid. No use getting hammered. You're a respectable woman, for God sakes. Schoolteacher. Pillar of the community and all that. And ye gods, I honestly believe that at last Mother is putting on her coat and crossing from the front hall to the bathroom for a final inspection. She's on her way, all right. I suppose she can't wait any longer, but it must be driving her crazy. Now Jan hears the kitchen door opening and her mother's careful footsteps on the stairs.

"Goodbye, dear. I'm off now," calls Mrs. Harper. "Have a nice time this evening."

"Yes, Mom. You too," Jan shouts. There is a long silence and then her mother's voice again.

"You will be careful won't you, Janice?"

Janice indeed! And delivered as abruptly as it was during my high-school years when Arthur Belt, his face blooming with acne, came by to take me to the movies. Poor Arthur! The homeliest boy east of the Don River, and bashful to boot. Yet my mother gave him a look you might reserve for a rapist. *You be careful, Janice.* Now Jan shouts again.

"Don't worry, Mom." Sitting down on the sofa she whispers, "I'm only going out with a married man who's an ex-con." The side door opens and closes and the Plymouth starts up with its usual roar. Mother's idea of starting the car in all types of weather is to floor the accelerator for ten seconds.

Five minutes to seven and Jan listens to the Plymouth backing down the driveway. And I wonder if she might just circle the block and come back, hoping for a peek? No, she has to be on time for her meeting. Still, Jan climbs the stairs and opens the side door. It's another cool, fresh September evening. Behind the Bonners' house a new moon is rising. Jan stands for a moment by the carport, hugging her arms and listening to the faint roar of the traffic from Crown Hall Road. At times like this Willowgreen Drive seems almost rural. Her father could never get used to it; he missed the bark of horns from Danforth Avenue. And here in Scarborough he found no place interesting to walk. What a sacrifice it must have been for him to move up here. And now that old house on Beech Avenue is probably worth a fortune. People are returning to the heart of the city.

Standing there, Jan wonders if she should invite him in for a drink. No, better not. Keep it fairly brisk and formal. After her talk with Harry Waggoner this morning, it's probably best that way. All week she'd tried to corner Harry and find out a little more about James Hicks. But these days Harry is a hard man to pin down. Not only does he run a big department, but there's also the football team. And problems at home. So most days he looks a bit distracted. Today, however, they both had spares the second period and the staff room was empty. Harry, a chunky, balding man in his late forties, was slumped over a table, drinking coffee and studying football diagrams. The season opener today at three.

Jan chose her words carefully and opened by thanking Harry for the Labor Day party. Since it was almost two weeks ago, Harry glanced up from his diagrams and gave her a funny look. "That's okay, Jan. I'm glad you enjoyed yourself."

"I talked to your nephew for a while," Jan said. "Is he still staying with you?"

Harry returned to his diagrams. "Jimmy? No. He just stayed over the long weekend. Helped me finish the family room. It was a change for him, too. He lives by himself and probably gets a bit fed up with that. Cooking his own meals and all that stuff." Harry marked some figures on a sheet.

"What does he do?" asked Jan. Like my dear old mother, she thought at the time. Mercifully, Harry Waggoner is a straight-forward and guileless man. You ask him a question; you get an answer.

"Nothing at the moment," he said. "He worked for an insulation company for a while, but they laid him off. He's on unemployment insurance right now. He's bounced around a lot of jobs over the past few years. Never really settled down into anything. He's had a rough time." Harry stopped and looked at the far wall. It was as though he were seriously considering James Hicks for the first time in his life. "I like the guy myself. And I feel a little sorry for him, so I have him over for a meal now and again. He's got some very good qualities. If he's interested in what he's doing, he'll do a good job for you. He laid all the tile in that basement bathroom. Well, you saw it. A beautiful job." Harry bent over his diagrams again. "Diane thinks he's lazy, but I don't agree. He's had some hard knocks. Got into trouble a few years ago and went to reformatory. And he doesn't have much education. Grade Ten, I think. I've tried to interest him in going to night school, but he doesn't think he could stick it out. And it's not that he isn't intelligent. He's a very curious guy. Interested in all kinds of things. Takes books out of the library. I went over to visit him once and saw all these books. He lives in that complex off Shaver Road." Harry shook his head as though baffled by another man's peculiar existence. "He's got a wife and a child, too." Listening, Jan looked up at the ceiling and rolled her eyes. I might have known. A good-looking man like that. Ye gods, Harper, another married one. "Jimmy and Gail don't live together anymore," continued Harry. "She ran off with some truck-driver, and I think that really shook Jimmy up. Pauline looks after the little boy. That's Diane'sister. I guess Dale must be eight or nine now." And Harry simply left it at that and returned to his diagrams. No messy questions like "Why do you ask?" etc.

In the bathroom Jan has a final look and finishes her drink. Looking into the mirror she says, "Well, for better or worse, Mr. Hicks, here I am." As she waits for him, she wonders what he went to jail for.

2

They go to a movie called *My Bodyguard*. Playing at the Plaza Cinema Three. It's only a ten-minute drive from Jan's doorstep. On the way Hicks asks her what kind of music she likes. At the time he's listening to Dave and Sugar run through "My World Begins and Ends With You." Jan tells him it doesn't really matter, but he says, "I'll bet you like classical music." So, he fiddles with the radio until he picks up a concert on CBC; it sounds like Wagner or Richard Strauss. A very stormy thing, and Jan moves the dial back to Dave and Sugar. Looking over at her, Hicks grins. He's dressed in the same outfit he wore last Saturday.

"You like country music?" he asks.

"Sure," says Jan. "Sometimes. If I'm in the mood. Why

not?" As they drive along, Jan watches the big white dice as they swing from the rearview mirror.

The movie itself is corny but entertaining and certainly no worse than most. Jan thinks that Hicks probably chose it because the story takes place in a high school and he thought she would enjoy that. Sitting beside him and thinking about this, Jan is touched. Basically the guy is kind, and she feels suddenly tender and protective toward him in the dark, crowded theatre. After the movie they go to the Jade Gardens. Hicks has nothing to say about the movie, but he's interested in what Jan thinks. When she says she found it a little hokey, he looks disappointed but says nothing.

In the restaurant the hostess seats them near the fountain and the little bridge. Here they can see the goldfish darting back and forth. Something to look at. Jan has a vodka and tonic and Hicks orders a shot of rye with a beer chaser.

"I don't usually drink much liquor," he says. "I really don't handle it very well. But I guess I'm a little nervous."

"Nervous?" says Jan, affecting her best Southern accent. She didn't play Blanche Dubois for nothing. Three nights running in the Eastview gymnasium in the spring of 1963. A smasheroo. Even beat out Max for the part. Surprised herself. "Why, James Hicks," she says, "are you telling me that I make you nervous? Little ol' me?"

Hicks drains his beer and says, "I'd like to get to know you a lot better. I think you're a tremendous person."

"Tremendous? Me?" says Jan, returning to her normal voice. "Well, I have feet of clay, dear boy. Besides, we've run this one through before, but the fact is you don't even know me."

"I don't have to know you." He is staring at his glass and picking at the label on the beer bottle. "I can just tell you're a good person," he says quietly. "A solid type of person. Dependable."

Jan laughs. "You make me sound like the best deal on a used-car lot." She lowers her voice and talks out of the side of her mouth like a carnival barker. Hamming it up. What's the harm? "Now here's a good, solid dependable job. Just the ticket for safe, reliable service. She's got a few miles on her, but still solid and dependable."

Hicks is not amused by this performance.

"Hey, stop that. I didn't mean that. I meant it as a compliment. You turn everything into a joke."

"Sure, why not?"

"Because underneath I think you're a very serious person. A person who thinks about things."

"What things?"

"All kinds of things. Important things." He looks down at the goldfish. "All the women I've known haven't a brain in their heads. They spend their time watching soap operas on television and things like that."

"And you think I'm some kind of intellectual, is that it?" asks Jan. She takes another sip of her drink. "Why? Because I'm a high-school teacher? James, I'm going to let you in on a little secret. Some of the dumbest people I know teach high school."

Hicks is attentive to all this but looks doubtful. "All the same," he says, "you must have to have something on the ball. I mean, you can't be stupid and get through university."

"To that I can only say balderdash."

Hicks signals to the waitress, who hurries over. And it's a great advantage dining with a handsome bloke like Hicks; we're getting the best service in the joint. Hicks orders another beer but no whiskey. Jan says she'll coast, and Hicks looks pleased. He frowns at the menu. He has the kind of bratty appeal of a John Travolta; several dames besides the waitress have been casting looks our way. And here you are, Harper, about to break egg rolls with this handsome ex-con who may have as many as eight or nine years on you. Let's hope he's at least thirty. And I wonder if he believes all that guff about improving the mind. Does he see me setting him out on the Great Books course? Tuesday nights we'll read Plato together at my place. On Thursdays we'll go over to his pad and study the Ming Dynasty. Is that how he really sees me? With Travers I could understand it. His wife is a bad-tempered, anxious woman. Living with her is a heavy trip, and so for a while I was the comic relief in his life. We laughed a lot. It was the thing we did most together. That and some pretty good sex. But mostly I made him laugh and forget about Madam Fang. And I accepted the role of court jester because in his own way Travers was a nice guy. Fun to be with. As for Bruce Horton, well that's not hard to figure. Bruce sees me as a pair of comfortable old slippers. A companion for Friday nights. Someone to sit with and watch Greer Garson and Walter Pidgeon in *Mrs. Miniver*. Old Shep Harper! But Hicks! Hicks is something else. And looking across at him I might as well entertain the naughty thought that I wonder what he's like in bed. Sometimes these good-looking ones are duds. Or so I read in some dopey magazine at the hairdresser's.

Hicks looks up at her. "Anything special you'd like?"

"Well no, not really," says Jan. The waitress is standing by with pad in hand. A kid of eighteen or so and giving Hicks this absolutely goofy grin.

"We'll have the dinner for two," says Hicks handing back the menus. He doesn't even look at her.

"Sure thing," says the waitress. Hicks holds his glass at an angle and as he pours more beer he asks Jan why she became a teacher.

"I think it was my father," she says. "He was a history teacher at Eastview Collegiate down in the city for forty-three years. He was a born teacher and devoted to the study of what he called the human story. Couldn't understand why people weren't interested in the Peloponnesian War. I guess he influenced me. I know he was very pleased when I decided to become a teacher.

As he studies his beer, Hicks looks gloomy. "My father never left me with any kind of feeling. I don't even remember that much about him except that he drank a lot. That's the smell I first remember as a kid. Somebody bending over me or playing with me and this boozy breath. He died when I was five years old."

"An accident?" asks Jan.

"Yeh. At a construction site up in Elliot Lake. You know, where the uranium mines are. The side of a wall collapsed on him. I remember we lived in this trailer camp. In one of those mobile homes. It was the middle of the afternoon and my mother was listening to the radio when this neighbour came running over to tell us there'd been an accident. I remember the funeral, too. He was busted up pretty bad."

"Any brothers or sisters, James?"

"No. After the accident me and my mother came down to Barrie, where she worked as a hairdresser. Then she met my stepfather, Fern, and they got married when I was about eight, I guess. Fern's got this small trucking business up there. A couple of gravel trucks and a bulldozer. My mother has her own hairdressing place, so they do all right." Hicks looks at her carefully. "They look after my son for me. I'm married, eh?"

The waitress lays plates of food in front of them and Hicks seems to welcome the interruption. After the waitress leaves he starts loading his plate. "My wife and me, we don't live together any more. It'll be three years in February. There's just nothing left there at all."

"Are you divorced then?" asks Jan.

"No," says Hicks. "We haven't got around to divorce. Gail lives with this guy over in Bramalea. Divorces cost money and she's not willing to share expenses. I don't know." He looks away. "We just never got around to it. We haven't spoken to one another now in over two years. It's just like we dropped out of one another's lives. She doesn't even phone my mother anymore. To ask about Dale. And you have to admit that is very unnatural for a mother. Gail is a very selfish type of person. Actually, I despise her. I mean, abandoning your child for a guy the way she did. There's certainly no way she's ever going to get him back now." He puts more food on his plate. "I just wanted to be open with you. So you know exactly what the score is. And this is it. I'm still married, but I no longer have one bit of interest in my wife. As far as I'm concerned, she might as well be dead." He wipes his mouth with a napkin. "How about you?" he asks. "How come you're not married?"

"Just one of those things I suppose," says Jan. "I often think it's a question of timing. Sometimes you're asked when you don't feel you're ready for it. Or maybe you're a little too unsure of the person who's asking. Other times you're not asked when you'd just love to be. I was once asked and said thanks but no thanks. I wasn't ready for it, and I don't think I missed out on all that much. The guy has since divorced and remarried." Jack Sullivan! She hasn't thought of Jack in years. Her first year at Scarborough Secondary, and Jack was in the English Department too. A large, solemn man with a beard. Very serious about politics. Very big in the anti-Viet Nam movement. A bit like Seth Calder really. But she did think seriously about it before saying no. Then Jack married some organizer for the NDP. Then divorced her and moved to British Columbia. Somebody told Jan he was now growing his own vegetables on Vancouver Island and was writing something. A novel? Or a book of stories? She can't even remember who told her all this. But she knows she couldn't have stuck it with gloomy Jack.

"I'll bet you would make an excellent mother," says Hicks. "Wouldn't you like to have children?" Jan reaches for a cigarette.

"I don't know. Sometimes I think I would and other times I'm absolutely sure I wouldn't. I know that sounds a bit wishy-washy, but I can't help it. This isn't exactly the dandiest world to bring kids into."

Hicks sips a little beer. "Maybe not, but I'll bet the world has never been all that great a place to bring kids into. I don't know that much about historical periods, but I'll bet there have always been wars and plagues and famines and things like that. It's part of human life."

"You're probably right," says Jan. "My father would probably have agreed with you on that." Hicks gives her a beautiful smile and she finds herself smiling back. Really, he's a very nice guy. Rough around the edges, and with a kind of coiled tension inside him. But there seems to be a basic decency there too. And this old-fashioned courtliness!

"Marriage," says Hicks soberly, "doesn't work for everybody. Some people are just not cut out for it. Or maybe they marry too young. Like my wife, Gail, for example. She was nineteen when we got married, and she was a very immature person. I'm not saying I was all that mature myself at twenty-one, but I was more mature than she was. After we'd been married a couple of years, we just couldn't put it on. We'd get mad at one another over the stupidest things. Like she wouldn't change the baby's diapers for maybe hours. I mean you could smell those diapers through the whole apartment. And so I'd come home for dinner, eh? And Dale would be dirty. And my wife would be sitting there watching some stupid game show on TV. I mean, it was crazy. So I would say to her 'Look, Gail.

You're twenty-one years old, and you've got a husband and a child. You've got some responsibilities around here. Now what are you watching that crap for when you could, for example, change the baby's diapers?' And in the oven she'd maybe have two TV dinners or some of that Shake 'n' Bake stuff. Nothing that takes a lot of time or effort. At that time I was working for this transport company. In the loading shed. And it was pretty hard work, so when I got home I'd be tired and hungry. And I would be faced with this situation. I mean, I will admit to you honestly that I have a hot temper, and so pretty soon we would be shouting at one another. And a few times it would get really bad. We'd call each other all kinds of names and I'm not exactly proud of myself for saying so, but I clipped her a few times, too. I'd just totally lose my head. The whole thing was a very bad situation. After the first two or three years. The first few years were fine.

"Or I'll give you another example of Gail's immaturity. We'd go to a party on Saturday night, eh? Gail had these girl-friends who used to party a lot. And soon as we'd get there, after a couple of drinks Gail would start looking around for someone to fool with. Just to get me jealous, see? And it wasn't hard for her to find somebody, because she's a very good-looking woman. So, after a while she'd pick up some guy and they'd start dancing. And before long she'd make it very obvious that she was, you know, kind of hungry. So maybe they'd do a little necking in the corner, or even go into a bedroom. So to spite her I would start fooling around too. I'd start dancing with some woman and maybe get a little familiar with her. It wasn't that I was all that interested in this particular woman. It was more like a contest between Gail and I. I suppose it was to see which of us could hurt the other the most. But these parties always ended in a fight. Either I'd get into a fight with somebody's husband or I'd go after the guy with Gail. It was a bad situation. I think sometimes maybe we were too young. But then you take my aunt and uncle. They're not exactly young anymore, and they just aren't getting along well at all. I mean, maybe I shouldn't say this because Harry teaches at the school with you, but my aunt is seeing this guy. I think he's a real-estate salesman or something. Wears some kind of coloured sports-jacket with a crest on it. I saw him at her place one afternoon when I drove by. I was going to go in for a coffee but I didn't bother. Harry's a nice guy and he's an educated man. I mean he's smart in things like mathematics, but there are some things he just can't see. He just can't see what's going on, and it's perfectly obvious. I mean the way she treats him and everything. I honestly think she's going to take off with this guy one day. Just like Gail did. But Harry can't see that."

"Maybe he doesn't want to see, James."

"How do you mean that?"

"I mean that sometimes people just don't want to see unpleasant things. They don't want to read the signs."

"I guess that's possible," says Hicks, finishing his beer. "I know this much, though. If and when I get married again, I'm going to make it work. It's going to work because I'm going to make it work no matter what. I believe that if you really want something to work, it will go for you." Hicks looks thoughtful. It's as though he's been inspired by uttering this statement. Now he smiles again at Jan. "Hey! You got a cat or something at home? Because we could ask for one of those little bags. There's a lot of food left here. They always give you too much in these places, and you hardly touched anything. I don't mind asking for one of those bags. It doesn't bother me."

"No cat or dog at home, James."

When they leave, Hicks grasps her arm firmly, and the touch of his hand on her arm feels good. The night is brilliantly clear. The sky is sprinkled with stars and overhead the new moon now rides high. In the car Hicks asks her to try for some classical music. "Fair is fair, eh. Your turn." So she finds some Mozart. A little string quartet. Very soothing. They listen to it as they drive across the parking lot in silence. When they stop for a red light at Crown Hall and Progress, Hicks turns to her suddenly and asks, "Hey! What would you do if you won a million dollars?"

Jan shrugs. "I don't know. I don't buy lottery tickets as a rule. Sometimes at school I'll go in with three or four others, but not very often. The odds are ridiculous."

"Maybe so," says Hicks as the light turns green. "But you can't win if you don't have a ticket. I spend a few bucks on them. You never know."

"That's true," says Jan.

"I worked with this guy at Cross-Canada Transport," says Hicks. "He used to spend forty or fifty bucks a week on tickets. We called him the ticket junkie. We thought he was crazy. And then you know what? Another guy and him won a hundred thousand. Fifty thousand each. Not bad. Me, I've never won more than fifty bucks."

They turn east off Crown Hall and are soon on the dark small streets. "And what would you do if you won a million?" asks Jan. Hicks seems to have his answer ready. It's as though he's given this question a good deal of thought. "Well, first I'd buy a nice house. Somewhere in the country. And I'd pay for it outright. No mortgage payments to those goddam banks. Excuse my language. Then I'd have Dale come and live with me. Maybe get a couple of horses for him and some other farm animals. The rest of the money I'd put in the bank and then I'd live off the interest. Then maybe I might go back to school. Not to learn a trade or anything but just to learn things. There are so many things I don't know."

"What kinds of things, James?"

"Things out of books. Like earlier you mentioned your father talking about that war? What did you call it?"

"The Peloponnesian War."

"Yeh! Well, see I've never heard of it. And probably I should have."

Jan laughs. "Why? Most people get through life quite nicely without ever having heard of the Peloponnesian War."

"Okay," says Hicks, "maybe that's true. But that's just an example of what I'm talking about. What I mean is that I don't think a person should go through his life being ignorant." He hesitates. "I've spent all my life around ignorant people. People who never think about anything. People you can't have an intelligent conversation with."

He seems hung up on this subject.

"But, James, you don't have to have a lot of money or even go to university to learn things. The public libraries are full of books. There are night classes at the schools."

Hicks shakes his head. "Yeh, yeh. I know all that. I go to the library a lot. But it isn't the same . . ." And Jan thinks, yes, the guy is looking for a structure. A framework to fit things into. Some kind of response. It's like trying to learn a language by yourself out of books. You need dialogue and encouragement and support. The man is so hungry to improve himself. But does he see me as his teacher? After a day in the classroom, all I need is another student.

Hicks seems talked out. He even appears to be brooding, so Jan says, "Well, I guess if I won the big million, I'd do some travelling. I'd like to go back to Europe and spend a year just wandering around. Italy and Greece in particular. Before they tear the old world down completely. Or put up more hamburger joints in the shade of the Acropolis. Only this time I'd go in style."

"You been to Europe?" Hicks sounds surprised.

"Yes. It's years ago now. Right after I graduated from the College of Education. A girlfriend and I spent six weeks backpacking through the countryside."

"Backpacking?" asks Hicks. "What's that?" He sounds a bit annoyed at not knowing.

"Well, hitchhiking with your sleeping bag and everything on your back."

"Jesus. You mean to say you once hitchhiked through Europe? Two women alone? That sounds crazy. You never know who'll pick up when you're hitchhiking. When I was a kid I used to get picked up by old fags all the time. It was ridiculous. Finally I just stopped."

"Well," says Jan, "maybe it was dangerous. But the funny thing is we never really thought about it that way. That summer Europe seemed to be filled with young people from North America hiking around. There was usually company. We just never thought much about the danger." Except once, Harper. Remember? Near the end of August in the wet, flat fields of Belgium. Stranded in the middle of nowhere in the evening. Drizzle and mist, and they stood by the side of the road watching the darkness surround them. Then an old white Volvo came down the highway and rocked to a stop. Inside were four Belgian soldiers, and she and Max hesitated. Still, the young soldiers seemed good-natured enough. So they got in. It was cramped inside the Volvo, and the Belgians smelled of beer and onions. The windows fogged up and Jan wondered how the driver could see anything. It didn't seem to matter; he was singing as he drove.

Jan and Max were in the back seat sitting on the soldiers' knees, and after a while one of them put his hand on Jan's thigh and squeezed it. The other one in the back, a big sergeant, started in on Max. It began to get tense, but they kidded their way out of it, with Max breaking everyone up by doing hilarious imitations of German villagers. The Belgians loved it and couldn't stop laughing. They let the girls out at the next village, and standing in the dark fog by a church, Max began to shake. She was almost hysterical. They crouched in the spooky old churchyard under a rain-cape while Jan tried to stop Max's trembling. She couldn't understand why Max was almost in pieces. But after she calmed down, Max told her. "Do you know how close we came to getting gang-banged back there?" she said. "And all the time that sergeant. The bastard put my hand on his thing. It was as big around as my arm and I stroked the son of a bitch all the time we were laughing and joking. He came in his pants, and all the time I kept thinking, at least it's better than having that thing inside me. Jesus, Slim, we're lucky. That was nearly a very bad scene." They slept in the church and next morning caught a bus for the boat-train to Ostend. The summer of 1968. Rioting students in Paris and Russian soldiers in Prague. It seems a century ago.

On Willowgreen Drive most of the houses are still lighted, but then it's still only a little after eleven. And at Number 21 the lights are blazing. Of course she will still be up. Waiting for a little peek at the mystery date. Hicks pulls into the driveway and stops. "I'd really like to see you again. I enjoyed myself tonight." He says all this quickly and defiantly. As though daring anyone to contradict him.

"Well I did too, James. And I want to thank you for a nice time."

Around them the Trans Am throbs, and in the background good old W.A. Mozart. Jan feels comfortable, even sleepy. There are worse places to be, but she should now say goodnight and get out of the car. Then Hicks asks her to go for a drive with him tomorrow. They could go some place out in the country. Jan sits up straight. "I can't tomorrow, James. I'm sorry. Saturday is a kind of ritual at 21 Willowgreen. My mother and I, we go shopping. And then I have all this marking to do . . ." Hicks nods. "Okay, I can understand that. What about Sunday?"

Jan can see her mother's figure just behind the front drapes. Just for an instant and then it's gone. And isn't it time you moved out, Harper? Ye gods, you're four years off forty and your mother is still waiting for you. An old question. She's been through it hundreds of times. Is she prepared for all the flak from Bobby and her mother? And what to say to Hicks about Sunday? Another date and she's more or less committing herself to something. What?

"I don't think so, James. Thanks anyway."

"Why not?" asks Hicks. He looks over at her. "You busy on Sunday too?" Like all bad liars, Jan feels trapped. "You said you enjoyed yourself tonight," says Hicks, "so why can't we do it again?"

She half turns to him. "James, I did enjoy myself tonight. It's just . . ."

"You wonder about me, right? I'm not a schoolteacher or an accountant or a lawyer or anything like that. So you're wondering about me. Wondering if maybe I'm on the level. Well, I'm out of work at the moment, okay? I don't have a job, but I'm looking. Something will turn up. Now I've levelled with you about my wife and son. I've explained all that. I can't help it if I'm not a lawyer."

"All right, James. I don't care if you're not a lawyer, for God sakes."

"Well, what is it then? What's wrong with me? Why won't you go for a drive on Sunday?"

"There's nothing wrong with you," Jan says and stops.

"Well then," says Hicks, "let's go for a drive on Sunday."

Jan feels herself letting go. Subtly repudiating something or other.

"All right," she says.

Hicks is grinning. "You mean it?"

"I mean it."

"Terrific. Two o'clock okay?"

"Two is fine." She reaches for the door.

"Hey! Wait a minute," says Hicks, jumping out and coming around to open her door. Standing by the car, he takes her arm again. "I really meant it when I said I enjoyed myself tonight."

"Thanks, James." In the shadows cast by the street lamp, Hicks's face looks apprehensive, and Jan wonders if he's thinking of kissing her. She's not sure she would mind. Instead he lets go. "I'll see you on Sunday at two."

"Fine," she says, starting up the driveway.

"Maybe you could bring that book and read some poems to me," he calls. He sounds very happy. "See you Sunday."

Without turning around, Jan waves an arm. When she gets to the side door, Hicks is backing out. He blinks his lights twice at her before driving away. Inside the door her mother is standing at the top of the stairs in her cotton floral housecoat. "Did you and Mr. Hicks have a nice time, dear?"

"Yes, Mom, thanks."

"Well, you certainly weren't late. Would you like to come up for a cup of Sanka?"

"No thanks. I'm tired."

"Well, you can tell me all about him tomorrow. Goodnight, dear."

Jan fits the key in her lock. "Goodnight, Mom."

3

It's still only half past eleven when Hicks drops in to the Puss 'n' Boots Club. The place is crowded and he's lucky to find an empty stool at the bar. Hicks has three quick drafts and is soon feeling good about things. One of the sets is nearly over, and on the stage a little blonde with tremendous jugs is grinding it out to some jukebox stuff. Terrible blaring music, thinks Hicks, watching the blonde push her twat almost into a guy's face. There's a table full of drunks right near the stage and everybody is cheering and laughing. Hicks feels a little contemptuous of all this. If it came to it, he wouldn't mind giving the blonde a bang, but the whole show strikes him as crude and vulgar. What with the loud rock music and the vulgarity, he doesn't know why he spends so much time in this place. Of course, the problem is that there is no other place around to drink. Just restaurants, and you can't see anything in a restaurant. Besides, Hicks feels like a fool sitting by himself in a restaurant.

In the far corner of the room Vicky Pruit is seated with some people. The party includes two black men in shiny suits. One of them wears a weird fedora with a big wide brim. Vicky waves to Hicks, but he doesn't let on that he notices. He's still thinking about his evening with Janice Harper. A very nice woman there. And it was not as difficult to talk to her as he had imagined. You have to level with a woman like that because she is too intelligent and sensitive to be snowed. With some chicks you can bullshit your way through, because all you want to do is give them a fuck or maybe borrow ten dollars. But with a woman like Janice Harper you've got to be level right down the line. Like tonight, for instance, when he gave her the news that he had no job at the moment. It didn't even faze her. Probably she appreciated the truth. Same with his story about his wife and son. The point is, thinks Hicks, that he levelled with her and she accepted him.

Hicks orders three more drafts. He feels good about the way things are shaping up with Janice Harper. Tonight they broke the ice. Got to know one another a little better. Next time they'll find out a little more, and so on and so forth. The worst thing you can do is rush things along because this could turn out to be a fine, permanent relationship. Maybe they'll even get married. Who knows? Hicks believes that Janice Harper would be an excellent influence on Dale. Hicks appreciates the fact that his mother looks after Dale. Food, clothes, toys, no problem at that end of things. But, for instance, the kid watches too much TV. Every time Hicks visits, Dale is watching TV. He even eats most of his meals in front of it, for Christ sakes. It doesn't seem to bother his grandmother or Fern, but Hicks figures it's not a good idea. You never see the kid reading a book, which might improve his mind. However, if Hicks and Janice Harper got married, Dale could come and live with them and Hicks would be willing to bet a thousand dollars that Janice Harper wouldn't let any kid eat in front of the TV. And Hicks would back her all the way. Even though Dale would probably kick up a fuss. But you can't give kids their own way all the time. And that's the problem with Dale. He's spoiled. His grandparents are too easy on him.

The blonde finishes her act and the crowd applauds. Hicks drinks some more beer and thinks about his Sunday drive with Janice Harper. He'll take her some place nice, maybe up to that conservation area near Claremont. Hicks worked up that way for a construction company. Fixing roads one summer. Used to drive up each day from the city in the back of a truck with a bunch of Wops. Hicks was the only guy who could speak English. At lunchtime they'd sit by the roadside and look at the farms with their white fences and racing horses in the fields. Peaceful. They could be there in an hour or so, and what would really be nice would be a picnic. The thought of it excites Hicks. He'll surprise her with a picnic lunch. Tomorrow he'll go over to Quik Pik and get some cold cuts, cheese, bread, and pickles. He's got beer at home, so put some of that on ice. If the weather is decent, it'll make a pleasant outing. A picnic lunch. A very attractive idea, thinks Hicks. She's bound to go for it.

"Hey, Jimmy! Where have you been keeping yourself? I haven't seen you around." Vicky Pruit stands beside him wearing very high-heeled shoes, pants, and a black satin shirt embroidered with spangles. She wears this cowboy outfit because her ex-husband used to play rhythm guitar with a country band and she's hung up on country singing and the whole lifestyle. The shirt is open and Hicks can see her long tits. Her dark hair smells like smoke. A good-looking woman, thinks Hicks, but stupid. He has told her numerous times that he doesn't like to be called Jimmy but she keeps forgetting. Hicks figures it's now pointless to keep mentioning it. But she's an awfully sexy-looking woman in her tight pants with her tits coming out of the satin shirt. She used to be a go-go dancer before she hooked up with the guitar-player.

"I've been busy," says Hicks.

"You been seein' somebody?" asks Vicky.

"Nothing special," says Hicks. "I'm just living a quiet life." Vicky smiles and leans in against the bar. She sneaks her hand between his legs and gives him a few strokes. Hicks grows hard as a stone. "You look nice tonight," says Vicky, rubbing his tool. "You been on a date? She couldn't have given you much of a time if you're sitting here all by yourself with this rock between your legs?"

Hicks brushes her hand away. "Hey, lay off that," he whispers. "You want me to drop a wad? I just had these pants dry-cleaned." Vicky laughs and gives him another little squeeze.

"Why don't we go to my place? I've got a bottle of gin. We'll party. Just you and me." Tempting. It has to be admitted. Hicks looks past her toward the corner.

"What about your friends over there?"

Vicky shrugs. "They're nobody special."

"You going out with niggers now?"

"I've gone out with Henry a few times. He doesn't own me."

"Which one is Henry?"

"The one with the hat."

"Is he a pimp?"

Vicky looks hurt. "Hey, come on, Jimmy. What do you take me for?"

"I don't know," says Hicks. "I just don't want any hassles."

"There won't be any hassles," says Vicky. "Look, why don't you go out to your car and wait for me? I'll tell them something. I have to go to the washroom or something like that. And then I'll be out in about five minutes. How is that?"

Hicks finishes his beer and slides off the stool. "All right," he says. He leaves without even looking at her.

In the parking lot behind the Puss 'n' Boots, Hicks sits in his car and watches a young guy vomiting. The guy's friend stands apart with his hands in his pockets. Looking at them makes Hicks feel old. When he was seventeen you couldn't count the number of times he threw up a night's beer. Also, he feels a little uneasy about the way the evening is turning out. The way he sees it, he is now more or less going with a very nice woman. And now, following a pleasant evening with her, he is going to fuck Vicky Pruit. In a way it's a serious betrayal. If a person is committing himself to a relationship with a woman like Janice Harper, then he shouldn't really go fucking the first woman who lays it out for him. Still, Vicky Pruit is Vicky Pruit, and even thinking about her in the spiked heels and the tight pants and the satin shirt is enough to give Hicks another hard-on. Looking at it in another way, too, a man has to be relieved of these physical longings. Hicks once read in a magazine that guys who don't get it regularly, people like priests and sailors, develop problems in their glands. Maybe even leading to cancer. It just isn't natural to go without it for very long. Yet he feels weighed down by guilt.

Maybe, he thinks, something could be worked out. A compromise. Instead of putting it in, he could ask Vicky to give him a blow job. She gives terrific head. Still, she might not go for that. It's a genuine dilemma, thinks Hicks, as he watches the sick kid and waits for Vicky Pruit.

Six

1

After her mother leaves for church, Jan relaxes. Her favorite time of the week. The blessed peace. The voice of the vacuum cleaner is no longer heard in the land. All quiet on the upstairs front. For years she accompanied her mother and father to church, but after her father's death she stopped. Her mother has tried in vain to persuade her to resume holy worship. Now, with her feet up on the coffee table, Jan smokes a cigarette and has a second cup of coffee. She parts her housecoat and examines her legs and long, narrow feet. One of her strongest points, those legs. Travers always said so. And her bottom isn't bad either. Blessed like her father with a tall, slender frame. Mind you, the chest is nothing to write home about, but you can't have it all, Harper.

This morning she feels a little spiky. Last night's sleep was only fitful. She can remember a bizarre dream in which she was riding with Hicks in the Trans Am. The police were chasing them, and they kept going back and forth along Willowgreen Drive while all the neighbours gathered on their lawns to see what the racket was all about. In her housecoat and hair curlers, Mrs. Harper watched these shenanigans from behind her picture window. The dream woke Jan up at four o'clock and, after that, sleep seemed to come and go. Now she walks to the window and looks up at a pale blue sky. Opening the window, she smells earth and petunias. Thinks about Hicks. A nice enough guy. Terrific looking. A little on the serious side, but vulnerable and eager to learn. Maybe too eager. And why, then, all this anxiety? Well, Harper, the guy is married, he's an ex-con, and he hasn't got a job. Nobody is asking for the neighbourhood Rotarian. In fact I wouldn't want him. But with Mr. Hicks it could get very complicated.

Yesterday for instance. Interrogation time. Where did you go? That's nice. And from then on, not so nice. Where does his family come from? What religion is he? *What is his education?* What does he do? Nothing, dear Mother, he's on the flipping unemployment rolls. Instead of which she lied and said he worked for a construction company. Finishing interiors. Laying tile and like that. Thank you, Harry Waggoner. A tradesman, said Mrs. Harper. She was not pleased. Her little rosebud mouth turned downward in disappointment. She still thinks tradesmen are somehow inferior to professional people. But that's by the by. The infuriating thing is that, at thirty-six, I'm reduced to lying about the man I go out with. I am a cowardly middle-class creep who is afraid of what my mother and others will think. And yet, Harper, face it, old girl. If you keep seeing him, sooner or later you're going to have to go out with other people. You saw how out of place he looked at Harry's party.

And then he's married. Do I really need that scene again? With Travers it was bad enough. When the little woman learned that Jan was seeing her husband, she got right on the wire. Those venomous phone calls. Jan listened with a scorched ear. "You think you're the first?" shrilled Mrs. T. "You're not even the twenty-first, Mizz Harper. You're just a little bit of recreation for him right now. In the end he always comes back to me and the girls." Then she called Jan a cunt. Which was surprising. Jan had never been called that before. Didn't really think it was a term women used. Well, you live and learn. Then one day, curious to know what a woman who would call another woman a cunt looked like, Jan drove out to Richmond Hill, hoping for a peek. She was parked down the street for an hour before she saw Vivian Travers and her two daughters coming home from shopping. Travers's wife was a peppy little bleached blonde in hip-huggers and sweatshirt. Smoking a cigarette as she unloaded groceries and ordered the girls around. The two girls, ten and twelve, were dolls. But Vivian Travers radiated an energetic hostility. Probably a compulsive type, thought Jan at the time. No wonder poor Travers needed to relax now and again.

So, when it comes right down to it, married is married. And Hicks is married. What if this wife of his decides she wants to move back in. It wouldn't be the first time. And I'll bet she's a tough little number, too. Jan sees herself being punched out by Hick's wife in the school parking lot some morning. The kids loving every minute, while principal Hornbeck looks down from his perch on high. And Bruce Horton rushes over to break it up, arriving just in time to get kicked in the trophies. Wonderful! And complicated. Yes, it could get very complicated. And who needs complicated?

2

Hicks drives along the freeway with his left arm draped out the open window like a truck-driver. With the windows rolled down, the car is filled with the rushing sound of the wind and the radio. Jan feels exhilarated but worried. She looks over at Hicks and listens to Billie Jo Spears singing "Rainy Days and

Stormy Nights." The radio is turned way up against the sound of the rushing air. And it has to be said that Hicks looks fantastic this afternoon in a pair of jeans and a dark blue shirt. The sleeves are rolled up past his elbows and Jan finds it hard not to star at his lean, brown arms. His hair seems to flow in the wind and he's wearing sunglasses. A real glamour-puss!

It's a glorious afternoon with huge white clouds riding across the sky. If only I could enjoy it all! But how can I enjoy it if I'm going to tell him that it's *tout fini* between us? He seems so pleased with himself; he's like a kid. Already he's talked about a surprise, and from time to time he looks over at her and smiles. Jan feels a mild dread. What's the surprise? One of those giant heart-shaped boxes of chocolate from Woolworth's? Ye gods, I hope not. I can't stand chocolates and I'll have to fake it.

Hicks turns north on a two-lane highway and soon they are in the countryside. While they drive along, Jan watches the long shadows darkening the fields as the clouds travel overhead. Then the shadows pass, and in the late summer afternoon everything is vivid under the sunlight. The air is rich and thrilling. Some of the leaves are already touched with colour. Mother Nature's Paintbrush! One of her teachers used to say that when they brought their crimson and yellow leaves to school. To tape into scribblers and label. Grade Three. Mrs. Jellicoe. An old maid and a distant relative of the famous English admiral. An old maid? I'll bet at the time she wasn't much older than I am right now. Of course, she looked older. Dressed like a Baptist. Severe suits and her hair pulled back in a bun.

As they turn down a country road, they dip into a valley and then rise to higher ground. An hour from Toronto and the countryside is like rural England with a horse farm here and there. A few cows. Even some sheep. Where sheep may safely graze. And I wish I weren't so damn nervous. When they pull into the conservation area they see only one other car, a Datsun wagon. But then the place is officially closed for the year, with the office and ticket booth boarded up for the winter. You can roam around but you're on your own. In the gravel parking lot a family stands by the Datsun, preparing to set off. The father, a tall, bearded professional type in hiking boots, is folding up a map. His wife and two kids, a boy and a girl about twelve, also look like serious walkers who mean business on the trails. They carry thermoses, and cameras for birdwatching. When Hicks pulls alongside, the man looks slightly annoyed. It could be the car. Or it could be Hicks's radio, which is still cranked up to full volume. "Let's Get It While the Gettin's Good." Sung by Eddy Arnold. The family hurriedly moves off toward the woods.

When the sun goes in behind the clouds it's chilly, so Jan puts on her suede jacket and stands watching Hicks open the car's trunk. Inside is a small food chest. "I thought a picnic would be kind of nice," says Hicks. He opens the food locker. "I hope you like cold chicken. I've got some potato salad here too. And some ham. Bread. Beer. I got a bottle of wine too. If you like it. I'm not much for wine." He looks over at her, smiling. "Well, what do you think? You don't look very happy. Don't worry. This stuff won't poison you. I didn't make it. Got it at the delicatessen." He snaps the lid shut. And, Harper you fool, you're going to cry a little.

"It looks great, James," she says, reaching into her purse for a Kleenex. Hicks looks over at her. "What's the matter? You got that hay fever again? Hell, I forgot about that. Maybe I shouldn't have brought you out here."

"No, no," says Jan, "we've had a frost. The ragweed's dead. It's nothing." He takes her by the arm. She can't read him behind those dark glasses. Sees only the black hair at the base of his throat. "Are you sure you're okay?" he asks.

"Yes, fine," she says, blowing her nose. "It's the old speck-in-the-eye bit. Not to worry." He bends to take the food chest from the trunk.

"Okay. There's a nice spot up there in those fields. You get a nice view of the country from up there. You take this blanket and I'll bring the food. All right?"

"Fine," says Jan. "This is really very sweet of you, James."

"You like the surprise?" he asks, grinning.

"Yes," she says. "Yes I do."

Holding her by the hand he takes her along a path toward a field of grey, dry grass. It's a bit of a climb, and they ascend wordlessly. At the top of the hill they can see the surrounding countryside as it darkens and brightens under the windy sky. Far below on the edge of the woods they can see the hiking family as it moves along the trail, stopping now and again to examine something. Jan spreads the blanket and sets out the food. Hicks opens a bottle of Black Tower, and they eat off paper plates. Around them the wind rushes past, and along the hillside the grass seems to flow in the moving air. As he eats, Hicks seems preoccupied, almost withdrawn. Watching him, Jan wonders if perhaps she didn't respond extravagantly enough to the picnic. Or maybe it's simply that he's touched by the scenery. She remembers his dream of wining the lottery ticket and buying a farm. Finally he says, "It's nice up here, isn't it?" He is still looking out across the small valley. "It's a lovely view," says Jan. "And at this time of the year, it's so quiet too." She has already decided to enjoy the afternoon; she'll tell him later when he drives her home.

They sit eating and listening to the wind in the grass until Hicks says, "How about driving up to Barrie with me next Sunday? I'd like you to meet my son. We could leave after breakfast. Have lunch at my mother's and I could introduce you to the family. Then maybe we could go out to dinner on the way back. There's a pretty good steak house not far from my mother's."

She should have expected something like this. If you don't discourage them early, some people invite you into their lives very quickly. Jan hesitates. "James, if you're out of work, all this must be costing you a great deal of money. Books, flowers, movies, dinners, picnic lunches. I mean, things are so expensive these days."

Hicks puts down his plate and leans back on his elbows. The wind flows through his hair. "You're always worrying about money. Don't worry about the money. I get by." He looks down toward the woods. "Manpower phoned me on Friday, and I have to see them tomorrow. Maybe something has come up. The insulation companies are hiring again, but I don't think I want to go back into that line of work. It's not healthy. You breathe in all those fibers when you're putting the stuff into the houses. They give you these little masks but they're not really much help. This guy told me that working in insulation is worse than smoking three or four packs of cigarettes a day. And I didn't quit smoking to ruin my lungs like that. So, I'll see what they come up with."

Jan watches him open a beer and take a long swallow. She tries to light a cigarette but the wind will simply not permit it, so she throws the cigarette and says, "James, I don't think we should see one another again." Hicks stops drinking and looks over at her. She wishes he'd take off those damn sunglasses.

"Why not?" he asks. She looks up at the big white clouds booming across the sky and thinks of Shelley. "O wild West Wind, thou breath of Autumn's being." That poem knocked her out in high school. Grade Ten. Naughty, mad Shelley. Probably a real fruitcake, but his words went to her head like wine. "I just don't think," she says carefully, "there's any future for the two of us together. Please don't get me wrong. I've enjoyed your company." *I've enjoyed your company.* Shit. How stuffy can you be, Harper? You sound just like an old-maid schoolteacher. Hicks is staring at her. His brow is knitted into a frown. She stumbles on. "It's so hard to put, James. It's just that I don't think we're particularly suited to one another." Hicks sits up and drops his hands across his knees.

"I'm sorry to hear you say that because I am feeling very serious about you. I told you before I think you're a tremendous person. I'm very serious about you."

"James, I just don't see how it could ever work." The wind whips away a paper plate and sends it flying through the air.

"It can work as far as I'm concerned," says Hicks. "I've known lots of women. Women have never been a big deal to me. I can tell you that in all honesty, and I don't want to sound like I'm bragging, because that's not what I'm getting at. But I've not met a woman like you before. I mean, I may not be educated like you, but I'm not exactly stupid either. There are certain areas in my life I want to develop. And I'm going to. I've made several mistakes in judgement. My marriage, for example. But I figure that's all behind me. I think I can get things sorted out." He looks at her again. "I thought that because you've gone out with me now three times, that you must like me."

Jan clasps her knees and rocks a little in the wind.

"James, it's not that I don't like you. And I certainly don't think you're stupid."

"Well, what's the problem then?" asks Hicks. "I don't understand why we can't go on seeing one another. Get to know one another better."

Jan begins to tidy up things by dumping chicken bones into a bag. The problem is to avoid hurting his feelings. He's a touchy man.

"How old are you, James?"

"I was thirty in June. Why?"

"I'm thirty-six," she says.

Hicks shrugs. "So you're thirty-six? So what? It doesn't matter. In fact it's ridiculous to even mention age. Lots of women now go with younger men. I read this piece in a magazine about that. It's becoming more and more common. I don't see that as a feasible excuse at all."

Jan senses an impatience sifting into his voice. She continues to sort out the remains of the picnic lunch. When the sun goes behind the clouds, she thinks of winter. The hiking family has disappeared into the woods and, far below, a camper truck makes a U-turn in the parking lot and drives away. Watching it, Jan says, "James, I can't see that we have very much in common."

He stands up and brushes crumbs from his jeans. He's angry all right, Harper. The party is definitely over.

"How do you know we haven't got anything in common?" he says, looking down at her. "You haven't given us a chance." Jan stands up and watches him snatch the blanket from the ground and shake it furiously. It makes a great flapping sound in the wind. "You might be surprised," says Hicks, "at the things we have in common." His voice is edged with bitterness. "The problem as I see it is that you think I'm some kind of a jerk. Because I'm not a lawyer or an accountant or a goddam schoolteacher. So you see me as a loser type. Right?" He stuffs the blanket under his arm. "Am I right, Janice?"

"James . . . that's not true."

"Bullshit. It's true. I can tell that." He grabs the food chest and, with the blanket tucked under his arm, strides away down the hill. Jan hurries to catch up.

"Now, James, wait a minute." He turns and watches her coming toward him.

"I never laid a hand on you," he says. "I treated you with respect." Jan stops and, looking down at his retreating figure, feels a flash of anger.

"Well, what do you want for God sakes?" she yells. "Brownie points for being a gentleman?"

Either he doesn't hear or he doesn't get it because he continues down the hill alone. When she reaches the car he is already sitting behind the wheel. The motor is running and radio is turned up full blast. Deafening. Hicks stares ahead. Even with the dark glasses his face is a study in grim and furious disappointment. He moves them out, the rear wheels spitting gravel as they leave the parking lot. Looking at him, Jan feels guilty. His surprise picnic is in shreds. She's ruined his afternoon. On the radio Johnny Rodriguez is singing "I Hate the Way I Love It." And Hicks is driving very fast.

The highway is busy with late Sunday-afternoon traffic as people return to the city after a day in the country. Hicks is a good driver, but he's driving too fast for a two-lane highway, moving out to the passing lane whenever there's the slightest opening. Then, slipping back in ahead of braking cars. He drives, in fact, like a man who hates the world and everyone in it. Oncoming cars flash their lights and horns blare in passing. Rocking through this late Sunday afternoon, Jan and Hicks listen to commercials for used cars, take-out chicken, and condominiums. Then Conway Twitty is singing "Happy Birthday Darlin'," and Jan feels overcome with anger. A richly satisfying wrath engulfs her and she feels suddenly glad to be rid of James Hicks and his gimcrack fourth-rate world with its muscle cars and whining cowboy singers. She imagines his apartment filled with supermarket paintings of rural scenes.

Hicks pulls out to pass a long line of cars. An oncoming driver flashes his lights and Hicks pours it on. For a terrifying moment it looks to Jan as though they might simply end their lives here on this highway. But at the last second Hicks squeezes in behind a panel truck. The northbound car sweeps past them. Jan is so angry she's shaking. "If you're not going to drive this car sensibly, then I want you to pull over and let me out. I'm not going to end my days overturned in some ditch with that goddam stuff playing in my ears." Hicks says nothing but pulls back to fifty and turns down the radio. After a moment he says, "If you want to try for something else on the radio, go ahead." "It's all right," says Jan, looking out her window. "It was just too loud."

They say nothing more until they reach Willowgreen Drive. Jan is already reaching for the door when Hicks grasps her wrist. "Wait a minute, Janice. Please." She looks at him. He's leaning over the steering wheel looking very tired. He's taken off the sunglasses and is rubbing his eyes with thumb and forefinger. "Look, I'm sorry," he says. "Back there. Driving like that. It was crazy. I was mad at you, so I acted like a punk. Just plain stupid. I'm sorry." Jan looks straight ahead. Her mother is at Bobby's for dinner, so she won't be staring out the window. Willowgreen Drive looks deserted. Everyone is inside watching TV football. The sun is now behind the houses and the front lawns are enclosed in shadows. Hicks says, "Janice, I don't think you've given us a chance. I mean, I know what I did back there on the highway was stupid. I admit that." And without knowing why, Jan suddenly feels like crying. She feels her eyes filling. You're overwrought, Harper. You were nearly killed back there. It's been a tense afternoon. Now she longs to be alone. A warm bath. A cigarette and a drink. A little Schubert. Piano stuff. And not too loud, please. Small mercies in a mad world. Hicks is saying, "If you like me as a person, then isn't that the important place to start? I mean, I am very interested in things like poetry and books and music. Like that Mozart on the radio the other night. I really enjoyed that. It's just that I've never been exposed to that kind of music. It's not that I don't appreciate its quality. I mean, it's lasted for several hundred years, so it's got to be good. Right? Same thing with Shakespeare and people like that."

"James, I have to go in now. I have a lot of work to do for tomorrow." She thinks her voice sounds a bit cracked. "I'm sorry if I spoiled your picnic." Hicks kisses her hand. It seems an oddly unaffected and perfectly natural thing to do. And, sitting ramrod straight, Jan stares ahead and feels his warm breath on her flesh. Still holding her hand Hicks says, "Look. If you don't want to come up next weekend to Barrie, I can understand that. Maybe that's a little premature. So how about we just go to another movie? Friday or Saturday night, whichever you're free. Any movie you like. You choose this time. We'll go downtown." Jan shakes her head. He just doesn't get it.

"No, James, I don't think so. I'm busy next weekend. I really have to go now." Hicks releases her hand. "Janice. Come on. You can't just go like that. Let's have another coffee at least." But she has the door open and outside the car she says, "Goodbye, James. And thank you."

As she hurries up the driveway she hears him calling to her. "I'll phone you tomorrow night. Okay?"

3

A few minutes later Hicks nearly has an accident. Going south on Crown Hall Road he slows for the red light at Richfield. However, he does not come to a complete stop before making his right turn. He's still confounded by the whole afternoon and brooding over the way things turned out. So he does not catch sight of the westbound Chevy wagon tooling through the intersection at about forty. The guy is obviously running the orange. Still, Hicks should have stopped and looked before making his turn. For a moment it's quite hairy. A really frightening screech of brakes as the wagon pulls around the Trans Am. Just misses Hicks. Luckily nobody else is at the intersection or there could have been serious trouble. Instead, the big car sways and rocks to a halt a half a hundred feet down Richfield Road. Hicks sees two kids staring out the back window. They look as if they've just gone through a wind tunnel. In the front seat a woman is holding her hands against her face. Hicks has to pass the wagon, and as he does, the driver, a guy about forty with a red face, rolls down his window and calls Hicks an idiot. Hicks would just like to get back to his place, but he stops and rolls down the window on the passenger side. After all, maybe he didn't stop, but the guy was running that orange. Leaning across the seat, Hicks gives the finger to the man. "Fuck you, buddy. You ran that orange at about forty-five fucking miles an hour." The guy's wife just stares at Hicks. He could be some monster from outer space the way she looks at him. "You didn't stop," the guy says, but his voice is subdued. Hicks looks fit and has at least ten years on him. Probably the guy sees an ugly incident in the making. Hicks yells at him, "You better watch your fucking step." And tramps the accelerator, looking in the rearview mirror. He knows the guy won't give chase. He'll take it out on his wife and kids. A miserable evening ahead for them.

In the late afternoon Richfield Road is quiet. The small factories and warehouses are closed for Sunday. Everything looks empty, and Hicks feels depressed and furious with life in general. You plan something nice, you lay out money for food and wine thinking this will please her. We'll just have a nice time. No fucking around, just talking and getting to know one another a little better. And what happens? A total fucking disaster. Now she doesn't want to see him anymore. Not good enough for her. And he gave it his best shot. Books, flowers, dinner, picnic lunch, and despite all this, everything goes to fuck. In the grip of this rage Hicks reflects on the idea that nothing ever works out the way you think it will. That's why it makes sense to believe in God or Fate or Whatever. That way, at least you got something to curse at. Or maybe try to get on the good side of. Probably cave men did that. Invented their gods and made sacrifices when things didn't work out. Or to ward off bad times.

At Transit Road Hicks turns left and sees the public library. In front of the library is an open area which has been cemented over to make a kind of square. Here, in good weather, people can relax. There are several slatted wooden benches bolted into the cement. They have also planted beds of petunias and hidden the trash cans in cemented cylinders. At lunchtime in the summer, four young women in long dresses turn up and play classical music while office-workers eat their lunches from paper bags. Now, of course, the little square is deserted except for a solitary figure who marches back and forth, waving his arms. It's that idiot Big John, and Hicks stops to watch the man. Big John sits down on a bench and points his finger at some invisible person. Hicks is too far away to hear anything, even with the window open. But then, the man never raves. He just mutters and cuts up the air with his hands. Crazy fucker. A man built like that could kill somebody one day. Now talking to the fucking wind. He's a potential menace to society and has no business walking around the streets.

As Hicks drives away, he ponders whether being crazy doesn't have certain advantages. For a start you don't have to worry about money. Insane people get looked after by the government so there's no worry about eats or rent. And when it comes down to it, you can really do whatever the fuck you feel like doing. If, for instance, you feel like waving your prick at some old lady in the A&P, you just go ahead and do it. Or maybe just take a serious shot at some guy who offers you lip. They'll put you away for a while, but then you act normal for a few months and you're back on the street like Big John. Of course, there are disadvantages too. No pussy for example. No woman in her right mind would fuck a big animal like that. He must jack off a lot, thinks Hicks.

Seven

I

The wind drives the rain in sheets against the windows. It's been raining for hours and there are now large puddles on the football field. Jan stands by the window, watching 12D write a content test on *The Mayor of Casterbridge*. The classroom smells of stale air and sneakers and exasperation. But they were warned two weeks ago this was the day. And every day for the past week she reminded them. Still the news was greeted with groans and shocked looks. Anthony Ellis, a seventeen-year-old malcontent from Trinidad and star running-back, looked up from his seat, his face bleak and arrogant. "Miss Harper. I read the book. And to my mind it is useless as an education tool. Who cares about a story written in old-fashioned language about people living in an English town a hundred years ago? This has nothing to do with my personal experience." Murmurs of approval all around as people sensed a shoot-out. If they could keep talking about it for ten minutes, then no test. Not fair. Not enough time. And, normally, Jan would have greeted an observation like Anthony's with a witticism. It was almost expected of her. She was supposed to handle these situations with deft humour.

One day she overheard a student say that Miss Harper is funny and fair. Perhaps not a bad epitaph for thirteen years of teaching. Only this morning Jan didn't feel like being funny or fair. So, when the star running-back got uppity she merely said, "Just do the test, Anthony. All right? Just do what you're told." Anthony Ellis didn't like that one bit, but he got on with it. Others gave her a puzzled look which said, "What's eating you this morning?" And Jan felt like screaming, "And why am I not entitled to a bad day now and then, damn it?" In fact the whole week has been bad. Her period is only a couple of days away. Then there are the letters from Hicks. And tonight the Harvest Dance for God sakes!

She watches Anthony Ellis filling in the question sheet, his handsome brow knitted in concentration. He knows the answers all right, but just wants to raise a little fuss. There's a chip glued to his shoulder. But his little scene at the beginning of the class has soured an already bad morning. They'll work their way through Hardy's novel over the next couple of weeks and a few of them will actually enjoy it. Most, however, will look on with numb indifference. Something else to get through. An ugly feeling of futility passes through her and she reminds herself to take it easy. Every teacher gets these feelings once in a while. It's just a bad day, Harper, so ride it out. She watches them frowning and scribbling away. Others stop to stare at the ceiling. As if the answers were there! It's a simple test, folks. To score well, all you have to do is read the fucking book. But reading a book! That's a major assignment for some of these kids. When she was their age she read all the time. Of course, there was no TV. At first her father wouldn't have one in the house. A highly suspect invention is how he put it, and Jan remembers being both angry and admiring because all her friends had TV. Not having one seemed unusually quirky. Finally he broke down and bought one. But not until 1962, when she was eighteen and in her last year of high school. Then *he* spent every Saturday afternoon watching reruns of *Leave It to Beaver* and *All-Star Wrestling*. Sitting in his sweater coat before the box, fully admitting that he was falling into hopeless decadence. God, how I miss him!

Watching the students, Jan hopes that most will take the period to finish the test. She doesn't feel like introducing the novel today. What she'd like to do most is go home, crawl into bed, and turn off the world. Also disconnect the phone, although he probably wouldn't call through the day. She hasn't answered the phone since Monday night, when she pleaded with Hicks not to call again. It didn't help. The phone kept ringing and she knew it was him. So, as soon as she gets home, she pulls the phone jack from the wall. She is thinking of an unlisted number. Getting in touch with the telephone company and arranging this is probably simple enough, but today it seems enormously complicated. The truth is I haven't the patience. There is a small fire in my chest, too, and why oh why do these sore breasts of mine go along with sexual hunger. I'm as horny as a bitch in heat. And always it's like this, damn it. The mysteries of the monthly cycle. Somebody must be doing a Ph.D. on it. She remembers a discussion in the staff room last spring. Mark Beamish sitting there in his gym shorts and tee shirt, his great hairy legs wide open. Talking, of all things, about menstruation. Mark also teaches Grade Nine health and is interested in these things. He'd "read up" on menstruation because his wife, Patty, always has problems with her period. Mark is the sort who doesn't mind letting it all hang out as they used to say. And his dear little Patty, all five feet of her, is rendered *hors de combat* once a month with menstrual cramps. Has to go right to bed for a couple of days. "And just think," said Mark, biting into a Mars bar, "what would happen if, say, the Americans elected a woman president, which might happen in the not too distant future. And suppose, for instance, that this woman president has to face some major crisis. Say, war with Russia. And suppose all this happens around the time of her period. Well, it stands to reason she may not be psychologically number one. So think about. All the pressure. She could get very emotional and make the wrong decision. And poof. Up she goes!" Norma Kirstead had already fled the staffroom, clutching a hiking magazine, her days of periods probably over and good riddance. But Judy Barowski, in gym bloomers, her face stormy, said, "You're out of your gourd, Mark, do you know that?" Judy likes to use expressions like that. Picks it up from the kids, I suppose. But she was hopping mad that day. Now, reflecting on that idiotic conversation, Jan believes that she could easily start a third world war today. Send Mark and his little Patty into orbit too. And why do big men choose such little tent pegs for wives. You see it so many times. Jan tries to picture them in bed. It must make for some weird positioning. Throughout it all, Mark would doubtless be thumbing through a sex manual, wetting his fingers as he turns the pages. And ye gods but my thoughts are in sexual turmoil today.

Watching the rain slash against the windows, Jan wonders if there will be another letter today. Or has he given up? Somehow she doubts it. The first one arrived on Tuesday. Another on Wednesday and again yesterday. She doesn't know quite why they leave her so rattled. Nevertheless, they do. Whenever she reads one, she feels surrounded by a vague panic. It's strange, because the letters are not in the least threatening. On the contrary, they are simple declarations of affection. Words most people want to hear. Why not you, Harper? In her mind she sees yesterday's letter. Words on a piece of lined notebook paper.

> 16 Terrace Court Gardens
> Unit 8
> September 26

Dear Janice:

Why won't you talk to me on the phone? I can't be that bad a person can I? I just want to tell you that I think I love you. I say I think because I want to be honest with you and I'm not sure I am yet. In love with you that is. Please let us talk together.

> *Yours respectfully,*
> *James*

Hicks! Hicks! You are bending my life out of shape with these phone calls and letters. Lay off, goddam it. But last night he invaded a dream. An erotic dream she can now only dimly remember. Except that his lean brown arms enclosed her and she awakened at five o'clock feeling moist and uncompleted. Lay there in the darkness with a thudding heart, listening to the rain. It's times like that when you feel you might just be cracking up. Here it comes at last. The nervous breakdown you've always read about in the women's magazines at the hairdresser's. Best to get up and get the coffee going. Turn on every flipping light in the place. Cook a helluva big breakfast of bacon and eggs. All of which she did.

And wouldn't it be nice to have someone to talk to about all this? I suppose I could always phone Ruth. But she's probably too busy grinding her goddam granola or worrying about poor old Seth. And Max? Too busy with the little French-Canadian dolly these days. Why don't I just go to Harry

Waggoner and ask him to get his nephew off my back. She can just see Harry's big, decent face opening in surprise. "You've been going out with Jimmy? I didn't know that." Of course, there's always Bruce Horton. "Bruce! My big teddy-bear protector, go around and talk to this guy, will you? Lay it on the line. Growl at him. Grrr!" Bruce! Who is still giving me these hurt looks. We've barely said ten words to each other all week. In fact, I've been avoiding him. And then this morning he appeared in my classroom before nine o'clock. In one of his expansive moods. Bruce is unbearable when he's in an expansive mood. This immense good cheer of his simply sets my teeth on edge. Bruce loves Fridays, and so he came in prepared to forgive and forget. Sat down on the edge of my desk and jingled the change in his pants. "Have you got problems with your telephone?" he asked. "I tried to reach you three or four times last night. Couldn't get through."

"I pulled the jack out accidentally," I said. "Just noticed it this morning."

"You should watch that," said Bruce. "In case of an emergency."

"Right, Bruce. I'll be more careful."

"I phoned your mom, but no answer there either."

"No. She plays bridge on Thursday nights."

"Ah. That explains it." And Bruce commenced to wander around my room.

Stopping by the window he looked out at the wet, grey day. "What a lousy day for the football game!" Then he jingled a little more change and said, "So. Are you all set for guard duty tonight?"

And I said, "Bruce, what exactly are you referring to?"

"Well, the Harvest Dance," said Bruce. "What else?" And oh shit! I'd completely forgotten about it. At the staff meeting at the beginning of the year, I'd agreed to supervise the first dance of the year. With Bruce. But it had totally slipped my mind. And now Bruce was looking at me with a puzzled frown. "Would you like me to drop by and pick you up?" he asked.

"No," I said, "I'll come along by myself, Bruce. Meet you here."

"I thought we might go out for a drink after."

"I'll see," I said, watching Laura Keyes timidly enter the classroom.

"Are we going to have that test today, Miss Harper?"

"That's about the size of it, Laura."

"You mean we are?"

"I mean we are."

She sneaked off to her little corner seat and opened her book, hoping I would notice how conscientious she is. Meanwhile Bruce continued to study me with the most stupefied expression on his otherwise amiable face. "Are you all right, Janice?" he asked.

"Yes, I'm all right. Why?"

"Well, you've sure been acting funny lately. Keeping to yourself. Not very friendly."

"Sorry about that."

He was on the corner of my desk again and now he bent low to whisper, "Are you seeing that salesman again?" I think we now had Laura Keyes's attention. Her eyes were still on her book, but I think her little left ear was aflame. Anyway, I whispered, "I don't really think that's any of your business, Bruce." By now the students were filing into the room, and Bruce stood up and straightened his dark-blue blazer. He looked, well, discomfited. Before leaving, he leaned forward on his knuckles to whisper, "Boy. You want to be careful going out with married men like that." And I'm going to the Harvest Dance with that man. Is there no fair play in the world at all?

• • •

Jan watches Laura Keyes's hand go up. She's finished the test and there's still ten minutes to go. And I'll bet the rent money she's got half the answers wrong. Jan walks down the aisle and bends across Laura's desk. The girl looks up expectantly. She would probably like me to pat her on the head. Emotionally she's still in Grade Three. Instead Jan whispers, "Do something else for the rest of the period. Okay, Laura?"

The girl nods knowingly. Secure in the belief that she's getting on with things. Life is proceeding in a nice straight line.

2

It's nearly ten-thirty when Hicks drives into the parking lot. He sees Janice Harper's Civic and, as it turns out, there's an empty space next to it. A good omen, thinks Hicks, parking next to the Honda and opening another beer. The school is ablaze with lights and a few couples are still going along the walk to the front entrance. Hicks can hear the rock music through the gymnasium windows. The half-dozen beers Hicks has drunk since supper make him feel about right. He can now coast along with the six-pack on the floor beside him. This is something he is proud of: this ability to put away a dozen beers over an evening and still function in a normal manner. The only worrying thing is that too much beer gives you a little belly. Sitting in the parking lot, Hicks decides he'll raise his set-ups next week to a hundred and fifty a day.

The rain is over and a powerful west wind has cleared the sky. From time to time a puff of this wind, travelling across the open schoolyard, rocks the Trans Am and makes the air sing. A cold sky of stars. Fucking winter is on the way for sure, thinks Hicks. Times are bad now, but winter is always ten times worse. In winter you can't buy a job. Some say there are jobs out west; Hicks has heard this in the Puss 'n' Boots. Out in the oilfields. Cold, hard work but fantastic pay. If you can stick it, you can easily make thirty thousand a year. Hicks thinks of Latimer and his girlfriend, who went out months ago. Wonders how they've made out. Probably doing better than he is. And everything going up price-wise, thinks Hicks gloomily, as he swallows the cold beer. Today, the superintendent, a little Englishman with tattoos on his arms, told Hicks that the rent would be going up as of the first of January. He also made a point of reminding Hicks that his rent was overdue. "You're behind a couple of months, Mr. Hicks. I suppose you know that. I know times are tough, but I'm getting some pressure from the owners." Hicks could see that the guy didn't want to make a hassle about it, but felt obliged to make his point. Just doing his job. If it was up to him, Hicks could stay in the place forever. But the owners! He made it sound like the owners are real pricks. So Hicks didn't take offence. He told the man he'd put something in his mailbox next week. However, this money business is worrying. If something doesn't soon turn up, the unemployment insurance is going to stop, and the next thing is welfare. A bunch of fucking social-workers nosing their way into your life. Asking how many times a week you pull your mutt.

Money fucking money, thinks Hicks. That's what clears the way. If you've got it, you're laughing at the rest of humanity. If you haven't, you're fucked, both ends and sideways. The world's a jungle with everybody scratching and biting and clawing away. If you're on the bottom of the pile, somebody's going to step on your face no matter what those old fuckers in the library say about things like socialism. In Russia and China, places like that, there's the top and then there's the rest of the people. In any case, the survival of the fittest. The weak get trampled. Only, thinks Hicks, holding the cold bottle between his legs, it isn't the physically weak you're talking about. He sees himself addressing those old geezers in the burnt-orange chairs at the library. What we're talking about here is the intellectually weak. It's what you got between the ears that counts in the stretch. The guys who make the big dollars are the guys who are mentally alert. People who've trained their minds to cope with every situation that comes up. What's mostly needed is a positive approach to selling your talents. And everybody has a talent, that's the thing to remember. In *The Dynamics of Power Personality* it says, "Every person has something to offer a prospective employer. *Find it and sell it.*" Sometimes Hicks thinks that's bullshit and sometimes not. How do you know about such things? Maybe the man has a very valid point. After all, he's a fucking millionaire, isn't he? Hicks looks across at the lighted school and swallows some more beer.

A Gremlin wheels into the parking lot and four teenagers get out. One of them, a boy who is maybe sixteen, looks toward Hicks's car and jogs over. As he approaches he yells, "Hey, Tommy! How's the man?" Hicks rolls down the window and looks out at the kid. He also lifts the bottle and takes a swig of beer. It stops the kid in his tracks. "Sorry, man. I thought you were somebody else. A friend of mine. Drives the same kind of wheels." Hicks says nothing to this. Just gives the kid this bored, stony look.

As they walk toward the school, the teenagers keep looking back at the Trans Am. Hicks figures they're talking about him. Wondering who he is. Maybe he shouldn't have shown the kid he was drinking beer. Showing off like that! A punk thing to do and Hicks feels mildly disgusted with himself. What if the kid tells the teachers and the teachers send around the cops to see about the strange guy drinking beer in the parking lot. Could be trouble. He could be picked up as some kind of weirdo who hangs around schools preying on kids. Hicks sees himself being grilled by the cops. Framed for some rape he never did but has no alibi for. It could happen. Those bastards can work you over pretty good when they have a mind to. Still, his uncle teaches at the fucking school. And, moreover, Hicks is now going out with one of the teachers. So, he figures he could talk his way clear of that one.

Opening another beer, he watches the kids vanish into the shadows by the side of the school. He tries to think of what it would be like to be in high school nowadays. For him, high school was a waste of time. His first year he sat in the back row. He can't remember answering a single question. Or ever being asked to. He was like a fucking shadow. For months teachers hardly knew his name; they completely ignored him. On the other hand, he didn't go out of his way for extra help. He remembers getting C's and B's. Same thing in Grade Ten. The thing was he never seemed to fit in anywhere. Everybody else was where he wasn't. Sports, dances, plays, clubs! Hicks remembers not caring at the time. Those things were all crap in his estimation. He left after Christmas in his second year.

Now he believes that he made a mistake. He should have stuck it out, because you're nothing if you haven't at least got high school. Sometimes he thinks Fern and his mother should have worked on him more. They were too easy about it all; the same way they now treat Dale. Yet, when he thinks about this, Hicks has to admit truthfully that he was a hard case in those days. You couldn't tell him fuck all. Always, when Hicks thinks about school and education, he thinks about his son. Worries about him. Jobs are disappearing left and right. There's a fucking machine for everything nowadays. What, for instance, will a kid like Dale do for a living in the next century? Which is only twenty years away. He's going to have to be sharp to find work, that's for sure. According to Hicks's mother, the kid's reports are good. But that doesn't mean too much. The first grades in school are a fucking snap. Colouring pictures and cutting figures out of cardboard all day. Everybody passes. Hicks can remember getting terrific grades when he was Dale's age.

Now he looks across again at the school and thinks about Janice Harper. He sees her as a student in school. One of the smart kids at the front of the room who knows all the answers. Hand up all the fucking time. He wouldn't have liked her then. But in those days he was just a punk. You have to grow up and learn to appreciate people who've got brains and know how to use them. Hicks huddles deep into his jacket. He hopes the dance will be over by midnight. She has to talk to him. She can't begrudge him a few minutes.

3

Behind the gymnasium the music pounds away. A quarter to eleven. Only another hour to go. Jan climbs the stairs to the main floor and walks along the hall. The dance is only a partial success. Mostly Grade Nine and Ten kids. Too tame perhaps for the older ones. Too bad, too, because Judy and Norm Barowski have gone to a lot of trouble over this harvest thing. Judy is a farm girl and at the staff meeting she made the point that today's kids are right out of touch with the whole food business. They think all food grows out of freezers. So she and Norm fixed up the gym with some pictures of rural life and put in a big papier-mâché cornucopia. Most of the grapes and apples and bananas were filched in the first half-hour. To be expected. Five years ago they wouldn't even have had a dance. But the kids seem to be more conservative now. Still, as Phil

Hornbeck reminded everyone over the intercom this morning, "We will continue to have school functions such as tonight's dance only on a probationary basis. Each of you must exercise personal responsibility for your behaviour." Pause. "Will Melvin Thorpe report to the vice-principal's office immediately." Had Melvin set fire to his locker again? wondered Jan.

Hornbeck and his wife have just left after dropping in for a few minutes to see how things were going. Good sports ever, they boogied a bit for the kids, coming up with a kind of old-fashioned Chubby Checker twist. The kids loved it and applauded. And Hornbeck's heavy presence kept them all in line. Hornbeck (Horny to the kids, of course) does his best, thinks Jan, listening to her footsteps in the empty hallway. I certainly wouldn't want to be principal of this zoo. As she walks along she feels a heavy sadness. It's not only the monthly depression; it's today's mail. First, a postcard from Max, who is spending a few days in the Laurentians. She sounded so happy. "The trees are gorgeous and the air is like wine. Life is beautiful, kid." And signed it "with love from Denise and me." And why should that be depressing? Ye gods, Max is entitled. She's had her share of rocky times. That nutty husband of hers who ran off with somebody's wife. But somehow it can't ever be the same between Max and me. Ever again. Then there was Hicks's latest letter. "I now know I love you. Please talk to me." How do you deal with someone like that? Because in some ways I wouldn't mind seeing him again. I keep seeing him in that dark shirt, damn it.

She hopes Bruce has put on fresh coffee. He and Norm Barowski are taking turns patrolling the hallways and watching the doors, the idea being that once kids leave, they can't come back in. This is supposed to keep them from sneaking outside for a joint or a beer. An imperfect system, but it seems to be working with tonight's younger crowd. The patrolling person is also supposed to keep the coffee pot in the staffroom going.

Jan is about to enter the staffroom when she notices Bruce at the end of the hallway near the front door. He's surrounded by four or five kids. Late arrivals. No one is supposed to be let in after ten-thirty. That's the rule, and if nothing else, Bruce knows his rules and abides by them. But in fact he is letting them in. They are following him down the hall as he hurries along looking full of business and very grim indeed. The kids seem pleased with themselves. Jan recognizes one of them, Ricky Laslo, a dim-bulb she had last year in Grade Ten. But something is definitely up, for Bruce looks terrifically agitated. What, she wonders, is the catastrophe?

"What is it?" she asks as Bruce goes past her into the staffroom. He is frowning. "Laslo says there's some man out in the parking lot drinking beer."

"That's right, Miss Harper," says Laslo, standing by the door with a smirk on his face. What a disagreeable-looking youth! thinks Jan.

Bruce has now gone over to the window that overlooks the parking lot, and holding his hands up to the sides of his face, he peers into the darkness. He goes up on his toes for a better look and, watching him, Jan finds herself growing faintly annoyed. Bruce is such a ridiculous fusspot of a man. And I never realized before what an absurdly huge backside he has! In those baggy grey flannels. Ye gods. "In the black Trans Am, Mr. Horton," says Laslo. "Just like Tommy Farlow's. Remember?"

And, listening, Jan feels a sudden and violent anxiety. It's Hicks, all right. He's waiting for her in the parking lot. She knows it as surely as she knows her own name. Still on tiptoes Bruce Horton says, "Yes, I can see the car now. Did you say he was alone, Laslo?" Behind Jan, Laslo says, "Ah . . . yes, sir. I think so, sir. At least I didn't see nobody else. You gonna phone the cops, Mr. Horton? The guy is drinkin' on school property." Laslo and his friends are having a good time; they see a little action in the offing. Bruce comes from the window looking worried and irritable. "Why don't you let me worry about that, Laslo? Okay? Now you and your friends trot along to the gymnasium. You're late, you know. You're lucky I'm letting you in." Bruce sounds petulant and aggrieved and Laslo shrugs at his friends. They wander away down the hall.

Lighting a cigarette, Jan watches Bruce rub his large jaw as he tries to parse things out. With Hornbeck gone, Bruce is now officially in charge. He knows Laslo will spread the news around the dance, and soon the gymnasium could be deserted, the parking lot swarming with students hoping to see police cars with lights flashing. Just like TV. Jan pours a cup of coffee and continues to study Bruce Horton. On his face now is a look of almost infantile self-pity. "What do you think?" he asks Jan. "Maybe I should get Norm and we could go out and see what's up before we involve the police." Jan sips the scalding coffee. And suddenly Bruce Horton is not only ridiculous but infuriating. A large Canadian boy with his antique cars and his comic books and his old movies and his collection of lead soldiers. Standing in his blue blazer and grey flannels, jingling the change in those wide pants. Fussing like an old woman. And she has spent so much time with him over the past two years! In people's minds they are now a team. Only this evening the Barowskis invited them up to their weekend farm one Sunday soon. Before the winter sets in. That's how people see them. Jan and Bruce. Bruce and Jan. She can't believe her voice is charged with such hostility. "I know who it is," she says.

Bruce looks across at her. Baffled. "What?"

Jan moves toward the clothes cupboard near the entrance. "I said, I know who it is."

"Who?" asks Bruce.

"It's James Hicks," she says.

"Who?"

"Bruce, excuse me, but you sound like a bloody owl. Who! Who! I said it's James Hicks. Harry Waggoner's nephew."

"Oh!" says Bruce. He looks relieved but puzzled. "Well, what the dickens is he doing out there in the parking lot drinking beer?"

What the dickens, thinks Jan. I didn't think anybody under sixty-five still used that expression. "He's waiting for me," she says, pulling her coat off a hanger. "Look, Bruce, I'm not feeling so hot. Can you and Norm run the rest of the show tonight? I'll deal with James Hicks. Don't worry your head about him. Everything is under control."

Bruce says something to all this, but Jan doesn't catch it. Already she's in the hallway, hurrying toward the door.

4

Jan feels she must look a little prim in her blouse and suit. Sitting in the Sundowner Lounge of the Holiday Inn among all these people in their slacks and sweaters and polyester leisure suits. She has just phoned her mother to say that she'd be staying overnight at the Barowskis'. It was Judy's idea to have some pizza after the dance. It could be a little late, so why not stay the night? Mrs. Harper dislikes any change in routine, and so sounded doubtful. What about shopping tomorrow? But Jan assured her that she would be back well before noon. So now, Harper, with that little deception out of the way, let the good times roll. And I'm going to have another Scotch in the company of handsome Mr. Hicks. Who continues to regard me with a bewildered look. He is clearly puzzled by developments. In fact I've got him completely foxed. He's been like this from the moment I leaned against his car in the parking lot and said, "All right, James. Let's go somewhere. Let's make a night of it." He certainly didn't expect that from the old schoolmarm, and he mumbled something about his place being a mess. I told him flatly that my apartment was out of the question. So that left a motel, the sordid haven for one-night stands.

They decided on the Holiday Inn off the freeway. She followed him in her Civic. He signed them in as Mr. and Mrs. James Hicks of Barrie, Ontario. And how do you like them apples back there at Scarborough Secondary? Where, right now, everyone will be scratching his pointed little head. And ye gods, suppose Bruce gets it into his head to drive to our house and talk to my mother? She hadn't thought of this. Nor would she put it past him. Well, I'll just kill him. That's all there is to it. Justifiable homicide. Sticking your nose into other people's business.

The waiter brings her a fresh drink. Hicks is nursing a beer as he looks around the big, dark room. From time to time he glances over at Jan. He probably thinks I'm a lush. A secret drinker. Not true, James old boy. I'm nervous and more than a bit depressed. It will all pass. Meantime, diversion please. Near the long, padded bar, the pianist, a Mae West type with tangerine-coloured hair, is belting out "I Left My Heart in San Francisco." The Sundowner Lounge is done up in black and red plastic with heavy lamps on the tables. The place is only half filled. Mostly businessmen. A few couples.

Jan lifts her glass. "A penny for your thoughts, James. And cheers!" Hicks raises his glass and gives her a faint smile. His heart is not really in it. He probably thinks a lady shouldn't do this. I've fallen off my pedestal. The guy is basically a blue-collar puritan. He probably sees me as the schoolteacher who must be courted in the style of the fifties. A kiss here and a grope there. Most of it in the front seat of the Trans Am. Ye gods, maybe I should wear crinolines for him. Jan looks away. Now if she could only talk to Travers! They used to come to joints like this for a drink. Ah, Travers! Where are you when I need you? Back home preparing for another winter with the Abominable Snowperson! Serves you bloody right. But if he were here now, they'd be having wonderful fun. Sneering all over the place like a couple of smart-aleck kids. Mae West at the piano for instance. Now starting in on "Tie a Yellow Ribbon to Your Old Something or Other." Some of the businessmen are singing along, and Jan reminds herself that this is one of Bruce Horton's favourite songs, bless his considerably rotund buttocks.

Two women in pantsuits walk by their table. Brassy, tough-looking dames in their thirties. On the prowl. One of them stares boldly at Hicks, who takes no notice. He's watching the businessmen. Or maybe he's just used to admiring glances from the ladies. But I should really put Hicks and his gloomy good looks out of sight. Put him in a box with a ribbon on it. Hide him in the motel room. That broad looks as though she could eat him alive. Or worse. She looks to have a dirty mind. The knowledge of utterly unspeakable acts. Hicks is making damp little circles on the table with his glass.

"I just don't understand why you're doing this," he says finally.

"Doing what, James?"

"Agreeing to spend the night with me. It doesn't seem like you. All week you ignore me, and now this."

Jan lays her hand on his arm and says in a low, throaty voice, "Maybe you have overwhelmed me at last." But Hicks is having none of this tomfoolery.

"Don't make a joke of this. Okay?"

Jan fetches up a sigh. "Well, okay then. Look, it might have something to do with several things."

Hicks looks up at her. "Like what?"

"I don't know, James. I've had a lousy week. I'm lonely. Let's be adults. This might look like I'm some kind of easy touch. But the truth, the whole truth, and nothing but the truth is that I've not had all that much experience in this line." She stops, wondering how much to tell him. "There's been a man in my life recently, but before that there was a long time when I sort of got out of the habit of men."

"What about this guy?" asks Hicks. "You said recently."

"We stopped seeing one another in the summer."

"Did you love him?"

"I don't know, James. We had a lot of fun together. It was good there for a while." She feels almost as though she's betraying something important by talking about Travers. "I'll be honest. I still think about him. I'm told these things take time." Hicks stares ahead, worrying over this old lover. It's hard to compete with a ghost. Jan touches his arm.

"Look. I think I can square tonight with myself. I'm just a little bored with my life at the moment. It happens to people."

"But do you like me?"

"Of course I like you."

Mae West is now pounding out "Volare," and one of the businessmen has stood up to lead the patrons in a sing-along. "Look," says Jan, "sometimes you have to take a few risks with your life. Somebody once said that a life without risk is like something or other. I can never remember those snappy little sayings, damn it. But there's also the old *carpe diem* bit that the poets are always harping on. Do you know that old chestnut

> *Gather ye rosebuds while ye may,*
> *Old Time is still a-flying;*
> *And this same flower that smiles today*
> *Tomorrow will be dying?*

Hicks smiles. Beautiful. "I like that. Who wrote it?"

"An Englishman named Robert Herrick."

Hicks finishes his beer. "When did he live?"

"Herrick? Let's see." She never does any Herrick with the kids. But she studied a few of his poems at university. English 310. Seventeenth-Century Poetry. "Around Shakespeare's time. A little later actually. He lived to be a very old man as I recall, so he was probably more cautious than those lines imply. Probably didn't believe half of what he wrote. Poets are notorious liars." Hicks is actually grinning at her.

"I like hearing you talk like that. Let's go up to the room. Maybe you can recite some more poetry to me."

"I didn't bring along a book, James. I didn't really think we'd need one."

"Come on," he says, putting down some money for the drinks and taking her hand.

Their room is on the second floor at the front of the motel. It smells of old tobacco smoke. Over the bed is a mural depicting a matador enticing a bull. Like the lounge downstairs, everything is in black and red. The old Spanish-hacienda look, thinks Jan. And the man (it has to be a man) who designed such places must have done his research in a Madrid brothel. Figuring, yes, this is what the average North American tourist would consider elegant. Ah well, Harper, don't be stuffy. You're about to enjoy a jolly sordid evening.

Hicks has gone to the bathroom, and Jan opens the closet door and hangs up her suit jacket. The hangers are attached to the clothes rack. In the good old days, hotels weren't so wary of being pilfered. Either that or a better class of people was travelling then. She remembers the first hotel she stayed in. The stately Château Frontenac in Quebec City. They drove all day from Kingston, where they'd spent the previous night at a cousin's. As they neared Quebec City her father grew more and more excited. He was going to give them all a lesson in Canadian history. They would tramp the Plains of Abraham, where Wolfe gave Montcalm the business. Bobby was nine or ten and he whined all the way. But for Jan it was exciting. Staying in that big room overlooking the St. Lawrence River. Watching the boats go up and down. On the morning they were leaving, she tried to boost one of those old wooden hangers with the hotel's name on it. A harmless little theft. Something to show Ruth Dunlop, who was spending all summer at her parents' boring old cottage in Muskoka. But her father saw the coat-hanger stuffed beneath her clothes in the suitcase and made her return it to the closet. Gave her a little lecture. An element of trust has to be established whenever you rent premises. We paid for the room, Janice, not the coat-hanger.

Now, of course, you can't steal them. Does that say something about how things are now and how they were in the summer of 1956? It sure does, Dad. And here's your loving daughter in a motel room. About to have sexual congress with a married ex-con. And I must find out just what he did time for. Ye gods, I hope not rape. Please don't make him brutal, God. That was perhaps the most wonderful thing about Travers. He was such a marvellously gentle and patient lover. And so funny about it too. Always said that sex was one of God's better jokes on poor suffering humanity. The absurd postures, the seriousness with which it's taken; all this struck Travers as hilarious. It tickled them both to talk about it afterwards. But Hicks? Jan can't see him joking about it. Which is fine so long as he isn't too rough. And I must tell him about these breasts of mine. Please handle with care. And I'm sure that's the shower running. The man is taking a shower. People are such creatures of habit. I wonder if he expects me to join him because if he does, he'll have a long wait. I tried it once and wasn't keen. Uncomfortable, and there's always the possibility of a nasty fall. And I wouldn't mind another Scotch, but I suppose it's too late for room service.

She stands by the window wondering whether to smoke another cigarette. He's a non-smoker and my breath must be like an old chimney now. Smelly old me and clean young him. She kicks off her shoes and stands looking out at the windy night. Below her is Hicks's Trans Am and her little Civic. His and Hers. Behind a row of tall, slender poplars is the freeway, and she can see the lights of the traffic hurtling past. The sound of heavy trucks is like a dull roar. She wonders whether she should get into bed. How do you do this with a non-talking type like Hicks? With Travers the first time seemed so easy. *Au naturel!*

A warm evening in May, and the bastard had fresh lilacs in milk bottles all over his funny little bachelor apartment. There must have been a dozen milk bottles filled with lilacs. The day before she had told him that lilacs were her favourite flower. He said they weren't a flower but a bush or shrub. They got into a silly argument over it. Then he got all these lilacs for her. The air was heavy with their rich fragrance. His ghastly little apartment had no furniture worth mentioning: a couple of plastic lawn-chairs, an old pine coffee table and dresser. In one corner a sheeted mattress. And a card table piled high with Travers's samples. *Basic Physics for Senior Students. Learning and Language. The Craft of Woodworking.* On the record player some Dixieland jazz. And at the stove in the little kitchen stood mirthful Travers. Cooking up some Oriental thing in his wok. Standing there in kimono and judo sandals, a dinky little fisherman's cap on the back of his head. He always needed a haircut and so his thick, greying hair curled down the back of his neck. And God, how that thick, curling hair did things to her. How she longed to touch it!

They ate their dinner sitting on the floor in front of the coffee table. And afterwards, half-crocked on saki, Travers said, "Why don't we get out of these clothes and do some pleasant and ridiculous things to one another?" Not perhaps the most romantic offer ever tendered but somehow it seemed just right, because behind the foolishness and the fun the very air was charged with sexuality. But that was Travers for you. Now James Hicks is another case, Harper. And the water's stopped; he's finished his shower. She shucks off her clothes quickly and climbs trembling into the cold sheets. Outside the wind presses against the glass and Jan lies there listening to her heart. I am in bed in the Holiday Inn waiting for a man I scarcely know. A complicated man. Probably never get to know a type like that. Something inside him smouldering away all the time. All that fervour of the autodidact who feels cheated and defensive. And I feel as though I'm on an operating table. Nerves, Harper. It's just nerves. Nevertheless, she is shivering violently.

When Hicks comes out of the bathroom he is wearing a towel around his middle. He walks around turning off the lights, and Jan sees only a dark, lean figure moving about the room. A naked prowler. When he climbs into bed she says, "My breasts, James." She can't believe her voice sounds so weak and timid. "They're very tender. They get like this before my period." Hicks's warm body smells of soap. He takes her in his arms and kisses her. "Hey! You're shivering," he says. "Relax. I won't hurt you."

And why has she started to cry like this? It's absurd. She's no schoolgirl. Here of her own free will. It's only a brief moment in a lifetime. Not to worry. But still the tears fill her eyes. And Hicks is gentle enough, kissing her damp face and imploring her to relax. Loving her in his way. And lying there she wills herself to yield to him. Let go, Harper. Let go. Yet somehow she finds it impossible.

5

Hicks lies awake with his hands behind his head. Looking at the ceiling. He thinks Janice is awake too, but he is somehow afraid to find out. It's crazy, but he feels shy toward her. He didn't satisfy her, he knows that. She didn't come, and when he thinks about it, he feels resentful. A little angry. Maybe she still likes this guy she talked about downstairs. Hicks wonders if she used to come with him. Maybe he has a bigger prick. But Hicks doesn't really think this is the problem. It's just that she couldn't seem to relax. It was like fucking a board. She's got nice legs, but a tiny little dry cunt and no tits to speak of. Of course, she said they were sore, so he didn't work on them at all. She's so different from Vicky Pruit, thinks Hicks. That big black bush of hers. She's fucked that nigger Henry and they have big pricks. Yet she always comes with Hicks, so he figures it can't be because he's inadequate. Thinking about Vicky Pruit excites Hicks. Maybe he should give it to her again. She's a nice woman, but she doesn't know how to fuck. On the other hand she could just be shy and nervous. Hicks can see that she's not used to this kind of arrangement, and he likes her for that. She's no tramp. Just a nice, respectable woman who is lonely. That can happen to anyone. Hicks feels a sudden rush of affection toward her and would like to take her in his arms. Still, she might not welcome it, and he doesn't want to be pushed away. She may already be regretting what she's done. She was crying, and that made Hicks feel bad. After all, it's no big deal. And it's not her fault if she can't fuck. Most likely she's had very little practice.

Hicks thinks of all the women he's known. Mostly tramps. You could get in their pants easy. If not the first night, then the second or third. The birth-control pill has had a lot to do with it and, thinks Hicks, that's probably bad in a general morality sense. But ten years ago it was even harder. He couldn't get into Gail until they'd been going out for weeks. Christ, the tussles they had in the back seat of that old Mercury! Then, after a while she agreed to beat his meat. Take it out of his pants and pound it damn near off. That felt all right for a while but got boring. And she wouldn't give head either. Just the hand-job! Then he finally got in one night at the drive-in. Afterwards she made an awful fuss. Went on about how it was all new to her. Crying her eyes out. What bullshit! Hicks knew she had had it from maybe two or three guys before him. Perhaps that started things off on a bad footing. But nowadays it's unusual to meet a woman who doesn't know much about fucking. Of course, the women he's met have come from a lower class than Janice Harper. She's the most educated woman he's ever fucked. And once she gets over this nervousness she'll probably be all right. Hicks decides that in a little while he'll eat her out. He's never met a woman yet who didn't enjoy that.

Hicks can hear voices and laughter and car doors slamming in the parking lot. The lounge must be closing and people are going home. Those businessmen who were up near the piano making assholes of themselves in their fancy suits. Hicks gets up and walks over to the window. Standing there naked, he looks down and watches the businessmen climbing into a big two-tone Olds. The driver guns the motor and takes off with a squeal of tires. The fuckers are drunk, thinks Hicks. But if a cop stops them, they'll be able to hire a smart lawyer to get them off. People like that never have to pay for their crimes in the true sense of the word. If you've got money, you're in there. No problem. And this fucking room costs sixty-four dollars. For one night, that's totally ridiculous. And if she thinks he can afford to pay for the whole thing, she's got another think coming. She'll have to help him. But there'll probably be no objection there. She seems like a generous type of person. Besides, schoolteachers make very good money.

Hicks hears Janice stirring in the bed behind him. Then she asks him to get her cigarettes on the dresser. Fucking cigarettes, thinks Hicks. A very bad habit. He hasn't smoked now in two years. It's the one unequivocal victory in his life, so he's proud of not smoking and can't help feeling a mild contempt for those who still do. Standing over her, he lights her cigarette. She is sitting up holding the covers against her. He can't make out her face in the darkness. But, standing there, he wants to reassure her that he is serious. That this is not one of those "thanks and see you around" sort of evenings. So, he takes her Bic lighter and, opening the flame, holds it under the palm of his outstretched hand. "You want to know how much I care for you?" he says. "See! I'll stand any amount of pain for you." It hurts like a son of a bitch, but a good part of it is mind over matter, the idea being to conquer pain. That always impresses people. It's like the karate books he's read at the library where it says you can master pain by just thinking of controlling it. That's how some of these guys can break a fucking brick in two with a chop. Whereas a normal person would ruin his hand. Mind over matter. These thoughts flash through Hicks's mind while he holds the flame to his hand. He can already smell his seared flesh. But Janice is horrified and pulls his hand away. Kneeling on the bed naked, she says, "God, James! What are you doing? Are you out of your mind?" She holds his hand while he looks down at her. "That," says Hicks, "is just to show you that I can put up with any amount of pain for you. I said I loved you and I meant it. So don't ever forget that."

Now he leans over and presses his hands against her shoulders. "Lean back," he says, looking down at her. "Go on. Lean back. I'm not going to hurt you." Quietly Hicks kneels on the bed and parts her legs. "Just relax, Janice," he whispers. "All right? I'm just going to make you happy, that's all." And as he kisses the inside of her thighs, Hicks feels aroused. Moving up he tongues her dry little hole. He'll teach her how to fuck. You can't expect things to go right the first couple of times. People have to get used to one another. You have to exercise patience. Hicks wonders if her former boyfriend ever went down on her. It's too bad if he didn't because Hicks can feel her starting to move with him. He can feel her hands now pressing the back on his head, and she's growling a little bit with the pleasure of it. He'll get her going with this and then drive it home. Put it right up there.

Part Two

One

I

Her two nieces are dressed for Halloween. Caroline, older and graver, wears a tall, pointed witch's hat and a long granny dress dyed black. Even at eleven years old she looks a bit sinister. In a yellow bunny-suit, eight-year-old Deborah is beside herself with excitement. Caroline is excited too, but keeps hushing her sister. The everlasting conflicts in family life. How wearing they are, thinks Jan, sitting in her mother's living room! The children have been in the house only ten minutes but already they are pressing their father to go. "Please, Daddy. It will soon be dark," says Caroline. "Yes, Daddy. Please," begs Deborah. Bobby looks flushed and oppressed. He's put on weight and Mother says he's been to the doctor about his blood pressure. This business with Marjorie is taking it out of him. Now he says to his daughters, "We'll go in a few minutes. All right? Now lay off."

The girls stand fidgeting near the piano. They are not pleased. But their grandmother, sitting on the edge of the knobby sofa, smiles over at them. Jan smiles too as Deborah stands waiting to be praised. All the vanity of the world in her small, pretty face. It's too bad that I can't feel warmer toward them. When Caroline was younger, I adored her; we were the best of friends. The kid went nuts every time I visited. All those marvellous picture books I used to bring her. *Dandy Lion. Make Way for Ducklings.* The *Babar* series. But as she grew older, she became more egotistical and demanding. On visits she was apt to come right out with it. "And what have you brought me this time, Aunty Jan?" The relationship cooled.

As for this younger one, I never did get close to her. From the beginning she was bratty and spoiled. We hardly knew one another. I suppose I should be more charitable. More forgiving. But I can't. To me they're just another pair of middle-class suburban brats who always get their own way. Growing up into a tough world and always expecting things to work out for them. Life's a department store. Help yourself!

Through the front window Jan watches the fading light of the late afternoon. She'll give them a few minutes and then leave for James's place. Meantime, there is this to get through. Bobby and his mother are talking about the American election next week. Bobby thinks Reagan will win easily, and Mrs. Harper thinks that will be a good thing. "Such a fine-looking man," she says. Bobby looks across at Jan; he would like to involve her in this conversation. But she knows that it's impossible for them to discuss anything without getting into an argument. So she pretends to make a fuss over Deborah's costume, feeling and examining the material. Marjorie must have spent hours getting these things ready. Fancy having the time and patience to do something like that. But then perhaps if I had children? Who knows?

Jan notices that as her mother talks she keeps giving Jan timid little smiles. These days her mother regards her with the sympathetic eye you might cast upon someone who suffers from a mild nervous disorder. Something you can't help but which is nevertheless faintly embarrassing. Like a facial twitch or a stutter. Sitting bolt upright, Mrs. Harper pats her hair and talks about politics with Bobby while judging when and how to bring the discussion around to her worrisome daughter. Jan knows that something is cooking. Ostensibly Bobby has dropped by to display the girls in their costumes to their grandmother and their aunt. But Jan would bet anything that her mother has really asked Bobby to come by and talk some sense into his sister's head.

Poor Mother! After all these years, she still thinks that my young brother will take care of me. Take care of *me!* Ye gods. She simply can't see that it's I who have been doing the looking after all these years. I couldn't count the number of times I loaned him money when he was bumming around trying to "find himself" as he used to put it. It was I who persuaded him to finish high school when he was all set to quit and hitchhike around the world. Hitchhike around the world at seventeen! In those days Bobby could get turned about on the subway. Dad was completely out of patience with him and admitted it. "Can you talk to that brother of yours, Janice?" All of this has apparently been forgotten by Mother. Or it simply went over her head. As far as she's concerned, Bobby is a man, and men are there to lean on when the going gets rough. It was ever thus. Whenever things got tricky, she would throw up her hands and say, "I can't deal with this. Your father will have to see to it." Perhaps she sees this as a permanent condition with women. In a tight spot, wring your hands and then ring for a man. Jan can't help it. She feels a dull, nagging anger toward both of them. Sitting there talking about the American election. And they get all their ideas from television talkshows. Of course, Mother reads the *National Enquirer* and the *Toronto Sun*. We mustn't forget that. And Bobby reads *Newsweek*. Jan feels like a defiant teenager as she lights a cigarette. Neither of them will approve of that. The girls are again bugging their father to leave.

"Look," says Bobby. "I've got an idea. Why don't you both go outside for a little while and show the neighbourhood your new costumes?"

"Can we trick-or-treat?" asks Deborah.

"Well, no. It's a little early for that," says Bobby. "Why not just go out and let Grandma's neighbours see what real Halloween costumes look like?"

"Okay," says Caroline.

"Okay," says Deborah, and receives a frown from her sister. They troop out the front door and can soon be heard talking on the lawn. Caroline is lecturing her sister on the need to stay clean. Deborah says it doesn't matter; it will soon be dark and no one will notice. Two fierce little wills locked in combat. Jan listens to them and smokes. The air around her seems blue. And she must try not to smoke so much at James's place; he scolds her about it.

"So how's school?" asks Bobby. Same old opening move every time.

"About the same as ever," she says. The old family awkwardness hangs in the air like fog. And are all families like this? wonders Jan. We are so inhibited with one another. Tight-assed Wasps. Nobody ever lays anything on the line and says here is what I want to talk to you about. Instead, it's all evasion. Indirection. Sidelong glances. Polite little coughs. Sighs. Everything is wrapped in some kind of artificial niceness that obscures genuine feelings of malice and reproach. Until somebody loses his temper and shouts and stalks out of the room. Followed by a month's silence. Easy, Harper. You've sucked that cigarette dry. The end is red hot. Must be a thousand degrees. Mother is looking down at her hands. Examining her nails.

Bobby finishes his coffee and says, "Mom tells me you've got a new friend." And there it is! A shot across the bow. Jan warns herself to be careful. Be civilized, Janice. They have your best interests at heart. Which is what every busybody since Day One has said to justify nosiness. "If you mean a boyfriend, Bobby," Jan says, "the answer is yes. I have been seeing a certain chap." This mock-humorous tone will irritate Bobby and confuse Mother, who never knows when I'm serious and when I'm not. It was always the same with Dad. Not once in her lifetime did she get one of his jokes. Bobby seems to be angling for a position. He shifts his weight in the chair and hikes one leg over the other. "What's he do, anyway?" The old question. As if he doesn't damn well know. Mother's doubtless told him everything she could winkle out of me.

"I'm sure Mother's already told you that he isn't doing anything at the moment. He is, in a word, unemployed."

Bobby purses his lips. "Well, what did he do? I mean before, when he was working."

"Why?" Jan knows she sounds rude but can't help herself. Outside, the little girls are into some heavy quarrelling about who will get more candy tonight.

"I don't know, sis," says Bobby. "I'm just curious." Jan stubs out the cigarette in her mother's huge glass ashtray. She'll be up in a minute to empty it. Rinse it under the hot-water tap and polish it with a dish towel. After I leave, she'll put out a bowl of vinegar to freshen the air.

"He worked for an insulation company, I believe."

"An insulation company?" says Bobby. He doesn't much like the sound of *that*.

"That's it." She can see that Bobby is growing annoyed by her tone. It never takes long. Storm clouds are gathering. Stay cool, Harper, and you'll be fine.

"Can't you do better than that?" asks Bobby.

Jan pauses and then says, "As a matter of fact, no. Not at the moment."

"Janice! Really!" exclaims Mrs. Harper. "What a way to talk about yourself! I'm sure there are some very nice men your age around."

"Name six," says Jan. "And don't include Bruce Horton, please."

Bobby leans forward, his jaw thrust out. His face is reddening. "I understand he's also younger than you."

"Yes sir, he is," says Jan. "He's just turned thirty. And, as you both well know, I'll never see thirty again."

"Well," says Bobby, leaning back in his chair, "if you're just going to make a joke of this."

"Please, dear," says Mrs. Harper. "Bobby's only trying to help."

"Help what?" asks Jan. "What exactly is the problem?"

Mrs. Harper gets up and comes over to take the ashtray.

"Mom is just worried about you, that's all," says Bobby. "She doesn't think this guy—What's his name? Hicks?—she doesn't think he's . . . suitable. I'm told he drives a souped-up car. And he has no job. He even has a criminal record, for crying out loud." The temperature is rising, and Mrs. Harper has fled to the kitchen, where she is running hot water over the ashtray. And Jan can see that Bobby is really very angry. If not with me, with everything. His job, his wife, his responsibilities, the whole shooting-match.

"How the hell can you run around with a person like that?"

"No taste, I guess," says Jan, wondering how they know that Hicks was in jail. Most probably that damn Bruce Horton told Mother. Bruce would have got it from Harry Waggoner. These days Bruce won't speak to me. Which suits me just fine. Harry Waggoner looks offended too. Everybody seems to be wondering what I'm doing. The next thing I'll be the talk of the student body. Probably already am. "Wow. Miss Harper is going out with this neat-looking guy who drives a Trans Am. He's about ten years younger than she is. He looks like John Travolta. Wow. Wow. Wow!"

"Are you serious about this guy?" asks Bobby. "He sounds like bad news to me."

"Serious?" asks Jan. "I don't know. Probably not. Anyway, what's with the interrogation, Bobby? I mean, this is 1980, for God sakes. People go out with people you know. It's not a large deal."

"Maybe," says Bobby. "But people like you don't usually go out with characters like this Hicks."

"Why not?" Old hypocrite Harper. You argued this all out by yourself only a month ago.

"Well, he's been in jail for starters."

"So he's been in jail! It happened years ago when he was just a kid. Lots of people get into trouble when they're young, Bobby." But he doesn't even flinch. Probably has forgotten how he and his friends almost ended up with a criminal record after one of them took his father's car without permission and wrapped it around a telephone pole. The judge just lectured them. Scared the hell out of them while they stood in court, nice respectable sons of middle-class parents. Looking properly contrite. What if it had been someone like James?

"We're just concerned about you, that's all," says Bobby.

"Well, Bobby, I'm old enough to look after myself, thanks all the same."

"Maybe so, but at your age, women sometimes do funny things."

"Ah, I get it now," says Jan. "You think I'm going through some middle-aged female thing. An identity crisis, as some people might put it. Perhaps you see me as the lonely, old-maid schoolteacher in her lonely old bed. Sex-starved and all that." And why am I going on like this? It's exactly how he sees me, and probably how everybody else does too. And maybe there is a simple chunk of truth in it. But was that poor Mother, gasping for air as she hovers near the living-room entrance straining to listen? I'll wager that's the first time the word "sex" has been uttered in this room. Bobby shifts his weight again and looks embarrassed. The conversation is an ordeal for him.

"Listen, sis. You've been doing some pretty damn funny things lately. You spent most of the summer going out with that textbook salesman. And he was married. What happened to *him* anyway?"

"He went back to his wife, alas."

Bobby looks pained. "Well, at least he didn't drive some muscle car. And at least he was . . ."

"One of us?" says Jan helpfully. "A respectable, middle-class bloke. Well, yes he was. You're quite right. But Travers was also a very naughty man. Nice, but naughty."

Bobby met Travers once. A hot Sunday in June, and he and Marjorie and the kids had dropped by to take Mother to church. While naughty Travers and I were dressed in swimming togs, headed for the beach. I was wearing a large straw hat, shorts, halter, and sunglasses. And we were laughing. Over what, I can't remember. But we had just come out of my apartment, where Travers had kissed my legs and feet. My feet, mind you. And there was Bobby and Marjorie and Mother and the girls. All in their Sunday finery. Travers tried to work his charm on them but they were having none of it. They looked very suspicious indeed, though Marjorie was clearly envious. She couldn't take her eyes off Travers who did look rather smashing in his shorts and tee shirt. And getting a little jealous buzz from dear, dumpy Marjorie was, I must say, deeply satisfying.

Now Bobby says, "This guy Hicks sounds like some kind of gigolo to me."

Gigolo. It's such a silly-sounding word. And it sounds even sillier in this room with the United Church hymnal resting on the piano. But I shouldn't be laughing, because Bobby looks furious with me. "James a gigolo? You think he's angling for my estate, Bobby? Waiting around for my superannuation pay? Is that it?"

"Oh Christ," he says. "Nobody can talk to you when you get into one of these crazy moods."

There is a commotion at the front door as both little girls come into the house stamping their feet. Deborah is crying and complaining that Caroline struck her. Caroline's tall hat is slightly crumpled. Their grandmother hurries down the hallway to soothe them. And Bobby shouts, "Oh, for God sakes, pipe down. We're going in a minute." And suddenly Jan feels sympathy and affection for her brother. Trapped into a marriage he no longer enjoys. Mortgage payments. Orthodontist's bills. The whole hopeless bit. But he loves his daughters and he does his best; he'll never leave Marjorie and the girls. Like his father before him, he'll do his duty. And in his fumbling, uncertain way he's tried to help here. He's responded to his mother's call for assistance, and all I've done is sat here mocking and ridiculing him like a silly, thoughtless teenager.

Jan stands up and puts on her new fall coat. "I have to go now, Bobby. Thanks for dropping by. And thanks for your concern. But don't worry. I'm a big girl now." Mrs. Harper stands in the entrance, holding the heavy glass ashtray and looking perplexed.

"I have such a headache, I don't think I'll go to the Club tonight."

Not go to the Friday Nite Club. Unheard of. She's trying to

make me feel guilty, damn it. And when I came home two hours ago, I felt great. Another week over. I sang in the shower like a bird. James is cooking a dinner for me tonight. I have no idea how it will turn out, but it has to be better than the Ponderosa or that goddam Jade Gardens where we always go. Now I feel the good mood totally evaporating. I'm supposed to feel terrible for going out.

"We've got to go too, Mom," says Bobby, coming into the hallway. Mother now looks afflicted. Everyone is leaving to have a good time and she's going to be left all alone. Which is ridiculous, because she can go over to the church and spend the night with her cronies.

"Why don't you just take a couple of aspirins, Mom, and then go along to your Club?" says Jan. "You know how much you enjoy it."

"Well, I know I do," says Mrs. Harper helplessly. "But I'm just not feeling up to the mark, dear."

"Just give the aspirin time to work and then go on. It'll do you the world of good."

"Maybe I will," says Mrs. Harper. "I'll see how I feel in an hour or so."

"Good."

At the doorway Jan kisses the little girls. Now that they are going, they're happy again.

"We're going trick-or-treating, Aunty Jan," says Deborah, who is usually not forthcoming. Now she is all smiles.

"That's great, Deb. I hope you and Carrie get lots of goodies. Don't forget to have your mother check the apples."

"We know about that," says Caroline, sounding very grownup. And ye gods, what a world! Razor blades in apples. The things you have to warn people about nowadays. Did it happen when I was a kid? Probably.

Bobby says, "Any time you want to talk, sis, just give me a call. Okay?"

"Right," says Jan.

Bobby now looks relieved that it's all over. He did his best. If his sister wants to go to the dogs, it's not his fault.

"Don't be too late, dear. Please," says Mrs. Harper.

"I won't, Mom," says Jan, stepping into the evening. As she walks across the grass, the air feels cool on her legs. It's the first time all week she's worn a skirt. James likes to see women in skirts and dresses, the cute old chauvinist pig.

As she backs out the driveway she can see Bobby and her mother standing at the front window. Watching. Always watching. And something is going to have to give, Harper, because these days she is beginning to get on your nerves. Always her eyes seem to be on you. At nights when I come in, even if it's three o'clock in the morning, it's the same thing. As soon as I'm in, I hear her toilet flushing. She wants me to know that I've kept her awake most of the night. But if I move out, it will break her heart. Jan backs the car out a little too fast. They wave to her as she leaves. And though she doesn't feel like it, she gives the horn a little toot.

2

It's almost dark, and now children are walking across lawns, alien little figures in white sheets and pirate outfits. Jan reminds herself to be careful. How awful it would be to hit a child! How could you ever recover from such an experience? In the front windows of houses, jack-o'-lanterns peer out at the darkening street. Jan drives slowly along Willowgreen Drive, mindful of the children, but thinking too of the last half-hour with her family. What do they expect from her anyway? How do they see her spending the thirty or forty years left to her? Is she supposed to take a vow of chastity like Norma Kirstead, buy a pair of hiking-boots? Tramp along the Bruce Trail every Sunday morning with her guide book and binoculars? Or would they like to see her married to Bruce Horton? Spending her weekends watching old movies or attending antique-car rallies. Ye gods! The wonder of it is that I've given so much of my time to that man over the past two years. James may not be the ideal fellow for you, Harper, but at least he isn't boring. If only he could get some kind of job, things might be better.

Driving south on Crown Hall Road she passes the shopping plaza. Thinks of Hicks. It's not just a job, Harper, and you know it. We are worlds apart, damn it. He tries. Everything from improving his grammar to listening to classical music. But I don't think his heart is really in it; sometimes it's so hard to open him up. Outside of bed, it's often impossible to find anything to talk about. When she thinks of Hicks in his apartment she can only shake her head. That squalid little place! All right, I can live with the disorder. I don't like it, but I can live with it. What I have trouble dealing with is the plastic flowers in the vase. That hideous black-velvet picture on the wall. He bought it at a flea market one Sunday. The cowboy songs. Everything he likes is tacky. And what can you say to that? It's a question of taste. With a touchy man you don't argue too strenuously about matters of taste. Unless he asks, Harper. If he asks, it's permissible to offer an opinion. But tread carefully, my dear, or he will give you one of those outraged looks. And what in God's name he will serve for dinner is beyond imagining! I've never seen him cook anything in his life.

Once, while he was sleeping, she looked into his refrigerator. Saw a box of Kraft Dinner, some rancid luncheon meat curling at the edges. Three eggs. For some reason the sight of these meager supplies made her weep. She stood by the refrigerator door with tears in her eyes. Then went into the living room and sat down beside him on the sofa bed. Stroked his sleeping face. Sentimental old me. At the same time he could manage things better. He blows too much money eating out and is always buying me things. In the past two weeks he's given her a Mozart recording. A good one too. The Berlin Philharmonic. A key-ring with a good-luck charm. A pocket diary with a perfectly dreadful little verse for each day. The beatitudes of some greeting-card-company hack. James! James! But at least he hasn't asked for money. And face it, Harper, you keep waiting for it, thinking, yes, the guy is hustling me and before long he'll be asking for a small loan to cover the car payments. But so far, nothing. I can't even pay for a meal.

She parks in one of the visitors' spaces at Terrace Court Gardens. One day when she was just dropping in for a few moments, she used somebody's space. When James found out, he was livid. He warned her not to do it again. One guy had all four tires slashed because he parked in another man's space. As James put it, "Around here, Janice, you don't give people any reason to be nastier than they already are." At the time she found it a bleak comment on human nature, but then he lives here.

When she knocks on his door, Jan can already hear Dolly Parton in the middle of "Starting Over Again." Hicks's neighbour to the right has her television on, and Jan can hear bursts of canned laughter. The walls in this place must be made of paper, and Jan often wonders if the neighbour can hear James and her in the sofa bed. Damn likely. The neighbour is a tough-looking blonde lady in her mid-thirties, who lives with her teenage son. Jan has met her a few times in the hallways and the woman has given her a funny little smile. A leering kind of smile that says, "I can tell you're getting yours, lady." It always leaves Jan feeling a little soiled.

When Hicks comes to the door, Jan hides her face behind her hands. "Trick-or-treat, mister," she says in a tiny voice. Leaning on the doorjamb, Hicks offers a thin smile. "How are things? Come on in."

"Thank you, kind sir," she says, sweeping past him and taking off her coat. She hangs it up in the hall closet. Not so long ago James would have done that. Ah well! The apartment smells like a quick-food joint and she follows Hicks into the tiny kitchen to see what he's doing. "I'm cooking up some chili con carne," he says. "I hope you like that." He stands by the stove, frying onions. And alas, James is not one for the small endearments. Now if she had been paying a call on Travers, he would have held her for a moment. Nibbled on her ear or laid one of those villainous kisses on her neck. Just harmless stuff, but designed to make you feel welcome and loved after a day in the trenches. But James saves everything for bed. A time and a place, etc. Oh, the hell with it anyway! On the radio Razzy Bailey sings, "I Can't Get Enough of You."

Jan stands in the kitchen doorway watching Hicks stir onions in a large iron frying-pan. He looks abstracted and annoyed. Without looking up he says, "You did say you like chili con carne, didn't you?"

"Yes, James, it's fine," she says, wondering why he didn't start dinner an hour ago. They won't eat now for ages. On the counter near the stove are cans of tomatoes and kidney beans and a great hunk of half-frozen hamburger. There are also several empty beer bottles and a thick cookbook which Hicks has propped against the toaster. Jan can see from the binding that it's another library book. There are at least a dozen library books in the place; most of them are on karate or judo or psychology. Weird when you think about it. None of them has a take-out card. She asked him once about these books, but he only shrugged; he obviously didn't want to talk about it, so she dropped the subject. When James doesn't want to pursue a particular subject, you drop it. But evidently the man steals books from the public library. However, we must learn to live with each other's frailties, Harper. Yet, watching him, Jan feels herself growing irritated. When he's brooding over something, everyone had better walk around on tiptoe.

She wanders into the living room and stands by the window, listening to the radio and looking down at the parking lot where several costumed kids are running among the cars. And please, dear God, don't let them flatten my tires. She could use a drink, but Hicks buys only beer. Hardly ever touches liquor. She wishes now that she'd stopped at the plaza and bought herself a bottle of Scotch. As if reading her thoughts, Hicks calls out, "Hey, I got you some wine. Do you want a drink of that before we eat?"

She walks back into the kitchen. "Thanks." Hicks is now stabbing the big brown lump of hamburger with a fork. Trying to break it up for browning.

"A lady might get in several drinks before we eat, James," says Jan. "Why didn't you thaw the meat first? It's only a suggestion." And a serious mistake, Harper. She can see his lips tightening.

"I didn't have time to thaw the meat. Okay?" Jan opens the fridge door and takes out the wine. A popular domestic rosé with a little duck on the label. Grape pop! The last time she had it was at Bobby's. Caroline's eleventh birthday, and they all sat around the dining room table wearing part hats while Marjorie poured this stuff into Styrofoam cups. Now Jan tears off the wrapping and goes to work on the plastic cork. Hicks looks furious as he stabs the meat. Looking over at him, Jan says, "Okay, James. I gather you didn't have a very good day. Do you feel like talking about it?" Hicks turns and gives her such a look of malevolence that Jan is stunned. It's like a blow. His eyes seem to burn with malice. "Do you feel like talking about it?" he repeats in a funny, distorted voice. "Do you know who you sound like, Janice? You sound just like one of those fucking broads down at Manpower. Do you want to tell me about it, James. Shit . . ." Again he chips away at the frozen meat, and Jan takes a swig of wine. The unvarnished truth is simple, Harper. Who needs this after a day's work?

"Okay, I'm sorry I asked," she says leaving the kitchen. Somebody on the radio is selling storm windows, and the only other sound in the apartment is the angry hiss of the onions and the meat frying. Then she hears him say, "They send me to Mister Gears." So he does want to talk about it after all. She returns to the kitchen. "Mister Gears?"

"Yeah," he says. "You've seen their commercials on TV, haven't you?"

"Ah yes." She remembers now. They fix car transmissions or mufflers or something. "So what happened?" she asks.

Hicks opens another beer from a case on the floor. "What a fucking run-around they gave me!" He takes a long drink and wipes his mouth with the back of his hand. He looks disgusted with everything. "I get there on time. Right at two o'clock. That's the time they told me at Manpower. But the foreman says I'm late for the interview. He says I was supposed to be there at one-thirty. So I says, 'Why don't you check it out with Manpower? They told me two.' But he wasn't interested, eh. He wasn't going to hire me. Right off the bat I could see he didn't like my looks. This guy's a foreigner, eh. And after we finished talking about whether I was or wasn't late, he says, 'Let me see your hands.' So I show him my fucking hands and he says with a laugh, 'Nice and clean, aren't they? When is the last time you do hard vork, meester?' I'm telling you, Janice. I nearly flattened the son of a bitch. I told him to shove his job. He only laughed. But I know what he's up to, eh. He wants to give the job to some other honky. His fucking brother-in-law or his cousin. That's how those bastards get ahead in this country." Hicks goes back to work on the hamburger and Jan sips her wine. What can you say to the man? What does she know about looking for work? She hasn't had to do it for thirteen years. And then it was easy. In those days you just finished your year at the College of Education and picked your school. She's never had to face the kind of humiliation that he probably encounters a couple of times a week. A proud man like that. It must be tough.

She longs to put her arms around him and comfort him. Tell him to forget it. But Hicks isn't the sort of man who forgets anything easily. It's all so complicated, and in a swift rush of feeling she wishes she were back in her own apartment. Alone with her music and her books. Alone to do what she'd like to do. With no one to answer to or worry about. She'd like to lose herself in something big like *Vanity Fair*. Or *Middlemarch*. Lord, she hasn't read those books since university. And this winter she is going to reread all of Eliot. Get a good biography and then go right through the woman's work. An excellent winter project.

The thought of ordering her life around these simple pastimes is inspiring. Simplify, Harper, simplify. Work at your job and be glad you have one. A couple of drinks before dinner and in the evening settle down with the good stuff. Holidays at Christmas and in March and in the summer. And who knows? With a little luck, a summer romance. Nothing too heavy. People make very satisfying lives out of such routines. She pours herself another glass of wine and goes into the living room. Hicks's hostility seems palpable. The overheated air almost crackles with his anger, and Jan feels the need for something soothing. Something that might enrich the moment and help to take him out of himself. Some music. "Music hath charms to sooth the savage breast," said some wise old scout. She picks up the Schubert record she bought him a couple of weeks ago. "Do you mind if I play this Schubert?" she calls.

"Who?" He looks around the corner. Frowning and holding a spatula in his hand. Jan shows him the record. "Yeah. All right," he says, coming into the living room to turn off the radio. Barbara Mandrell.

"Well," says Jan, "I could have done that. If you don't want to hear this, just say so."

Hicks stops and looks at her. "Just play it, Janice. All right."

He returns to the kitchen and Jan sets the record on the turntable. Schubert's Symphony No. 8. He said he was interested in serious music and wanted to know more about it. So fine. One night last week, listening alone to this symphony on the radio, Jan began thinking of him. The passion and the tenderness of the music moved her. In fact, it reminded her of Hicks. So, next day she went to A-1 Records and bought him a copy. It was the least she could do after all the things he'd given her.

When she gave him the record, Hicks was delighted. He was happy as a kid with a new toy and could hardly wait to hear the music. And when he did, he listened thoughtfully, staring at the wall. Afterwards he wanted to know why the music reminded her of him, and Jan did her best to explain. Said she saw violence and gentleness in both the music and the man. It was hard to put; she was working more on feelings than anything else. But Hicks was touched by her gift and said he was going to look up some books on this Schubert. Find out more about him. When she asked him if he liked the music, he said he did. But there was something about his answer that made her disbelieve him. Now, listening to the symphony, she wonders if she is irritating an already irritated man. Sitting down on the sofa bed, she lights a cigarette. Over the music she can hear him banging his pots and pans around like a frustrated housewife. He doesn't really want to cook the damn dinner; his heart clearly isn't in it. So why not admit defeat and forget about it? But it's probably too late to suggest they go out. He'll be offended and sulk for the rest of the evening. So here you are, Harper. You told yourself a month ago it would get bloody complicated. And now what you really want is simplicity and order. So get thee to a nunnery, Harper. Go!

There is a loud knocking at the door, and Jan calls to Hicks. "That will probably be kids looking for candy. Do you have any, James?" He doesn't answer and so she gets up and goes around to the kitchen. He is dumping a can of beans into a pot. "Do you have any candy in the place?" she asks. Perhaps the music is a little loud; she's aware of perhaps talking too loud. Hicks now regards her with a baffled, angry stare.

"Candy? What the hell would I have candy in the place for, Janice? I never touch it. It's bad for the teeth."

"That's all very true, James," says Jan, "and congratulations from me and your dentist. But it happens to be Halloween and there are children at your door. See, there's this old custom. Been around for years. It's called trick-or-treating." Shut up, Harper. Stop being a smart aleck. He looks enraged.

"Well, shit. Halloween! I forgot, goddam it. I don't have none. Tell them."

Jan gives him a mock salute. "Aye, aye, Captain." I don't have none. Ye gods.

When she opens the door, she looks down into a variety of masks and costumes. Grotesque faces look up at her. Frankenstein, Richard Nixon, Miss Piggy. Shopping bags are held open. "Sorry kids," says Jan. "I'm afraid we just forgot about Halloween this year." They move off down the hallway, but not before Frankenstein mutters, "Fuck you then, lady." Jan is meant to hear it and she does. And closing the door she feels both dispirited and querulous. Of course, you hear it every day in the school corridors, but that kid can't be more than ten years old. And somehow that makes his ugly little rebuke more depressing.

Hicks now looks around the corner from the kitchen. "Turn that down, eh!" he calls and disappears. Eh! Eh! Thinks Jan irritably. Why do so many bloody Canadians have to finish nearly every sentence with eh? Angrily she twists the reject button and watches the needle stop and lift from the record. The apartment is left in silence except for the hissing and sputtering of Hicks's dinner. Jan lights another cigarette and stands again by the window in the living room. Hicks comes back around the corner holding a dish towel.

"I said turn it down, not off."

Jan inhales deeply and continues to look out the window. "Can't you be a little more polite, James? I mean, it doesn't cost anything to be civil." She is standing now hugging her elbows and she turns to look at him.

"Civil!" he repeats exaggerating the last syllable. "Are you worried about my manners, Janice? Is that it? Well, don't worry about my manners. Okay? I just told you a simple thing. That's all. I just said turn the music down, not off. Just a simple request." Jan stares at him.

"It wasn't a request at all, James. It was in fact an order. It seems you don't know the difference."

Hicks doesn't quite know how to take her. "So what the fuck is all this about? What did I do now?"

"Nothing, James," she says. "It's just that I'm getting a little tired of all this Attila-the-Hun approach."

Hicks shakes his head as though he can't hear properly. "Who the fuck is Attila the Hun? What are you talking about?"

"What I'm talking about is simple. I'm getting tired of orders. I'm getting tired of f— this and f— that. When we first met you were polite. You spoke like a civilized human being. Now, when something upsets you, when everything just doesn't go the way you want it, it's f— this and f— that. And I'm tired of it."

Hicks surprises her. He sweeps the dish towel before him and bows. "I'm sorry, your ladyship." But the comic gesture doesn't come off; he's simply not built for the light touch. "Between you and I," he says, "I didn't know my language was offending you."

"Well it is offending me," says Jan. "And for the record, it's between you and me, not you and I. Me is in the objective case. Object of the preposition between." She knows she sounds pedantic and stubborn but can't help it.

Hicks suddenly throws the towel onto the sofa. "I don't give a fuck about your prepositions and your objective case."

"Well, let me remind you that you're the one who wanted to talk good, as you put it."

"I talk all right, goddam it." The shout is violently conclusive. Followed by an appalling silence as they both stare with dislike at each other.

Then Jan walks toward the hall closet. "James, this just isn't working tonight. I'm going home."

She opens the closet door and reaches in for her coat. Hicks raises his arms and then drops them to his side. His voice is very low.

"All right, Janice. I'm sorry. I'll put that record on again." He bends over and puts on the record while Jan climbs into her coat. Hicks looks up at her as the ominous opening chords of the Schubert symphony fill the apartment. "Come on now,

Janice." He reaches for her arm, but she feels that a barrier has been passed. The whole thing is impossible.

"Let go of my arm, James. Please. I want to go."

"No you don't," says Hicks. "Look, I said I was sorry, didn't I? I've got our dinner cooking." Jan tugs at her sleeve.

"James. Please. I do want to go. Don't you understand English?" Hicks looks at Jan carefully.

"I understand English, Janice. Don't fucking worry about that, all right? But I am cooking your dinner and you are going to stay and eat it. Now take off your coat, please. It's going to be all right." His grip has tightened on her arm.

"It's not going to be all right, damn it," she says. "Now let go of my arm."

Instead, he begins to pull her toward the kitchen. "Come on now, Janice. I'm getting dinner ready for us."

"Damn it, James. I don't want your dinner. Now let go." Jan pulls her arm free, but Hicks now grips her by the elbow.

"Don't give me any bullshit. Okay? You're going to stay and eat that fucking dinner and that's all there is to it." He begins to pull her across the room while she tries to hold onto the wall. She hears her voice rising. "Let go of me." But he continues to pull her toward the kitchen, and she realizes that each of them has now embarked on an elementary and perilous course that neither intends to alter.

"I want you to sit down in the chair," says Hicks. "I'm going to pour you a glass of wine and then we're going to eat dinner."

With her free hand she strikes him across the chest several times. "I want to go home." She's aware of sounding like a furious, thwarted child. But in the kitchen he holds both her wrists and shakes her.

"Just stop it," he says. She wills herself not to weep. There will be no tears shed over this nonsense.

"Let me go, you bastard." Is she shouting? It's hard to tell. She can hear the Schubert and feels Hicks's grip tightening. Her wrists seem burned and numb. They are now maneuvering awkwardly in the tiny kitchen. Ludicrous! A crazy kind of dance. "Janice. Settle down, goddam it," says Hicks. Again she struggles to free herself, but Hicks suddenly pushes her down hard onto one of the plastic chairs. She can feel the shock travelling up her spine. Above her, Hicks points a finger at her face. "Now you just fucking sit there. Don't move. We're going to have our dinner and everything is going to be just fine."

Sitting at the kitchen table in her new fall coat, she realizes with relief that this has to be it. It's time to get out of this whole thing. It was foolish to get mixed up with him; everyone but her was right. The truth hurts, but there it is. Hicks has opened another beer and he's taken the bottle of rosé from the refrigerator. Now he places a glass of wine on the table in front of her.

"Okay now," he says. "Drink your wine and cool off. The food won't be ready for a while. Just relax and listen to the music and drink your wine. Come on now." He holds the glass in front of her. "Drink some wine, Janice. Be nice." She stares at the glass, and Hicks bends toward her. She can feel his breath on her face. "Drink this fucking wine, Janice," he says. His voice is thick with rage. She lifts the glass and takes a small sip. Above her he says, "That's better. Everything's going to be just fine. Now let's take off your coat." He stands behind her and she feels his hands on her shoulders. He could be dealing with a madwoman or some hopelessly wayward child. "Come on now. Let's take off the coat." And sitting there she feels diminished and humiliated. Never has she felt so totally abased. She's hardly aware of her own voice. "Take your hands off me, James. Please." She hears the music and hears him say, "Come on now, Janice. Just take the coat off, eh? He is tugging at her coat when she drives her elbow into his stomach. She hears him grunt. It's only a matter of reaching the door. A few seconds. Surely there will be someone in the hallway: the kids in their Halloween costumes, the woman next door.

Behind her Hicks is cursing, and by the sofa bed in the living room he has caught her again by the elbow. Jan sees his raised arm only as a blur. Feels a scream gathering in her throat but hears only the blow along her face like an explosion. As she falls against the sofa bed she wonders absurdly whether he closed his fist or used one of those karate chops. It doesn't matter because her flesh is seared. Branded with pain. Lying there, she sees only a dazzling brightness. It's odd, but she's never been struck before by anyone's hand. Not intentionally. Her mother and father didn't believe in touching their children. And she can't remember any schoolyard fights, though she did receive a blow like this in high school. An accident.

Hicks is now holding her against his chest, saying he's sorry. He is weeping, and she can smell his sweat. Yes, in high school she got a knock like this. A basketball game. She can't remember the team, but they wore red uniforms. She was jumping for the net when a girl on the other team brought an elbow down against her cheek. That flaring pain was just like this. She remembers falling backwards against the polished floor. Looking up through a blur at the dancing legs. Then everything slowly emerging into focus. A ring of worried faces gazing down at her. Max, her face flushed, and Ruth, her thick glasses steamed and tied to her head by a ribbon. The girl in the red uniform saying over and over, "I'm sorry. I didn't mean it." And the referee, a woman with short grey hair, asking her if she was all right. The sweaty smell of that old gymnasium. And somewhere among the spectators, her father looking on with worried eyes. Now Hicks is rocking her like a child and saying, "Oh God, Janice baby, I'm sorry. I'm so sorry. I didn't mean to do that. I'm so sorry."

He takes her into the bathroom and wrings out a washcloth. Sitting on the edge of the bathtub in her fall coat, Jan presses the damp cloth against her cheek. On his knees, Hicks holds her other hand and repeats his contrition like a litany. When they return to the living room, Jan feels only a remote calm. As Hicks folds down the sofa into a bed, she looks at the grey sheets and listens to Hicks's sorrowful words. When he undresses her she feels somehow disabled and hollow. Overhead a jet roars, and Hicks covers her bruised face with his hands. She's aware that he's still weeping, but it doesn't matter. The thing is to endure. Return to a calm place.

As he enters her, Jan tries to get a fix on something tranquil. A line of poetry. A field of snow with a solitary dark tree. A nocturne by Chopin. Her father in his chair. Reading of Greeks long dead.

Two

I

From his small office Jorgenson turns off the floodlights. Only the office light and the big yellow-and-blue Sunoco sign are left on. In the darkened garage, Hicks wipes his hands on a piece of waste and walks out to the pumps. A cold night, and along Crown Hall Road the traffic is thin. An hour ago it was bumper to bumper, as northbound commuters moved slowly homeward. Hicks stood watching the traffic and looking, too, at the waning light of the November sky. Now the sky is black and filled with stars. Hicks picks up the bucket of empty oil-cans and carries them around to the back of the garage, where he empties them into the big red waste-container. They fall clattering against the empty steel bottom.

When Hicks walks into the office, Jorgenson is sitting at his little desk listening to the radio and counting the day's receipts. Jorgenson is a short, burly man. The long peak of his John Deere cap is pulled low across his brow. In the lapel of his jacket is a plastic poppy for Remembrance Day. In a long-ago war, Jorgenson flew fighter planes. The best time of his life as he told Hicks on Hicks's first day on the job. As he counts the bills, Jorgenson moves his lips and puts down figures in a black scribbler. Without looking at Hicks he says, "You sweep up?"

"Yeah," says Hicks.

"Disconnect the air hose?"

"Yeah."

Same fucking questions now for a week. You'd think the guy would know that Hicks is aware of the routine by now. But maybe, thinks Hicks, Jorgenson just feels it's a big deal being boss. "Okay," says Jorgenson, working with a pocket calculator. "Back the truck into the first bay and you can go." He adds, "And take it easy," as Hicks again steps out into the cold night.

In the cab of the big GMC tow truck Hicks feels good. It's a beautiful machine. Two days ago Jorgenson sent him out in it for the first time. A woman with a stalled Pinto in the shopping plaza parking lot. Hicks enjoyed the experience. Now he listens to the powerful motor and is careful not to race it. On his first day Jorgenson told him to back it in, and Hicks gunned things a bit. Never heard the fucking end of that. So now, carefully and slowly, he inches the truck back into the garage. The GMC is Jorgenson's baby and he keeps it in top condition. Worries about it the way some men worry about their kids or their dog. Still, Hicks doesn't hold that against the man. In fact, he understands perfectly.

Now he turns off the ignition and the parking lights and sits in the dark truck. He can hear the music from Jorgenson's radio. One of those "Remember When" programs. Bing Crosby and people like that. Jorgenson is a hard man to figure. Seems to want the upper hand on you all the time. Like this afternoon, for example, when this friend of Jorgenson's came by for gas. A regular customer, balding, about Jorgenson's age and driving a blue Dodge. While Hicks filled up his tank, Jorgenson came out and started talking to the man about the war.

Jorgenson said, "We made it safe for these young guys. Right, Dave? We took it to the Jerries and I'll bet guys like this young fellow here don't know the first thing about the war." Then he said to Hicks, "I'll bet you don't know much about that war, eh?"

"No," said Hicks. "Not much."

"What did I tell you?" said Jorgenson. The man in the Dodge nodded and looked at Hicks with faint disapproval. Hicks wasn't wearing a poppy. He checked the Dodge's oil and listened to them going on about the Second World War and what a great experience it all was. But what was he supposed to do about it? They were talking about events that happened years before he was born. Yet Jorgenson had felt the need to make Hicks look bad by saying what he said. And that, in Hicks's estimation, was an ignorant thing to do. On the other hand, the man sometimes could be thoughtful. One day Hicks had no time to pack a lunch and, noticing this, Jorgenson gave him a sandwich from his own bag.

When Hicks leaves, he doesn't bother to say goodnight to Jorgenson. From the first day Hicks could see that Jorgenson is a man who doesn't set much store by things like that. Driving home, Hicks reflects on how tired he is. He's still not used to working all day, and what most people don't realize is that while pumping gas, you're on your feet a great deal of the time. It's busy most days, too. Jorgenson has a good location, though he worries all the time about the self-serves. Anyway, as far as Hicks is concerned, sore feet or not, the job will have to do for now. Certainly it's better than nothing with Christmas coming up.

He's told her about the job in several letters which he can see her throwing in the garbage without opening. She's had her phone changed, too. It's clear she doesn't want anymore of him, and who can blame her? He never should have hit her like that. What a stupid thing to do! For maybe the hundredth time, Hicks goes over the evening and fiercely reproaches himself. Wishes somehow that he could pull the whole day back in and do it over. Starting with that foreigner at Mister Gears and then the chili dinner. What was he trying to do with that? He knows he can't cook shit. He should have taken her out some place nice. Any place would have been better than his crummy apartment. Again and again Hicks sees Janice leaving his place. Moving about and trying not to wake him. But he could see her long, pale body as she stooped to pick up her clothes. Then, when he turned on the light, he saw her swollen cheek and the discoloured eye. He'd begged her to stay and talk, but she just shook her head and he couldn't press her. If it had been Vicky Pruit or even Gail when she was younger, he could have talked her into staying the night. Then made things up the next morning. But Janice is a different type of person altogether, thinks Hicks, as he drives down Crown Hall Road. And she had to go into the school on Monday with that eye. A very hard thing to do for a respectable woman.

To atone for his sins, Hicks has played over and over the record she gave him. He now knows large parts of it by heart. He listens to it hungrily, trying to find himself in the music. Now and then he does catch a glimpse of what she was talking about. Or he imagines he does. It's easy to fool yourself in these matters. He even went to the library and picked up a book on Franz Schubert. It was written by some professor and was heavy going, so Hicks skipped along as he read. He gathered that this Schubert was a fat little Jew who lived in Germany a long time ago. Mostly a sad life right through to the end, and he died when he was only thirty-one. Yet he could come up with a piece of music like that! The book also said that this Schubert wrote over six hundred songs, but Hicks isn't sure he believes that. How could a guy write that much if he died so young?

As he pulls into the parking lot, Hicks can't think of anything good about his own life. He's so tired of coming back to this place and eating something in front of the TV. For a moment he sits and thinks of how nice it would be to come home to a good dinner. With a woman there and maybe kids. For a while it worked with Gail, though she was no good in the cooking department. Still, she was there when he got home. And when Dale was a baby, Hicks enjoyed fooling around with him. He can remember the boy taking his first steps, and thinking about this, Hicks reminds himself that he should see his son. Spend some time with him, maybe a weekend, soon.

As he gets out of the car, Hicks notices the dark van with the scenery painted on the side panels. Even in the dark he can make out some mountains and a lake. Then from the van's cab comes a series of low, stuttering farts. Or maybe just imitations of farts. Hard to tell. Hicks then hears Brian Latimer laugh. A wild sort of giggle. It used to get on Hicks's nerves.

"Hey, Hicksy! What do you say, man?"

Hicks walks over to the van. He can see the outline of a figure wearing a hat. The glow of a cigarette.

"What the fuck are you doing here, Latimer?"

Latimer opens the door and climbs down, a tall, thin character about Hicks's age. Now rigged up in cowboy gear. Denim jeans and jacket. High-heeled boots. A big light-coloured cowboy hat sits on his head. Hicks has to laugh. "Latimer? Where did you get that fucking hat? It looks ridiculous."

Latimer laughs and takes off the hat. Makes a short bow. Then, settling the hat back on his head, he does a little sparring around Hicks, feinting a few punches and bouncing one lightly off Hicks's shoulder. "What do you say, Hicksy? How are they hanging? What's that you're wearing anyways? A fucking grease-monkey suit?" Hicks shrugs, feeling vaguely ashamed without knowing why.

"I thought you were in fucking Alberta."

Under the large hat Latimer is grinning. "So I was, Hicksy. So I was. But that don't mean I'm going to stay in fucking Alberta for the rest of my natural days." He turns abruptly to the van. "So how do you like my new wheels?"

"Okay," says Hicks. He's never been big on vans. Latimer strikes the door.

"It drinks fucking gas, but it can dangle right along when you want to get there. You can sleep in it too, eh. So you can save on motels and things like that." They are now walking around the van. Inspecting it like a salesman and his customer. Hicks's voice is scornful.

"Pretty fucking cold sleeping in there tonight."

"Well," says Latimer, "you know what I mean. In the summer."

On the back window is another little scene. The sun coming up or going down. Latimer has been drinking and smells like a fucking brewery, thinks Hicks. He asks Latimer about the woman he left town with last spring. Latimer gives a rueful little laugh. "Gone, man. Gone with the fucking wind." He has now opened the back door and is crawling around inside the van. As he crawls, he talks. "She took off with this young guy who worked in the rigs way the fuck up north." Latimer stops what he's doing and on hands and knees looks back at Hicks. "We met this guy in a bar in Edmonton. And he tells us he's been working two years way the fuck up in no man's land. Saved all his money. Never spent a fucking nickel. He showed us his bank book. He had forty thousand dollars in that bank account. He was only twenty-one fucking years old, Hicksy. Can you believe it?" Again he begins to root about in the van.

"I got something for you here," he says. "I brought you back a present."

As Latimer rummages around, Hicks stands behind him and looks into the van. Sees a camp bed, some battered suitcases, a couple of sleeping rolls, some beer cartons, a copy of *Penthouse*, a box of cornflakes. Latimer's worldly possessions. On hands and knees Latimer gropes his way through this junk and emerges finally with another cowboy hat, identical to his own, only dark. He stands up, blowing dust off it. "There you go, man. Try it on." Hicks holds up the large hat in his hands. It might as well be some strange animal that bites. He never wears a hat of any kind, even in winter. But now he gently places the hat on his head. It feels strange. Latimer settles it at an angle. "Looks great, Hicksy. You're a real fucking dude."

"Shit, Latimer," says Hicks, laughing. He takes the hat and looks at it disbelieving. Latimer has always been generous, and in a way Hicks is glad to see him. But there is the business of the old apartment they shared. Latimer did run out on him. Left him holding the fucking bag. So, the air has to be cleared before they can proceed. "You shouldn't have run out on me like that," says Hicks. Latimer also realizes this has to be squared away, so with his hands in his jeans he looks away across the parking lot.

"I know that, man, but I did leave you that big fucking TV." He pauses and shrugs. "But you're right, Hicksy. It was that cunt Audrey. She talked me into it. She didn't like you, man."

"I didn't exactly care for her either," says Hicks.

"Well, fuck her anyway," Latimer says. "Look, I got some beer. What do you say we get a load on?"

Bending down, he hefts a case of beer toward Hicks. "Put that fucking hat on, man, and take the beer." Hicks clamps the hat on his head and takes the case of beer. Latimer tucks another case under one arm and locks his van before turning to Hicks. "Now, Hicksy, lead me to your palace." Together they walk across the parking lot, and Hicks asks Latimer how he found him. "It was easy," says Latimer. "I remembered that you used to fuck that go-go dancer, that Vicky. So I went over to the Puss 'n' Boots this afternoon and she was sitting there with a couple of spades. She must be getting tired of white meat and now wants a big drumstick, eh." Latimer's laughter sounds insane to Hicks. "But you used to put a lot of pipe in her pants, as I recall. Anyway, she told me where you lived. You can't escape old Detective Latimer that easy."

They walk along to the entrance of the building before Latimer says, "This Vicky told me she hasn't seen you around lately. Figures you must have a new lady." Hicks says nothing to this but merely shifts the case under one arm while he opens the front door. When it comes right down to it, Latimer is an asshole. Always has been. Still, he's company. Somebody to talk to. Opening the door, Hicks stands aside and lets Latimer pass. They walk across the small lobby to the elevator. With Hicks hoping that nobody will see them wearing these cowboy hats.

2

The restaurant has only half a dozen tables and is at the rear of the health-food store. You step through a beaded curtain and here you are in the back room. And isn't it like Ruth to suggest a place like this! I should have been more assertive, damn it. However, according to Ruth they serve the most *authentic* vegetarian food in town. But ye gods, Toronto has dozens of excellent restaurants, and I allowed myself to be talked into coming to this soup kitchen. All the way downtown to sip this hideous concoction of vegetable juices. And look up at the sign that says "Thank you for not smoking."

Ruth certainly looks grumpy. She hasn't said ten words since we've met. I hope it's not poor Seth's thesis; I couldn't bear two hours of that. Jan studies the handwritten menu. It may be a great place to eat but the world hasn't yet discovered it. The only other patrons are a couple huddled over their soup. Both young and dressed in jeans and having an intense conversation about recycling newspapers. The waiter, a young, effeminate man, keeps looking over at me. I wonder if my eye is still noticeable. I wish Ruth would get on with the ordering. She's been staring at the damn menu now for ten minutes. Sitting in her batik kaftan and reading every blessed word through her bifocals. And for God sakes, Harper, stop being so nasty. You're having dinner with one of your oldest and dearest friends. But the waiter keeps looking at me. I know a slight yellowing remains, but you can't possibly see it under this make-up. Nothing like a week ago when I walked around sporting my famous shiner. The talk of the school for all of one day. And yet it was strange how everyone believed my absurd story about the washroom door in the restaurant. Banged open right against my face. Even Mother, with her fiendishly suspicious mind, went for it. But then she just seems relieved that Hicks is no longer around. Perhaps no one can see me as the sort of woman who gets punched out by her boyfriend. Too outlandish. Not Janice Harper.

Jan sips some vegetable juice and thinks about Hicks. Poor James. She can still see his face on that awful night. He looked forsaken as he pleaded with her to stay and talk. And for a moment she considered it. The man was so obviously sorry about what he did. She wonders now whether she should have read his letters. There is something *awful* about throwing away unopened letters. She can see him in his apartment writing those letters. Sitting at the little kitchen table writing on his lined notepaper. Looking for the right words to say he's sorry and asking her to have another meal with him at Burger King. Now the waiter comes over to the table and smiles at them. "Have you decided, ladies?"

Ruth looks up. She seems a bit dazed. Finally she says, "The soup is always good, and tonight it's black bean. That's very good. What about some of that and the vegetable casserole and salad? With some twelve-grain bread and herb tea. How does that sound to you, Harp?"

"Sounds great, Ruthie."

"Thank you," says the waiter and heads for the kitchen. Ruth sips some juice and frowns. "I think something should be done about this Rembrance Day business in the schools. Don't you?"

"Pardon?"

"You know," says Ruth. "Remembrance Day. Poppy Day."

"Oh yes. Poppy Day. That's what we used to call it when we were kids." Today all the teachers were wearing little plastic poppies. There was a small tray of them on the secretary's desk outside the principal's office.

"Morgana," says Ruth, "came home at noon wearing one of those poppies. Apparently the whole school spent most of the morning watching films on war. I think the whole thing is sick. It's just another example of how we glorify war. I intend to bring this up at next month's meeting of the PTA." Ruth sounds very angry. And where, I wonder, does she get the energy for all this indignation. She's forever fulminating about something or other; there are always petitions to sign or meetings to attend.

In the sixties there were the anti-Viet Nam demonstrations. Outdoor rallies to support blacks in Alabama. Fair enough, and Jan went along with all that. She can still see Ruth sitting on the spiky grass in a cotton granny-skirt. Hugging her knees and swaying back and forth as she listened to "We

183

Shall Overcome." Tears leaking from her eyes. But always too fervent about things. Too righteous. At heart, a Puritan scold. Now she says, "I just don't think it's right." Pushing out her lower lip. Just as she used to do twenty-five years ago in the schoolyard at King Edward Public.

"Well," says Jan, "I don't think it's actually celebrating war as much as remembering people who fought and died in it. I mean, let's face it, Ruth. The Second World War. Old Adolf and Tojo and Mussolini. Those guys were very bad actors." And is Ruth actually making small grunting sounds in response to these remarks? Little woofing utterances of displeasure as she looks down at the soup now placed before us.

In many ways Ruth is an unattractive person. Lumpish. Always has been. Max used to say that Ruth reminded her of that grey modelling clay we used in school. Now she appears to be sulking, so Jan asks about Seth and the children. The question seems to provoke her, and she blows furiously on a spoonful of soup. "His parents are coming up this weekend. He didn't bother to tell me this until an hour ago. They'll be here on Friday afternoon and the place is an absolute mess. I have three meetings to attend this week, and there just isn't time. Well, he's just going to have to hire somebody to do it, that's all. I don't know where we'll find the money, but it's going to have to be done. He's known they were coming since last Sunday. Says he forgot." She bends over to work on her soup. So that's it. There's been a tiff in the Calder household. Poor old forgetful Seth has irritated his wife. It's funny. When Ruth feels like it, she confers on Seth's vagueness a playful and fond reverence. Sees it as a touchstone of scientific genius. Seth is far too preoccupied with important scientific matters to bother with the small change of everyday life. However, it seems that living with a genius can sometimes be a nuisance. But I'm damned if I'm going to spend the next hour in this place listening to the trials and tribulations of the Calder household. The fact is that Ruth's ill humour is making me cross and mischievous. She's such a graceless woman. Hasn't even asked about Mother.

"Has Seth ever laid a hand on you, Ruth?" I already know the answer to that; Seth is simply not the type. Still, you never know, and it's always fun to speculate. Ruth looks up, uncertain that she's heard correctly.

"What?"

"I said, has Seth ever hit you?"

And is that a small, bitter smile tucked around the corners of her mouth? A little crimping of the flesh that says he wouldn't dare? Oddly enough those are her very words.

"He wouldn't dare," she says.

The waiter arrives with the food, and for a moment Ruth seems to have forgotten all about it. Yet you would think that such a question would be of interest, since she sees so much of it at the Women's Distress Clinic. Now, however, she is busy helping herself to casserole and passing the bread. Anger has certainly not dulled her appetite. The food is very good, but I'm not hungry. I'm feeling stubborn and persistent. Offended by Ruth's incuriosity. I feel like a terrier bothering an old tortoise.

"What would you do if he did?"

She hasn't forgotten. Not a bit of it, for she says quickly, "He just wouldn't, that's all."

"Yes, Ruth, you're probably right." I picture myself as some authors describe villains who plunge daggers into people. Smiling wickedly. "But what if he did."

Ruth chews her food and looks thoughtful. "I'd discuss it at the Clinic with some of the other volunteers. Then talk it over with Dr. Weems. Dorothy is our liaison at the Clarke. Then we'd probably invite Seth in and ask him to explain his behaviour. I mean, we have these sessions all the time. There are a lot of men who take out their aggressive hostilities on girlfriends and wives. Even on mothers." Yes, and Seth would go along too, thinks Jan. She can see him trudging along in his sand-coloured corduroy pants and baggy sweater. Sitting in a chair surrounded by a dozen women who are grilling him on why he slugged his wife. Now James! That would be out of the question, Harper. I cannot see him in those surroundings. For that matter I wouldn't want to see him in those surroundings.

"The incidence of aggressive behaviour in the male population is on the rise," says Ruth. "It's a question of urban alienation."

And she doesn't even bother to enquire as to why I asked the question. She's more interested in talking about social priorities and municipal funding. Just another well-off busybody, middle-class social worker with a heart of stone. But I have needs too, Ruth, damn you. I'm supposed to be your best friend. Well, the other night a man named James Hicks gave me a black eye. I looked just like one of those women who come to your goddam Clinic on Saturday night after taking a belt from their common-law husband in the beer parlour. And I'm no masochist. I didn't like getting hit. It hurt like hell. Now he sends me letters in which he probably says he loves me. What do I do about this, old friend? He loves me. And sometimes I miss him telling me that.

3

"Take a look at that, Hicksy, and tell me if you've ever seen anything like that in your fucking life. Go on, man. Look at it!"

Hicks and Latimer sit at the kitchen table in their underwear and their cowboy hats. Under the kitchen light Latimer's pale, pock-marked face looks greasy. But Hicks has trouble focussing on anything, and he realizes with regret that he's drunk. He holds the photograph before him and sees only a blurred image. A slash of red. Some fingers. None of it makes any sense. On the radio Gene Watson sings "Nothing Sure Looked Good on You."

It's three o'clock, and in four hours Hicks has to be at work. He feels bloated with beer and pizza. Disgusted with the evening's excess.

"What the fuck is this, Latimer?" he asks, angrily squinting at the picture. Latimer's face is filled with sly humour.

"Guess," he says, grinning.

"Fuck off," says Hicks.

"That's Audrey's snatch, man," says Latimer happily. "I took a close-up."

"What?" Hicks is amazed. Even drunk it seems a weird thing to do. But that's Latimer for you. The fucker is half crazy most of the time. Now Hicks studies the photograph more closely, mildly repelled yet fascinated too. He can now make out the fingers spreading apart the vulva.

"For Christ sakes, Latimer," he says.

Latimer takes off his hat and runs a hand through his stringy blond hair. Laughing, he places the hat back on his head. "We got fooling around one night and decided to take some pictures. Look at this one!" He shows Hicks another picture of Audrey, a blocky twenty-year-old brunette. In five years she'll be fat as a pig, thinks Hicks. In the picture she is on the floor on hands and knees with her ass up in the air. Looking at her, Hicks feels a little flutter from his prick.

"You're a fucking pervert, Latimer. Do you know that?"

"No harm done, Hicksy," says Latimer. "She didn't mind doing it. In fact she said it was a turn-on. I showed them to the kid she ran off with. Maybe that's what got him going. Anyway, she'll go through his money like shit through a goose.

And she'll fuck him ragged. Hicksy, that woman could fuck a man *to death*!"

Hicks looks around his kitchen with hopeless disgust. The sink is filled with dirty dishes and the table and counter are covered with empty beer bottles. A few crusts are scattered along with Latimer's cigarette butts on the pizza box. The garbage can is overflowing. And there is Latimer in his cowboy hat and black jockey shorts. Carrying around pictures of an old girlfriend's twat. From start to finish a loser, thinks Hicks. Yet, watching Latimer open another beer, Hicks wonders if he's any better. In four hours he'll be pumping gas for Jorgenson. Where's the future in that? Lately his life has not improved in any direction. Except for that book on Schubert, he hasn't read anything for two weeks. Hasn't done his exercises either, and in fact feels sluggish and defeated.

Looking at Latimer he feels a wave of despair pass over him. Feels contempt for Latimer's lazy acceptance of everything. His unfailing optimism. Things somehow always work out for Latimer. He rides with the times and seems to possess a kind of luck denied to others. Over the years he's been involved in any number of things. Yet, except for that stretch in Guelph, he's avoided jail. An easy sinner, and around him Hicks always feels righteous.

"Latimer," says Hicks. "Taking pictures like that." Hicks searches for the words. "It's bad taste. You hang around with chicks like that and you're not going to go anywhere. I mean, a woman like Audrey is just a tramp." Listening, Latimer takes no offence. It's impossible to insult the man. Instead he just laughs, and Hicks has the uneasy suspicion that Latimer is mocking him. Earlier Hicks mentioned that he had been seeing a nice woman who is a schoolteacher. He felt proud talking about Janice. Now he feels the urge to tell Latimer more. "You should get to know a different kind of woman, Latimer.

Now this woman I was going with, Janice Harper. Now she has something on the ball. A schoolteacher. And she is a very nice person." It appears that Latimer is only half listening.

"Where is she now, Hicksy?" he says. "Did you actually entertain the lady in this place?"

Hicks considers dropping one on Latimer, but he knows he's too drunk. A foolish move anyway. Where does it get you? But you can't have a sensible conversation with a person like Latimer. From start to finish the man is an asshole. And now Hicks feels trapped, because earlier he agreed to let Latimer stay on until he got settled away. Latimer said he would pay half the rent and it seemed like a good idea at the time. Now Hicks is not so sure. All he feels now is an overwhelming fatigue. When he stands up his legs are unsteady.

"I'm going to bed, Latimer. I got to go to work in the morning."

Latimer raises his beer. "Here's to all good citizens who get up in the morning for work. Here's to you, Hicksy!"

In the living room Hicks pulls out the sofa bed. Picking up the Baby Ben he winds it slowly. It's an effort to turn the tiny crank. He remembers to pull out the alarm knob and sets the little clock on the floor beside him. Lying on the cold sheets, he hears Latimer call out to him.

"Now listen, Hicksy. If we're gonna sleep together, you stay out of my underwear, you hear?"

Hicks lies there listening to the laughter. It seems like you could peel it off the walls. It's like Latimer never left. Been living here all along.

Three

1

Jan lays the parcels on the coffee table and peels off her coat, feeling mildly triumphant. At least it's a start. But she doesn't feel in much of a Christmas mood. Perhaps it's the weather. Christmas is less than three weeks away, but the cloudy mild day is like April. Weather affects people too; nobody seems to be in much of a festive humour. In the stores people had a glazed look as they examined things. Outside Sears, Santa Claus gave his little hand bell a feeble shake and actually yawned as Jan passed him. Outrageous!

Jan looks at her purchases. A jumper and blouse for Caroline, and for Deborah an impossibly expensive doll that does everything except take out the garbage. Or so the saleslady said. Jan picks up the packaged doll and looks at the huge blue eyes and yellow hair. "Listen, cutie pie, you better do everything she said because you cost me a bundle." Normally she gets a kick out of choosing the right gift for the right person. But it's getting harder each year, especially with the girls. They have so much. Well, Aunty Jan has done her best, kids. And for your mother, a large pepper-mill. Marjorie is a tough customer to buy for; she accepts everything with such elaborate praise and gratitude that you never know whether to believe her or not. Marjorie is, I'm afraid, a gusher. So that leaves Mother and Bobby, Max and Ruth. The paperboy.

Jan kicks off her shoes and goes to the kitchen to make coffee. The house is wonderfully quiet. So quiet, in fact, that she can hear the faint buzz of Bob Bonner's electric saw in his basement workshop. Mother has gone out for the afternoon. This morning she was so excited she was like a little girl. The Friday Nite Club has organized a small choir and they're off now singing carols in a nursing home. Ironic when you think about it. Most of the Friday Niters are in their mid or late sixties and it probably won't be long before some of them will be going into those places. Mother is only sixty-two and still full of beans. Most days she has more energy than I have. But five to ten years down the line, who knows? What if she were to have a stroke and become severely disabled? What would we do with her? It's something she and Bobby have never talked about. Whoever talks about such dreadful things until they happen? Somehow Jan can't see her mother in one of those places.

She goes back to the living room and, standing there, surveys the blouse and jumper, the doll and pepper-mill. She feels vaguely cheated. Not one of the damn things is worth the money she paid. Ah well, Harper! What are you saving your money for anyway? *Your* old age. What a thought with Christmas drawing near! At least this year we'll eat Christmas dinner upstairs. I never feel at home at Bobby's. I can't help it, I just don't feel comfortable. It's odd, because both Marjorie and I try so hard. Maybe that's it; we try too hard. She wants to make me feel at home and I want to be the perfect guest. Yet we seem always to be meeting in doorways. Bumping into one another on the stairs. Exchanging nervous smiles as each of us tries to figure out why the other is behaving so like an imbecile. Last year I spilled that damn cranberry cocktail over her Christmas tablecloth. It was perfectly stupid on my part. Yet Marjorie apologized to *me*. We spent half an hour consoling one another. I shouldn't have helped set the table. I should have stayed in the living room with the girls. The maiden aunt who is always in the way. It might be nice to do something different for a change.

She returns to the kitchen and, pouring hot water into a cup of instant coffee, thinks of the Christmas she spent with Max in Nassau. Was it seven or eight years ago? They left on Christmas Eve afternoon. Flying from snow and evergreen trees to sun and shore. In the airport bar they drank martinis, so when they boarded the plane they were a little tight. A pair of swingers. High above the clouds they had another drink, touching glasses while Max winked and in her best Bogey imitation said, "Here's looking at *you*, kid!" Wearing a flat tweed cap with that wonderful red hair tucked inside. What a striking creature is old Max!

On Christmas morning they rented snorkels and flippers and paddled through the clear, green water examining the striped fish. In the afternoon they lay on the sand until the sun disappeared and the warm day turned overcast and humid. Later, Jan tried to call home, but she couldn't get through. Either the lines were busy or, as Max suggested, the operator was both stoned and incompetent. Max's haughty manners got them into trouble. In the dining room they were given a poor table in the corner. Served cold sweet potatoes and slabs of dry turkey by an insolent waiter whom Max loathed on sight. The feeling was mutual. On the table was a little plastic Christmas tree. On a stage at the other end of the dining room, a three-man steel-drum outfit played "Jingle Bells." Both Max and Jan agreed that it was the worst Christmas of their lives.

Yet maybe it would be different in some other place. Say, a ski lodge. With snow and a big stone fireplace and eggnog or mulled wine. All that corny stuff. Of course, Max now has her little friend. And why do I keep thinking of her as little? For all I know she might be six feet tall. But somehow I don't think so. I'll bet she's dark and petite and very good-looking. And I still find it hard to believe that Max is a lesbian. I know her marriage to that jerk never amounted to anything, but she did have boyfriends now and again. Though when I think about it, she was never really much interested in boys. In high school she only went out with a couple of guys. Of course, she was always so busy. Running the Drama Club or the school paper. Captain of the basketball team. But we slept together dozens of times. From the days we spent at one another's houses over weekends. All through Europe that summer. Holidays together. And not once did she make a pass! Ye gods, make a pass—that sounds so old-fashioned. Maybe I should feel insulted. But I don't. Max sees me as a friend, not a lover. Which is fine. But I wonder if it will ever be the same between us? I hope so, because I love that wacky dame.

Jan drinks her coffee and flips through the *TV Guide*. At nine o'clock Channel 10 is showing *Some Like It Hot* with Jack Lemmon and the late Marilyn M. Not a bad flick! She's seen it a couple of times and it's good for a laugh. And if I skip a drink before dinner, I can have a couple while I'm watching that. On the other hand, maybe I shouldn't have a drink at all. What was that article called in last weekend's magazine? "Ten Signs of Alcoholism." Number One: If you drink alone. But what the hell are you supposed to do if you *live* alone? Anyway, if you heed the advice in all those articles, you'd be afraid to get out of bed in the morning. Don't drink. Don't smoke. Don't eat eggs. Don't use spray deodorant. Don't wear pantyhose. They're supposed to cut off the air supply to your crotch, for God sakes. Don't live. All written by killjoy doctors who jog, and never think they're going to die.

When she hears the knock at the door, she thinks immediately of Bruce Horton. Old Bruce has been thawing out lately. Yesterday he invited me to next Friday's movies. A Christmas show. Double feature. *Going My Way* with Bing Crosby and *Miracle on Thirty-Fourth Street*. Heartwarming stuff, if not exactly thrilling. I said I'd think about it. Now he may feel the time is right to start dropping in again for coffee. Mooching around for some of Mother's butter tarts. But when she climbs the stairs to the door, she sees Hicks's dark head on the other side of the glass. His face is pensive and averted as he stares at the ground. Around him is the grey light of the late fall afternoon. Standing there in a new topcoat, he looks like a catalogue model. His hair has been styled. Staring out at him, Jan can feel the blood rising to her face. She takes a deep breath before opening the door.

"Hi," says Hicks. He smiles as he hands her the flowers. Roses again. Red as my heart's blood. There must be two dozen of the damn things wrapped in white tissue paper. She shakes her head in mild astonishment.

"James! What's all this about?"

Hicks shrugs. He still shrugs. I remember his goddam shrugs. I have dreamed about those shrugs. "I wanted to bring you some flowers," he says. "And I'd like you to meet someone."

He stands there as though challenging her. What a bloody nerve! At my door in his new clothes and fresh haircut with his goddam roses and just like that I'm supposed to drop everything and go somewhere to meet someone. And Harper, stop trembling.

"James. This is not exactly giving a lady fair warning." Another of his shrugs. "You'd better come in," she says, and Hicks follows her down the stairs and into her apartment, glancing around with the look of a bashful man in strange surroundings.

"Who do you want me to meet anyway," asks Jan, putting the flowers on the kitchen counter.

"It's a surprise," says Hicks. And my but don't we sound sprightly! This is not the old glum James I remember. Could he be on speed or something? How do people act on speed? Christ, I'm thirty-six years old and there's so much I don't know. And I wish my heart weren't pounding so hard. I think I can actually hear the racket going on inside my chest.

When she goes into the living room, Hicks is standing by her bookshelf examining her books. "Well, you look as if you're going to a ruddy wedding," she says. "I can't go out like this."

"You look great," says Hicks.

"In these jeans I look great? Okay, I look great. But this is still short notice, James. A bit cheeky if you don't mind my saying so."

Hicks is holding a book. "Hey, I remember some of this stuff, believe it or not. Between you and me. The objective case. Right?"

"Correct. Now just who am I supposed to be meeting?"

Hicks puts the book back on the shelf. "Aw come on, Janice. I said it was a surprise. I want to surprise you. Okay?"

"I hate surprises," she says as she heads for the bathroom. She knows she sounds a bit harsh, but he doesn't seem to mind. This persistent cheerfulness. It's so unlike him. Did he win a million in the lottery, I wonder. He seems so glad to see me.

She looks in the mirror and scrubs furiously at her face. Wondering why she is bothering with this. Because I want to. Because I don't want to spend the rest of this ruddy afternoon by myself. Because, because, because . . . because of the wonderful things he does. The old song from *The Wizard of Oz*. Ye gods, he walks in the door and I'm acting like a schoolgirl. My face is blazing, damn it. She applies lipstick and a little

195

eye-shadow, wondering whether she should change her blouse. She could do with a little freshening up, but the hell with it. He can like me or lump me. Hump me? Oh for God sakes, Harper, stop this foolishness. And who in Heaven's name does he want me to meet?

Before they leave, Jan arranges the roses in the pickle jars. Sitting on the sofa in his new coat Hicks watches Jan move about the apartment. When they walk down the driveway he squeezes her arm and says, "God, it's good to see you, Janice." He's excited. More excited than she's ever seen him. He tells her about his job. "It's nothing great, but it's better than hanging around on unemployment. And Jorgenson is okay. He's all right to work for."

"Where are we going, James, for goodness sakes?"

"How about a coffee?"

At first she can see no one in the Trans Am. Then she sees the boy. He's slouched in the front seat, a handsome, dark-haired eight- or nine-year-old. A little chunkier than Hicks. His mother's genes, I suppose. The boy is frowning as he watches them approach the car. I can see his father in that frown. Hicks steers her around to the passenger side and opens the door. "Hey Dale! I want you to meet a good friend of mine. This is Janice." The boy nods. Unimpressed. And I wonder how many *friends* his father has introduced the kid to over the years? Now he mutters "Hi" and looks out the front window.

"Hi, Dale." And do I sound unnaturally birdy? A little like Mother. Chirp, chirp, Harper. "You're gonna have to get in the back seat, Dale," says Hicks. Wordlessly Dale climbs into the back. While Hicks walks around to the front of the car, Jan can feel the boy's hostility burning through the back of her neck. But I'm damned if I'm going to humour him with idiotic questions about school and life with Grandma. And why did

James ever think that this was such a great surprise? And why did I not have enough gumption to say get lost? When Hicks gets in the car, Jan actually glares at him. "How about some ice cream, Dale?" asks Hicks, looking at his son in the rearview mirror.

"I'm tired of ice cream," says the boy. Hicks starts the car.

"When I was a kid, ice cream was a big deal."

"So?"

"So, don't be lippy."

As they move along Willowgreen Drive, Hicks says, "Janice and I are going to have some coffee. You can have whatever you like. A piece of pie. Doughnuts."

"You said you could get tickets for tonight's game," says Dale. His voice is filled with reproach. Something is up and I've walked right into the middle of it. More fool you, Harper. Now Hicks says, "I said maybe, Dale. Maybe."

But the boy is persistent. "On the phone you said we'll go to the Gardens on Saturday night. I can get tickets. That's what you said."

"The hell I did," says Hicks irritably. His good humour has vanished. "I said 'maybe.' *If* I can get the tickets, which obviously I couldn't. So knock it off about the tickets, Dale. Okay?"

Jan looks out at the suburban bungalows and their dead grey lawns. Such a colourless time of the year. Why doesn't it snow? They drive in silence through the empty streets and move south along Crown Hall Road to the shopping plaza. "We'll go to Mister Donut," says Hicks. "Is that all right with you?"

"Fine, James. Fine," says Jan, looking out her window. She feels as though she's been a part of the family for ten years.

"I told him on the phone," says Hicks, "that maybe I could get tickets. Maybe. There's this guy who comes into

Jorgenson's on a regular basis. Drives a Lincoln. He's got these season tickets and I told him how Dale likes hockey and how he plays in a little league up in Barrie. He's good too. How many goals you scored already this year, Dale?"

"I don't remember."

"Come off it. Your grandmother gives you a buck every time you score a goal. So how much money have you made?"

The boy sounds bored out of his head. "I don't know. Thirty-five dollars, I think."

"Right. So anyways, this guy in the Lincoln said how would I like to take Dale to see the Leafs play. And I said terrific. Well, I thought he meant tonight. But maybe he said some night. I don't know. He could have said some night. And he didn't come by yesterday, so there you have it." Hicks looks again at his son in the rearview mirror. "What you've got to understand, Dale, is that people like this guy in the Lincoln, they've got season tickets, eh. You have to be rich to have these season tickets. So the average man doesn't stand a chance of getting into those games. Only rich people can afford them, see?"

"You shouldn't have said then," says unforgiving Dale.

"Okay, I shouldn't have said, but I did. I'm sorry."

The doughnut shop is crowded, but they find a table in the corner. Sitting there, Jan thinks of that long-ago Saturday in September when Hicks first sat across from her and the young waitress couldn't take her eyes off him. The girl no longer works here. Jan and Hicks have only coffee, but the boy eats jelly doughnuts and milk, wiping his mouth on the sleeve of his windbreaker. He looks unrepentant and insolent. A sulking type who bears a grudge. A bad enemy, thinks Jan. When Hicks ask him what he'd like to do for the rest of the afternoon, he only shrugs. "I don't know."

Hicks turns to Jan. "I'd like to take him to that Science

Centre. They say it's an interesting place. And you can learn something. But he says he's not interested in science. Everybody should be interested in science, for Christ sakes. That's where the future is."

Jan sips some coffee. "It's a great place, Dale. Lots of fun. I've taken my two nieces there and they really enjoyed it."

"See!" says Hicks.

"I don't want to go," says the boy, and Hicks gives his son an angry look.

"You don't see enough things like that. All you do is watch television."

The boy eats his doughnut and looks down at his plate. He seems so glacial and remote, thinks Jan. "You're not going to learn anything," continues Hicks, "unless you use your head once in a while. Hockey and television. That's all you ever think about." Listening, Jan feels sorry for the boy. Who needs a lecture like this on Saturday afternoon? James comes on too strong with his son. I'm not a parent, but even I can see that. However, Dale is a tough little number, and he's not about to wilt under his father's words. Instead he looks grim and determined. You can almost see the stubbornness settling along his jawline. His obstinate silence only seems to confuse and annoy his father, who says finally, "Well, you're going to the Science Centre and that's all there is to it." The boy continues to look down at his plate. A half-eaten doughnut.

"I won't get out of the car," he says quietly. "You'll have to drag me out of the car."

"Well, I can do that easily enough, by Christ," says Hicks. Jan covers his hand with hers.

"James. Look, it's no good. If Dale doesn't want to go to the Science Centre, it's pointless to drag him there. He's never going to learn anything that way. Or enjoy himself, which is probably more important. It doesn't make any sense."

"He's not learning anything anyway," says Hicks irritably.

"Maybe not, but you can't force people to learn. You just turn them off."

She looks across at Dale. "You're missing out on a great experience, Dale, but maybe another time. You've got lots of time to go to the Science Centre." She says to Hicks, "Why don't you take him to a movie? There must be a movie he'd like to see." For the first time the boy lifts his head and regards her with solemn interest.

Hicks is relieved by the suggestion, but he's not about to let Dale off the hook that easily. "Janice is a schoolteacher. She teaches in a high school. She knows what she's talking about." He hesitates and then says, "Today we'll go to a movie. But sooner or later you're going to visit that Science Centre."

2

Airplane is playing at Plaza Cinema Four and the place is crowded with youngsters. The only seats left are near the front, and so they sit staring up at the monstrous figures on the screen. Behind them the laughter of the audience bursts over the darkened theatre. Dale is no laugher, but he clearly enjoys the movie's foolishness and snickers away in mild approval. Hicks too looks pleased, and now and then a smile plays across his face. From time to time Jan sneaks a look at them. In the bright light from the screen she is struck by the similarity of their profiles. They even sit the same way, slumped in their seats with the watchful and suspicious expressions of slum kids at a party. The mystery of genes! When she was ten or eleven she remembers watching her father come into a room. Although he was not an exceptionally tall man at six feet, he used to dip his head a bit as he came through a doorway. And now I do the same damn thing! Strange!

When the movie is over it's nearly dark, though the plaza is lighted up and still filled with shoppers. Hicks stops at Colonel Sanders, and driving back to his apartment, Jan feels a vague contentment. The three of them are somehow united in a comfortable silence, and she sits there smelling the French fries and feeling the warm cardboard bucket on her lap. Coming home from the movies with a Saturday-night take-out dinner. A pleasantly dull experience, and she wonders if this is what it feels like to be married.

Hicks has made an effort to clean up his place. The rug has been vacuumed and the kitchen and bathroom have been tidied. Stacked in one corner of the living room are several suitcases, a duffel bag, a sleeping roll, and an electric guitar. Hicks explains that a friend is staying for a while. However, he's away for the weekend. Wearing a big cowboy hat, Dale lies on the rug in front of the TV eating chicken and drinking Pepsi. In the kitchen Jan and Hicks sit at the table. They drink beer and eat chicken and play Scrabble. Hicks bought the game a week ago and is consumed with excitement. He sees the game as an enjoyable way to improve your vocabulary. Educational. He and Latimer have played nearly every night, though Latimer is not much interested in word games. Still, as Hicks tells her. "You have to give the guy credit when you consider he only has Grade Six or Seven." Jan asks Hicks where he met Latimer and Hicks says, "Latimer? I met him up in Guelph. We seemed to hit it off from the first day, though I don't know why. We don't have all that much in common. I mean, Latimer can be a real jerk. Still, he's okay too. He'd give you the shirt off his back."

Hicks puzzles over his tray of letters. "But he can't play this game, that's for sure. Now Miss Schoolteacher, how about this one?" Using nearly all his letters he spells *chapter*. In fact, he's surprisingly good at the game. He keeps watching Jan, expecting her to put together huge words instead of the puny things she must settle for. She tells him that she's hopeless at games like this, but he doesn't believe her. Imagines she's just having a poor night. Hicks tells her that he's also learning how to play chess and hopes one day to teach Dale. So they play with these small lettered pieces of wood while Dale watches the hockey game.

At eleven o'clock Hicks rolls out the sofa bed, and, watching him smooth down the sheets, Jan feels such tenderness toward him that she wants only to touch his face. When Dale comes from the bathroom he is wearing white pyjamas with blue elephants on them. In these pyjamas he loses altogether that look of sullen defiance. He is, after all, thinks Jan, only a little boy. Watching Hicks bend over the bed, she has a pang of envy for those who have children. Moments like this must be the most satisfying of all and the odds are long that she will never experience them. Hicks and his son do not touch. He says only, "Have a good sleep, Dale." The boy, hands folded across his chest, stares up at his father and says goodnight.

In the kitchen Hicks turns on the transistor very low searching for a station that plays classical music. Before long he finds some too, a nice little flute thing by Telemann. Jan has already mentioned phoning a taxi, but Hicks suggests that there is time enough for that. So they sit at the kitchen table and listen to Telemann. They can also hear the television from the apartment next door. A siren somewhere in the night. Without saying much, they wait for Dale to sleep. Without discussion they have entered into a harmless little conspiracy. But the boy too seems to be waiting. They can hear him turning over restlessly.

Is he holding out against them, wonders Jan? Probably he suspects mischief between his father and his girlfriend. The kid is nobody's fool.

In time, however, small boys fall asleep. He's had a busy day, explains Hicks, shyly telling Jan how much his son enjoyed riding in Jorgenson's tow truck. Hicks went into the service station this morning and took the kid for a drive around the block. Hicks didn't think Jorgenson would go for it, but when he asked him the boss said go ahead. His beloved truck, too! According to Hicks, this Jorgenson is a puzzling man.

In the living room they stand looking down at the sleeping boy. Dale's face is mashed against the pillow. A faint snore coming from his open mouth. When Hicks takes Jan in his arms, she whispers a protest. What if the boy should awaken and discover them on the floor? A terrible risk. But she badly wants him too, and on the floor under a blanket they hungrily embrace. As Hicks kisses her he says, "I'll never let you get away again, Janice." And how good it feels to be loved, she thinks, as he touches her! So why am I so frightened of this man?

3

The clerk at Rings & Things is a snotty English bitch. Or so thinks Hicks as he stands by a glass counter examining a tray of diamond rings. The English bitch stands behind the counter with her arms folded across her chest. Not a bit fucking interested in serving him. When he first came into the store, he stood there for several minutes while this bitch talked to another clerk. Except for Hicks and the two clerks, the store is empty. Skinny blonde twat with her fancy accent. They come over here and first thing you know they think they own the fucking country.

Hicks believes that if he'd worn a suit, a shirt and tie, he'd have received better service. But he came straight from work, and his work pants and windbreaker are spotted with grease and oil. Although he washed his hands, they still look grimy. But so what? She's only a salesclerk in a jewellery store. Big fucking deal! But then, in England people like her look down their noses at working persons. They classify people over there by the way they talk and dress. Hicks doesn't know where he read or heard about that, but he knows it's true. Common knowledge. Now he takes a ring from the tray and pretends to study it. Money-wise the fucking things are out of sight. Still, he asks how much for this one. "That one is twelve hundred," says the bitch. She seems to enjoy announcing these ridiculous prices. If only she'd turn her head he might have a go at palming one. But she is watching him like a fucking hawk. "Perhaps," she says, "you might try a shop which carries a less expensive line. I'm afraid we just don't have anything very interesting under a thousand dollars."

"What you mean," says Hicks slowly, "is that maybe I should try fucking Woolworth's. Right?" The woman doesn't fall over hearing this, but does colour slightly. Snotty little stone-faced English cunt, thinks Hicks. And before he leaves the store, he calls her just that.

4

Murray Ford winds a long scarf around his throat. "Have a super holiday, Janice my love!" Everyone it seems has left but me. Even Bruce, who went off without wishing me happy holidays. But then I'm out of favour again. "You too, Murray." Murray stands in front of the small mirror which is on the back of the staff closet door. He is adjusting a black beret.

With his smart new overcoat and the English university scarf and the beret he looks youthful for a man of forty. Murray has good taste. Bless his heart. This morning he gave me a bottle of perfume, "a most provocative fragrance by Max Factor." Which reminds me of that old high-school joke. One of Max's no doubt. What happened to Helena Rubenstein? Max Factor. Ho. Ho.

Putting her feet up on the low table, Jan sips her tea and watches Murray fiddle with his beret. The man is impossibly vain, but in a way it's forgivable, even touching. "I hope you have a naughty old time," says Murray, dipping at the knees to give the beret a final tug. He then twirls on his heels and looks down at her. "I'm told by little birds that you have a new beau." Jan feels herself colouring. "Awfully good-looking, I understand," says Murray, looking outrageously mischievous. "Well, all I can say is that I'm glad someone around here is leading an interesting life. Besides me, of course. It's encouraging to know that the English Department is holding its own. Now if we could just get someone for Norma." He stops to whisper, "How about some rough trade for the poor old thing? Say, the leader of a motorcycle gang?"

"Oh Murray, for God sakes," says Jan, laughing.

Murray pecks her on the cheek. "See you in January, love," he says, waving goodbye.

"Yes, Murray. Take care. And thanks again for the perfume."

But Murray is gone. For Murray the Christmas vacation is a time for clearing out of suburbia fast. Not for him the home and hearth. As he once said to her, "My dear. I simply can't bear the turkey-dinner scene. All the little nephews and nieces! My cretinous brother-in-law! It just won't do." So he spends a week in New York going to shows and concerts and galleries. Probably with his friend Colin. Good for you, Murray. Enjoy!

The staff room smells of stale smoke, but it's quiet and the hot tea is good and it feels just fine to sit here with my feet up and two glorious weeks of holidays staring me in the face. For a moment Jan imagines she's alone. But then she notices Harry Waggoner bent over a desk in the far corner. Writing something. Harry looks exhausted and ill. Obviously he's having a rough time of it. The word is out that Diane has left him. What a time for a family to break apart! Now he looks so defeated. Even the children seem to be taking it better, though it's hard to tell with the Waggoners. They're such a reticent crew. I don't know about the girl, but Brad was in class this morning and he acted quite normal. It's funny how I keep forgetting that young Brad Waggoner is James's first cousin. He even looks a bit like him. James's cousin! But why should that stroke me as odd? Why shouldn't James have uncles and aunts and cousins just like everyone else? Yet it does strike me as curious. Perhaps because he seems to be so alone in the world. He gives such an impression of privacy and singularity. A man no one has ever been close to. Strange! And when he comes to dinner tonight, I suppose I will have to introduce him to Mother. Well, dear Mother is just going to have to damn well get used to him.

In the end she got used to Travers. Even to his car starting up at three o'clock in the morning. Ah Travers! My old flame. My old summer romance. Where are you and how are you? Back with Lady Bitch and the two lovely daughters, I suppose. Putting up the Christmas lights and all that stuff. Fickle old me, I hardly think of you nowadays. The flame has burned out, though I had a curious dream about you the other night. You were on a sailing boat, wearing your faded cut-offs and that dinky little blue cap I liked so much. Waking up, I remembered how one day you told me you wanted to sail around the world. Chuck everything and buy a small boat. You said you'd take me along as first mate or cabin girl or something. We'd see the coral reefs off Australia. Sail past the junks in Singapore harbour. Wearing soiled white clothes and looking like old Humphrey Bogart and Katharine Hepburn in *The African Queen*.

"You must love this place," says Norma Kirstead, coming into the room.

"Oh, hi Norma." Jan looks up at the heavy-set figure in the grey suit. She's carrying her coffee mug and a large book.

"No, I'm just relaxing. Easing myself into the holidays."

Norma strides across the room to the tiny sink. "Well, I can think of better places to ease it than this." She lays down the book and begins to run hot water over her coffee mug. Carefully drying the mug, she hangs it on the third hook from the corner. I've seen her take someone else's cup off that third hook and put her own mug on it. Totally compulsive. And is that what happens when you live alone for twenty-five years? Your life becomes a quest for trivial order: plumping cushions, straightening tablecloths, arranging books, rinsing coffee mugs. A place for everything and everything in its place. One of my mother's favourite expressions. Norma comes back toward me. The book under her arm is *War and Peace*. "You're not going to read *that* over the holidays, Norma?"

"Yes I am," says Norma. Such a steadfast and persevering soul. "At any rate," she says, "I'm going to get a good start on it. I haven't read the darn thing since university and I've always been meaning to go back to it. So I thought to myself the other day, why not start over the holidays? You might say I'm getting started on my New Year's resolutions." Norma seems immensely pleased with the prospect of getting on with her resolutions. "Are you staying home for the holidays?" she asks.

"Yes. How about you?" I seem to recall having this conversation with Norma last year. And the year before that. I wonder if Norma remembers too. It's hard to tell as I watch her stuff the book into her old leather briefcase.

"Yes. Of course I'll spend Christmas Day at my brother's." She taps the briefcase. "But I'll be spending most of the time with the cats and the Count." She looks indeed very happy. "Goodbye now," she says. "Have a nice holiday, Janice."

"Yes, goodbye Norma. You too." She didn't even say goodbye to Harry, who still sits in the corner. What's he doing? Grading tests? Maybe Norma didn't even notice him.

She has laid up her Raleigh Traveler for the winter, and so she will walk the eight blocks to her apartment building at the east end of Progress. A nice place too. Airy and bright and filled with plants and books. When I first met her, I thought she would live in some old apartment building downtown. Some severe place with dark wood paneling. Filled with her dead parents' furniture. Not a bit of it. Norma lives on the top floor of a huge apartment building. When the weather is fine, she can see south to Lake Ontario. On her balcony she watches birds through heavy German binoculars. She says it's amazing the variety of birds you can see even from the balcony of a suburban building. Her apartment is done up in soft cream colours and has a great curving sofa with several fat cushions. The whole effect is feminine and sensuous. Which I have to admit surprised me. The only object in the place that is remotely masculine or old-fashioned is a cylindrical basket in the hallway. This holds Norma's walking sticks. She bought the basket in Burton-on-the-Water during a summer walking-tour of the Cotswolds. Off she went by herself, absolutely undaunted. She's already talking of going to Andalusia next summer. For the rest of the year she lives in that big chic apartment with her two Siamese cats, Wordsworth and Coleridge. And she'll have a perfectly contented holiday with her cats and her walks and her birdwatching and her Tolstoy. She keeps herself busy and she has told me that keeping busy is the key to contentment. Could I be satisfied with that kind of life in my fifties? Who knows? And ye gods my feet are swollen. Is there too much salt in my diet, I wonder? There's always some damn thing.

Jan eases her feet back into her shoes and stands up. For a moment she looks over at Harry Waggoner. He has stopped marking and now sits at the card table, staring at the wall. Jan walks across to him. She warns herself to be careful. Sometimes people don't appreciate this. "Harry," she says, "I'm sorry . . . about things." Harry turns and looks up at her. "Oh, hi Jan. Yes . . . well." He looks down at the test papers. "Well, these things happen to people, you know. You hear about them all the time." He examines a marking pencil as though he's seeing it for the first time. "Diane is an awfully good-looking woman. I don't know. I guess she got tired of me. I'm not very lively, I guess." And to Jan's horror, he laughs. It's a short, terrible laugh, nearly a snort. Harry! Harry!

"You shouldn't sell yourself short, Harry."

Again he laughs his desperate laugh. "Oh, I don't know, Jan."

"Well." Jan finds herself foolishly patting the man's shoulder. A Merry Christmas is out of the question, Harper. Harry's shoulder is like bedrock. "Take care, Harry. See you in January."

"You bet, Jan," says Harry, looking up at her blankly. And I wonder if he's taken a tranquilizer. But then Harry looks this way most of the time. And he's horribly right about himself. He isn't a very lively person. Maybe that's why his wife left him. Men often think it's sexual, but there are worse sins than sexual neglect. Boring a person must surely be one of them.

In the parking lot she feels the cold wind pressing against her face as she walks toward her Honda. She wonders is she has time to clean the oven. What an awful job! But the damn thing is filthy and will smoke when she broils the steaks. Is there something else she could prepare that wouldn't need the oven? The decisions in your life, Harper!

Four

I

When they first mentioned it an hour ago, Hicks thought they were crazy. Yet he's still listening. When you're talking about money, it doesn't cost anything to listen. Latimer's long, skinny frame is hunched over Hicks's coffee table. He and his friend Ronny Gregg are sitting on the sofa bed drinking dark rum and Coke. Gregg's girlfriend sits apart from everyone in one of Hicks's basket chairs. She has her knees up and her denim legs are spread so that you can see the outline of her crack. Her toenails and fingernails are painted black, for Christ sakes. Hicks guesses the girl can't be more than sixteen or seventeen. A little blonde runaway with nice tits. Not bad looking. She's drinking Coke from a can and humming along with Mickey Gilley, who is singing "True Love Ways." She seems to be paying little heed to this talk about robbing a bank, but she shouldn't be here listening anyway, thinks Hicks. To him it seems somehow unprofessional. Yet Hicks doesn't think there's much use in pressing the point. Gregg would probably take offence, and Hicks wonders if he could handle the situation. Gregg strikes him as one of those ugly men who are as tough as they look. He's about Hicks's age. A bit shorter, but beefy, with heavy, tattooed arms. However, he's running to fat and has a little beer gut hanging over his belt. And that, decides Hicks, is what he'd work on. That little gut!

When Latimer brought Gregg and his girlfriend to the apartment an hour ago, Hicks received the strong impression that Gregg did not like him. Hicks could feel this hostility between them right away, even though they hadn't said a word to each other. However, he let it pass, because these things sometimes happen and anyway there isn't anything you can do about them. He's been around guys like Ronny Gregg before, and nearly always they give him a hard time because, as Hicks figures it, they're jealous of his good looks. So they nearly always feel uneasy about their women in Hicks's company. But what guys like this Gregg don't understand is that Hicks couldn't care less about this dopey little teenager. Sure, he'd throw a fuck into her if the opportunity arose. But she's almost certainly not worth any hassle. Yet it would be pointless to say this to Ronny Gregg, who is really a very ugly man with his sloping brow and slab-like face. Nearly bald too. A brutal-looking fucker. Right now he is again explaining the advantages in knocking over this trust company on Monday morning. Talking about the fact there are only the manager and four women working in the place. As he listens, Hicks drinks beer and looks out his streaked window at the blue December sky.

Gregg has drawn a rough diagram of the shopping plaza, and to Hicks this seems both foolish and unnecessary. In any case, he knows the shopping plaza better than anyone in the room. The trust company is at the end of one wing of the plaza. Next to an alleyway. On the other side of the alleyway is the back wall of Canadian Tire. He's walked past there hundreds of times. Yet Gregg points to the map. "There you have the side of the Canadian Tire building. And the trust company here, eh. With this alleyway between them. We park behind the place and walk up the alleyway." Hicks studies Gregg's flat, heavy face. Such a face could take a lot of punishment before breaking up. Hicks also figures Gregg for the sort of man who would use that brutal-looking head of his for a weapon. He'd butt you in the stomach with that head. Gregg thinks they could scoop up at least twenty thousand dollars in a minute. He swallows some rum and Coke. "Me and Brian can be in and out of the fucking place in sixty seconds." Hicks can't help himself.

"How do you know that there's twenty thousand dollars in there? I mean, it seems to me that unless you know somebody who has worked in there, that kind of information would be very hard to come by. For all we know, there's only a couple of thousand dollars in that branch. What I'm saying here is simply this: Is it worth the trouble?"

Gregg looks disgusted as he says to Latimer, "Brian, I thought you told me this fucking guy would be interested?" The girl now looks over at them. T.G. Sheppard is singing "I'll Be Coming Back for More." "But all I get," says Gregg to Latimer, "is fucking negative stuff from this man." Latimer shrugs and Gregg turns to Hicks. "Listen to me. Do you know what's coming next week?"

"Sure," says Hicks. "Christmas, for fuck sakes. Everybody knows that."

"All right. Fuckin' Christmas. Right. So . . . people are gonna need money, right?"

"Could be," agrees Hicks. He's beginning to enjoy himself. The truth is he feels light-headed. This is his fifth beer and he's had no breakfast.

"Never mind fucking could be," says Gregg. "People are gonna need money. Everybody runs short just before Christmas. All banks are going to be loaded next week, even little branches like this one here."

"Ronny is right, Hicksy," says Latimer. "Those fuckers will have lots of cash on the premises next week. Those drawers will be filled with bread. What do you want, son? Some fifties? Some hundreds? Want to buy the little lady a new pair of oven mitts? Just help yourself here." Latimer is dealing out imaginary money and the girl is giggling. She sees Latimer as a character.

Now Latimer gets up and goes to the corner of the living room, where he kneels down and rummages through an Adidas bag. After a moment he holds up a pair of Quebec licence plates. "It's a good set-up, Hicksy. We're gonna use these Quebec plates so they'll think we're a bunch of frogs. A lot of frogs come in and work the Ontario banks this time of year. Gangs of them, man. Some of them did a bank the other day. That one up in Aurora. You read about that one, Ronny?"

"Yeah."

"Well, the cops figure it was some guys from Montreal. They got more fucking bank robbers in Montreal than anywhere else in the world. So on Monday morning, I come on with a froggy accent in the place." Latimer now stands over Gregg's girlfriend and, making a pistol of his right hand, points it at her. "Gimme dat goddam money, s'il vous plait." Breaks her right up. What an asshole, thinks Hicks. But it might work. "Look, Hicksy," says Latimer, "this is strictly a run-and-grab thing. We're not greedy. We just want fifteen or twenty thousand. A little Christmas shopping money. And like Ronny said, it won't take us more than a minute to scoop that up. All you have to do is keep the old motor running and get us back to the van. Then we split. In half an hour you'll be back changing somebody's oil."

Gregg looks bored and contemptuous; he doesn't like the idea of persuading anybody about anything. Hicks drinks some beer and thinks about Monday. He wonders if Latimer has ever done anything like this before. Gregg probably has.

Gregg is a tough fucking customer. No doubt about it. But Hicks has never done anything like this in his life. These guys are going to use guns. Armed robbery is not the same as hustling hot colour TV's or boosting the odd little thing from the trucks at Cross-Canada Transport. Still, he'd be in the car. He doesn't have to go in the place, so nobody will see him. From start to finish, according to Gregg, the whole thing can be done in twenty minutes, and then he'll be back at Jorgenson's. Nobody is going to look for a guy pumping gas six blocks away. Still, it's a helluva risk. If it doesn't work, you could be looking at a long time. Hicks wonders if he could handle another stretch. Living among those morons would drive him crazy in no time flat. Sometimes he believes he'd kill himself rather than go back in the bucket. But they promised him a quarter of whatever they get. And a quarter of twenty thousand is five thousand dollars. Jesus! It would certainly solve a lot of problems money-wise. For a start he could pay off all his debts, including the fucking car. It would be his outright. He could buy Janice the ring for Christmas. Give it to her Christmas Eve. A nice touch.

Take her out to dinner at one of the big downtown hotels. The candlelight-and-wine scene. Put the ring by her plate without a word. She'd want to know where he got the money, so he'd have to make up something about an uncle dying or what the fuck ever. Not difficult. And, of course, sooner or later he'll have to get in touch with Gail about a divorce. But it's time he was getting on with that side of his life anyway. It's time to put things in order, and a few thousand dollars would certainly help.

Hicks suddenly feels good about things. The morning seems enriched with possibilities. "Open me another beer, will you, Latimer?" he says. "And get Gregg here another drink too." Hicks feels a sense of fellowship stealing over him. These are not bad people. Certainly there are worse types around than Latimer. Even Gregg, though basically an unattractive type, probably has his good points. You have to take people as they are. It only makes sense.

Hicks figures that one of the first things he'll do with the money is move to a nicer place. Get a two-bedroom in one of those new buildings over on Chester Green. He'll talk it over with Janice on Christmas Eve. It's a very good time of the year for making plans, thinks Hicks, as he listens to Johnny Cash and Waylon Jennings sing "I Wish I Was Crazy Again."

2

Jan throws a box of macaroni into her cart and reflects on what a creature of habit she's become. So, as you get older, Harper, you'd better watch this compulsive stuff. There was no reason to endure this crowd today, you could have done all this on Monday morning when most of these good burghers will be at work. As it is, the A&P is jammed. The line-ups at the cash registers are horrendous, and needless to say, only four of the ten registers are in operation. And ye gods, if somebody doesn't turn down Perry Como mumbling about being home for Christmas, I'm going to scream. I wonder what people would do if I simply blew a gasket. Is that what gaskets do? If it comes to that, what the hell is a gasket? Bruce was forever going on about gaskets for his cars. "The Nash needs a new gasket, I think." Wonderful! But what if right here, in front of the frozen foods, I went ape. I can see the headline. *Schoolteacher Goes Berserk in A&P. Throws Cans at Supermarket Loudspeaker.* Oh, calm down, Harper. Think pleasant and serene thoughts. A snow-capped mountain and an old, wrinkled Oriental gent smoking a pipe of opium. Stoned out of his sage old skull. O Wise Father, how do I get through this festive week? Take heart, daughter. Think of eternity. The peace of infinite space. Right, O Learned One. Meanwhile, look at the price of this goddam orange juice. It's absolutely criminal.

She hesitates by the case of frozen juices and wonders whether she shouldn't just forget about it. Abandon the cart here and now and come back on Monday. It'll take at least another hour to get out of this place today. Behind her a short man in a zip-front jacket with a bowling crest on the sleeve says, "Excuse me." Very sarcastic. Jan, who is six inches taller, moves to one side, and the little man wheels his cart recklessly past other shoppers and disappears into the baked-goods section. And where are the manners nowadays? Where are the gentlemen hiding? On the other hand, I was blocking the aisle. She picks up some orange juice. Mother likes her orange juice and says she needs the vitamins. So okay!

Mother, Mother. Who today abandoned her Saturday morning routine for the first time in ten years. "Oh no, dear, not today. Gordon is coming over at eleven and we're going to go over a few songs. Besides, it'll be so busy. Gordon said he'd take me Monday or Tuesday. But you go right ahead, dear." All this delivered in such a breezy manner. But then, outrageous as it may seem, I do believe that dear Mother is in love. If not in love, at least infatuated. Her heart has been smitten. My mother! At sixty-two! Well, stranger things have happened, I suppose. But it certainly answers the question of why she has spent nearly every night for the past three weeks rehearsing with the Happy Choristers for their singalongs at the old-folks nursing homes. It seems that Mr. (please call me Gordon) Rutherford is a Happy Chorister too, bless his freshly barbered white head. They met a month ago when he joined the Friday Nite Club.

I met his yesterday afternoon when I came home from school. His clean little two-tone Chevelle was parked in the driveway. And once inside the house, I heard the voices singing together: a pleasant light tenor and Mother's spirited soprano. They were singing "Silver Bells," and in my apartment I stood listening. They sang well together. Who could he be? So, after I took the steaks from the fridge, I listened again as they sang "White Christmas." James was coming over and I was determined to have Mother meet him. Get it over with. The idea was to invite her down for a glass of juice before she left for the Friday Nite Club. So, I went upstairs and knocked lightly on the living-room archway.

Mother was seated at the piano in a new mauve dress. She'd just had a new permanent too, and she was wearing little mauve earrings. Earrings for God sakes! I hadn't seen Mother in earrings for fifteen years. Standing behind her was this dapper little character in polyester slacks, light brown sports jacket, and yellow cardigan. One of those peppery little fellows whose bounce and fizzing good spirits make you forget just how small he is. Gordon Rutherford can't be more than five-foot-three. I felt like an Amazon standing beside him. Looking down at his fresh, pink face and smelling his Old Spice. He has the clearest blue eyes I've ever seen in a man, and he seems to carry with him a kind of willed authority. Perhaps to make up for his size. Anyway, he squeezed my hand and said, "It's a great pleasure to meet you, Janice." Then he reared back on his heels and fixed me with such a look of admiring affection that I wondered briefly if he might have once enrolled in Mr. Carnegie's famous course. Whatever, there he was, magnetic and male and working something on Mother, who looked agreeably flustered. She was girlish. I might have come upon them necking on the sofa. She was actually blushing, and looking at her, I caught a glimpse of how she must have seemed to my father in 1942. Sweet-faced and amiable and possessed of that innocence peculiar to persons who are fundamentally unconfident and capricious. No wonder Lorne Harper was smitten. And now this little guy, so brimming and sassy, was already treating her with proprietary affection. "Janice. Your mother does not eat enough to keep a bird alive. She says she worries about her weight. What nonsense! She could carry ten extra pounds. She's got the figure of a forty-year-old woman, and there's no use being bashful about it, Lillian."

At first I saw him as a retired salesman. An old word-slinger in hardware or yarn goods. But not so. He is in fact a retired railway conductor. "Worked for the CPR for forty-three years." And a widower. "My wife passed away exactly three years ago this coming January. Cancer. As a matter of fact it was exactly the same week that your poor father was taken. I thought that was a remarkable coincidence when Lillian told me." All this offered freely and without embarrassment. Gordon Rutherford is, as they say nowadays, up front about things.

When I asked them down to meet James, Gordon reared back on his heels and declared that it sounded like a wonderful idea but he was taking Lillian over to the Crock & Block for supper. Then they had to "skedaddle" to some senior-citizen place if they wanted to be in time for the concert. And it just wouldn't do to be late, since they'd been asked to sing a medley of popular Christmas songs together. In agreeing, Mother seemed not to give a hoot about James Hicks. "Gordon's right, dear. We really have to run along. You and Mr. Hicks enjoy yourselves. If there's anything in my fridge you need, just help yourself." So there you have it, Harper. A month ago she was fretting over you as though you were sixteen years old. Now she doesn't care if you have Jack the Ripper in for tea.

Working from her list, Jan throws article after article into her basket and in a half-hour she reaches the end of a line-up, moving in just ahead of the fellow in the bowling jacket. In fact she cuts him off and grins fiercely. *And a Merry Christmas to you too, my friend.* But the man takes no notice. He gazes past her. It's as though his anger is spent, and now he only looks unhappy and bewildered. In a moment he is fishing in his wallet, looking for the dollars to pay for his groceries. And he must be shopping for a large family because his cart is loaded. Where is his wife, I wonder? Sick? Drunk? Flown the coop like Diane Waggoner? Or maybe working at the K-Mart to help keep things going. Jan sees a couple of teenagers at home. Lying in bed. *Exhausted* after a late Friday night. They'll be up in time to sass their father. No wonder he looks confused by the world. Watching him, Jan feels genuine sympathy for the guy. Life can be such a tangle. There's a great deal to be said for simplicity. So, Harper! Why did you not say something last night when James kept going on about marriage and family and how wonderful it all could be?

Five

I

Latimer is phoning from a motel on Lakeshore Boulevard. He moved out of Hicks's apartment a few days ago and is now staying with Ronny Gregg and his girlfriend. Latimer sounds high, though it's often hard to tell because he seems crazy most of the time. "Hicksy, Hicksy," says Latimer. "Are you relaxed, man? Are you loose as a goose for tomorrow? We're going to do our big thing tomorrow, Hicksy, and we got to be relaxed."

"I'm all right," says Hicks. "Don't worry about me." The phone awakened him and now he looks at his watch. It's five-thirty. When he looks around the corner of the kitchen, Hicks can see the sky through the living-room window. A rich, dark blue. And a solitary star. This morning he heard on the radio that today is the first day of winter. Some guy said that the earth in its orbit passed a certain point just before noon. That makes it officially winter, even though there's still no snow. All this news about celestial traffic intrigues Hicks. To him, it seems important to know about stuff like that. If you think about such things seriously, it's a way of getting your mind off your troubles. Puts things in perspective. So he reminded himself to get out a library book on the planets and stars because it was just something else he didn't know about. At times Hicks believes that all the goddam knowledge in the world could smother a man. Was Latimer moaning at the other end of the line? "Hey Hicksy man. Are you there?"

"I'm here."

"Do you know what Cheryl is doing to me now? As of this very minute?"

"What are you talking about, Latimer?" Hicks looks up at the evening star.

"Listen," says Latimer, "this chick is something else, let me tell you. Right now, Hicksy. I am sitting in a chair in my birthday suit. Do you remember when you were a kid and bare-assed, your old lady would call it your birthday suit? My old lady did anyways." Latimer sounds like he's grunting.

"What the fuck are you talking about, Latimer?"

"What I'm talking about is sitting in this chair in my birthday suit while little Cheryl is giving me some of the sweetest head of my short life. That's what I'm talking about, Hicksy." Hicks strains to listen. Hears some kind of weird, snuffling noise. Hicks can't believe his ears. Is that little broad actually blowing Latimer while he talks on the phone?

"Are you giving me the fucking gears, Latimer?" asks Hicks, stirred by the image of the girl kneeling in front of Latimer's long, pale body. Hicks remembers her breasts, her pouty little lips. Jesus Christ!

"It's party time, Hicksy," says Latimer. "We're having a party. We're smoking some mean grass, too. It's pure fucking gold, believe you me. Why not drop over? There's plenty for all. This girl is an artist, Hicksy. Seventeen years old and she's an artist. What's the world coming to? I just don't know how old Ronny gets them."

"Yeah," says Hicks, feeling left out of things. "And where's King Kong now?"

Latimer lets out a yelp. "King Kong?" he shrieks. "Oh, I love it, Hicksy. Fucking King Kong. That's beautiful, man." Hicks can hear Latimer telling the girl about it. Looking out at the sky, Hicks wonders if there is any life on those distant stars. He guesses not as Latimer says, "Cheryl doesn't know who the fuck King Kong is, Hicksy. Can you believe that? They do not educate the youth of today. Listen, don't worry about old Kong." He starts to giggle. "God, I love that! King fucking Kong! Anyway, don't worry about him. He's zonked out on blue bombers."

"What the fuck are blue bombers?" asks Hicks. "I don't want to work with no hop head."

"It's just Valium, man. Ten milligrams. They make him sleep. King Kong has trouble napping, Hicksy, so he pops a little Valium. He'll be fresh as biscuits tomorrow. Right now he's gone for twelve or fourteen hours. Anyway, he doesn't give a shit if you have a little taste. He even told me and Cheryl to have some fun. No harm done."

"He doesn't dig me."

"Maybe not, but don't worry about it. Ronny's okay. I've told him you can drive and that's all he cares about. So come on over. Listen, Cheryl digs you. She says you remind her of that movie actor John Travolta. She told me that, Hicksy. So come on over. It'll relax you. The three of us will do something interesting. Get a pound of Crisco and go nuts."

Hicks laughs bitterly. "You're out of your fucking tree, Latimer. Do you know that?"

"Maybe so, Hicksy, but you gotta have some fun. While you're beautiful and young. Listen man, Cheryl wants to talk to you. Here now, Cheryl. You sweet-talk my old friend Hicksy."

Hicks stands waiting by the phone. He can feel his heart racing and knows it's crazy. She's just a little tramp. Could be carrying a dose of clap. Christ! Explain that one to Janice. Yet he can see the girl with her pointed breasts, sitting naked on Latimer's knees. Then he hears her giggling and saying "Hi." She laughs again. "Do you want to come over?" Sounds zonked out of her mind.

"Are you sure you want me over there?" asks Hicks. "What are you doing anyway?"

"Just foolin' around," says the girl, laughing. "I think you're really good lookin'. I wouldn't mind doin' it with you if you want." Hicks listens to the two of them laughing.

Latimer says, "This could be a very depraved scene, Hicksy. Rub-a-dub-dub, three folks in a tub."

Hicks looks up at the cold winter heavens. It would only take a half-hour to get over to the west end. But a party like that can be murder on your system. You start drinking and doping; it could go on for hours. Not that he cares that much for dope. It only gives him a headache. The point is he has to be at work tomorrow by seven. Has to be alert too. Anyway, how can he justify fucking around with trash like Cheryl if he's serious about Janice Harper? She's the only good thing that's happened to him in the last ten years. So, going over to that motel makes no sense at all. Relieved, he tells Latimer to forget about it. Latimer seems to be yawning. "Suit yourself, man." Hicks feels suddenly nervous and wary. Tomorrow they are going to rob a bank for Christ sakes.

"Have you got the car, Latimer?"

"We've got the car, Hicksy. No sweat." Latimer now sounds languid. Probably shot his lump and is now ready for a sleep. Fucking party! Big deal!

"What have you got?"

"Big fucking Chrysler, Hicksy. 'Seventy-six or 'seventy-seven. Eight pipes. It'll step along."

"What's the rubber like? We don't want any fucking flat tires."

"The rubber's okay, Hicksy. You worry too much. You know that?"

"That's a big car," says Hicks. "Probably handles like a fucking steamboat."

"Beggars can't be choosers, Hicksy. The point is nobody is going to notice it's gone for a while. We got it at the airport. The owner's in Florida. Trust me, man."

"Okay. I trust you," says Hicks. "But this thing has got to go right."

"It'll go right."

"You and King Kong better lay off the grass and booze. We got to be awake tomorrow."

"No problem. Like I said, you worry too much, Hicksy. Ronny knows what he's doing. He'll hold our hands."

"I don't want anybody holding my fucking hands. I just want people to do their job right."

"Just drive, Hicksy. All right? That's all you have to do. You don't have to go into the fucking place and play stick-em-up." For the first time Latimer sounds annoyed.

"I know what I have to fucking do, Latimer."

"Good man. Now why don't you go over and bang that schoolteacher friend of yours? It'll relax you. You sound all uptight, Hicksy. Get yourself a good fuck and a good night's sleep."

"Tomorrow at nine-thirty, Latimer. Don't be fucking late. I've only got an hour."

"No sweat, Hicksy. Sleep tight. Don't let the bedbugs get under your foreskin. It's a bad scene."

Hicks hangs up the phone. Standing there he can still feel his heart thumping away. Maybe he is too tense. He has to get some sleep tonight, that's for sure. He has to be sharp as a tack tomorrow. Perhaps he should go over and see Janice. He hasn't talked to her since Friday night, when she cooked that nice steak dinner for him. But in bed she seems to hold back. Why? Sometimes she comes and sometimes she doesn't. She won't talk to him about it. She won't even talk about their lives together. And just when he thought things were starting to work. How the fuck do you figure out women?

Hicks dials Janice's number and gets a busy signal. The hell with it. He decides he'll go over and talk to her anyway. Maybe later they can go to bed. Her period is coming up and it makes her a little bitchy. At the same time she seems to want it more. So he'll give her a good fucking. It'll take his mind off tomorrow.

2

The girl at Pizza Hut says the order will be delivered in half an hour. Meantime Jan prepares a green salad, while on the sofa in the living room Max sits cross-legged next to her friend Denise Payette. Everyone is a little high, having drunk a good part of the wicker jug of *vin ordinaire* brought by Max from Montreal. Now Max sits on the sofa in a magenta blouse and vivid yellow slacks. When she moves her head, the long, reddish-gold hair spills over her face. Her gold earrings flash like sunlight. She looks terrific, and it's so good to see her. A complete and happy surprise. Just the ticket for a blue Sunday, thinks Jan, as she takes lettuce and green onions and peppers from the crisper.

When she first saw the yellow Renault with its black racing stripes in the driveway, she had no idea who it could be. Then out stepped Max in a fur-topped leather coat. And from the other side her friend, who now sips red wine. A pretty little thing in jeans and a red short-sleeved jersey with the word *Allons* lettered in black across her chest. Her dark hair is cropped like a boy's. She looks like a little *gamine* as she gazes around Jan's apartment with open and affecting curiosity. She has never been to Ontario, and so it is all *une grande aventure*. As she says this she laughs, showing her small, perfect teeth.

They are on their way to Florida and decided to break up the journey with a surprise visit to Slim's. They plan to spend Christmas week at Miami Beach with the sun and the sea. All done on impulse, according to Max. Originally they thought of skiing in the Laurentians or Vermont. But they've already done that scene, and besides, it's so damn cold and it will be winter for months. So why not get away from Santa Claus and all that Christmas-tree bullshit? Listening, Jan recalled their Christmas together in Nassau but didn't mention it. So only yesterday, said Max, she began making frantic arrangements: phoning travel agents, trying on old swimsuits and summer clothes, digging out beach towels and suntan lotion. Packing. It was all hectic fun. As she talked, Max seemed radiant, and Jan felt envious. Max is truly in love and it shows. So, for two hours they've drunk wine and talked.

Jan mentioned her mother's romance, and Max found it hilarious. She wanted to know all about Gordon Rutherford and whether she could meet him. But right now they are out to dinner. Again. It's the third time this week. Max is delighted.

"So! This little guy is giving her the real rush is he? That's terrific, Slim." Watching Max from the kitchen, Jan feels affection for her old friend. She seems to be having a run of luck. After years of hiding these feelings, she is now out in the open, and the best of British luck to her. And how she dotes on the little thing! Fills her glass carefully so as not to spill any. The girl seems to regard Max with fond amusement. She smiles at all her jokes, but I wonder if she gets them all. Her English is good, but she is not the witty type. She's a quiet little sit-in-the-corner-and-watch person. With that dark, pretty face of hers someone will always come over to light her cigarettes. And so petite! Her wrist looks no wider than a ruler. I could put my fingers around her ankles. She appears to have no breasts at all. I'll give them the bed tonight; I'll take the sofa.

While Janice works on the salad, she and Max talk about the death of John Lennon two weeks before. "God Almighty," says Max, "is it really twenty years ago when we watched those guys on the *Ed Sullivan Show?*"

"Well, maybe not twenty, Max," says Jan, chopping green onions. "But sixteen or seventeen. Didn't they make their big splash over here in 1963?"

On the sofa Max shakes her head and the earrings sparkle and flash. "1963! Jesus Christ. The year Kennedy was shot!" She looks over at Denise. "And you, ma chérie, would hardly remember *that*? Why, you were still probably getting your little knickers dirty on the streets of La Pocatière."

Denise smiles and says something in French. For some reason Jan suspect it's lewd. In any case, Max laughs and pours more wine from the great wicker jug. In fact Max is getting tight. "We should phone old Futz," says Max. "Wish her and that drippy husband of hers a Merry Yule. Futz used to like the Beatles, didn't she?"

"I think," says Jan, "that she was more into Peter, Paul, and Mary. Pete Seeger. Bob Dylan. Those kind of people."

"Oh Christ, that's right. I remember now. Futz was big on songs about some guy working on the railroad or in a lumber camp. How is she anyway?"

"About the same," says Jan. "I had dinner with her a few weeks ago. In this funny little health-food restaurant. She keeps busy. God, does she keep busy! She spends a couple of nights a week at this Women's Distress Clinic. And then there's the PTA. The Ratepayers' Association. Seth and his thesis. The two children of course."

Max takes a sip of wine. "Old Futz Dunlop. God how I used to get her goat! Do you remember that disastrous year we lived together? Of course you do. Who could forget it! Remember how I used to throw out that yogurt crap and those smelly cheeses she'd keep in the refrigerator? She used to get furious. God, how did we ever imagine we could live together? If it hadn't been for you, Slim, we'd have been at one another's throats. You were always the pacifier. The one in the middle. Old diplomat Harper. Diplomacy's a talent I've never had, alas."

Jan puts the salad on the counter and returns to the living room for more wine. She's feeling just about right; the old blues have been chased away. At least for a while. And it's good to be talking over old times with Max. Max is in good form, and as long as she doesn't get too drunk everything will work. A drunken Max is not nice. Right now, however, she is looking good. Or so thinks Jan, watching Denise get up and go to the bathroom. When the girl disappears, however, Max's mood shifts dramatically. She shakes her head. "God, Slim, I love that little creature. She's my whole life. If you only knew what it was like!" Jan feels embarrassed and faintly annoyed. *If you only knew what it was like!* Why shouldn't she know what love feels like? People who say such things immediately place you on the sidelines. You've never been in the game, so how could you possibly know what it feels like to play? "She seems very fond of you, Max," says Jan, pouring herself a glass of wine. Max shakes her head again. "Shit. Don't bet on it. Listen, all that stuff about deciding to go to Florida over the past couple of days is just a crock. The truth is that for the past month I've been on my knees begging her to come with me. On my knees, Slim! Can you picture me on my knees? I've actually made a glorious fool of myself. Cried like a baby. Thrown tantrums. And I can't bloody help it." Max lights a cigarette and smokes furiously. "She kept saying she wanted to spend some time with her parents in La Pocatière. But I know differently. She'd spend a couple of days with them and then hustle back to the city to be with her theatrical friends." Max blows smoke at the ceiling. "She's stagestruck. Wants to be a fucking actress. Half the little salesclerks in Montreal want to be actresses these days. They want to be in the movies like, what's her face, Micheline Lanctôt. The woman who made that film *Les Bons Débarras*. So Denise is into this small theatrical group, and there's this director who is giving her the rush. She denies it, but old Max wasn't born yesterday. I can tell. He's giving her the rush all right, and he happens to be filled with the old Gallic charm. You know the type? Tall and lean. Pockmarked face. *Gaunt*. Working-class background. A Gauloise in his mouth all the time. Giving off all these artistic vibes in his jeans and black turtleneck sweaters. And in case you're wondering, old friend, our little Denise can swing both ways. I sometimes think I'm just a little adventure for her. She's very big on little adventures. Anyway, there you have it."

Max looks away and gulps some wine. "How can love possibly compete with ambition? Some poet must have asked that fucking question somewhere along the line. Come on, you're the English teacher. Console me with some pithy quote."

"I can't think of any at the moment, Max." And I wonder if Max's visit is all that accidental? She never talks about other friends. She's forever complaining about the bitchy, lonely, competitive world of department-store fashion. I may be her only friend, and she wanted someone to confide in.

"Anyway, not to worry," says Max. "At least she's mine for

the next week." Max takes an enormous breath, and ye gods I hope she doesn't burst into tears. A tearful Max can be a trial. And everything was going so damn well. "I'll tell you this, though, Slim. I honest to God don't know what I'd do with my life is she left me. I just don't think I could stand it." And yes, there are the tears. A few at least, for Max quickly wipes a fist across her eyes. And what can you say after all? In the circumstances you must rely on clichés. On the most trite expression of sympathy.

"Well," says Jan finally, "you'd probably live, Max. People do. Or most people. Somewhere, every hour of the day, someone is walking out a door." To this Max offers a large snorting laugh and digs through her handbag for a tissue. Blows her nose hard.

"Slim, you're a real philosopher. Always so cool and in control. I envy you, by God."

Looking shyly around, Denise enters the room. Her face is scrubbed and she smells like soap. She could pass for one of my students. Max gives her a hug. "And here is our angel. My God, I'm starved! And you must be too, ma chérie. We haven't eaten anything since breakfast. Where is that wretched pizza, Harper? In Montreal it's at your door in ten minutes."

"Well, this is the suburbs, Max. The Sticks."

"Never mind that anyway," says Max. "I've an idea. Why don't we get started on the salad?"

"Okay," says Jan, getting up and heading for the kitchen.

"And more wine," says Max grandly, holding up the jug.

When the doorbell rings Max yells, "We eat. They have heard my cries of hunger. And don't anyone move, Maxine is paying for this. No arguments. Where the hell is my purse?" She gropes at the side of the sofa. "Right under my feet of course."

From the kitchen Jan watches Max walk toward the door.

She holds herself erect, clutching her handbag and looking very like a woman who has passed the afternoon in a bar and must now get home *sans contretemps*. No tripping or bumping into chairs or tables. A dignified exit. Max seems now propelled along by a terrible concentration and, watching her, Jan realizes that Max is really quite drunk. But then she's safe here. She'll eat and probably crash early. I'll have to entertain the little one. How? Frowning at the thought, Jan pours oil and vinegar over the salad and tosses the greens with large wooden forks. How Travers used to enjoy making salads! Made damn good ones too.

As Jan carries the salad into the living room, she sees Max coming through the doorway, holding James's hand. Hicks stands there in jeans and a windbreaker looking bewildered as Max says, "Janice, my love. This is *not* the pizza man, or so he informs me. In fact this handsome devil claims to be a friend of yours. Now is this true or do we call the cops? He may be a rapist." She stops to pat Hicks's arm. "Don't mind me, darling. I'm a little tipsy. I've driven from old Montreal today and I've been into the vino. And by the way, Janice my love, just who the hell is this gorgeous creature?" On the sofa Denise might well be asking the same question. For the first time all evening she actually looks interested in what's going on. But Jan feels only furiously confused. Why couldn't he at least have phoned? How dare he assume that her door is open to him all the time? The man can be such a clod.

She walks across the room and puts the heavy wooden bowl on the coffee table. Max is now escorting Hicks to a chair, and Jan suspects the worst. Max is filled with dangerous mischief.

"Now, Janice," she says, "I want the absolute truth. Is this gorgeous creature actually yours? You naughty old thing, you've been holding out on Aunty Maxine."

Jan feels a surge of pure malice flooding through her. "You

never *asked*, Maxine." Max lays a hand against her chest.

"Mea culpa, my dear, mea culpa." She looks at Hicks. "Okay! So, just who the hell are you anyway, mister?" She pats his knee and laughs. "Don't take me seriously, darling. I'm an old kidder from way back." Hicks looks nervous and threatened. He might as well have dropped in on some mad Tupperware party. Now he looks across at Jan.

"I phoned. Your line was busy."

"Max," says Jan. "This is a friend of mine, James Hicks. James, Maxine Ross." Hicks nods. "And a friend of Max's," continues Jan, "Denise Payette. They're on their way to Florida. They're staying over tonight."

But Max is up to no good. She sits on the edge of James's chair and says, "We're having an old-fashioned hen party, James." She pauses. "James! So formal. Why not Jim or Jimmy?" Max bends down to peer into Hicks's embarrassed face. "No . . . no. You're not a Jimmy. You look too serious to be a Jimmy. You're a James all right. Anyway, James," she says straightening up, "we're having a hen party. When Janice and Aunty Maxine were kids . . . we grew up together, you see. On old Beech Avenue. When we were kids we used to have these pyjama parties. We all sat around in our pyjamas and played records and talked about boys. Do you remember those parties, Janice my love? Friday nights?"

She touches Hicks on the arm. "We had nicknames for one another, you see. *Les sobriquets*, Denise my pet." Smiling, Denise says, "Ah yes!" She's curled up on the sofa and looks amused by all these shenanigans. Her feet are tucked beneath her and she eyes Hicks over the rim of her wineglass. A born flirt. And Max is being uncommonly tiresome. "There was old Futz Dunlop," says Max. "She's now married to an American draft-dodger. And of course I was called Red. That's not hard to figure. And Betty Chalmers. What in God's name ever happened to Betty, I wonder? Anyway, she was called Boop. Betty Boop. And James, what do you suppose we called our Janice?"

On the sofa Denise laughs quietly but Hicks looks uncomfortable. He simply doesn't know how to deal with someone like Max. Nor does he like guessing games. Jan tries to get him off the hook.

"How about some salad? That pizza should be along any minute now."

But Max is not about to give up her game, and so now she again taps Hicks lightly on the arm.

"Well, James. What do you think? What do you suppose we called Janice?"

"I don't know," says Hicks, looking very grim.

"Come on now, guess," says Max.

"I don't know," repeats Hicks like a dull child.

"Well, Christ Almighty, James, you might at least guess something. Anything."

"He doesn't want to guess, Max," says Jan. She can feel the heated blood in her face. "Anyway, it isn't important to anyone but us. I mean, who cares about pyjama parties on Beech Avenue twenty years ago? And who cares what we called one another?"

"I care, goddam it," says Max. She gets up from the arm of Hicks's chair and advances across the room in her straight-backed way. "And," she says, bending down to refill her wineglass, "I think . . . I believe that one could at least be a good sport and enter into the spirit of things by guessing. It seems to me that isn't too much to ask. Of course, you have to be a good sport." She pauses to sip some wine, looking over at Hicks. "After all, if you're interested in someone, I should think you'd want to know something about her. Is that not right, James? Would you say that is a reasonable statement,

Mr. . . . God, I'm sorry but I seem to have forgotten your last name. It's awfully careless of me and I do apologize."

"His name is James Hicks, Max," says Jan. "And you're not being very funny. Now for goodness sakes let's eat some of this salad. That pizza should be along any minute." Jan begins to fork salad into bowls.

"Well, we called her Slim," says Max. "You might at least have shown some interest and guessed. We used to play basketball together, Mr. Hicks. One year we went to the city semifinals. What year was that, Slim? 1962? 1963?"

"I can't remember, Max," says Jan.

"God, I remember one game. It was against Riverdale, I think. I had twenty-seven points. And you weren't too far behind me, Slim. I think you had twenty-two or twenty-three. We were the whole offence. And stout old Futz was back on defence. The toughest guard in the goddam city. Built like a Mack truck. I should phone old Futz."

When the doorbell rings, Max again announces that she will pay for the pizza. Denise now uncurls herself and carries the wine jug and a glass to Hicks. "Would you like some wine, James?" she asks. Watching her, Jan senses the little vixen in her. Poor old Max doesn't stand a chance; it's just a question of time. And Christ, I hope she doesn't fall down the stairs. If only she'd shut up, too! Then Max comes down the stairs and into the apartment carrying the pizza and doing a crazy cha-cha-cha step. Singing to the tune of an old song, "Heat Wave." "We're having a party. A hen-pecking party." She stops. "With only one cock present. Oh, excuse me, Mr. Hicks." Denise is laughing. "I do tend to get a little vulgar," says Max. "You must bear with me." She looks at Denise. "You liked that, didn't you, little one? That mention of cocks. Ah, there I go again."

Jan takes the pizza from Max and carries it into the kitchen.

She feels furious with them all. With Max and her drunken, stinging cruelty. With that little tart, who is just along for the ride. A little opportunist who will use anybody to get what she wants. A grabber at life's feast! And with Hicks. Who sits there like a bump on a log. Unable to sense that this is broads only and he's jamming the airwaves. Zero sensitivity. He hasn't even taken off his goddam windbreaker. Jan narrowly misses slicing her finger as she divides up the pizza. For a moment, as she stands there listening to Max talk about high-school basketball twenty years ago, Jan feels a terrible wave of bleakness passing through her. It's almost physical and, leaning against the counter, she reminds herself to take it easy. The dreadful cycle is having its way with you, Harper, but in a few days all will be well. Still, there's this evening to get through. And why doesn't he take a hint? She looks over at Hicks sitting in the chair. He seems to be regarding the two ladies from Montreal as though they were rare pheasants in an aviary.

"Do you want some pizza, James?" asks Jan.

"Yeah, sure," says Hicks without looking at her.

"Of course he wants some pizza," calls Max, who, drunk or not, appears to miss nothing. "And I shall help serve it, my dear," she says, coming into the kitchen.

"Never mind," says Jan, sweeping past her with two plates. "It's all ready. Let's eat."

"Righty-o," says Max. "And more vino for all."

3

Standing in front of the stereo, Jan glances through her record collection. Some music has to help. But what in God's name can she put on to satisfy the members of this little gathering? The little one probably enjoys *les chansons de la belle province*.

Unfortunately I don't stock them. Nor do I have any Merle Haggard or Loretta Lynn for James. Poor old Mozart and company might be considered a little effete under the circumstances. Max likes old show tunes. *Hello, Dolly. West Side Story.* But some of that is too bloody hectic for my nerve ends.

She settles finally on the sound track from *Manhattan*, and behind her Max applauds. "Terrific kid. Great party music. George Gershwin. Now there is a man I would really like to have met. Gershwin and Noel Coward." The ritzy penthouse music fills the apartment as the four of them eat their pizza. From time to time Max looks over at Hicks. He's an irresistible puzzle to her. Finally she asks, "And what is it you do, James?"

Jan imagines that Hicks is unclear as to whether he's been asked a serious question. He looks at Max suspiciously.

"Do you mean what do I do for a living?"

"Why yes," says Max, smiling. "That's the generally accepted meaning of the question, I believe." Jan feels a solid thump in her chest. Max is spoiling for a fight, and beside her little Denise, interested again, looks over at Hicks.

"I work in a garage," says Hicks flatly.

"Oh!" Max says. "How interesting!"

Watching Hicks slowly chew his pizza, Jan can feel her quickening heartbeat.

"No, it's not very interesting," says Hicks. "Pumping gas, changing tires, draining old batteries. It's really very boring."

"How terrible for you then!" says Max, settling back with her wine. She now regards Hicks with calm dislike. "If it's so boring, James, could you not find something better? Or at least more *interesting?*"

Hicks pops the last of the pizza into his mouth and slowly finishes his wine. In some compelling way, all three women are staring at him. Demanding an answer. "I'm too stupid, I guess," says Hicks. "I only went to Grade Ten, eh."

"What a shame!" says Max. "But of course there's always night school, isn't there? I mean, if you want to improve your little lot in life."

"Yeah, I guess so," says Hicks. "I've thought about it." Is this affected boredom a defence or does he simply not care? wonders Jan. But his face looks stony, and she guesses he's furious.

"And how, pray, did you two meet?" asks Max, looking now at Jan.

"What business of is that of yours?" asks Hicks. For a few seconds the question lies in the air like a bad odour. Max smiles at him.

"I was merely asking, James. You mustn't take offence so easily. I was only trying to make conversation. It seems to have withered on the vine, so to speak, since your arrival. No offence intended."

The strings of the Buffalo Philharmonic fill the air with a lovely old tune called "Someone To Watch Over Me," and Denise leans back against the sofa and closes her eyes. A little kitten whose attention easily wanders. Is she thinking of her tall, gaunt director in his jeans and black turtleneck? Hicks sits in the chair with his hands folded across his chest.

"How about a coffee, Janice?" he asks.

"Yes, Janice," says Max, "hop, hop to the kitchen and get the man some coffee."

Hicks looks across at Max. "Why don't you just shut up?"

Max makes a face, and Jan feels enormously frustrated by both of them.

"I'm still eating, James," she says. "You know where the coffee is."

Max won't shut up. "That's telling him, kid. Listen, James old boy, the days of women heeding men's beck and call are drawing to a close. The little barefoot woman in the kitchen is a creature from the past, dear boy. At least in these climes."

Listening to all this, Hicks frowns before saying, "Why don't you shut your fucking mouth? All I've heard from you since I've come in is yak, yak, yak."

"Tut, tut. Such language, James. Your friend, Janice my dear, appears to be an authentic primitive. Why don't you take off your windbreaker and tear your shirt for us? Our very own Stanley Kowalski. In living colour." She looks over at Jan. "My dear, I didn't know you went in for such rough trade."

Jan stands up. "Oh for God sakes, Max."

"Women like you," says Hicks sternly, "shouldn't drink. Do you know that? You can't hold your liquor. Drunken women disgust me."

"Do tell," says Max. "Just listen to Tarzan here declaim on the evils of drink. While he uses gutter language. Why don't you just amuse us by beating your breast and dragging poor Janice into the bedroom? Or maybe you would prefer to drag little Denise?"

"Well, I certainly wouldn't drag you, that's for sure."

"Thank God for small mercies," says Max.

At the kitchen sink Jan rinses her plate. In this situation would a primal scream not be permissible? I could scream loud enough to wake the neighbourhood. Drag everyone from in front of their television sets! Hicks is now standing behind her. "If I'm not welcome here, then I'll go." Jan does not turn around. "I do have company, James. An old friend. You might have phoned."

"I did phone. I told you that. The fucking line was busy." They are whispering like conspirators.

"Please don't use that word again," says Jan. "You could have waited. You could have tried again. I was only ordering pizza, for God sakes." She can feel his breath on the back of her neck.

"If you think more of that drunken dike than you do of me, then I'd like to know that. I wanted to see you tonight, Janice. I love you and I need you tonight, goddam it."

Jan can feel her eyes filling. And God I'm not going to do something stupid now and bawl? "She's an old friend, James. One of my oldest. She's had too much to drink and she's not at her best. But she's under a strain. She's not usually like this." She feels Hicks's hands on her arm. His lips touch the back of her neck.

"Please come with me, Janice. Just for half an hour. We'll go for a drive."

"I can't leave these people, James. They're my guests. Can't you understand that? I only see Max three or four times a year."

"But I love you, Janice," he whispers. "Does she love you the way I do? I love you and I want you tonight. I want you to give me half an hour of your time." Jan shakes her head, willing these ridiculous tears to stop. In the living room Max is singing "I've Got a Crush on You, Sweetie Pie."

"Turn around and look at me, Janice, please," says Hicks. "Please now. I just want to look at you." She turns to face him and he grips her arms. "Your friend in there tried to make a fool of me. All night she's tried this. Who is this Stanley guy she's talking about?"

"A character in a play. It isn't important."

"It's important to me. I don't like being made to look like an idiot."

"You're not an idiot, James. Nobody called you an idiot. God, I'm so tired of all this. I just want some peace, James. Just peace and quiet."

Hicks's face is watchful and angry. "I don't like being made to look like a fool. And I don't fucking have to put up with it.

That bitch is lucky I didn't drop one on her."

"James, let go of me please. I don't like being handled this way." She whispers the words with such fierce energy that Hicks releases her arms and steps back. Standing there, he holds up his hands as if in surrender.

"All right. If you think more of that dike friend of yours than you do of me, then I better get out of here." He turns to go and then stops to look at her once again. "I needed you tonight, Janice. But you got no time for me, I can see that. I'll see you around." He heads for the door, zippering his jacket as he goes, and watching him, Jan reminds herself to let him go. This is the very thing you've been looking for, Harper. This, in fact, is it. You've known from Day One that it could never work out, so it's all for the best.

Yet, she hurries after him. Max is dancing by herself, swirling about the living room and singing while Denise watches her with a little smile. When Jan steps outside she can see Hicks's dark figure walking down the driveway. His hands are plunged deep into his pockets. She calls after him, "James, wait. Please. Call me tomorrow." Without turning around he says something. It sounds like "Yeah, yeah." She can't be sure. Standing by the doorway she hugs her arms and listens as the car door slams. Hicks backs out of the driveway and then squeals the tires as he guns the car past the front of the house. Shivering, Jan listens until she can no longer hear the Trans Am.

4

Hicks prowls his apartment. One minute he thinks he should have punched that red-headed bitch in the mouth. Broken the teeth right out of her head. But then he seriously questions the worth of that. What's the point? You can't go around beating up women because they make you feel like a half-wit. It just doesn't make sense, no matter how tempting. All the same, the bitch was asking for it, thinks Hicks, as he sits on the sofa bed to calm himself. She didn't like him; he could sense that. From the very minute he walked in the door he could tell. Goddam dike. And drunk too. Is there anything more disgusting than a drunken woman? How can Janice tolerate such people? An old friend! To Hicks this news was a genuine disappointment.

Walking around again he feels a frenzy overtaking him. Tomorrow he is going to participate in a bank robbery. A bank robbery, for Christ sakes! So how is he going to get any sleep feeling this worked up? Because, if he's going to be alert tomorrow, he's going to need sleep. If that red-headed bitch hadn't been there, he could have gone to bed with Janice. That would have relaxed him. Hicks thinks now of Latimer and that horny little teenager, Cheryl. Probably they are now all stinky and fucked out. Sleeping like babies. He should have listened to Latimer. Hicks wouldn't have minded some of that Cheryl. Gobbling the man while he talked on the phone!

Again Hicks sits down and stares at the wall. He thinks that maybe with the money tomorrow he should get away somewhere. Just fuck right off. Go out to British Columbia or someplace like that. Yet what's the good of such a plan? He doesn't know a fucking soul out there, so how would he get started? He can guess what would happen. He'd go to a bar and meet a broad. She'd be down on her luck with the husband gone. First thing you know, he would be shacked up with her. And when the money ran out, he'd be driving a fucking truck or something. Thus, agitated and depressed beyond words, Hicks ponders these maters. He doesn't, in fact, know what to do. And that is it in a nutshell, he thinks. I don't know what the fuck to do with my life. My life has no shape or direction to it.

For a terrible moment Hicks feels almost maddened by despair. Wonders if he's losing his mind. Then he goes to the record player and puts on the Schubert symphony. Standing there, he listens to the music. Tries to parse things out. What, after all, is in this gloomy stuff that reminds her of him? But listening to the symphony only makes Hicks feel worse. How could she have a friend like that drunken, red-headed bitch? In a rage, Hicks tears the record from the turntable and hurls it across the room. Watches it bounce off a wall and hit the floor. It wobbles around before settling. A small black wheel. Fuck her music and all the bullshit books he can't make head or tail of.

On top of the fridge is the list of books she typed up for him. But what is the point? thinks Hicks, staring at the titles. Somehow he just can't stay with these things. *Madame Bovary*. Who the fuck is she? *Great Expectations*. He saw a copy in the library. Who could read such a long book? It would take forever. The one by the Russian he tried. *Crime and Punishment*. The title appealed to him and he started in on it. This moody young guy, a university student, kills an old lady with an axe. But Hicks got only twenty or thirty pages beyond the crime before bogging down badly. He tried to skip-read the rest of it but it was impossible to follow the story. The language was so complicated. Those long Russian names. He couldn't keep them together in his head. The whole thing left him stupefied and staring at the walls. Wondering how people can read such books, let alone enjoy them. Or get something from them. *But what exactly?*

And why, wonders Hicks, does none of this rub off on him?

Or affect him in the remotest way? In a spasm of anger he shreds the list and watches the pieces of paper fall to the floor. A moment later, feeling panic around his heart, he dials Janice's number. Listens to the dial tone and hears her voice. She sounds unhappy, and he himself feels choked with grief. He tells her he's sorry he tore up the street while leaving. Hangs up without saying another word.

Six

1

Hicks is grateful for the raw, cloudy day. He feels better about stealing money in weather like this. It doesn't make any sense, but still he feels it. If the day were bright and sunny, he would definitely feel more threatened. So, driving down Crown Hall Road he is thankful for the grey sky and the few snow flurries in the air. However, the day did not start well. To begin with, he slept only three or four hours last night, and most of that was only fitful. He'd doze for a while and then wake up to turn on the light and look at his watch. After five o'clock he didn't close his eyes. At twenty minutes to seven he was parked in the lot waiting for Jorgenson to arrive. Then Jorgenson was grumpy. Claimed to have forgotten about Hicks's phone call yesterday in which he told the man he had a bad tooth and had arranged a dentist appointment for a quarter to ten this morning. Under the long, peaked John Deere cap Jorgenson had looked suspicious. Figured maybe Hicks was pulling a fast one. Still, he gave him the hour off.

Now Hicks turns west on Hewlett Road and drives past the apartment buildings lining both sides of the street. It's like a small city of apartment buildings, he thinks, as he looks out at the white towers. Yesterday morning he drove from the trust company to the apartment building three times. About ten minutes, but add another two or three for Monday-morning traffic. At the outside, fifteen minutes. According to Gregg, fifteen minutes in the same car is stretching your luck. Gregg seems to know what he's doing, and in some ways the apartment-building garage is a good idea. But there are some risks involved. Sooner or later the cops are going to find the car and start asking questions. Yet Gregg's friend who lives in the place says they can ask all the questions they like but they can't prove a thing. Gregg will give him five hundred for passing along a copy of the garage key. Money well spent if you believe Gregg.

The place is called Lorelei Towers, and when he moves the Trans Am down the ramp, the door opens immediately and Greg is standing there waving him through the darkened garage. Gregg's friend told him that spaces 24, 25, and 26 would be free all day. By the time Hicks has stopped the car next to Latimer's van and got out, Gregg has hurried over. He's wearing Greb workboots, jeans, and a heavy red-plaid shirt. Hicks is already pulling off his coveralls. Underneath he's wearing a bush jacket and jeans. Quickly he folds the coveralls and puts them on the front seat of his car. Gregg nods at him.

"How are you feeling? You ready to make some money today?"

"I'm ready," says Hicks.

"Good man." Gregg gives him a pair of gardener's gloves. "Put these on and don't take them off until you're back in your own car. Okay?"

"Okay," says Hicks.

"We better fucking move," Gregg says. "Before someone comes down here." He taps the back of the van. "You okay in there?" Hicks hears only a muffled reply. "Okay," says Gregg. "Just lay low. If you hear people coming and going, forget about it. And don't play that fucking radio. Okay?" There is another muffled reply and then Gregg, slapping Hicks on the back, points toward a beige Chrysler with Quebec plates.

After the Trans Am the Chrysler feels like a goddam truck, thinks Hicks, adjusting the seat. Gregg opens the front door and slides in beside him. From the back seat comes a light punch on Hicks's shoulder. Latimer!

"How are you feeling, Hicksy babe? Are you loose?"

"I'm okay, Latimer," says Hicks, starting the car.

"How does it feel?" asks Gregg.

"A little sloppy after mine, but I'll get used to it."

"Okay," says Gregg, handing them each a yellow hard-hat. "Put these fucking pots on. If anybody's interested, we're three construction workers."

Gregg clears his throat. "Now listen, Hicks. The goddam gas pedal is a little touchy on this motherfucker. I don't know what it is. Too much gas going through the line maybe, I don't know. I fucked around with the timing yesterday, but it didn't help any. And I didn't want to take it to a garage. So just be careful. No heavy-foot stuff because it'll jump ahead like a fucking jackrabbit. And we don't want any squealing tires. Save that shit for those assholes on TV." Gregg holds a small plastic bottle and takes off the top. "Anybody want a jellybean before we go?" Hicks looks across and sees Gregg sprinkling small blue tablets into his gloved palm.

"What the fuck are those?"

"Valium," Gregg says. "Slows down the system. They work in about ten minutes. They can make you dopey later, but they're just the trick in the short haul. You better take one, Brian, you fucking wire."

"Don't mind if I do," says Latimer. Gregg seems to have

swallowed two or three. They both drink from a can of Coke.

"You want one, Hicks?" asks Gregg.

"No."

"You haven't had any booze have you?"

"In the morning? Are you fucking crazy?"

"Okay. I'm just asking." Gregg looks at his watch. "Okay. That place opens in twenty minutes. Let's go. And watch that fucking gas pedal."

"Just let me drive, Gregg. Okay?"

"Okay. I'm just reminding you."

"Okay, I'm reminded," says Hicks.

As they move up the ramp into the grey morning light, Latimer beats softly with both hands against the back of Hicks's seat.

"This is going to work, guys. No fucking problem."

They drive east on Hewlett to Crown Hall Road and then north toward the shopping plaza. As they move easily through the sparse traffic, Hicks wonders where the guns are. Probably in the Adidas bag on the floor between Gregg's legs. Not too smart if you're stopped by the cops. But then, why should they be? Fucking guns, thinks Hicks. Guns are trouble; he's never liked them. In reformatory he couldn't stand hearing guys brag about using guns.

Gregg half turns in his seat toward Latimer. "Okay. The three things again."

Latimer groans. "I know the three fucking things, Ronny. All right? That's all you've talked about all weekend. So relax."

"I'm relaxed," says Gregg. "Don't fucking worry about me being relaxed. I just don't want anybody to fuck out on this. We can make ourselves some nice money this morning if nobody fucks out."

"Nobody is gonna fuck out, Ronny." Latimer sounds irritable, and for a few moments they drive in awkward silence. It's as though doubt has entered the Chrysler and poisoned the air. Hicks can feel his palms moist inside the gloves. Wonders vaguely if anyone would think it odd to see a man driving with gloves on.

Stopped for a red light at Richfield, Hicks looks out the side window and sees a man reading a newspaper by a bus stop. A seat, well-dressed older guy. Looking at him, Hicks wonders where he's going. It's too late for work. Maybe *he* has a dental appointment this morning. And Hicks thinks how easy it would be just to open the door and climb out. Leave the fucking car right here in the traffic. Gregg would have to slide over and drive it. But when the light changes, Hicks taps the accelerator and moves them on.

Gregg tries again with Latimer. "Okay. One more time. The three things."

"All right, all right. Christ!" says Latimer. "For a start, no names."

"Right. No matter what happens, we don't mention any names. Now that sounds simple, but it's not as easy as you might think. Sometimes a little thing can fuck you out and you just forget. What happens is you fall back on habit." Gregg pauses. "I was on a job once. In fucking Moncton. And this guy I was working with started to get nervous. He thought he saw one of the tellers moving or something. So what the fuck does he do? First thing you know, he says 'Hey Ronny, I think she's touched something.' I'm telling you. It can happen easy."

"Don't worry about me," says Latimer.

"I worry about all of us. Number Two?"

"Number Two," says Latimer, sounding bored, "the froggy accent. We're Frenchman, hokay? By gar and all dat?"

"Don't lay it on too fucking thick. Okay?"

"Yes, yes, yes," says Latimer.

"And last?"

"At the slightest sign of trouble we get the fuck out.

"You got it. I won't give a fuck if you're shovelling hundred-dollar bills into your bag, we get the fuck out if there's a whiff of trouble."

"I got it, Ronny. Don't worry."

"Don't fucking call me Ronny anymore today. Okay?"

"Yeah, yeah."

Gregg looks over at Hicks. "How is it handling? You gonna be all right?"

"It's all right. Like Latimer says, you worry too much."

"If you don't worry," says Gregg, "you can end up in the fucking bin for a long time, man. Just remember that."

"Can we be a little more fucking positive, Ronny, please?" says Latimer.

"I told you not to call me fucking Ronny anymore."

"All right for fuck's sakes. Sorry."

They can now see the shopping plaza on their left. The parking lot is only half filled with cars. "Brian," says Gregg, "make sure your piece is tucked well into your belt before you go in. Okay?"

"I will do that," says Latimer, "if will you stop calling me Brian."

Gregg makes a gruff barking sound. Hicks figures it just might pass for a laugh. "All right. Sorry. But be sure of your piece. I worked with a guy once. And we go into this credit union. The place has got maybe five customers plus the staff. And as soon as we get inside the fucking door, what happens?"

"Your fucking pants fell down," says Hicks, turning into the plaza.

"Well no," says Gregg. "But this guy's piece fell right out of his pants. It's laying there on the floor. And you know what?

Nobody even fucking noticed. But we got lucky that time, so just make sure you got it well tucked in."

"Was that the same guy who called everybody by name?" asks Hicks.

"Nah, that was another guy."

"You've worked with some real winners, haven't you?"

"Don't be fucking smart, Hicks. I'm just trying to point out how, if you're not careful, things can go wrong."

"Wrong, wrong, wrong," says Latimer. "That's all I'm hearing today. Nothing is going to go fucking wrong."

By Gregg's watch it's five minutes to ten, and already a few people are standing in front of the trust company. Gregg quickly sizes them up. An older couple, who are probably cashing pension checks. A younger woman. A teenager, looking half frozen in a denim jacket. He's maybe eighteen. Gregg reminds Latimer to keep an eye on the kid, though usually there are no hassles from the customers. "Basically," says Gregg, "the average guy hates fucking banks. They're into his ass for a mortgage, a car payment, the fucking TV. He figures they're already ripping him off, so why should he risk his neck for their money. Anyway, banks don't encourage that kind of behaviour. Still, we'll keep an eye on that fucking kid and make sure he doesn't do anything foolish. I mean, you never know about people. They can be unpredictable. The worst kind are old ex-army types who get all up fucking tight about law and order and that kind of bullshit. All right Hicks, let's move this fucking thing around to the back."

Hicks goes to the end of the shopping plaza and wheels in back of the buildings. Behind the A&P two guys are unloading a truck. Putting boxes on a moving belt.

"Just look straight ahead," says Gregg. "Just give them your profile." But as they pass, the men on the loading dock don't even look their way. At the rear of the trust company, Hicks stops and backs the car to the entrance of the alleyway beside Canadian Tire. He kills the engine.

"Okay," says Gregg. "Here we go then." He reaches down and opens the bag. Takes out two black woolen masks with eyeholes. "Now we put these on the minute we're inside the door. Okay?"

"Right," says Latimer.

Gregg now hands Latimer a small black pistol. To Hicks it looks like a toy.

"Now keep the fucking safety on while you got it in your pants. We don't want you to blow your nuts off." He lifts his shirt and tucks another pistol into his belt. Looking back at Latimer, Gregg's pale grey eyes appear milky.

"You ready?" asks Gregg.

"I'm fucking ready," says Latimer. "Let's do it."

Gregg looks once more at his watch. "Okay. They're open now. Let's go."

In the rearview mirror Hicks watches them as they walk up the alleyway toward the front of the plaza. Just a couple of working guys, but carrying athletic bags. For the first time in years Hicks feels like having a cigarette. Sitting in the Chrysler he can hear the plaza loudspeakers. "Rudolph the Red-Nosed Reindeer." Through the mirror he can also see to the other side of the parking lot and Mister Donut where he had his first coffee with Janice. And what would Janice think if she knew what he was now doing? Well, she mustn't find out, that's all. No reason why she should. He'll phone her later. Make up somehow for last night, though he can't see how he was in the wrong about anything. It was that red-headed dike who did all the damage to the evening.

Gregg and Latimer have now disappeared around the corner and Hicks takes several deep breaths to calm himself. This he learned from *Essential Karate*. In tight situations, breathe deeply for control. Something to do with the fucking oxygen level in your system. Again he feels the urge to jump from the car and run. Just burn it down this road behind the stores. Go out the other side and walk back to Jorgenson's. But then how would he explain his car in that apartment-building garage? No, he is in it all right. For better or fucking worse. He tries to picture what is now going on inside the trust company. Comes up with a television show. Women screaming, gunshots, bells and sirens, the place soon surrounded by yellow cop-cars.

Starting up the car, Hicks now wills them to hurry. What if this fucking boxcar stalled on him? He tries not to think about it. In fact there's no good reason why it should. The timing's a little fast, but that's no problem. He wishes now that he'd taken one of those pills. Guys his age are dying of heart attacks every day. Stress! He read an article about it in *Time Magazine*. "Heart Disease: Number One Killer." Still, he figures he's in pretty good shape. He's not overweight and doesn't smoke. All things considered, a heart attack is unlikely. Again he checks the mirror. Where can he run if things go haywire? Head for a crowded store is probably best. They can't fucking shoot you in a crowded store. Sears or the K-Mart. Inside the gloves his palms itch. The loudspeaker is now playing "Silent Night." Hicks's favourite carol, but who can enjoy anything under these circumstances? He curses himself for getting involved in the whole thing.

Then, incredibly enough, he sees Gregg and Latimer walking quickly toward the car. And watching them come down the alleyway, it crosses Hicks's mind that they didn't go through with it after all. At the last minute something must have gone wrong and they called the thing off. Hicks is glad. Without a word Latimer slides into the rear seat and Gregg moves in beside Hicks, stuffing the bag between his legs.

"Okay," he says. "Move it now. Nice and easy. Take off the

fucking hats. Brian, get rid of that shirt." Gregg is already shucking off the heavy work-shirt. Astounded, Hicks puts the car in gear.

"You guys really did it then?"

"Of course we fucking did it," Gregg says, stuffing the workshirt and hat into the bag. In the rearview mirror Hicks can see a couple of men and the teenage kid in the denim jacket. Gregg, too, is looking back at them. They are standing at the other end of the alleyway. Hicks turns right, moving in behind Canadian Tire.

"We just robbed a fucking bank, Hicksy," says Latimer. "We are genuine fucking desperados." Brimming with mirth Latimer socks a fist into his palm.

"Shut up, Brian, for Christ sakes," says Gregg. "I think a couple of people back there seen the car. You better do your job, Hicks, and get up to that fucking garage."

"Don't worry about it."

But coming toward them along the narrow road is a delivery van and Hicks has to pull over to let the truck pass. The driver, a kid, is so close you could touch him.

"Fuck," says Gregg as the van goes by and Hicks pulls back on the road.

On the other side of the Canadian Tire building Hicks turns right and comes out to the main parking area of the plaza, heading for the exit on Crown Hall Road. They can now see that a small crowd has already gathered in front of the trust company.

"Just drive nice and easy, Hicks," says Gregg. "Just get us there now."

But at the exit a little more bad luck as they find themselves stuck in behind a car on a red light.

"Okay," Gregg says, "just take it easy and don't panic. In a minute this place is going to be crawling with cops."

Gregg seems worse now than before the robbery, and Hicks decides it is because the situation is now out of his hands. Everything is now up to Hicks.

"Who's fucking panicking?" asks Hicks.

"Okay, okay!" says Gregg. Now they can hear a siren, and Hicks feels sick to his stomach. "Here they come, the fucking bastards," Gregg says. Maddeningly, the light stays red. "Come on, you cocksucker, change!" The man's nervousness has an oddly calming affect on Hicks. He's in charge now.

"The green is always longer on Crown Hall. I told you that. It was one in ten we'd get a green on this exit."

"I know what you fucking told me," says Gregg. "There. It's green. Move it, for fuck sakes."

Ahead of them an old man in a spotless twenty-year-old Plymouth makes a slow, elaborate left turn, cranking the wheel around in the short, jerky manner of the aged and arthritic. Hicks turns right into the southbound traffic. He thinks he can hear another siren. Maybe two or three more.

"How did you like my froggy accent, Ronny?" asks Latimer. "Wasn't that something, man?"

"You were okay, Brian," says Gregg. He seems more relaxed now that they are moving. "In fact you were damn good for the first time out."

"Hicksy," says Latimer, "the whole thing went smooth as greased shit. I can't believe it. I actually robbed a fucking bank."

There are three lights before they turn west on Richfield. The first is green, and Hicks stays in behind a fast-moving van in the curb lane.

"How much do you figure we got?" he asks.

"Hard to tell," Gregg says. "We did okay. Maybe fifteen or twenty. My bag's half full."

"Mine too," Latimer says. Thinking of the money leaves Hicks elated. Money makes you happy. It really does. Never mind all the horseshit you hear to the contrary.

"Jesus," says Latimer, "everybody was shaking like a fucking leaf in there. You should have seen me, Hicksy. Fuckin' Jean Baptiste Dillinger."

"I just hope," says Hicks, "that fucking driver didn't get too good a look at us."

Gregg agrees. "That was bad luck."

At Meadowbank Hicks follows the van through an orange light. Gregg sounds nervous again. "Don't ride that fucking guy's tail, Hicks. You're pretty close."

"Relax, Gregg," says Hicks.

"Just fucking get us to the garage. Okay?" says Gregg. "Don't tell me to fucking relax. I was in that bank back there while you were playing with yourself in the car."

"Hey, hey, hey," says Latimer. "Come on, you guys. We're fucking rich. Let's have no shit now. Is there no honour among thieves, for fuck sakes?"

Traffic southbound is light. And then, just before Richfield they see the police car burning northward. The cherries are flashing and the driver gives the siren a bust to clear the intersection.

"Down in back, Brian," Gregg yells. "Be cool now. He'll probably go right by us. We're just another fucking car to him."

Hicks watches the yellow car with its flashing roof-lights coming toward them. He stays behind the van, which has now stopped. The police car goes whizzing past them, and Gregg and Latimer look back while Hicks studies the rearview mirror. The yellow car continues northward, and Latimer says, "We're laughing, gents."

"Not fucking yet," says Gregg. "I'll feel better when we get to that fucking garage."

The light turns green, and Hicks makes a right turn on Richfield. Remembers that Sunday in September when he nearly wiped out here against the station wagon. The look on those kids' faces! It's only a few short blocks to Transit Road. In planning their route, Hicks suggested Transit because it's a quiet through-street running parallel to Crown Hall but without lights. You can drive six blocks before the first stop-sign at Merida Drive. As he turns left onto Transit Road, Hicks can see the Public Library on his left. The street is deserted except for a delivery van stopped in front of the library with its lights blinking.

"Those cocksuckers will soon be all over these streets," says Gregg.

Hicks now wants only to get to that underground garage. He remembers feeling like this as a kid. Walking along a dark street by yourself. But what are those rustling noises in the bushes? Are those really footsteps somewhere behind you? No matter, because you break into a run. Fucking overdrive all the way home. As he accelerates down Transit Road, Hicks thinks he sees the man walking along the street. Later he will dispute this with himself many times. Certainly, though, when the man steps out in front of the parked van, Hicks has no chance to stop or avoid him. There he is, heavy as a fact, and the Chrysler hits him at fifty miles an hour. Hicks sees the lumber-jacket and the large, astonished face. The man is wearing a toque for the weather, but also white sneakers. Crazy for December. Carrying an armful of books against his chest like a schoolgirl. When he is struck, these books fly everywhere, their pages opening upon the air like wings.

"What the fuck!" cries Gregg. Behind them the man hits the street twice before lying still. On the library steps a woman runs down to the sidewalk holding her arms above her. She could be screaming. At a bus stop an old man turns to watch the Chrysler speed past. Gregg seems crazed. "You fucking idiot! You hit somebody!"

"I didn't see him," says Hicks, surprised at how calm he feels. "He stepped out in front of that truck. I couldn't stop."

He slows down and turns east on Merida. These quiet suburban streets are somehow comforting. He watches a woman putting garbage in a pail at the side of her house. "Fucking fuck," says Gregg. "Latimer tells me you can drive a fucking car and you wipe out a guy. Jesus Christ."

Briefly Hicks feels like ramming the car into a pole. Getting out and killing Gregg. Stomping the son of a bitch to death. He can't think of anything more pleasurable than kicking Gregg in the head. But his voice is still level when he says it was an accident.

"I couldn't fucking help it. He walked out in front of me. He's not all there anyway."

"Just get us to that fucking garage. Okay?" says Gregg.

Over the roofs of the bungalows they can now see the row of apartment buildings on Hewlett Road. "We're nearly there," says Gregg. He is breathing noisily.

"It wasn't Hicksy's fault, Ronny," says Latimer. "I saw the fucking guy. He just walked right out in front of that truck. There was nothing Hicksy could do about it."

For no reason he can think of, Hicks says, "I know who he was." He turns on to Colchester. Two more short blocks. Gregg looks pained and disbelieving.

"You know who the fuck he was?"

"Yeah. I mean, I don't know him personally, but I used to see him around the library. A big goony bird. Reads a lot of fucking books and is always talking politics or religion. Stuff like that. Talks to himself. Fucking crazy."

"Well, he ain't crazy no more," says Latimer. "He is fucking dead. He bounced off that road like a fucking Indian rubber ball. I saw him, man."

Hicks sees the books and a white sneaker passing his eye. Feels again the thump of metal against flesh. "Well fuck him anyway," says Gregg as they descend the ramp into the basement of Lorelei Towers. "The main fucking thing now is to get out of this car." He sticks the key in the lock and the garage door slowly lifts. Once underground, everyone feels easier about things.

2

Jan has put on heavy slacks and a rollneck sweater, but still she is cold standing in the driveway saying goodbye to Max and Denise. The Renault's motor roars on automatic choke, and the driveway is filled with sharp, gassy air. A few snowflakes settle on the little car's windshield. In the passenger seat Max looks haggard. But she has dolled herself up with large, dark glasses and a kelly-green kerchief. This get-up she calls her Joan Crawford morning-after look. Behind the wheel Denise is in jeans and a suede jacket with leather elbow-patches. On her head sits a little tweed cap. She could pass for a young man.

From over on Crown Hall Road comes the sound of sirens. "Christ," says Max. "Is Toronto on fire this morning?" Listening, Jan thinks of a fire or some awful car accident. And so near Christmas! What a time for serious trouble! Max reaches out to grasp Jan's hand. "You'll catch your death of cold out here, Slim, so we'd better say goodbye. Listen, I'm sorry about last night. I was loaded. God, I can be such a pain in the butt when I drink too much. I hope all is forgiven."

"Of course. Don't worry about it, Max. It was good to see you. Both of you."

"Well," says Max. "From here on in, it's a glass of plonk before lunch and one decorous martini before evening chops." Looking up, she smiles and squeezes Jan's hand. "And listen, kid, apologize to that friend of yours, will you? I'm sure he's a very nice guy and I behaved very badly. As usual. Ah well . . ." She gives Jan's hand a final squeeze. "Goodbye, Janny. Say goodbye to your mom again. I enjoyed coffee with her this morning."

"She'll wave to you from the front window," says Jan. "Say hello to the palm trees for me."

"Will do."

With great care Denise backs out of the driveway, while Max blows a kiss. "I'll call you when we get back," she yells. "Come down to Montreal for the weekend this winter. Maybe we could go on to Le Carnaval. Think about it."

"Yes, I will, Max. Goodbye. Merry Christmas."

Max rolls up her window and says something to Denise as the car backs out onto the street. Then Max is waving fiercely, though no longer to Jan but to Mrs. Harper, who is now standing by the front window. And at ten o'clock in the morning already dressed in a fuchsia pantsuit. Indeed, she made us all look dowdy as we sat around the living room drinking coffee. Mother insisted on having us up this morning. She was very interested in seeing Max again. And I wonder what she made of Denise? Would she see the lesbian connection? Would my mother know what a lesbian is? Surely she would. In any case, it made no difference. She was all charm, moving around with truly terrifying cheerfulness. Pouring cream and adding lumps of sugar. Asking about Montreal and coyly answering Max's questions about Mr. Rutherford. Oh how coy Mother has become! Mr. Rutherford is working some kind of magic on her.

Opening the side door, Jan doesn't know whether to feel happy or resentful. But how can you resent your mother's happiness, Harper? Yet the truth is that Mother has reverted. She has turned the clock back forty-five years and is now acting like a cute little seventeen-year-old in love. Well, why not? Gordon Rutherford seems a nice enough fellow. He's certainly no con artist. He can't be after Mother's money; she doesn't really have any. Besides, Gordon has a handsome pension from the railway. So what have we here but a dapper little guy who's seen the apple of his eye. And wants a bite. A little guy who doesn't want to let the grass grow under his feet. Or over his head. Fair enough. And he's neat as a pin. Probably changes his socks and underwear every day. An absolute must if he's going to hook up with Mother. He also goes to church and has a nice tenor voice. What more can you ask for when the leaves are falling in the autumn of life, Miss English Teacher?

From the other side of the kitchen door Jan hears her mother calling. "Would you like another cup of coffee, dear?"

"No thanks, Mom," calls Jan. Talking through bloody doors. We've always done a lot of that in this family. "I have some things to do."

"Please yourself, dear. There's plenty left if you want some."

What things, Harper. She walks down the stairs to her apartment feeling depressed. Is this nothing more than the sadness accompanying the departure of guests? You're alone again. Well, last night for a while you wanted to be alone. So here you are, kid. What's the big deal? The thing now is to get busy. The best remedy for the old blues is hard work. And this damn place is a mess. I'll vacuum the joint from top to bottom. Wash and wax the kitchen and bathroom floors. This afternoon I'll go over to the plaza and finish Christmas shopping. Perhaps buy a small tree. The prices are hilarious, but a little tree would look festive in that far corner.

She stands in the centre of the living room, remembering her mother as a young woman. Whenever she was confused or depressed, she would attack household disorder and dirt. Not that there was ever much of either. But away she would go in the house on Beech Avenue. Pulling around that old bomb-shaped vacuum cleaner. Brushing ceiling corners with a rag-covered broom while she listened to *Pepper Young's Family* and *Ma Perkins*. Wearing an old polka-dot dress and ankle-socks, her head covered in a kerchief pinned up in some cunning way. You saw women like that in the rotogravure sections of magazines. Working in munitions factories or ship-yards during the Second World War. Rosie the Riveter. And now she's overhead in the fuchsia pantsuit. Looking like a Fort Lauderdale swinger and humming along with Mitch Miller and the gang. "Chestnuts roasting on an open fire." Waiting for a phone call from the conductor. Well, take heart, Harper. It's never too late for love.

3

In the back of the van, Gregg and Latimer quickly count the money, arranging the bills in neat piles and keeping score on a piece of paper. Now and then Latimer swears softly and admiringly at the money in front of him. Gregg is fiercely intent as he arranges tens and twenties and fifties, snapping rubber bands around the stacks. The girl sits on the floor Indian-fashion and watches the men count the money. When they hear the garage door lifting, they all freeze. But it's only a woman in a Mustang. They listen as she parks and then gets out and, carrying a bag of groceries, walks to the door leading into the building. Then they go back to the money.

Hicks now wants only to be away from these people. He doesn't care if he ever sees them again. He just wants to get into his own car and clear out. He sees the row of tools hanging on the wall in Jorgenson's garage. Wishes he were there now, looking at them.

Gregg sniffs and totals the figures on a piece of paper. "We got twenty-two thousand and fifty-six dollars."

"That's not bad for half an hour's work," Latimer says. "Not bad at all."

Gregg doesn't sound impressed. "We'll forget the fifty-six dollars. Here, Cheryl, you take it." He hands the money to the girl. "All right, we'll work around the twenty-two." He looks at Hicks. "Your share of this is five, but you don't fucking deserve five after the way you drove that car today. Me and Brian did our job. The fucking thing went like clockwork, and then you fucked out and hit that guy. Five thousand dollars is a lot of money for fucking out on a job."

The air in the van seems laden with bad feeling. The girl stirs uncomfortably. Hicks says nothing. Listens to Latimer talk. "Come on, Ronny. We said he'd get a quarter. That was the deal."

"That was the fucking deal, all right," says Gregg, staring at Hicks. "But he fucked it up, Brian. You know that. Now there's a guy lying dead on the road because of this cocksucker. And we're all going to feel some real fucking heat because of that. And now you want to give him five fucking thousand dollars?" Gregg appears to be growing increasingly outraged by the injustice of it all.

"It was an accident, Ronny," Latimer says. "Nobody could have seen that guy. Without any warning he steps out in front of that truck. Hicksy had no chance at all. And you heard him say the guy was fucking nuts. He was jaywalking, the stupid fucker."

"How do we know the guy was fucking nuts? That's what your friend says."

"Well, from what I saw of him, he looked nuts to me. Wearing running shoes in the winter, for fuck sakes. But it doesn't matter anyway. The fucking point is it was an accident. Now give the man his money and let's get the fuck out of here."

In the damp gloom of the van Hicks and Gregg stare at one another and Gregg says softly. "I say the job is worth three thousand dollars. He did a three-thousand-dollar job for us, Brian." Hicks can now feel the blood rushing through his ears.

"You owe me fifty-five hundred dollars, prick, and I want it."

"Three," repeats Gregg. "That's what the job is worth. You fucked out on us."

"Come on, Ronny." Latimer sounds exasperated with the world in general. Hicks has picked up a jack shaft from the floor of the van.

"I want my money, you ugly fucking prick. Fifty-five hundred dollars."

"No fucking way," says Gregg, looking at the jack shaft. Not a man you can threaten. The girl now looks frightened.

"Listen, you guys," says Latimer. He is really talking to Gregg. "This is fucking bad. We got to get moving or we're gonna get our asses fried." He starts suddenly counting hundreds and fifties. As he counts he talks. "We said we'd pay the man a quarter of whatever we got. That was the fucking deal, Ronny. You know that, man. So why fuck things up now? You were the one who was always harping about timing. This has to be done in three minutes. That has to be done in two minutes. We should be out of here by now, man. So let's cut the bullshit. We'll give Hicksy his money and get the fuck going." He hands over a thick wad of bills to Hicks. "There's five thousand, Hicksy. You better split."

Hicks knows they owe him another five hundred but doesn't feel it's worth pressing for. The point has been made, so he stuffs the money inside his shirt.

"He don't fucking deserve it," says Gregg, but he offers no resistance. It's as though he's made his point too; now the matter has been taken out of his hands. Also a victory of sorts.

Hicks opens the back door and steps down. Watching him, Gregg says sullenly, "You're fucking robbing us, you bastard."

"Fuck you, Gregg," says Hicks.

Gregg gives him the finger and Latimer says, "All right, let's get the fuck out of here." He closes the van door without saying goodbye to Hicks. It's preposterous, but Hicks feels slighted.

When he reaches the Trans Am he crouches by the side and climbs back into his coveralls. Once inside the car he feels safe again. He's stripped off the gloves and his hands are ice, but he's safe. In a few seconds he watches the big garage door slowly lift. Half expects to see the neighbourhood surrounded by yellow cars, cops across the street kneeling with rifles, some guy in a topcoat yelling through a bullhorn, "Come out of there with your hands up!" That's what fucking TV does to your mind, thinks Hicks, turning east on Hewlett. In fact, the street is quietly normal. And why shouldn't it be? There is no reason in the world why they should be looking for a man in a Trans Am. He touches the five thousand dollars inside his shirt. Through his rearview mirror he can see the van coming out of the garage and turning west on Hewlett. The three of them will head north to the Macdonald-Cartier Freeway. Going to Cornwall where, according to Latimer, they'll spend Christmas with some of Gregg's friends. Hicks is glad to see the last of them. He doesn't want to see any of them ever again. Not even Latimer. Fuck him, he didn't even say goodbye. Still, Latimer helped out with the money. Without Latimer it could have got ugly back there.

Hicks knows he's late and Jorgenson will be pissed off. Probably sulk for the rest of the day. But there is no way Hicks is going to speed up. The last thing he needs right now is some cop pulling him over for speeding. Hicks sees himself reaching for his driver's licence and five thousand dollars spilling out onto the street. He reminds himself to take it easy. Fuck Jorgenson anyway. In a couple of weeks he'll tell him to shove the job. Not in as many words maybe, but he'll tell him just the same. At Crown Hall Road and Hewlett Hicks sees the police car. Parked at a Texaco station with two guys sitting there looking out at traffic. Going north on Crown Hall, Hicks sees two more. They pass him without a glance.

It's over now. They robbed a fucking bank. Hard to believe. If only that stupid son of a bitch hadn't stepped out in front of that truck! Because Gregg is right. That puts a whole new light on things. It's not just a bank robbery anymore. They killed a man. *He* killed a man. Hicks again sees the books flying through the air. But he stepped right out in front of that van. Probably the son of a bitch was thinking of some great political theory to save the world. Hicks remembers the man waving his arms on the empty library steps that Sunday afternoon in September. What the fuck goes on inside a head like that? For a moment Hicks considers that at least he didn't kill a normal man. But that idea doesn't sit well either. Whatever was going on inside his head doesn't really matter. What matters is that Hicks killed him.

If that hadn't happened, things would have been perfect. They robbed a bank, but so what? Banks have lots of money. Probably the insurance will cover that. They got away and nobody got hurt. Then that idiot steps out on the road. Hicks figures that if he'd been driving along on routine business and had hit the guy, the cops would probably dismiss the charge. Taking into consideration the guy's mental state. On the other hand, he hit the man at fifty miles an hour. If he'd been doing the speed limit, could he have stopped? "Fuck it," says Hicks aloud, and the sound of his voice startles him. It was just bad luck, that's all. Chance. A guy is daydreaming and he steps out in front of a van at the very moment you're passing by. Just bad luck. Pulling into Jorgenson's, Hicks thinks about good and bad luck in everyday existence. How do you figure it? Luck is luck. There's good and there's bad. And that, decides Hicks, is all there is to it.

Seven

I

The elevator is out of order, and so Jan opens the heavy firedoor and takes the stairs to Hicks's apartment. Listens to her footsteps in the empty, malodorous stairwell. When he called her, he was drunk. Unusual for James. He likes his beer, but he's no boozer. But there he was on the phone sounding very drunk indeed. And not happy drunk either. Imploring her to come over and see him. What in God's name is eating the man. Even last night he acted funny. Wanting her to go out for a drive. Something is on his mind.

Maybe his wife is back on the trail. Bear in mind, Harper, that Christmas time is family time. People get sentimental and start believing the words on Christmas cards. I want my husband and son back. We'll toast marshmallows in front of the fireplace and watch the Christmas-tree lights. But then he told me he's finished with her. A stupid woman, so he says. He hasn't seen her in nearly three years. Do I believe him? Maybe yes, maybe no. But if it is wifey trouble, then I'm gone. Vamoosed. I don't need the aggravation. Travers's little housemate with her juicy vocabulary was quite enough for one year, thanks very much. But maybe Dale is in trouble.

Whatever, James sounded really loaded. Which in itself is not so good. Not much fun visiting a drunken man. And he better not pull any funny stuff, because I ain't in the mood. If he so much as lays a finger on me, it's permanent exit for J.H. But face it, hypocrite, drunk or sober, you're glad he called.

On the second floor she passes a fat man in tan pants and undershirt. On his feet a pair of broken-backed slippers. He is carrying his day's garbage to the incinerator at the end of the hall. Somewhere a baby howls. God, is someone beating the child? And from behind the doors comes the sound of TV sets. She knocks at the door several times before he opens it and stands wavering before her. Drunk as a skunk, by God. He can hardly stand, and his face looks somehow lopsided. Somewhere between a foolish grin and a frown. Still wearing his work clothes. Blue shirt and pants, but barefoot. Which is oddly touching. Those long, white feet have always struck me as incredibly sexy. However, you can forget about any of that, kid, because the man is obviously too far gone for any love games. Pity, too, because I rather feel like it.

Jan stands looking at Hicks. "Well, may I come in, James? Or will I carry on a conversation from out here in the hallway?"

Hicks opens his arms to her. "I love you, Janice. Come here!"

Jan closes the door and they hold each other very tightly. Hicks smells of liquor and sweat and grease. He kisses her hair and tells her again that he loves her. Over his shoulder she can see his work-boots and heavy grey socks. Abandoned in the middle of the living-room floor.

"James? What's the occasion? Christmas is still a few days away."

He turns from her and walks unsteadily toward the kitchen. "Sit down, Janice. I'll make you a drink. I've got some rye."

"A small one, James. Please. Rye gives me heartburn."

"I'm sorry I haven't got anything else," says Hicks. "Just rye and beer. I'm really sorry."

"Well, don't worry about it. When was the last time you had something to eat anyway?"

"I don't want anything to eat." Jan makes a face as she follows him into the kitchen. As usual the sink is filled with dirty dishes. An open case of beer sits on the kitchen table next to a half-empty bottle of rye whiskey. "The place is a mess, isn't it?" says Hicks, slumping into a chair and staring at the floor. Jan stands over him. It's mothering time, kid. Well, why not? Everyone needs some of that once in a while.

"What's with all the booze, James? You're not exactly jumping up and down with joy, so what's the problem?" Hicks presses his face against her stomach.

"I'm glad you came over, Janice. I'm really glad."

"Okay, you're glad. And I'm here. But I'd like to know what's going on. Why are you so unhappy? What is it? Is there something wrong with Dale?" Hicks shakes his head. "Your wife? The job? Did you lose your job?"

Hicks continues to shake his head, while Jan strokes his thick, dark hair.

"Well, when you feel like telling me about it, tell me. Right now I'm going to clean some of this up. Today I am Miss Cleaning Lady. You should see my place. It's like a commercial for a TV cleanser. All day I've been on my hands and knees. The place is spotless. But look at these hands. Never mind the knees." Hicks still looks at the floor. Well, she never could get much of a rise out of him. She turns toward the sink.

"I smell," he says.

Jan turns to look at him. "What?"

"I stink," Hicks says. "I can smell myself."

"So you stink? So what? You've been working all day. The

sweat of honest toil and all that. Take a bath. It'll probably do you the world of good. It'll help to clear your head. You've had enough to drink, James. You know that."

Hicks stands up. "Okay, I'll take a bath. Good idea. You smell so nice and I stink. You must be disgusted with me."

Jan stacks the plates on the counter. Not a clean one left in the place. "Come off it now, James. Stop feeling sorry for yourself. Take a nice warm bath. Not too hot. And for God sakes don't fall in the tub and crack your head open."

After he wanders from the kitchen, however, Jan considers that very possibility. In fact he could fall headlong into the tub and kill himself. Or scald himself. Ye gods, the things that can happen. As she hurries to the bathroom she can hear the heavy rushing flow of the water. When she opens the door, the room is filling with steam, and Hicks is lowering himself into the tub. He seems much thinner than when she first saw him naked. And looking at him, she is moved. There is something vulnerable about a naked person trying to cleanse himself. Jan turns down the hot water and rolls up the sleeves of her denim shirt.

"All right, chum, I'm going to give you a bath. You really do need one."

Kneeling beside him, she begins to soap his back and neck. "You're the best thing that's ever happened to me, Janice," mutters Hicks. "I love you very much. You have to believe that."

"All right, I believe it. I'm Wonder Woman. Now lean back." She scrubs his feet and legs. Watches amused as his penis stirs. They are so like little boys. Sometimes. It's hard to believe they can swell the way they do. But right now forget it, little friend. You're drunk too.

The water is so grey that she drains the tub and refills it. Rinses him off using an old margarine container. Under the pouring water his hair is sleek as seal fur. When she finishes she towels him dry and finds a pair of bikini jockey-shorts. Helping him into these she says, "Très sexy, James." Hicks smiles vaguely as she gives his penis a playful yank. "Shame on you for leading a lady on like this." In the living room she pulls out the sofa bed and smooths down the sheets. Does he never change his bedclothes? Staring down at the bed, Hicks looks like a man reprieved from the depths.

"Beddy time now, lover," says Jan. "And when you wake up, you'll feel a lot better. Now take these." She hands him three aspirin and a glass of water. Hicks swallows the pills like an invalid. As she covers him with the sheet he says, "Lie down beside me, Janice." Jan sits by the side of the bed.

"You're in no shape for fun and games, chum."

"I don't want fun and games," says Hicks. "I just want to hold you. Come here."

Jan lies down beside him, and arm in arm, they lie in silence. At first she does not believe he is weeping. But when she touches his face she can feel the tears. Something is deeply troubling the man, but there's no point in asking him. He'll tell me in his own good time, I suppose. Right now, it seems enough to hold him. Old Mother Harper. But wouldn't I want it, too, if something were troubling me? How many nights have I had the shakes and wished someone were there? Just to hold me. Well, here I am, Hicks, you goddam moody, good-looking hillbilly with your desperate attempts at self-improvement. From where she lies she can see a copy of Will Durant's *The Story of Philosophy*. Stolen from the library, no doubt. That bloody pathetic list I made up for him! But he's so eager to learn. What? She feels Hicks relax into sleep. And it's not unpleasant lying here beside him. Even in this godawful place. She can hear the television from next door. A Christmas special starring those good folks from *Little House on the*

Prairie. A warmhearted Yule on the old homestead. The turkey's in the oven and all's right with the world. At home Mother and Gordon are watching the same hooey. Sitting on the chesterfield, eating Christmas cake and drinking Sanka. Probably holding hands like a couple of teenagers. While I lie here beside my lover, who has fallen asleep, drunk, and weeping. No wonder Dad found life damn strange.

She remembers visiting him during those last weeks. For a dying man he was remarkably cheerful, and looking down at him Jan wondered more than once if in fact he was ready to call it a day. Certainly the last forty years of human history had given him a great deal of trouble. He couldn't get a handle on all the evil. Knew it had been around since before Moses, but still had trouble with the size of the problem. Endlessly fascinated and repelled by the complexities and contradictions in humanity. Cranked up on his narrow hospital bed, the history teacher talked to his daughter about these things. The flesh under his eyes was yellowed with disease.

"Janice, I've never been able to grasp the paradoxical nature of man. A failing on my part, and I admit it. Even after all those books, I still can't come to terms with it. The tyrant tends his orchids and the torturer goes home to play with his children after a day's work." He lays back against the pillow and sighed. "These years on earth we call life. Let me tell you, it's a damn strange trip. In fact I wouldn't mind that on my headstone. *L.G. Harper. 1912–1978. He Found Life a Damn Strange Trip.* Do you think you could persuade your mother and Bobby?" Smiling as he said this. Knowing full well what they'd say. And I wish I could have arranged it for him, but I didn't even ask them. Didn't want to get into a family fight. Settled for *Beloved Husband of Lillian Hurst.*

Beside her, Hicks's ragged breathing grows more even as he

settles into a deeper zone of sleep. He snores a little. Lying on the sofa bed, Jan listens to the television noises and Hicks's breathing.

2

Awakening, Hicks can't recall why Janice is lying beside him asleep and fully clothed. It takes a while to remember things. The apartment building is quiet, and Hicks waits for the bad memories to return. Yesterday lies upon him like a heavy stone. He sees again the man's shoe and the books cast into the grey air. All day at Jorgenson's he expected the cops to arrive and take him away. After work he bought a paper at the Jug Shop, then stopped at the liquor store for whiskey. After that, many things are unclear. He can't even remember phoning Janice, though he remembers her being here. He had a bath and she helped him to bed like baby. Jesus!

The Star had the story on the front page, and Hicks can remember reading about it. The paper carried the man's picture. Only it didn't look like him at all. The guy in the paper looked normal. It was some kind of graduation picture, because he had long hair and was wearing a gown. His name was John Hepworth and he was twenty-eight years old. Graduated in philosophy from the University of Toronto in 1974. Lived with his parents over near Hillcrest Boulevard. Not so many blocks away, thinks Hicks, remembering the article. Hepworth's father was quoted as saying, "John was a good boy. He read a lot and tried hard to understand things. Mostly he wanted to make the world a better place to live in. In college he was on the wrestling team and he used to work with the Big Brother organization." He also lifted weights and studied yoga. Mr. Hepworth said it was hard to lose your only son this way, especially at Christmas.

His wife was not available for comment.

Hicks also read that there were two witnesses to the accident: a woman coming out of the library and an elderly man waiting at a bus stop. Both of them said Mr. Hepworth was struck by a large brown car. They couldn't identify the make because the car was travelling too fast. The man thought there were two people in the vehicle, but the woman said she thought four. The police figured it was the getaway car from the trust-company hold-up, and it was only a matter of time before they found it. They were already working on a number of important clues. What clues, wonders Hicks? And so they find the Chrysler? So what? Nobody left any prints. Hicks remembers reading all this several times while he drank the whiskey with beer chasers. A deadly combination. No wonder he got blasted. Now he thinks about Latimer and Gregg and the girl. They must have made it to Cornwall by now, and so maybe everything will work out. This Hepworth guy is dead, and that's too bad. But there's nothing anyone can do about that now. It was an accident pure and simple, and accidents happen to people. He was in the wrong place at the wrong time. Hicks gets out of bed and goes into the kitchen.

Holding the transistor against his ear, he dials for news. It's a few minutes before three and so he waits, standing in the dark listening to Tammy Wynette and George Jones sing "Two-Story House." When the three o'clock news comes on, he presses the little radio against his ear. But there is nothing about the robbery or the accident. Instead there's a fire in a west-end apartment building. A shooting downtown. More trouble where the Arabs live. Hicks puts down the radio and goes back into the living room. He sits on the sofa bed and stares down at Janice. Considers what a good person she is and how lucky he is to have her. Maybe he can persuade her to move away from here. They could go out west. Teachers can always get jobs, and he could go back to school. Learn a trade. Like welding or pipe-fitting. He's always been good with his hands. Between the two of them they could make a very good dollar. And he has five thousand to stake them, plus whatever she has. Later, when they are settled away, he could get the divorce worked out and send for Dale. It all sounds plausible and, looking down at Janice, Hicks is overcome with tenderness. He watches as she stirs but does not awaken. Taking her hand, he makes a silent vow to protect her from all harm. All the women he's known in his life! They're nothing compared to her.

3

A diamond as big as the Ritz! Isn't that the name of a short story by Fitzgerald? I seem to remember reading that one in university. That American Literature course under Professor Gullickson. What an old curmudgeon! No sense of humour. He only gave me a B as I recall. Well, it's not as big as the Ritz, Harper, but ye gods it must have cost him a fortune. I hope he didn't go to some shady finance company and put himself in debt for the rest of his natural life. But where else would he get the money for a rock like this?

She frowns at the diamond ring in its little plush case on the coffee table. Overhead her mother's piano thumps resoundingly as Gordon Rutherford sings "Joy to the World." And I think I can also hear Marjorie's chirpy little pipes dropping a note in here and there. Like me, Bobby knows he can't sing, and so I expect he's sitting in Dad's old armchair, folding the *Star* and waiting for dinner. I really don't feel like going up and making merry, but Mother was her usual insistent self. If I'd refused she would doubtless have complained over the entire holiday. Besides, she knows I have nothing better to do tonight.

"Just a little dinner party," she insisted. "So you children can get to know Gordon a little better. We're not even going to have the girls. Marjorie's arranged for a baby-sitter. So there'll just be the five of us. And I've bought a bottle of wine." My mother in a liquor store buying wine! That seems perilously close to loose living. I can't picture it. But that's what the woman said. All this because tomorrow Gordon is flying to Vancouver to spend Christmas with his daughter and her family.

"A chance to see the little ones," as he put it, presumably referring to his grandchildren.

Jan takes a drink from her second Scotch and leaning forward, elbow on knee and fist sunk under chin, studies the diamond. Intimidating damn thing in many ways. Nice to be asked, of course, even if the ring was disguised as a Christmas present and handed through an open car window.

"Just a Christmas present," he said. "A surprise. I hope you like it."

A strange way to propose marriage. After all, the man has been known to send a lady flowers. And do I really want to share my life with someone who can act so peculiarly? A nice tough question, Harper. Because I'm still irritated with him, damn it. Phoning me an hour ago to say he was dropping by, and would I come out to the driveway. He was in a hurry. On his way to Barrie to spend Christmas with his mother and Dale. Fair enough, though he might have told me this morning when he sobered up.

In the driveway he handed her a package through the open window. "Merry Christmas," he said. Sitting there behind the wheel with his hillbilly music twanging away and those goddam velour dice swinging from the mirror.

"I hope you like it. It's a surprise."

"Dandy. Why didn't you let me know when you were going

away? I haven't bought your present yet. This makes me feel like a shit."

"Don't worry about it. Look, Dale's in this hockey tournament up there. So I thought I'd stick around for a few days and watch him play. He's pretty good."

"Good for Dale." And there went the dinner she had planned for tomorrow night. Christmas Eve and all that. She had bought a duck. Never cooked a duck before but thought she'd give it a try. The damn thing is now thawing in her fridge. Is it possible to enjoy eating a duck by yourself?

"I'll call you," he said.

"Do that little thing."

"Ah come on, Janice." He took her cold hand. "I want to see my son at Christmas. You can understand that."

"You might have told me before this." She was dying to make him feel bad by telling him about her little dinner, but she let it go. She could smell the beer on him and in fact there was an empty case in the back next to shopping bags filled with Christmas presents.

"What about work?" she asked. "You've got all this time off?"

"Yeah, Jorgenson said it was all right."

"You've been drinking," she said. "You'd better be careful. It's spot-check time, chum."

"I'll be careful." He squeezed her hand. "I hope you like your present."

She bent down and kissed him on the mouth. When she straightened up she could see him grinning, the handsome bastard. From the house they could hear the singing.

"What's that?" he asked. "A party?"

"My mother is having us all to dinner."

"That's nice."

"It's okay."

It was chilly standing there, and she didn't want him to go. "Will you do me a favour, James?"

"Sure. What?"

"Get rid of those bloody dice."

He looked at them as though he were seeing them for the first time. "Why?"

"Because they look stupid. Only cowboys and high-school kids have things like that in their cars." He shrugged as he unhooked them. Threw them in the back of the car.

"They're no big deal." Jan felt terrible, but couldn't help herself. Snob Harper. "I'll phone you tomorrow."

"Right."

"I love you, Janice."

She squeezed his shoulder. "Drive carefully." Watched him back onto the street and drive away with nary a squeal of tires.

When she took the package inside she had a feeling that it was a ring. Still, it amazed her. And should she wear it upstairs? It really is a dazzler. But that's a cheap stunt. It almost certainly would ruin Mother's little party. And the questions, ye gods, the questions. And who, pray, has the answers? Not I, said the little red hen.

Jan gets up and takes the ring to her bedroom. Puts it in the drawer beneath her underwear. In the bathroom she combs her hair. Already the music has stopped, and as she opens the door leading upstairs she hears her mother's voice.

"Are you coming, dear? Dinner's almost ready."

"Yes, Mother. I'm coming right up."

Part Three

One

1

I hate New Year's Eve. I always have and I expect I always will. All the hand-wringing and tears that went into this evening in days of yore. Waiting by the phone during the week after Christmas. Hoping some clown would ask you to a party. The shame of it when you weren't asked. "You mean you didn't go *anywhere* New Year's Eve?" The question put by some bubble-brained little floozie who was already filling out her angora sweater in Grade Nine. Like Mavis Faraday. Ye gods, I haven't thought of Mavis Faraday in twenty years. You could feel the temperature rising when she walked into the classroom. Probably she's now a blowsy housewife with four kids. Overweight and married to some dope. I certainly hope so. But even in university, New Year's Eve was a big deal. You felt like a leper if you didn't go some place where everybody drank too much rye and ginger ale and put on funny hats and blew party tooters. At midnight all the guys tried to cop as many feels as they could manage in a minute.

In the Trans Am Jan shifts her weight and looks out at the freeway traffic. They are heading west to some party in Rexdale. She thinks he said Rexdale but she can't be sure. And he's certainly in no mood to be helpful. Hasn't said a ruddy word since we left my apartment. The warm car smells of his shaving lotion. Doubtless to cover up the smell of booze, because he's been drinking heavily. And that, together with this brooding, does not augur well for the evening, Harper. But I can guess why he's moping. I haven't said anything about the ring. Not on the phone all week and not today when he picked me up. The ring lies between us. An undiscussed subject. But this past week has been very good for settling accounts, as my father used to say. I've had the entire week to myself. Plenty of time to think. And what I think can be put simply. It was nice to be asked. Thanks very much, but no thanks. Because the more I think about it, the more I'm convinced I'd be making the mistake of my life. Now if I can just find the courage to tell him all this!

When Jan thinks about telling him, she's filled with dread. In her handbag the ring seems to weigh a pound. The truth is I could do without this party, which he invited me to at four o'clock this afternoon, damn it all. I should have said no. Told him I had palsy or rickets. What I should have been was out of the apartment, because I had a feeling he would call New Year's Eve. But where would you go, Harper, on this night of nights in a young woman's life? Probably I could have phoned Ruth Calder. Ruth and Seth are not big on New Year's Eve either. We could have sat around and eaten cashews and raw cauliflower. Drunk a bottle or two of low-calorie beer and talked about the perils of acid rain. Or, I could have gone to the Film Society with Bruce Horton. Suave old, darling old Bruce. Who phoned this morning at eight-thirty, for God sakes, and asked if I'd like to see *Gold Diggers of 1933* and *Little Caesar*. The Film Society was planning a party too. Sandwiches and wine would be served at intermission. I could see the egg-salad sandwiches on the paper plates and the Cold

Duck in the plastic cups. A cone-shaped paper hat on my head. I told Bruce I would have to miss out on the fun. I lied about some prior arrangement and didn't feel a twinge of guilt. Because, as I approach 1981, there seem to be a few things that need straightening out. Time is marching on, Harper, and you've reached a point in your life when you should no longer have to do certain things if you damn well don't feel like doing them. And one of those things is almost certainly attending any more meetings of the goddam Film Society. The harsh truth is that Bruce Horton is what used to be referred to as a drip. And I'm through with drips. I'm also through with good-looking moody types like Mr. Hicks, though I must say there will be things I'll miss. Oh yes, indeed!

The drinks and the warm, sweet air of the car make her feel a little groggy. That third Scotch was perhaps a mistake. Now and then she glances at Hicks, who is hunched over the wheel in a new suit that glows in the dark. With a peach-coloured shirt and a wide tie. Patent-leather shoes. Where did he find this get-up? In Barrie, Ontario? In fact, he looks like a well-heeled hood; he must be ringing up one godawful credit bill somewhere. Which is another thing to consider, kiddo. No, this is definitely the last tango. And somehow tonight I've got to tell him.

Jan closes her eyes. Let him sulk. Lord knows I've tried. I've asked him about his Christmas, his mother, and his son. Now you can't ask for more than that in the personal-interest line. And all I've received for my troubles so far are grunted replies. So, all right. If that's the way you want to bring in the New Year, fine and dandy. Maybe I can find somebody to talk to at this party. He hasn't even told me who's throwing the damn thing. Just old friends, he said. Girlfriends, I wonder? That would be cheeky. Well, no matter, Harper. Ride out the evening and then it's au revoir. Get your life back into some recognizable shape. Join an exercise class or take up a craft on Tuesday nights. Now the exercise class is not a bad idea, but let's forget about the batik rods and the potter's wheel. I don't really care for craftpersons as they now like to be called. Fanatics most of them.

It seems that for a moment she dozes. When she awakens they are off the freeway and on a wide, empty street of gas stations and small factories. Looking out, Jan sees only a few cars and a bus stopped by a glassed-in shelter. Alone, the driver is having a smoke. Jan takes out a cigarette. It will probably annoy Hicks. He doesn't like the smell of cigarette smoke in his car. Well, to hell with him, and his car too. Jan strikes the match so hard that only a sliver of light flares briefly. She tries again and, looking down at the trembling flame, realizes how furious she is. The entire goddam day! First, the drip phones at eight-thirty in the morning. And then lover boy here just before dinner. I shouldn't have come. I should have stayed home. Got mildly potted and gone to bed. *I hate bloody New Year's Eve*.

She wonders if perhaps she shouldn't give up smoking. But then everyone and her old Aunt Sally will be giving up cigarettes tonight. At least for a week. Besides, you can't give up a good-looking man *and* cigarettes all in the same night. Totally unreasonable. Hicks turns down a street on either side of which are several large white apartment buildings. Jan counts a half-dozen on her side of the street. Huge boxes filled with people, some lighted here and there by Christmas trees on balconies. Hicks turns in at the sixth one and stops in the parking lot. When he cuts the motor, they can hear laughter and music from windows. There seem to be several parties in progress.

Hicks reaches into the back seat and pulls out a pint of rye from a paper bag filled with liquor. Unscrewing the top, he takes a swig.

"You want a drink before we go in?" he asks. We're like a couple of kids in the school parking lot before the dance. He should know by now that I hate rye. Still, a small one may do no harm.

"Why the hell not?" asks Jan, taking the bottle. The whiskey scorches her throat. Ye gods, the Indians were right to call it firewater. Hicks stares straight ahead.

"Thanks," Jan says, handing back the bottle. He takes it without looking at her.

"I wish you wouldn't swear like that," he says.

Jan looks over at him. "I beg your pardon."

"It sounds cheap. You're supposed to be an educated lady." Jan takes a deep drag on her cigarette.

"I see. Is that how I've been billed tonight? The educated lady?" She talks slowly with a mild tremor in her voice. "James, in a few months I'll be thirty-seven years old. I don't think I need anyone to tell me what to do and what not to do. It's one of the advantages of running your own ship. Now, if I say a naughty word now and again, it's because I bloody well feel like saying it. If that offends you, that's just too bad." It's been said. A little sententious, Harper, but it's been said. And you've probably risked getting your teeth rattled.

Hicks continues to stare ahead as he sips more whiskey. "If you're gonna be in that kind of mood, we're gonna have a great time tonight, aren't we?"

This is amazing. Simply amazing. Jan shakes her head. "Mood? I've been in a mood? Good Lord, defend the innocent. You're the one who's been grunting replies all night, James. Ever since you came by it's been yes, no, maybe. I guess so. That is not civilized conversation, so don't talk to me about moods, chum." Jan reminds herself that she's skating on very thin ice. This is an unpredictable man, and he's half loaded. In the shadows she can hardly make out his face.

"I gave you a ring worth two thousand dollars last week," says Hicks. "And you still haven't said nothing about it. Not on the phone. Not today. Nothing. Jesus Christ." He slams his palm against the steering wheel. And that one was meant for you, Harper. But at least it's out. I've hurt his feelings and I'm sorry. Damn it, I *am* sorry.

"Can we talk about all this later, James? Please?" Jan reaches over to touch his arm but he knocks her hand away and opens the door. Grabs the bag of liquor from the rear seat and says, "Let's go."

So there's to be little in the way of chivalry tonight, thinks Jan as she opens her door. Standing by the car, she watches Hicks fire the pint bottle against a garbage container. It explodes like a gunshot. Seconds later someone calls down from a balcony. A voice in the night. Filled with rage. "What the fuck do you think you're doing, you asshole? Clear out or I'll call the cops."

2

She catches up to him in the lobby, where he holds open the buzzing door. In the elevator he stands clutching the bag of liquor and staring up at the lighted numerals on the panel. Even though the night is cold, Hicks has not worn an overcoat, and so he now stands angry and aloof in his shiny suit and patent-leather shoes. Looking at him, Jan is mysteriously touched by his flashy good looks. His childish vulnerability. Again she reaches for his arm.

"James. Please. Let's try to have a good time tonight."

He ignores her hand as they stop at the tenth floor. "I'm going to have a good time," he says, walking out of the elevator. "You can do whatever the fuck you like." She follows him down the long hallway toward the noise of a party. When the apartment door opens, the sounds burst upon the hallway: a shockwave of laughter and talk and Engelbert Humperdinck singing "Take Me in Your Arms." Or is it Tom Jones? The woman at the door is in her middle thirties. Not bad looking. Heavily made-up and wearing a champagne-coloured dress. A lot of blonde hair and all of it lacquered into a beehive hairstyle that is right out of 1963. She puts her arms around Hicks's neck.

"Jimmy! We're really glad you could make it. Gary and me have been wondering about you. My God, we haven't seen you in ages!" She stares over Hicks's shoulder at Jan, and Hicks turns.

"Uh. This is Janice Harper. A friend of mine. Janice, this is Marlene Thayer."

"How are you?" says Marlene, sticking out her hand. "Nice to see you. Come on in." She takes Hicks's arm. "Where the hell have you been keeping yourself anyways?"

"Here and there," says Hicks.

"Listen, Jimmy, you won't know too many here. Most of them are Gary's friends or guys he works with. But they're all real people."

I hope so, thinks Jan, following them into the dark, smoky apartment. I hate a party that doesn't have real people. Makes conversation so difficult. Marlene Thayer suddenly turns and comes back to Jan.

"Say, gimme your coat, Janet, and I'll put it in the bedroom for you. The drinks are across the room. The punch is really good." She stops to peer at Janice. "Well, you're certainly not the usual type we used to see with Jimmy. He said on the phone you were a school teacher. That's really nice. Gary and me are really glad you could make it."

"Thanks," says Jan. "How long have you known . . ." But

the woman has fled with Jan's coat, squeezing past several big men who are leaning against a wall smoking and drinking. As they talk they watch a few couples dance. Hicks has disappeared, and so Jan walks past the men, who are in their late twenties or early thirties. They all look overweight. Packed tightly into their polyester leisure suits and open-necked shirts. Some have large, drooping moustaches and thick sideburns. The women are clustered on the other side of the room near the windows and the balcony. Some are in pantsuits and others in party dresses. A few more beehives in evidence. When Jan passes the men, they appraise her briefly and then again turn to one another.

She stands alone by a long table covered with white cloth while Engelbert belts out an up-beat version of "I Need You." On the makeshift bar is a bowl of pink punch, an ice-filled tub of beer, and several bottles of whiskey and vodka. Jan helps herself to a Scotch and looks across the room at the men, who seem to be killing themselves by telling one another jokes. Jan can't get over their size. Filled from childhood with French fries and doughnuts. Gallons of Coke and now rivers of beer. How huge North Americans must seem to the rest of the world! It was one of the first things she noticed when she and Max were in Europe that summer. How comparatively small most European men are! In Spain, in France, in England, you rarely encountered big fatties like these characters. Never mind the poor little Third Worlders living on their fifteen cents' worth of maize or rice every month.

Hicks is now dancing with a sexy redhead in a gold-lamé dress. Looking cool as he circles her with eyes downcast. The redhead is a showboat who shakes her arms and writhes like Salome at Herod's court. She's kicked off her shoes, and in stocking feet her legs look thickly packed with muscle. She smiles at Hicks and says something to him. Gets a shy smile.

The bastard. He's charming her buns off. And never once has he danced with me! A blessing, perhaps, because I can't dance. All those little steps and the finger-snapping. It just makes me feel silly.

A little blonde in a mauve dress passes through the dancing couples, holding an empty glass. She can't be more than five-foot-two. Her hair has been frizzed into some weird kind of Afro. The little woman looks annoyed. Jan sees her as a sawed-off version of the old TV character Maude. The same wide, cruel mouth and vulgar cockiness. Little Maude stands at the bar and slowly fills her glass with punch. In fact she's quite drunk. She looks boldly up at Jan. "I'm Tiny Haverman. My real name is Tina, but I'm called Tiny. I guess you can figure out why." Jan has a good six inches on her and feels uncomfortable gazing down at a person who looks as though she'd like to make something out of something.

"Hi," says Jan. "I'm Jan Harper."

Tiny Haverman raises her drink. "Happy New Year."

"Thanks," says Jan. "The same to you."

They stand watching the dancers. Tiny Haverman sways as she sips her drink. "I'm married to that turkey over there in the light-brown suit. Who did you come with?"

"He's dancing now," says Jan. "With the lady in the gold dress."

Tiny Haverman looks across the room and snorts. "Lady? Terry Beal? You gotta be kidding. Terry may be something, but she's no lady, believe you me. She'll fuck anything in pants. You better watch your boyfriend there or Terry'll have his shorts in her handbag by eleven o'clock." She hesitates. "Your friend there is the best-looking man in the place. He reminds me of some movie actor. I can't remember his name."

"I know who you mean," says Jan, wishing that Tiny Haverman would go away.

"Is he any good in the sack?" asks Tiny.

"I beg your pardon."

The woman looks offended. "I beg your pardon," she says. "I said, is he any good in the sack?"

"He's fine," says Jan, finishing her drink.

Tiny Haverman again studies Hicks. "On a scale of ten, what would you give him?"

"I don't really know," says Jan. "I never really thought of it that way."

"You haven't, eh," says Tiny Haverman. "Well, I think about it all the time. Well, no, that's not true. I don't think about it all the time. Only when I've had a few drinks. Sex isn't everything, you know."

She says this with such an air of defiance that Jan wonders if the woman is looking for a fight. A quarrelsome little drunk. Best to agree with everything she says and look for an exit. Damn you, Hicks, for leaving me like this.

"Sometimes," says Tiny Haverman, "good-looking guys like him aren't worth a poop. Or so I've been told. I've only got old Larry over there. He's more interested in playing games than giving me a fuck. In the summer it's softball and in the winter it's hockey. That turkey's always tired. Tired and full of beer farts. That's the story of my life in bed. I haven't had a climax in years."

Jan reaches for the bottle of Cutty Sark and half fills her glass. And one ice cube only, please, because I believe I'm losing my reason. However, Tiny Haverman isn't finished.

"Larry used to be a six. For the first couple of years he was a definite six. Now he's not much better than two or three. That's when he bothers. We've been married fourteen years."

"That's nice."

"Some of the old zing is bound to go, I suppose," says Tiny Haverman, frowning at the dancing couples. She pours more punch into her glass. "How old are you anyways, Janet?"

"Excuse me," says Jan. She slips through the kitchen, praying that the bathroom is unoccupied. It must be down this hallway. Fortunately it is empty, and, locking the door, she sits on the pink toilet-cover and lights a cigarette. Takes a large swallow of her drink. That crazy woman! These awful people! And Hicks! Playing the perfect bastard. And it's not even eleven o'clock. I'll go mad before midnight.

From the other side of the door somebody gives a great shout; the voices seem to be growing louder by the minute. Jan gets up and examines the medicine cabinet. As good a way as any to see how people organize their lives. Nail-polish remover. Cuticle scissors. Preparation H. Children's aspirin. Where are the kids? At Grandma's probably. An aluminum strip of Polident tablets. Who wears the false choppers, I wonder? Him? Her? Both? She closes the cabinet door and studies her face in the mirror. I look anxious and haggard. And I didn't dress correctly. This goddam grey thing is more suited for a funeral.

Her heart quickens as someone rattles the doorknob. On the other side of the door she can hear laughter and male voices. Feels her face burn as she hears one of them say, "Who brought that dog in the grey dress?"

"The guy dancing with Doug's wife."

"You gotta be kidding."

"I'm not kidding. I saw them come in."

Sitting down again on the toilet seat, Jan feels an old, familiar sadness stealing over her. Listening to the voices, she remembers other New Year's Eves. Reading a seven-day novel from the library. Trying to ignore the clock and not think about her friends at dances and parties. Sitting up with her mother to watch Guy Lombardo and his Royal Canadians bring in another year. While her father quite sensibly went to bed after the eleven o'clock news. Well, to hell with it anyway. When it comes down to it, to hell with these fat clowns and their frustrated wives. And to hell with Hicks too. Let him paw that dame in the gold dress at midnight. Just don't come running over next Tuesday asking what book will improve your mind in January. Try Zane Grey. As for his two-thousand-dollar ring, I'll send it to him by registered mail. The main thing now is to get out of here. I suppose a ruddy taxi would be damn near impossible tonight. But I have to try. I am not going to stick it out here for the next two or three hours of my life.

She takes a last drag on her cigarette and flushes it down the toilet. Considers finishing her drink, but it's too potent. I might fall on my face. So she leaves it on the toilet tank and, opening the door, finds herself staring at three men. They are leaning against the wall.

"Hi there, honey," says one of them, grinning at her.

"Fuck you, buster," says Jan as she walks past them down the hallway. And please, dear God, not into a closet after that timely riposte. The bedrooms have to be down this way. Behind her the men are cracking up.

"Did you hear that, Rick?"

"What's eating her?"

"Maybe she's a ragtime baby tonight."

More laughter, and my God it's so easy to hate them, thinks Jan, as she tries a door. The room obviously belongs to a teenager; the walls are covered with posters of rock stars. In the room across the hall Jan can see a clothed male body lying on a small bed. "At the end of the hall, honey," calls one of the men.

When she opens the door at the end of the hall, she sees three men and a woman sitting on the bed on top of the coats. They are watching a dance show on TV and listening to a dirty story told by one of the men. As she roots for her coat, Jan hears the end of the story, which involves that tireless couple, the travelling salesman and the farmer's daughter. Some things never go out of fashion, thinks Jan, finding her coat. Rather touching in a way. On the TV screen some old-timers are shuffling around to the rhumba. Or is it the samba? It could be a fucking jig for all I know or care. In a corner of the screen the countdown to midnight changes each second. It now stands at 57:03.

One of the men now notices her. It's the storyteller. "Hey, can you find what you're looking for, little lady? Say, what's your hurry anyway? My name's Gary Thayer. I live here. It's my party."

Jan puts on her coat. The other three people are staring at the television.

"Where are you off to anyway?" asks Gary Thayer. "It's New Year's Eve. In another fifty-six minutes it will be 1981."

"That's wonderful news, Mr. Thayer," says Jan. "Have you got a telephone, by the way?"

"A telephone?" Gary Thayer scratches his head. "Well, sure I got a telephone. Hasn't everybody? But Holy Jeez, I don't know if you'll be able to hear yourself think in this place. The telephone's in the living room. It's on the floor by the sofa. We moved the tables out, eh? For the dancing."

"Forget it," says Jan. "Happy New Year, Mr. Thayer. And thanks for the party."

"Well Jeez, sure. And you too. Have a nice time." He turns away to the other guests as Jan makes her way down the long hallway.

The men have left and now standing outside the bathroom door are Marlene Thayer and another woman. They don't even notice Jan as she passes them. Marlene Thayer is knocking on the bathroom door.

"Tiny? Are you okay in there? Are you gonna be okay? Tiny, listen. Use the bowl. Okay?"

The front room is now crowded with dancers wearing party hats. The music is deafening. Hicks is dancing with a lanky brunette, but he notices Jan and, snatching off his little hat, comes hurrying after her. At the door he puts his hand on her shoulder. She can feel his fingers through the cloth of the coat.

"Where do you think you're going?" he asks. His face is glistening with sweat and his tie is loosened.

"I'm going home, James. I'm going to find a telephone and call a taxi."

"You're not going home," says Hicks. "I'll take you home when the party's over."

"I want to go home now, James. Please take your hand off my arm."

"Don't be a fuck now, Janice. It's New Year's Eve, for Christ sakes. I want you to stay here. Come on, we'll have a dance."

"I don't want to dance. Now let go of me." They stand by the doorway, staring with hostility at one another.

"Don't give me a hard time, Janice. Okay? I've had enough fucking aggravation today."

Jan feels consumed with rage. Thinks about how good it would feel to strike his face.

"James, if you don't let go of my arm, I'm going to scream so loudly that it will bring this goddam party to a halt. I mean it."

Hicks gives her a bitter smile and releases her arm. "Thank you," says Jan, opening the door.

He follows her into the hallway. "How are you going to get fucking home at this time of night? You'll never get a taxi for Christ sakes."

Jan walks ahead of him. "Just leave it to me. All right? Go back to your party and leave getting home to me."

But when she reaches the elevator, Hicks is still beside her, straightening his tie. His face pale and serious, he watches thoughtfully as she presses the button. Leaning on his arm against the wall, he looks down at the floor and says nothing until the elevator arrives.

"All right," he says, stepping in with her. "Okay, I'm sorry. Listen, I acted bad back there. I know that and I'm sorry."

She listens to Hicks explain. "Janice, listen to me. I've been waiting all week for you to say something. All fucking week. I give you this ring and what happens? Nothing. You don't say nothing about it. I want to marry you. You know that. I thought we had something good going between us."

The elevator bumps to a halt and Jan walks ahead of him into the cold, clear night. She can hear his footsteps behind her on the pavement.

"I'll drive you home, for Jesus sakes. You can't get a taxi out here this time of night."

3

In the car Jan looks at the empty winter streets and touches the case in her handbag. Finally she puts the case over the lighted dials on the dashboard.

"James, I'm sorry, but I just don't think it would work. I've thought about it all week, believe me. But I just can't see it working." There. It's out. At last. Hicks is driving fast, hitting a series of long green lights.

"It could work," he says.

"No, it couldn't, James," says Jan. "We've had some good times together. Wonderful times. But I just can't see it working in the long run." He says nothing to this, and they drive in silence until they take the eastbound ramp to the freeway.

"You think I'm a real jerk, don't you?" he says.

Jan looks out the side window at the lights of the city. She can sense a weariness in her voice. "No, James. I don't think you're a jerk. God, I wouldn't have been seeing you over these past few months if I thought you were a jerk."

"Bullshit."

"No, it's not bullshit." She turns toward him. "Look, we just haven't very much in common. That's not hard to figure out, is it? We live in two different worlds. I know that's a cliché, but it happens to be true."

"So what?"

"So everything. Look, people have to have some common ground. I mean besides sex. People have to share some common interests."

Words, words, words, as Hamlet says. Always so inadequate. And he doesn't want to hear this.

"We could make it if you wanted to make it," says Hicks. Jan says nothing. "But you don't want to make it. Right? I mean, that's it right there, isn't it? You just don't want to make it."

"It's not a question of wanting anything, James. It's looking at things as they are. And as I see things, we have little in common. Not enough anyway for a lifetime." She can feel the bitterness seeping into her voice. "Look at that party we just left. God!"

"There was nothing wrong with that party," says Hicks. "People were just having a good time. They work hard all week, so they deserve a little recreation. Anyways, it's New Year's. People are supposed to party on New Year's Eve. Your problem back there, Janice, was your goddam superior attitude. Instead of enjoying yourself, you stood around the place with your nose in the air, thinking you were so much better than everybody else." Jan looks out the window.

"And while I'm doing all that, you're doing your best to ignore the fact that you came with the 'dog in the grey dress' as one of those charmers put it. Shaking your trim little buns with that sexy number in the gold dress. But that's all right. After all, it's New Year's Eve. But the real problem, James, can be put this way. How did you ever imagine that I could enjoy myself among people like that?" She takes out a cigarette.

"Don't smoke anymore, eh," says Hicks. "You're like a goddam chimney. All night I've been inhaling other people's cigarette smoke." Jan drops the cigarette into her handbag. "There was nothing wrong with those people," says Hicks. "They were just ordinary people."

"Yes, yes," says Jan angrily. "Just ordinary people. Real people as your friend Marlene, the charming hostess, said. Before she fucked off without introducing me to a single person."

Hicks looks across at her. "You talk dirty, Janice, but you know something? You're a snob."

"So I'm a snob."

"Those people," says Hicks, "are every bit as good as you are."

"Maybe," says Jan. "And I recognize their right to exist. But I don't want to go to their goddam parties. They haven't any manners and they haven't any taste. Those fat clowns with their dirty stories and their snickers."

"Yeah? So? What's that got to do with us?"

"It's got everything to do with us. They're *your* friends, James."

"And you think you're so superior, eh. Just because you went to college and teach high school."

"It has nothing to do with going to college, for God sakes. Can't you see that? As for feeling superior, you're damn right I

299

feel superior. I feel very superior to that little frizzy-haired blonde, talking about her sex life and throwing up in the bathroom. You better believe I feel superior to such people."

"Which means you feel superior to me, right? Isn't that it? Isn't that just what we're talking about here?"

"I'm talking, James. You're shouting."

His rage seems to thicken the air and she warns herself to shut up. Look straight ahead at the empty highway.

"Answer me, Janice," says Hicks, looking over at her. "That's it, isn't it? You feel fucking superior to me. I'm just an asshole who never finished high school. A jerk who finds your fancy books and your nice music boring. Right?"

Jan wishes she could smoke a cigarette. "Maybe, James, I don't know. Please don't shout. I don't want to talk about this anymore. It's pointless. I just want to go home. Please."

Hicks has rolled down the window and the cold, rushing air makes Jan gasp. He grabs the ring from the dashboard and throws it out the window. Shouts at her in a terrifying voice.

"Well fuck you then. I don't fucking care. I don't give a fuck if you don't want to marry me, you fucking creep. Who'd want to marry you anyway? Every time I fucked you I dreamed I was fucking somebody else. Do you know that? Every time." Then he is slapping at her with his right hand. "Every time, you ugly bitch. I can get better women than you any time."

Jan holds up her hands to ward off the blows. Watches through brimming eyes as the tall highway lights flicker past. After a moment Hicks stops striking her and is silent. He rolls up the window and hunches over the wheel. The Trans Am surges forward, and Jan sees them hitting a guard rail and spinning out of control. Rolling over. The brutal sound of tearing metal and her own screams. Then blackness and silence. Afraid to look at him, she still covers her face with her hands. She can hear him panting beside her, and after a while he turns on the radio. They listen to dance music all the way home.

When the car stops in front of the house, Jan glances over at him. He stares ahead, and in the half-light his face looks dazed and obscure. She slides out quickly. Running up the driveway, she fears he will follow her. She listens for his footsteps. Only when she is behind the locked door does she feel safe.

4

Hicks awakens from a dream of death. Lying fully clothed on the sofa bed, he stares out the window. Sees the edge of a neighbouring building and beyond that the dark winter sky. Listens to a baby crying somewhere in the building. The child's sobbing is persistent and frantic. A sound that could bore a hole in your skull. Where is its mother, wonders Hicks? How can she sleep through that?

He tries to remember the dream. It had something to do with death, and so now he thinks of John Hepworth lying beneath the grey grass and the snow. Hicks wonders what it feels like to be dead. The idea of a hereafter he rejected long ago. He remembers the year he went to Sunday School at the Gospel Tabernacle. The teacher was a pale, homely young woman who carried a large white Bible. All the time she talked about Heaven and Hell. But the whole idea of those mythical regions was too fantastic for Hicks. Even at ten years of age. Everlasting fire or a golden city in the sky! Neither vision made any sense at all. Instead, death must be nothing. You feel nothing. But *you* doesn't exist. *Feeling* doesn't exist. So you are left with nothing. John Hepworth lies under the grass and snow, but he doesn't in a way because he no longer exists. He is nothing. Forget even about the *he*. Just nothing. Lying in the darkness, Hicks tries to get a handle on the idea of nothing.

Two

1

The supply teacher is about Jan's age. A stocky woman in navy slacks and a grey wool sweater. With her short, dark haircut she looks a little butch. But she has an open, attractive face. Her dark eyes look amused and skeptical. Jan watches the woman sip coffee and smoke. She takes long, deep drags, and absently flicks ashes on the floor. She is listening to Murray, who offers a kind of splendour this morning with his green check jacket, his lime-coloured slacks, and his brown suede loafers. Not bad for a grey January morning. The staff room is noisy with conversation. The first day is always the same. People are talking about holidays and Christmas presents. And about John Trimble, who broke his leg in two places while skiing in the Blue Mountains.

Murray beckons Jan to come over and she walks across the room. "Janice, my love, I want you to meet someone." Murray's eczema is bad this morning; there are vivid patches of it along his brow and neck. The poor man's nerves are on the loose. He tries so hard to give off an air of light-hearted unconcern, but in fact he's a terrible worrier. Now he hugs his mark book against his chest.

"I suppose," he says, "that you've heard about Trimble. I told the silly ass that sooner or later he was going to break his neck in that ridiculous sport. Well, it seems he's managed to break a leg, and so he won't be with us for a while. So here we have Liz Barton, who is going to replace him. Liz, this is Jan Harper, my right-hand person in the department. And please note, ladies, my use of non-sexist language. Just don't let me hear either of you referring to me as the goddam chairperson."

Jan and Liz Barton both laugh, and Murray's eczema seems to flare before Jan's very eyes. Strange women always put him into a state. And then John Trimble's accident! Not a smooth beginning to the term.

Liz Barton looks wryly amused by Murray, and Jan quickly decides that she likes her. Murray talks about texts and mark books before abruptly excusing himself.

"I have to run now, my dears. Liz, if there's anything you want to know, Janice is the one to ask. Bye now."

Both women watch him hurry toward the door, a flash of colour among the drab corduroys and tweeds. Liz Barton puts down her coffee and lights a fresh cigarette off the old one. In a chair near by, Judy Barowski wrinkles her nose in disgust. But if Liz Barton notices it, she doesn't let on. She blows smoke out of the side of her mouth and, picking some tobacco from her lips, wipes her hand across her pants.

"Well," she says, "he seems like a nice little fruit. What's he like to work for?"

Jan smiles. "Murray's a pet really. Don't let all that affected stuff fool you. He knows his job and he's a terrific teacher. Some of the dumber kids make fun of him, but the smart ones respect him. Just watch them flock around his classroom door when there's a major test coming up. He'll expect you to work hard and, no doubt about it, he can be demanding. He can also be bitchy and unreasonable. But he'll back you up if you feel you're being pushed around by anybody. Whether it's the jock department, who wants their big star basketball player excused from an essay date, or the vice-principal, who doesn't really think we do anything useful in the English Department anyway. Whoever it is, Murray will be right there with you. He may not look it but he's absolutely fearless. He has a will of iron and he believes passionately that we are the most important department in the school. For this he sometimes gets a lot of flak."

Liz Barton blows some more smoke at the ceiling. "Yeah. I figured him for somebody like that. The last guy I worked for was a real turd."

She does not elaborate on this but continues to smoke, casting about the room with those shrewd eyes. Liz Barton doesn't miss a trick. A tough little survivor who's been around, and Jan wonders about her. There's nothing on her pudgy little ring-finger.

The bell for opening classes rings and Liz says, "Well I guess it's into the trenches."

Jan says she has the first period free. "But if you need anything, Liz, just let me know."

"Thanks. It's Janice, isn't it? Well, if I do need anything you'll hear me holler." She takes a last drag on her cigarette and drops the butt into her coffee cup. "I can holler pretty damn well. I've been doing it now for a dozen years." She picks up her books and shifts them under one arm. "The funny thing is I don't know why I stick to teaching. I'm getting sick and tired of it and I often think I'd like to try something else before it's too late. The horribly subversive truth is that I don't like teenagers very much. There, I've said it to another teacher and you're not even horrified."

Jan laughs.

"They're such self-centred little bastards," says Liz. "It's all me, me, me. My daughter is fifteen and a nice enough kid. Not perfect, but nice enough. But Lord, the demands that child makes on me. The entire world revolves around her and not the other way around. Well, they're all the same. Maybe it's a part of growing up. Hell, I was probably the same way when I was fifteen. The funny thing is I can't remember much about being fifteen. Probably I spent most of my time mooning over boys. And being just as selfish as Jenny is now." She looks at Jan carefully. "You're not married are you?"

"No," says Jan.

"I didn't think so." She shifts the books to her other arm. "Maybe some time after school we could go and have a drink or something?"

"Yes," says Jan. "Sure. I'd like that."

"Good. Well, I'll see ya."

Jan watches her walk from the room. A forthright, oddly likeable little creature. Maybe a new friend? Jan looks down at the cigarette butt floating in the coffee cup. Well, she won't win many friends around here with habits like that. But then Liz Barton doesn't look like the sort of person who would much care one way or the other. When Jan looks up she sees Bruce Horton smiling at her from across the room. Bruce looks happy this morning; he's glad to be back. Two and a half weeks of taking his mother for drives and playing Chinese checkers with her must be taxing. Even for Bruce. Jan picks up the coffee cup and carries it over to the sink. Bruce would find the dead, unraveling cigarette disgusting. He'd want to know who did such a revolting thing. He'd demand explanations. And this morning Jan doesn't feel up to explanations.

2

When Hicks picks up the telephone, he hears Latimer's scornful high-pitched laughter.

"Hey, Hicksy! How are they hanging?" Hicks is pleasantly surprised to hear from his friend. "Latimer! Jesus! What do you say?"

"I didn't know if you'd still be in that place, old buddy," says Latimer. "I thought you might have moved by now." Looking out at the cold winter sunlight, Hicks too wonders why he hasn't moved.

"What time is it there anyway, Hicksy?" asks Latimer.

"It's nine o'clock in the fucking morning, Latimer. Why?"

"Jesus. Is that right? It's only six o'clock out here. The sun's just coming up, for Christ sakes." Out where, wonders Hicks.

"Is it cold up there, Hicksy?" asks Latimer. He sounds tickled by everything.

"Yes, it's cold," says Hicks. "Where the fuck are you anyway?"

"You'll never guess," says Latimer.

"Okay, I'll never guess. So why not just fucking tell me?"

"We're in Las Vegas," says Latimer.

"No shit?"

"No shit, man. Staying at this big fucking hotel. It's fancy, Hicksy. A hundred and fifty bucks a night. We're going in style. I been up all night playing blackjack. I lost about forty dollars. Would you believe at one time I was eight hundred dollars ahead of the fucking house?"

"I can believe it," says Hicks, who despises gambling.

"Cheryl is still downstairs in the casino. Playing those fucking slot machines. It's crazy out here."

"Where's Gregg?" asks Hicks.

"Ronny? He's back in Cornwall. Living with some chick he used to go with. They met at this party Christmas Eve, and it was all lovey-dovey again. She's got a couple of kids. He bought one of those trailer homes. A nice place, but he paid too much for it."

"And you're with the girl? Jesus, I thought she was Gregg's girl."

"Nah. She likes me more, Hicksy. I'm better hung than Ronny." Hicks listens to another burst of laughter. "We're married, Hicksy," says Latimer.

"Married?" Hicks is astonished. "You married that kid?"

"Fucking right. We're on our honeymoon. I bought this new van. You should see it. It's got everything. We're going to California in a couple of days. But it's fun here. Christ, we went to this show last night. A big floor show, eh? You sit around having this fancy meal with wine and all kinds of shit and on the stage are a couple dozen of the most beautiful chicks you've ever seen. Showing everything, man. Bare fucking ass. And so good-looking, Hicksy. I tell you I nearly threw a lump sitting there eating this big dinner. Then they had this singer come on. I can't remember his fucking name, but he used to be big and you still see him now and then on TV. Anyway, he comes on and he was good too. Cheryl was just sitting there squirming away watching this guy."

"Good for Cheryl," says Hicks bitterly.

"So how are things with you, Hicksy? Are you still taking out that schoolteacher?"

"No."

"Well, there's lots of stuff around. You've never gone short, you old stud." Hicks takes a moment to cough. A harsh, barking sound. "You're not still pumping gas or something fucking stupid are you?"

"No."

"You should get out of that place, Hicksy. Do you know it was eighty degrees here yesterday? We sat around this big pool. Cold drinks served by chicks in bikini bathing-suits. I'm telling you, man, you can't beat it."

Hicks can hear his neighbour's television. Somebody talking about carbohydrates. Tries to concentrate on whether they're supposed to be good for you. Loses the drift as Latimer says, "I've lost all track of time, man. What fucking day is it anyway?"

Hicks tells him it's Thursday.

"Good for Thursday," says Latimer. "Thursdays are nice. And what's the fucking date?"

"Jesus, Latimer. It's January the eighth."

"Is that right? God, I've been married now for five whole days. My rambling days are over, Hicksy." More insane laughter and then Latimer says, "So nothing new up there, eh? I mean about the little job we did."

"No, there's nothing in the paper about it anymore."

"You know something, Hicksy? I think we got away with that one."

"They found the Chrysler in the garage. But that's as far as they got."

"Well, we left it clean, eh. Wearing fucking gloves was a smart idea. I was worried about that car. I kept thinking of that friend of Ronny's. But maybe we got lucky, eh?"

"Maybe," says Hicks.

"Well, Hicksy, I better let you go. I am so fucking tired, man. Been up all night."

"Take care, Latimer."

"No problem. Listen, next time you're screwing one of those girlfriends of yours, think of your old married pal, eh. The old ball-and-chain man." Latimer is still laughing when Hicks hangs up the phone.

Sitting at the kitchen table, Hicks thinks about Latimer. People like Latimer seemed destined to survive. Things always appear to fall into place for them. They don't worry about life but maintain a happy, optimistic outlook. It's like in some of the books Hicks has read where it says you must establish a positive approach to things in general. For a person like Latimer this is easy. Without trying or reading books he can do this because that is his nature. The very idea of Latimer reading a book on, say, psychology is laughable. Other people, however, have to work at being happy. Hicks figures he's the type who has to work at it.

3

Walking across the school parking lot, Jan thinks of the opening lines of Emily Dickinson's poem.

> *There's a certain slant of light,*
> *On winter afternoons,*
> *That oppresses, like the weight*
> *Of cathedral tunes.*

Two or three of them actually liked the poem. Which isn't bad for last period on Friday. Listening to her boots creak, Jan wonders if perhaps it was on just such a colourless afternoon as this that those lines came to Emily Dickinson as she walked in the bare New England woods. A dark-clothed and solitary figure in the midst of that pale winter light.

Jan is still thinking of the dead poet when she sees the Trans Am. It's parked a half-block away on the other side of Graymore Road. Groups of students crossing the street temporarily block the car from her sight. But she knows it's Hicks, and getting into her car she feels a little light-headed with anxiety.

She wonders if he's been parked there on other days without her having noticed him. Is he following her each day through these suburban streets? An eerie thought! But perhaps not. It's so easy for your imagination to run wild in these circumstances. Be calm, Harper. Think of Emily Dickinson walking in the woods with her head full of words. Anyway, he hasn't done anything. There is no law that says you can't park on the street and watch another person drive home from work. Or is there? How the hell do I know?

As she leaves the parking lot she is afraid to glance at the Trans Am, which is to her right. However, her turn is to the left, and so, as she drives east along Graymore, she checks the rearview mirror to see if he is following her. Soon, though, other cars are behind her, and when she turns onto Crown Hall Road she is caught up in the thickening late-afternoon traffic. Still she feels pursued. This has ruined my Friday afternoon, she thinks as she drives along.

Gordon's Chevelle is parked in the driveway behind her mother's Plymouth, and Jan is annoyed. He could have parked the damn thing on the street. Now I'll have to come back out when he wants to leave. Well, I'll leave the keys in the car; he can move it himself. Lately the little railwayman has been spending a great deal of time around the place. He and Mother are the chief organizers of a charter bus trip to Florida. On Monday fifty members of the Friday Nite Club are heading south for some "fun in the sun" as Gordon puts it. Right now he and Mother are probably huddled across the dining-room table checking brochures and maps. Going over last-minute details. Mother will be cooing and billing like a little dove. And Harper, for God sakes, stop being so snide. She's happy, isn't she?

Sitting in the car, Jan thinks of her father and the annual trip to Florida during the Easter holidays, as they used to be called. The long and tedious drive south along the Interstate with her and her father taking turns behind the wheel every two hundred miles. Getting off the big highway south of Washington and driving past the motels and filling stations until they found a vacancy sign. She always felt faintly ridiculous watching her father sign the register. Requesting a separate room for his daughter. They shared expenses, so why did it never occur to her to sign her own name? Strange! She was a tall, gawky woman in her twenties who still tagged along with her parents. In the restaurant she imagined that people were staring at her with pitying eyes. Lying in the room next to her parents, she could hear them moving about. Unpacking their travelling bags and talking about the trip. The dry murmur of their voices came through the walls. Lying there and listening to them, feeling headachy from the long day in the car and the smell of gasoline.

On a beach near Fort Lauderdale, her mother, in black tanksuit and rubber bathing cap, stepped timidly into the sea while her father sat under a palm tree reading Mark Twain or Stephen Leacock. His holiday authors! Dressed like a man in an old photograph with his light trousers and white shirt and hard straw hat. I could see him with his foot up on the running board of an Auburn. In the cool evenings they walked around the town and what her father saw only displeased him. Old-timers sporting jazzy clothes and doing things. Busy at shuffleboard or lawn-bowling under the lights. Winnebago owners wearing baseball caps and discussing mileage. It all confirmed his view that North Americans have never learned how to act their age. A frivolous, immature civilization.

Plenty of knowledge but no wisdom in sight. Too much American know-how and not enough American know-why, etc., etc. He could go on about it. And now he's been in his grave over three years. I wonder what he would think if he could now see Mother with her dapper little boyfriend making holiday plans.

Sitting in the car, Jan realizes that all this time she has been waiting to see if Hicks will drive past the house. Looking in the rearview mirror, she half expects to see his car. When she doesn't, she's not sure whether she feels relieved or disappointed. And that's something to think about. But really, it's much better this way. There's no future with the man in the Trans Am, Harper, and you know it. Opening the car door, she's certain that Emily Dickinson would agree.

4

As Hicks drives past the school, he listens to Barbara Mandrell sing "Crackers." Janice's Honda is four cars ahead of him, but still he can see it turn down Crown Hall Road. On the sidewalk, groups of teenagers are huddled into their bomber jackets and parkas, hurrying toward McDonald's and Harvey's in the shopping plaza. Looking at them, Hicks feels a mild resentment. Their whole lives are ahead of them! Yet, in a way he's glad he's not seventeen now. He doesn't like the look of things ahead. What are these kids going to work at, for instance?

Earlier this afternoon Hicks had an argument in the Puss 'n' Boots Club about this very thing. His adversary was a skinny character in his thirties who wore glasses. A regular at the Puss 'n' Boots, a barfly named Dave. The story had it that he was busted once for peddling dope. He told Hicks that in the next twenty years he would see some tremendous things happening in the world of technology. Unbelievable things that would change the way people looked at reality. This Dave character used words like "reality" and "perception" a lot. He talked about silicon chips and laser beams and all kinds of shit Hicks had vaguely heard of but didn't know much about. In fact, the guy was smarter than Hicks had figured. And all Hicks had on his side of the argument was a stubborn lack of faith in man's good intentions. Anyway, he drank too much beer and got himself turned around. Boxed in by this guy, who was very good-natured about it all. He kept insisting that they were not having an argument but a discussion. Hicks left with the feeling that the man did not have a very high opinion of Hicks's intelligence.

Now, driving down Crown Hall Road, Hicks regrets ever having talked to the dope peddler about the future. What does either of them know anyway? They're just a couple of assholes who spend their afternoons drinking beer in a dark bar. Hicks also regrets having drunk so much beer; now he feels sluggish and crapulous. And it's not yet four o'clock in the afternoon. Without knowing why, he drives a familiar route south on Crown Hall to Richfield and then along to Transit Road and the Public Library. In the parking lot behind the library he sits and looks out at the raw afternoon. Since the accident he's avoided the place.

At this time of the day Hepworth's cronies, the old men and oddballs, have left. Gone to wherever it is they go at the end of a day. Instead, the place is filled with teenagers, mostly girls in jeans, who sprawl across the long reading tables and copy things out of books. A couple of them look up with interest when Hicks comes in and whisper to themselves. Fucking jailbait, thinks Hicks, as he walks among the fiction stacks. Taking down a copy of *Crime and Punishment*, he goes to a chair near the tall windows overlooking Transit Road. Sitting there, he tries again to puzzle out the story of the Russian student who buries the axe in the old woman's head. It's tough going, and again Hicks feels perplexed and irritated by the tedious conversations, the incredible names, the monstrous detail of the story. Reading it, he feels angry enough to write obscenities in the margins or tear out pages by the handful.

The library is overheated and Hicks unzippers his jacket. After an hour he takes it off and reads in his shirtsleeves. Struggling with the novel, he reads on, stopping now and then to stare at his reflection in the darkened window. He sees a gaunt figure holding a heavy book.

Three

I

"I thought I was in bad shape," says Liz Barton, "but did you check out that blonde in the purple leotards? My God! I mean I know I may be a little, let us say, rotund. But that woman was actually gross!"

Jan laughs as they drive through the mild January night. A thin drizzle beads the windshield. Earlier the radio forecast freezing rain and this worries her. She's terrified of slippery streets. Always pictures herself sliding out of control into a nine-car pile-up. Right now she'd like to drop Liz off and drive straight home. But she allowed herself to be talked into a drink. As Liz said, "I think we've earned a drink. I know it's cheating, but what the hell! One miserable bottle of low-calorie beer can't kill us."

Jan is tired. The first exercise class has taken more out of her than she could have imagined. She really is out of shape. Her weight is all right, but those last few laps around the gym left her flushed and breathless. She resolves to cut down on the cigarettes. She doesn't really feel like a drink but is going along anyway. For Liz's sake. Behind Liz's breezy manner she's quite let down and needs the company. All night, the fitness instructor, a perky, trim little number with a bobbing ponytail, singled out Liz for special scolding. So perhaps a drink might not be a bad idea, thinks Jan, as they drive through the wet, black streets.

"Why do I do this to myself every year?" says Liz. "I'm thirty-seven years old and you would think that by now I would recognize the simple and unassailable fact that I am destined to be fat. And that little bitch told me that I had to lose twenty-five pounds. Twenty-five pounds, for God sakes!"

Liz now mimics the little gym instructor. "'Twenty-five pounds, Mrs. Barton. Absolutely essential.' Is she out of her cotton-pickin' mind? I couldn't lose twenty-five pounds if my life depended on it. Ten yes, I can see ten. Even fifteen, if I bear down and grit my teeth and hate everyone in sight. But twenty-five! The woman is mad. Turn right at the next light." Liz yawns. "And what about some of those things we were supposed to do? Who dreams up these tortures anyway? My God, I'm no ballerina!" She again mimics Miss Dean. "'All right girls! Now everyone up on her tippy-toes. Right up.' And how I wish the dear little thing wouldn't say 'tippy-toes.' And what about that one where you're supposed to pretend you're a goddam tree being 'buffeted' by the wind. The woman did actually say 'buffeted,' didn't she? I must say that surprised me. But really! A tree in the wind? Isn't that what kids do in kindergarten? I felt about five years old. Maybe next week we'll do our exercises to a rhythm band. And suck in that tummy, Mrs. Barton. Why did she single out my tummy? I was sucking *my* tummy in. By God, was I ever! And that blonde dame in the purple tights had *her* tummy out to here. She looked eight months gone, for crying out loud. I need a drink. And when it comes right down to it, I wouldn't mind a Big Mac and a large fries either. Here we are, Janice Harper. Pull in immediately."

The Malibu Motel and Tavern is near the freeway. In the parking lot you can hear the traffic rushing past. The lounge is chrome and plastic with a padded bar in the shape of a horseshoe. On a little platform near the bar a pretty young woman in a long red dress sings "I Want to Make It with You." The place reminds Janice of the Holiday Inn where she and Hicks spent their first night together. The lounge is only half filled. A Wednesday-night crowd of middle-aged couples sitting at the tables and watching the girl in the red dress. Along the bar a few men are looking at a soundless hockey game on TV.

Jan asks the waitress for a Scotch and water.

"You cruel bitch," says Liz, ordering a bottle light beer. They sit in silence, listening to the girl finish her song to light applause. After the waitress brings their drinks, Liz tells Jan that the Malibu is an old watering-hole. She and her husband used to come here on Friday nights when the place was livelier.

"But don't get me wrong," Liz says. "I'm not here on my sentimental trip. It just happens to be handy." She looks around the long, smoky room with her mocking eyes. "Actually, it's quite a crummy place. Crummier than it used to be." She sips her beer. "There was a group of us every Friday. Four couples. We used to have our own table over there on the other side of the room near the stage. There was a little platform out front where you could dance. It was all right. A night away from the kids. We all had young kids then. I never see those people anymore. They've all moved away. Actually I ran into one woman a few months ago. In the Eaton Centre. And she didn't even recognize me. God, I was embarrassed. It's all this weight, I guess."

They watch the singer finish another song and step down from the stage, holding her long dress and taking tiny, cautious steps in her high-heeled shoes. She's replaced by Muzak. Liz glances over her shoulder into an empty booth.

"They used to serve these little dishes of peanuts with the drinks." She shrugs. "Well, I guess I'm going to have to stop thinking about food." She looks at Jan. "You skinny types. I hate you. I'll bet you can eat anything and not gain an ounce."

"It's true, I'm lucky," says Jan, smiling. "I've never had a weight problem. My father was tall and slim, and I take after him. But when I was in high school, did I ever wish I carried more weight. Especially up front. Ye gods, I was just like a bean-pole."

Liz laughs. "Well, I never had any problems in that department. Every boy in the school was dying to get his hands under my sweater. In high school I was what you called 'stacked'. It's funny how people are built. You're probably like my husband. Jack can eat a three-course dinner and a half-hour later go to the fridge for a piece of chocolate cream pie. He's six feet tall and never in his life has he weighed more than a hundred and sixty pounds, the son of a bitch."

Jan smiles and lights another cigarette. Take that, Miss Dean! And another Scotch would go down rather nicely, too. She now feels pleasantly tired.

"If you're wondering," says Liz, "Jack and I split three years ago. Three years ago next month actually. We haven't divorced. Maybe he'll come back, I don't know. I'm not sure I want him to come back." Sooner or later, thinks Jan, everyone has her story to tell. And sooner or later everyone gets around to telling it.

"Thirteen years of marriage down the old tube," says Liz, finishing her beer. "Let's be madly decadent and have another drink. I'll do a couple more push-ups when I get home. Girl Guide's promise. But just one more. I promised Jen I'd be no later than eleven-thirty."

Liz waves to the waitress, who comes over and takes their order. "At thirty-four," she says, "Jack suddenly decided that he was suffering from some kind of mid-life crisis. I said, 'Jack, you've got at least another six years. Wait until you're forty, it's more fashionable. People will be more sympathetic. Meanwhile, stop reading *Time* magazine and the weekend papers.' But would he listen to his chubby little wife? I should say not. My life is passing me by. That was his line. Where has my youth gone? I'm not getting enough. Or, I'm not getting as much as I think other people are getting. Well, of course, he didn't exactly say that, but that was what he was getting at. So he started to tart himself up in sporty clothes. Began to wear medallions around his throat and eye the senior girls. Jack's a teacher, too. Phys. Ed. And he began to do weird things. He read *Jonathan Livingston Seagull*. He went away on weekends to those encounter sessions where people sit around and talk about what went wrong with their marriages and why they can't get it all together and so on and so forth. Group sessions where you rap with your fellow penitents under the eye of a psychologist who is probably the most fucked-up person in the room, but who is too clever to let on. So he started going to these things, and what with the youthful clothes and the weekly hair-styling appointments and all the rest of it, life began to take on new meaning. He started reading people like Richard Brautigan and Kurt Vonnegut. Jack finally discovered the silly sixties ten years after they were over." Liz takes a long swallow of beer. "I knew he was starting to get a bit on the side, as I believe the vulgar expression has it. You can always tell if you have half an eye open. The perfume that lingers, the strands of hair, the scratches on the shoulder blades, the phone calls about seeing the basketball salesman. All the stuff you see on the soapers. It's all true. And I won't say some of it wasn't my fault. Damn it all, I mean look at me. I'm fat. I used to have a terrific figure, but now I'm fat. It has to be said. So, he's bored with me in bed, I guess." She looks away. "Hell. I told him to get out and get his own place where he could fuck the little student teachers who visited the school. I don't regret it, though it was hard on Jenny. And I'm sorry about that. She misses her father. She sees him a couple of times a week, but it's not the same." Liz gives Jan a shrewd, appraising look. "Am I boring you, Janice?"

"No, of course not," Jan says, looking across the room. "I'm sorry." A man has just got up to leave, so Jan can now see a couple seated at a table. The man's back is to her but Jan can feel a quickening in her blood.

"I'll bet," Liz says, "that you weren't even listening to my tale of woe. I admit it's fairly trite."

"No, listen, Liz. It's not that at all." Distracted, Jan continues to stare at the man's back. "I heard everything you said. It's just that I think there's somebody sitting over there I know. Or used to know."

"In this place?" says Liz, looking across the room. "Who or what?"

Jan is now certain. That thick, curling hair at the back of his neck. He always needed a haircut. How odd it is to think of the number of times she touched that thick, curling hair! When he turns to order fresh drinks, she sees his profile. It's Travers all right. Still cheating on the dragon lady! After telling me he was finished with all that! He had to think of his daughters, etc., etc. The son of a bitch! And here he is in the Malibu Motel and Tavern with yet another one. She's young, too. Probably no more than twenty or twenty-one. He'll charm the knickers off her in no time. I wonder if he's already booked a room in the joint. And even from this angle the bastard looks terrific in that tweedy sports-jacket.

Looking at her old lover, Jan feels furious. But why? He didn't promise anything, Harper. But he did say was he was through with roaming around! Ha! Words on the wind! And wouldn't it feel good to walk across the room and empty this drink over his head?

"Well," says Liz, "whoever it is, you're looking daggers. Your eyes are bugging out of your head, Janice. So, do I now have to play twenty questions? So I'll play! Animal, vegetable, or mineral?

Jan smiles grimly. Feels ashamed and foolish. The truth is she doesn't want Travers to see her sitting here with Liz Barton. A couple of middle-aged dames in sweaters and slacks. Cooling off after exercise class. She wouldn't mind if he saw her sitting here with Hicks. How would you like them apples, Travers? Hicks has ten years on you. But what a base thought! Liz is now her friend. Why should she care what Travers thinks? Taking out kids like that! Pathetic.

"There's a guy over there I used to go out with," Jan says. "For a few weeks last summer. He had a wife and kiddies at home. And by the way, that little brassy blonde he's with is not his wife."

"Which one are you talking about?" asks Liz, looking across the room. "Do you mean the guy in the tweed jacket with the blonde?"

"The same."

"Hey, he's a real doll!" Liz's voice sounds amused and wondering.

"And I'm not exactly Jane Fonda? Right?"

"Hey, come on, Janice! I didn't mean that."

"Yes, you did. But don't worry about it. Let's get the hell out of here."

In the parking lot Jan guns the engine to warm up the car. Beside her, Liz relaxes into another huge yawn. Jan looks over her and says, "Can I ask you a personal question, Liz?"

"Why not?" Liz says. "My life is, to coin a phrase, an open book."

"What do you do for sex anyway?"

Liz watches the windshield wipers clearing the rain. "That's an easy one. I masturbate." She leans forward, bulky as an Eskimo in her heavy coat. "Listen, for the past couple of years, I've been having this sizzling affair with Burt Reynolds. The things we do, my dear, are not for innocent ears. But I don't know. To tell you the truth, old Burt is starting to look his age. He's still a gorgeous hunk of man, mind you, but I've been looking over some younger stuff. Of course, when they're over the hill, I just throw them on the ashheap. Old Heartless Barton, that's me." They are still laughing when they leave the parking lot.

2

Jan looks up from the essay entitled "The Failure of Relationships in *Death of a Salesman*." She closes her eyes and rotates her head, listening to the ominous creaking in her neck. Nearly eleven o'clock. Have I been at this damn stuff for three hours? Well, put a little gold star in your conduct book, Harper. And go make some fresh coffee! Only three more of these things to go and then the rest of the weekend is yours. Hallelujah!

In the kitchen she waits for the water to boil and takes down her mother's latest postcard. There are three of them Scotch-taped to the refrigerator door. Three cards in eleven days! You can't say she isn't dutiful about writing. She is still having "a wonderful time." Gordon is proving to be "the life of the party." The "gang" is on its way to St. Augustine to see something "historic." The weather has been cool, and folks are worrying about the citrus crops. Lately it's warmed up, though, and they are now enjoying temperatures in the low seventies. The low seventies! Ye gods! When I came home this afternoon, the temperature on this last Friday of the last month of 1981 was exactly twelve degrees on the good old Fahrenheit thermometer that Dad put up in the carport ten years ago. Low seventies indeed! The picture on the card shows a bosomy young creature in a bikini holding a hamper of oranges. Who picked out that card, I wonder? Naughty little Gordon?

Taking a cup of coffee back to her bedroom, she sits down at her desk and stares at the pile of marked essays. After school she'd asked Liz if she felt like a movie tonight. But Liz had laundry to do. Every piece of clothing owned by her and her daughter was dirty.

"Janice, I am now wearing a pair of panties that look sexy enough, if you consider homemade fishnet sexy. You can put your entire hand through the holes in my underwear. But they're the only clean pair I could find this morning. I just have to come to grips with this." Now Jan is glad. She feels proud of her evening's work.

A ringing phone late at night pierces the nerves. Fills the air with an urgent summons. Startled, Jan thinks immediately of her mother. Something has happened in Florida and she will have to listen to Gordon or Bobby convey frightful news. When she picks up the receiver, however, she hears Hicks's voice.

"Hello, Janice. How are you?" He speaks with an extravagant courtesy. She guesses he's drunk. In the background she can hear traffic noises.

"I'm fine, James." Absently she touches her face. "It's very late, James. Why are you calling me?"

Hicks sounds formal and remote. He seems to be choosing his words with immense care.

"I have to see you, Janice. It's extremely important. I have to come over and see you."

He's drunk all right, thinks Jan, and the thought of him in the apartment leaves her stricken with dread."

"James, please. That's not a very good idea."

"Janice, I have to see you. I love you."

"James, no. Listen to me. We've said everything we have to say to one another. Why can't you just leave it alone now?"

"No," says Hicks. "That's not right at all. We haven't said everything there is to say. I have to tell you that I'm sorry." Jan can hear a heavy vehicle pulling away. A bus?

"It's all right."

"It's not all right. It's not all right at all," says Hicks. "I am sorry about the way I spoke to you in the car on New Year's Eve. The way I treated you . . ."

"It's all right, James. I know you didn't mean it. We were both upset that night. Let's just forget it."

"I do not want to forget it," Hicks says. Jan detects a sullen obstinacy in his voice.

"James, it's after eleven o'clock. I'm very tired."

"You don't understand what I'm trying to tell you, Janice. What I said in the car. All those things I said about you. They were not true. Not one of them was true, so help me God."

"Don't come over, James. Please!"

"I'm only five minutes away," he says. "In a phone booth at the shopping plaza. I have to see you, Janice."

"Don't come over, James. I don't . . ." But he has already hung up and she is left holding the phone and staring at the next essay. "Why Willy Loman Is a Failure." Panic swarms about her heart, and yet she sits at the desk reading the opening sentence of the essay.

"Willy Loman's attempts to comunicate are seen in the first page when Willy tells his wife, Linda, about the acident he nearly had." She circles the misspelled words. Five minutes away! What can you do in five minutes? Turn off the lights and hide! But he knows I'm here. He'd probably pound on the door until I let him in. If I went upstairs to Mother's, he'd do the same thing.

She thinks of going next door to the Bonners'. They're home. I can see their kitchen light. But what could I say to them? Knocking on their door at this time of night? Can I hide in your house? An old boyfriend is making a drunken nuisance of himself. She can see Bob and Betty Bonner standing in their doorway listening to this. Gulping down their surprise. Betty's little-girl voice. "Are you kidding, Janice? You gotta be kidding." And Jesus Christ, what do you do? I could let him in, I suppose. He might be all right. If I humour him, he'll be all right. Give him a drink and after a while he'll probably go to sleep. But where does that leave you, Harper? He'll be here in the morning when you wake up and you're right back on the merry-go-round.

For a moment she is seized with fury. Goddam him to hell! Why doesn't he leave me alone? I said I didn't want to see him and I mean it. But the stupid man can't take no for an answer. Almost without thinking about it she picks up the phone and dials Liz Barton's number. The phone seems to ring forever. Is she asleep? Liz looks the type who could sleep through an earthquake. My ruddy luck! But Jan hears Liz's voice.

"Yeah?" She sounds a little vexed. Well, it is late.

"Liz? It's Jan Harper."

"Jan?" says Liz, genuinely surprised. "I thought it was Norman again. Jenny's boyfriend. What's up?"

Jan knows her voice is breathless and hurried. "Can I come over to your place, Liz?"

"You mean now?" Liz sounds mildly amused by the idea.

"Yes."

"Well sure, I guess so. Why not? I'm just ironing all the

damn washing and watching an old Elvis Presley movie. It's not the most exciting place in town."

"Listen, Liz, I don't care. I just have to come over. Okay?"

"Sure. Come on over. Any time, Janice."

She moves quickly now. Switching off lights as she hurries from room to room. Grabbing her keys and cigarettes as she stuffs an arm into her winter coat. Thankful that she's still wearing a sweater and slacks. An hour ago she'd thought of putting on her pyjamas. When she steps out into the cold, clear night, she prays she won't meet him as she's backing down the driveway.

The steering wheel is freezing to the touch, and she's forgotten her gloves. Her hand shakes as she inserts the ignition key. She listens, disbelieving, as the car emits a low, growling sound. She tries again. Hears a weaker growl. The final whimper of a stone-dead battery. It's been hard to start for the past two weeks and she's been meaning to take it into a service station. One of those chores that always seems too damn inconvenient. I'll do it tomorrow, etc. And now this cold night had killed it. Damn. Goddamn! She reminds herself to stay calm. Tries once more and gets only a click. Bastard. Bastard. Bastard. How long is it now since he's called? Maybe, after all, she should go to the Bonners'. Or take her mother's car! The keys to the Plymouth are in her mother's kitchen. In a little bowl on the shelf above the sink. But the car hasn't been started for nearly two weeks. Would the damn thing go? For that matter, is there time? It must be five minutes since he phoned. Then the headlights of a car are blazing down the driveway and lighting the carport. Jan ducks and lies across the front seat. Feels hopelessly foolish as she listens to the heavy throb of the Trans Am's engine. Then the headlights go out and the motor stops.

Lying across the seats, she hears the car door slam and his footsteps on the asphalt. Lurching and uneven. The footsteps of a drunken man. She listens to him knocking on the outside of the aluminum door and calling for her.

"Janice? It's me, James! Can I come in and talk to you?"

Slowly she raises herself and looks out the car window. With his arms outstretched, Hicks leans against the side of the house. His breath smokes the air as he coughs into his fist and again calls to her. Knocks and implores her to open the door. "Come on, Janice, I want to talk to you. Open the door, eh."

Jan sinks down across the seats again and listens as Hicks begins to hammer the door with his fist.

"I want to talk to you, Janice. Let me talk to you, goddam it." Staring at the rubber floor mat, she prays he will leave. The Bonner's side-door light comes on. They must be wondering what in God's name is taking place. Hicks is now yelling for her to open the door, and she hears Bob Bonner calling from his doorway.

"You better get away from there before I call the police. Miss Harper obviously doesn't want to talk to you."

Jan closes her eyes as she hears Hicks say, "Shut up. Mind your own fucking business." Poor Bob. He wouldn't say boo to a goose. Has anyone ever spoken to him like that, I wonder?

"I'm going to call the police," says Bob Bonner. He sounds shaken. Jan then hears the terrible sound of shattering glass.

"Well, fuck you then," shouts Hicks. "Fuck you all."

She listens to his retreating footsteps. Hears the car door open and slam shut. He backs down the driveway without lights and takes off down Willowgreen Drive. She listens to the sound of the powerful engine fading into the night. Bob Bonner is now walking around the driveway and talking to his wife, who must be standing in their doorway. Jan hears Bob Bonner say, "I'd better see if she's all right." And dear God should I now get out of the car and walk over to my own door and thank Bob for his help? Just a little personal problem, Bob. Nothing much to it. Or stay here? Ye gods, the situations you can find yourself in! She listens to Bob Bonner knocking gently on her door.

"Are you okay in there, Janice? Is everything all right?"

He knocks again, and Betty Bonner says, "Maybe she's not even home. There are no lights."

"Well, her car's here," says Bob, and Jan closes her eyes. What can she possibly say if he comes over and looks in to see me crouched like this in the front?

"Well, maybe she's out with friends," Betty says. "You better come in now. You're going to catch your death of cold."

"I wonder who that fellow was," says Bob. "He was drunk as a skunk. And he's broken the window in the door here. There's blood all over the place."

"Well, never mind that. Come in. It's freezing. It's her problem, Bob. If he comes back, we'll call the police." Jan can hear Bob now walking toward his door.

"It beats me. Who was he, for crying out loud?"

Then, the thankful sound of their door closing. The side light goes out. They'll be talking about it now. She can imagine them making coffee and talking about it. Now why would Janice Harper be mixed up with someone like that? I always thought she was so quiet and reserved. An old-maid type actually. It just goes to show that you never really know people, etc., etc. But what do I care what they're saying? The main thing now is to get myself out of this ridiculous predicament. And be thankful he didn't find me.

She shivers. Every day you read about lovers' quarrels erupting into violence and death. You wonder how such things can possibly happen. How can people lose control of their lives like that? Well, now you know, Harper, now you know. The thing

329

to do is wait ten more minutes. Give the Bonners time to settle down and go back to the late show or whatever it is they were doing. Then I can get back to my apartment and have the biggest drink in the world. Then call a cab and get over to Liz's. Thank God for Liz. I'd never sleep a minute in my place tonight.

Trembling in the freezing air, she waits. Tries to ignore the ache that has begun to invade her spine. When she does get out of the car, she is cramped and stiff with cold. She steps carefully through the broken glass. Sees the dark spots of blood near the door. James! James! Behind locked doors in the apartment, she sits. Still wearing her winter coat she smokes and drinks a large Scotch. Feels her heartbeat slowing down. The woman at the cab company said the best they could do was twenty minutes. More likely a half-hour. It's Friday night and the taverns are emptying. There's always a heavy demand at this hour of the night, blah, blah, blah. Nowadays everyone has a fucking excuse for not doing his job properly. She feels enormously depressed by Hicks's visit. Senses how fragile is the order in a person's life. And this apartment offers no refuge tonight. This is her home, yet she feels unsafe in it. The very air seems charged with menace. My overheated imagination perhaps. But still!

After pouring herself another drink, she locks the apartment and climbs the stairs to her mother's place. She's only been up twice since her mother left. To water the plants. The house smells of old wax and emptiness. She walks into the hallway and turns on the outside light for the cab-driver. Stands there listening to the hum of the refrigerator. In the living room she sits on the piano bench and sips her drink. Peers at the faint outline of her graduation picture on top of the piano. Janice Harper in mortarboard and gown. Looking severe and studious. About to set forth on life's perilous path. As some idiot no doubt said in the 1967 convocation address. 1967! Ye gods!

· · ·

The cab arrives in twenty minutes. Driven by a brooding black man whose hair is got up in oiled ringlets. Some kind of Rastafarian character, who rockets her through the empty suburban streets without a word. A light snow fell earlier in the day, and lawns sparkle under the starlight. They are almost to Liz's house before Jan realizes that she is still holding her drink. She downs it at once, a great thumping glass of Scotch and water that leaves her eyes misting. Sitting there, she wonders what to do with the empty glass. Give it to the Jamaican as part of the tip? She finally stuffs it in her handbag.

3

Jan follows Liz down a hallway cluttered with winter boots. Liz is wearing jeans and an old tee shirt. On her bare feet are rubber thongs. She has set up the ironing board in the living room in front of the TV. On the screen the late Elvis Presley is crooning a love song to a demure little blonde in a starched white dress. Elvis whispers the song in the girl's ear while she gazes down at her hands. She looks very embarrassed by the whole thing.

Liz's house smells of ironing. Piled on chairs and chesterfield are stacks of jeans and blouses and nighties and underwear. On a table near the ironing board is a king-size bottle of Coke, a glass, and a bowl of potato chips. "And don't you dare say a word, Janice Harper," says Liz, popping a chip into her mouth. "I have fallen off the wagon and I don't care. If I have to spend all Friday night ironing three weeks' washing, then I'm going to have a few perks."

Her small white teeth break another chip. "Want some calories?" Smiling, Jan shakes her head as she removes her coat and lays it on top of several brassieres, each one big enough to fit three of her. "How about an alcoholic drink, as my mother would say?" Liz is giving her the once-over all right. Those shrewd eyes are studying Jan.

"No thanks, Liz," says Jan, sitting down on the chesterfield next to the brassieres. Liz sighs.

"You'll excuse the mess, I'm sure. I'm a rotten housekeeper."

"Don't worry about."

"I'm not," says Liz. "Are you sure you wouldn't like something? I'm not much of a drinker, but there's some stuff here left over from Christmas. I have a little rye. Some rum. How about a rum and Coke?"

"No, really, Liz. I'm fine thanks." In fact she feels a little drunk after that big drink in the taxi. When she looks up, she is startled to see a girl of about fifteen staring at her. A pretty girl with long, dark hair. She is knotting the belt of her housecoat and looking rumpled. Her attractive, plump face is creased with sleep.

"Hi," she says. Her voice is weak and distant. "I heard voices, Mom."

"Hi hon," says Liz. "This is Janice Harper. She teaches with me. My daughter, Jenny." The girl smiles at Liz. A pleasant-looking kid.

"Can I have some Coke, Mom?"

Liz looks up at the ceiling. "I thought I'd seen the last of you tonight. Well okay. But then back to the sack. All right? It's past twelve o'clock."

The girl goes to the kitchen for a glass while Liz sits down in a chair opposite Jan. Kicking off her thongs, she tucks her feet beneath her and sips her Coke. They both watch Jenny Barton filling her glass. She is looking at Elvis, who now holds the blonde girl in his arms, obviously intent on planting a kiss upon her lips. Liz looks over at her daughter.

"Jennifer? Please!"

"Okay, okay," says Jennifer, giving the television a final, sidelong glance before she leaves the room. Liz shakes her head.

"She'll be sixteen next month. A very difficult age. Especially for her rapidly aging mother."

The warm house and the Scotch have left Jan mildly dazed. She sits on the chesterfield sunk into herself. Sees Hicks leaning against the side of the house, his breath smoking the air. Liz has gone for the chip bowl and now returns to her chair, placing the bowl on the floor beside her.

"Are you sure you don't want any of these? They're very good. Salt and vinegar. Chuck-full of additives. Tomorrow my fingers will feel like knockwurst."

Looking over at her, Jan realizes that behind all the wisecracking, Liz Barton is fundamentally shy. It's possible she may even be troubled by this visit. After all, they don't really know one another that well. A month of working together. A few nights at exercise class. Perhaps coming here was presumptuous. The thought is depleting.

"That kid of mine," says Liz. "You know, I wonder about twenty-five times a day whether having kids is everything it's cracked up to be." She drinks more Coke. "It's just a damn good thing you didn't pop in here two hours ago. Jenny's in love. In love? My God! And I wish you could see what it is she's in love with? If you'll pardon that oddly shaped sentence! But Norman! Now Norman is something else. A born loser. You can tell at a glance. This skinny little eighteen-year-old human. A drop out with all of Grade Nine. I think he bags groceries at Super Save. But they're madly in love. I think he wants to marry her. The idea leaves me in a cold sweat. So we had it out tonight. I told her to be in by eleven, and she came in at ten in a tearing rage. It seems that Norman was upset by this eleven o'clock business and they had an argument. So in she came, and oh the tantrums and slamming of doors! It would have given you a taste of family life, you lucky maiden lady." Liz eats another chip. "I just hope to God she's not having sex with that little weasel. I told her everything about it years ago, but I won't put her on the Pill. Not at fifteen years of age. It just doesn't seem right, damn it. But if he knocks her up, I'll kill him. That's it, pure and simple. I'll just kill him. When you've got a kid Jenny's age, all you do is hang on. It's survival. You find yourself counting the months, hoping they'll avoid a major disaster, a car accident, a pregnancy. Until they reach nineteen or twenty and hopefully get some sense. And now aren't you glad you're not a mommy?"

Listening, Jan begins to understand how essentially goodhearted Liz Barton really is. She's too well-mannered to come right out and ask what's wrong. This runaround about her daughter is only a way of making me feel better. Probably their quarrel was no more than standard warfare between parent and teenager. And by telling me about it, she's inviting me to consider how lucky I am not to have these problems.

"Sometimes," says Jan, "I think I've missed out on something by not having had a family."

Liz regards her empty glass. "Well, to be truthful, it's kind of nice when they're little kids. I mean around four or five when they're out of diapers. They're a pain in the butt, no way around that. Mommy, can I have this? Mommy, can I do that? But for a few years it's nice. I mean, before Jack decided to become a beachboy, it was mostly nice. Now it's mostly not nice. And sometimes I just wonder what's ahead. I know she's going to leave in a few years, and in a way that's fine, though I know damn well I'm going to miss her. Maybe it would be different if I could see somebody walking with me down the golden road to the old folks' home. But I really don't. I'd have to lose a good fifty pounds before I can see some guy asking me to share his bed. And I just don't think I'm up to all that self-denial. The daily grind of it. I don't think so." She pauses. "My mother keeps saying, 'Now Jack will get over this phase and come back. You'll see.' As if it were that simple. She just assumes I'll take him back. But why the hell should I? The son of a bitch has been having the time of his life, and then some day the young girls are no longer interested in him and he comes back to his Elizabeth. Who needs it?"

Liz looks across at Jan and frowns. "Okay, Janice," she says. "I've practically stood on my head telling you about *my* problems, now what do I have to do? I'll ask if you like. But first let me say that you look like hell. If you don't want to talk about it, fine. We can watch TV. As a matter of fact there's a program coming on in a few minutes with one of my favourite people. Good old Hardy."

"Thomas Hardy?"

"No, Miss English Teacher. Oliver Hardy. What do you think I am? An intellectual?" Jan has to laugh. It sounds cracked and dry.

"Or," Liz continues, "you can watch me iron the rest of these clothes. That's very exciting. Or, I can fix you up in the spare bedroom. Economy rates but no breakfast. We're out of everything, even bread. Tomorrow's shopping day. There might be a can of soup."

"Oh Liz, I'm sorry," Jan says. "Coming in on you like this without any explanation. It's just that I've had this strange night."

"I figured."

"You probably wouldn't believe me if I told you."

"Try me."

Jan lights a cigarette. "Well, this friend . . . let's just say a former friend . . . came calling tonight. He was drunk. And very violent. He smashed the window in my door and swore at the neighbours. I was hiding in my car. I know it sounds crazy."

"No, no, not at all. In fact, it sounds absolutely fascinating. You've got me hooked already." She shakes her head wonderingly. "Another man in your life? You really are something, Janice Harper. First, you point out this great-looking guy in the Malibu the other night. Now you mention a guy trying to get at you in your apartment. You seem to lead a very interesting life. And I have to confess that you've certainly fooled me. Frankly, I thought you were the quiet, bookish type. Living at home. Driving Mother to church on Sunday morning. Your very own hymn book!"

Jan smiles. "But I really am like that most of the time. Not the church business, but quiet and, I suppose, bookish."

"Except when drunken men come breaking down your door in the middle of the night. Right?" Liz stoops to finish the last of the chips. "Look, Janice. I know I sound foolish and unsympathetic. But I don't mean to be. It's just my way. You have to get used to me. How about some coffee?"

"I'd love it."

"Okay," Liz pushes herself out of the chair and pads barefoot across the rug. The heaviness of her footsteps makes small china objects tremble.

"I've only got instant," she calls from the kitchen. "I'm too lazy to make the real stuff, and anyway Jenny doesn't like it. Can you believe that?"

She talks across a divider that separates the kitchen from the dining room. Jan has to look around a corner to see her.

"So tell me about this character who breaks windows in your door. Who is he anyway? What's he look like? How did you meet him? I want details, woman, the more sordid the better. And turn off that goddam TV, will you?"

Smiling, Janice gets up and turns off the TV. Suddenly it feels good to be here talking to Liz Barton. Telling her the story. Jan wonders if she can tell it right. It's a matter really of convincing someone that the things that happen to you are seldom what you expect. Or something like that.

4

Hicks can't remember being this cold. The weather has entered his bones and remains locked within him. He feels like one of those statues you come upon in a deserted parking lot on a winter day. Looking out the car window at the empty streets, he wonders if being this cold is like being dead. You feel nothing. Not even his shattered hand, which lies in his lap like something apart from him. A pale, wounded thing. The jagged line of black, crusted blood runs over his knuckles. Last night it pulsed with pain. Hurt like hell. Now he makes a fist and watches the dark crust open and the fresh blood ooze forth.

Down the street behind a row of apartment buildings the sun is rising. The sky is lighting up with pale fire. Hicks tries to remember how long he's been here. It was still dark when he stopped driving around the block and parked here. But trying to fit together parts of last night seems an impossible task. He spent many hours in the Puss 'n' Boots Club; he knows that. Vicky Pruit was there. They drank together and she wanted him to go back to her place. She was wearing jeans and a satin cowboy shirt. Black and white. She kept going on about this movie, *Coal Miner's Daughter*, and what a great picture it was. Had to do with the life story of Loretta Lynn. Vicky had seen it a half-dozen times. She was crazy about it, and Hicks grew tired of listening to her talk about this movie. But that was in the afternoon!

When he left the Puss 'n' Boots it was nearly dark, and he stopped in at The Frying Pan for a bite. Yes. He stayed there for a long time. Had several drinks with his meal. He vaguely remembers leaving the waitress a ridiculous tip. It was perhaps a ten-dollar bill. Maybe even a twenty. She was a friendly, plain girl with acne, and Hicks felt sorry for her. Saw her as the kind of girl who would never get laid by anyone interesting. Then he phoned Janice and went to her place. Smashed his fucking hand on her door. What a stupid thing to do! Somebody was going to call the cops, so he got out of there. He remembers going back to the Puss 'n' Boots, but they wouldn't serve him. That's it. Another part of the evening falls into place, and Hicks is filled with shame. They made a big fucking deal of it. That new nigger bouncer put the arm on him and hustled him past the tables. Embarrassing. On the stairs Hicks stumbled, and the nigger was twisting his arm, hurt hand and all. Black bastard!

After that, it is all terrifyingly vague. He must have driven around for hours. And drunk like that! Crazy! Then he came here and went to sleep sitting up. He watches an empty bus go down the street. The rising sun now emerges between two apartment buildings and everything is bathed in its light. The morning assumes an elusive radiance. Across the street the windows in the cop station blaze with this enriching light. In the parking lot three yellow patrol cars seem briefly afire. Very nice, thinks Hicks. Early morning is very nice. Six-thirty is an innocent hour. The night's troubles are over and most people haven't yet got out of bed to fuck up things.

Hicks thinks of John Hepworth lying under the snow. In cold weather like this he wouldn't go bad so fast. Probably look the same until the spring. Hicks tries to picture the man in his tomb. Eyes closed. Wearing a dark suit, with the big hands folded across his chest. Hicks dimly remembers his father lying in a coffin like that. Now he sees Hepworth's great, pale head. Like a giant mushroom in the dark. Not feeling the cold or anything. Nothing!

Outside the air smells fresh. No gunk in it yet. When Hicks was a kid, he enjoyed this time of the day. On a Saturday, while his mother and Fern slept, he would take his sleigh to a school on the next street. There was a little hill in the schoolyard, and there he would ride his sleigh. He remembers the air smelling just like this. Dale likes to get up early on Saturday mornings too. Only he doesn't go sleigh-riding or things like that. If there isn't a hockey game, he sits in front of the television watching cartoons. Even on a beautiful day like this he will sit in front of that fucking television and watch cartoons. Hicks figures his son is probably doing that at this very moment.

As he walks across the street, Hicks sees the brilliant colours vanish into ordinary daylight. The sun is high enough now that the windows in the cop station are just windows again. The patrol cars are the same sickly yellow. When he opens the heavy glass door, the heat of the building strikes him like a blow. This modern, neutral space looks deserted except for the two cops who are seated behind a long counter. They are in shirtsleeves and are drinking coffee from plastic cups. One is big and bald and middle-aged. The other one is young, with short black hair and a moustache. The police radio is turned low. A background squawk. Both cops watch as Hicks approaches the counter. The big one gets out of his chair and hikes up his belt. He frowns at the man in jeans and windbreaker with the busted hand.

"What's your problem?" He is staring at Hicks's hand. Hicks speaks slowly. He wants to get it right.

"I killed this guy," he says. "It happened weeks ago. Back before Christmas. I ran over him."

The young cop now looks up from his newspaper and stares at Hicks. But Hicks ignores him. He is trapped instead by the steady, bitter gaze of the older man, who now says, "You want some coffee, fellah?"

Four

I

"I think," Miss Harper," says Dr. Han, "that it might be a good idea if you were to go off the Pill for a while." Her mild, pleasant voice comes from below this ridiculous paper "gown." If I raise my head just a bit, I can see her dark little head. Her black hair is now streaked with grey and pulled severely back into a bun. What a taut and precise little creature she is! Like some impossibly perfect machine. Functional and efficient. And that metal contraption she has just inserted feels like an ice cube. You would think in this day and age that they could come up with something made of plastic. Everything else is. As she prods me she says, "To give your body a rest. Let it return to its natural cycle. Of course, it's entirely up to you."

Now Jan feels the swab being inserted. And is it possible, I wonder, to be in a more ridiculous position? I suppose there may be some freakish types who enjoy this kind of thing. Flat on your back with your feet in these stirrups! Jan looks at her legs and knees. Those legs still look pretty good, Harper. And my whole front end open to the little doctor's intelligent black eyes. But then it's only once a year. Besides, there's nothing particularly special about your privates, Harper. The doctor has seen tens of thousands of front ends and back ends in her time. Below her, Dr. Han says, "I can fit you with a loop. Or I can recommend other methods. Not today of course. You'd have to make another appointment. Now nice and still, please."

Lying there, Janice remembers her first internal examination. She was fifteen, but still no period. All her friends were menstruating by then. Mildly worried, her mother took her along to old Dr. Thomas, the family physician for over twenty years. He'd taken out Jan's tonsils, treated her for mumps, and fixed up a mysterious rash of warts that had appeared the summer she was ten or eleven. But this was different. There she was in his office, which was over a store on Danforth Avenue. She could hear the streetcars go clanging by and devoutly wished she was on one. While her mother thumbed through old copies of *Life* and the *Saturday Evening Post* in the dark, somber waiting-room, Jan lay naked under a cotton gown, holding her breath, while the old doctor's large, hairy hands prodded her rib-cage and felt her breasts. Not that there was much to feel: two little rose-tipped buds growing at a maddeningly slow pace on her bony chest. Still, a man was feeling her breasts. A slow, heavy old man. And then he put his hand inside her and felt around. Incredible!

Afterwards, while dressing, Jan caught a glimpse of her flaming face in a mirror. Listened as the doctor explained to Jan's mother that everything was perfectly normal. Janice was just reaching puberty a little later than most young ladies. In those days doctors called pubescent girls young ladies and pimply youths young men. So there was nothing to worry about. She would probably start getting cramps within the next few months. And the old geezer was right. Two months later she was buying Midol and sanitary napkins. But those large male hands on my body! It took me a while to get used to the idea. But at least old Dr. Thomas had cotton gowns for his patients. Not these goddam paper things that rasp your skin and stick to your bottom. I suppose the idea is you can throw them out. No laundry bills. Makes economic sense. Efficiency always makes economic sense. Even while making life in general more unbearable.

"You can get dressed now, Miss Harper," says Dr. Han, coating a piece of glass with the smear and carefully encasing it. A little piece of me off to the laboratory and please, dear God, let there be no problem.

"Take your time dressing," says Dr. Han. "I'll be back shortly."

Jan sits up and swings her legs over the side of the examining table. Stares at her long, pale feet. Against the window a slashing rain is driven headlong by a bitter east wind. A miserable Monday in March. What a lousy day to be sent to prison. Is there such a thing as a *good day* to be sent to prison, Harper? As she starts to dress, she thinks of Hicks in the courtroom this morning. That hooded, obscure look of his. He seemed thinner than she remembered him, too. Now and then he looked around the courtroom. But like Meursault in *L'Étranger*, he seemed like a stranger at his own trial. Uninterested in what was taking place, his eyes passing over the people who had come to see him condemned for his crimes. An old couple, who sat in the back and left quietly after the sentence was pronounced. The dead man's parents? A handsome woman, maybe fifty, in a pantsuit. Clearly James's mother. Beside her, a dark, heavy man in a polyester suit with black hair combed straight back. He looked to have Indian blood in him. And a pretty blonde woman sat next to James's mother and whispered things from time to time. She looked indignant and upset. Prepared to quarrel with the authorities if given half a chance. James's wife? And sitting apart from them, alone, was another woman. A dark-haired woman, good-looking in a tough, flashy way. And me, of course. All these women in James's life! Now he goes to live among men.

It's perhaps not so unusual for a law-abiding woman of thirty-six, but I had never set foot in a courtroom before this morning. And there I sat listening to James's court-appointed lawyer doing his best. Typical of James to refuse any assistance and allow himself to be defended by this overweight young man in a blue pin-stripe suit, who is obviously just beginning his career. He was easily outclassed by the Crown Attorney, a grey-haired gent with a long, foxy face. He'd been around, and he wasn't having any truck with the young lawyer's appeals to the bench for mercy. The fat young lawyer kept talking about the accused's remorse and how it should be a mitigating factor in sentencing. It seemed to be the only thing he could get a hook into. *Remorse*. One of those words you see in books all the time but seldom hear spoken. There are many words like that. Recalcitrant, for instance. Or egregious. Who has ever heard anyone use the word egregious in serious conversation? But there was the fat young lawyer in his blue suit going on about *remorse*. He must have used the word two dozen times. The accused had given himself up. The accused was willing to accept the consequences of his actions. The accused was showing *remorse*, and would the court be mindful of this when passing sentence?

The elderly Crown Attorney arose and took this word *remorse*, transformed it into an adjective, and shook it to death like a cat with a mouse. Turning the word to useful ironic purpose, he clearly impressed the magistrate. *Remorseful* or not, the accused had killed an innocent man while driving at an excessive rate of speed in the act of fleeing from an armed robbery in which he was a participant. Furthermore, *remorseful* or not, the accused had taken more than five weeks to confess his responsibility for these serious crimes. Moreover, *remorseful* or not, he had stubbornly refused to reveal the identity of his accomplices, who at this very moment were at liberty, no doubt "living the life of Riley on their ill-gotten gains." The old guy had a way with homely language.

In the end the magistrate sentenced James to eight years, and the prisoner left the courtroom without looking at anyone. In the corridor, Jan overheard the fat young lawyer as he talked to the family.

"Eight isn't bad. Don't worry about it. If he watches himself, he'll be out in two and a half. At the most three." He looked to be in a hurry as he stood there buttoning his raincoat. Beside him, James's wife looked pale with anger but said nothing. They all watched the lawyer run down the steps and into the rain.

Now Jan brushes her hair with short, furious strokes. So he wanted to pay for his sins. Okay! But he could have had someone better than that fat puppy to represent him. James! James! Now probably handcuffed to some policeman and travelling through the grey rain to a life behind walls. Looking in the mirror, Jan sighs at her long, plain face. She remembers him throwing the ring out the car window on New Year's Eve. Paid for with the loot, no doubt. And out the window! How can you deal with a person who does something like that? She puts the brush in her handbag and looks at her watch. Two-thirty. She could go back to school and collect some junk to mark. But to hell with it. She told Murray she'd be gone all day.

Now Dr. Han hurries into the room. She wears little half-moon glasses for reading. They hang by a chain across her small, neat bosom. When she puts them on, she means business. So now she consults Jan's folder.

"Well, you seem to be in good health, Miss Harper. It would be better of course if you'd stop smoking, but that is your decision. Otherwise, everything looks normal. We'll send the Pap test over to the lab today. If you don't hear from me by Thursday, you can assume that everything is fine."

They stand by the door. Jan looms over the doctor, who sticks out her hand. A fine, strong little instrument of a hand.

"So I'll say goodbye and see you next year." She pauses to take off her glasses. "Unless, of course, as I said before, you would like to consider an alternative method of birth prevention. You can think about it and, if you wish, make an appointment. I'm sure we can find something comfortable for you."

"Thank you. Goodbye, Dr. Han."

"Have a nice day, Miss Harper."

2

For the past week she was awakened at daybreak. Just as the birds are getting their act together. Lying there, she can hear a cardinal pumping away. The cheerful robins of course. And the crows making a racket in the pine tree behind the Bonners' house. Once or twice she has got up and stood by the window to watch these big black fellows wheel in a grey sky above the pine tree. The window is held open by an old shampoo bottle. Standing by it, she gets a whiff of earth smells and feels exalted. Caught up in a brief, goofy affection for life. Returning to bed, she tries to remember dreams in which Hicks holds her in his arms and frowns at her in that way of his.

These early morning awakenings leave her tired and light-headed by the middle of the afternoon. So she has taken to eating a banana before the last class. Bananas are supposed to replenish your blood sugar and ward off fatigue. So they say!

And what was that old song her father used to sing? You heard him now and then in the bathtub. "Yes, We Have No Bananas." That was it! She thinks about this as she drives to school looking out at the small grey lawns in front of the bungalows. In another couple of weeks the grass will be green and the maples and poplars will break into leaf. Already the willows are palely touched with yellow. This morning the sunlight felt strong on her face when she stood for a moment by the side of the house.

Driving north on Crown Hall Road, she tries to remember if she's forgotten anything about the shower. It's been settled that Gordon will take Mother to Crock & Block and have her back by eight. Gordon is enjoying himself these days. Tickled half to death by all these female goings-on. How he loves the company of women! Knows they admire his dandified ways. He'll shine tonight surrounded by all those old dames from the Friday Nite Club. And thank God for Marjorie, who will bring over the sandwiches while Mother and Gordon are having dinner. Marjorie will be at those sandwiches all day, and a very good thing, too, because I'm not proficient at that line of work. Cutting bread into little stars and trimming crusts. Impaling olives and Red Rose pickles on fancy toothpicks. Making twenty-nine incisions in a radish, so that arranged on a plate it looks like—what? A radish that has been put to the paring knife twenty-nine times. Such tasks require the patience of an ox. Which, luckily, Marjorie has. My own little mother getting married in two weeks and flying off to England on her honeymoon! My mother on her honeymoon! Ye gods, I'm going to have to get used to that idea.

As she turns west on Graymore, she looks out at the students walking through the spring sunlight to school. In a few weeks another school year will be gone, and my word, don't they just fly by! Especially after you're thirty! As Max says, "None of us is getting any younger, Slim. So enjoy! Enjoy!" Marvellous Max, who thrilled Jan on the phone the other night with the news that she was returning to Toronto. She was wildly excited by the idea. "I got this terrific promotion, so I'm coming back to Hogtown, kid. Move over and make room for Ross. Listen, there must be some snooty exercise club we can belong to. Where we can fire the old basketball around again. Wait till they see us in action!" She sounded so happy. And not a word about her little friend, so that must be over. Max was strictly gung-ho all the way. "And I'm going to make your mother's shower on Friday, too. I'll get an afternoon flight, and don't bother coming out to the airport. I'll take the limousine. What the hell!" It will be great to see her, and I hope she and Liz get on. I think they will; they're both funny, and they should get a kick out of all those old trouts tonight. About poor Ruthie I'm not so sure. But she did sound glad to be invited. Seth is having his thesis examined next week. At last! But the "anxiety level" in the Calder household is high these days. Well, Ruth will have to find someone else to bore with the details because I intend to enjoy myself tonight. Max will insist on spiking our coffee with what she calls "brown-paper goods." Most likely J&B.

When Jan turns into the school parking lot she can see Bruce Horton. He is standing with four or five students beside his 1931 Ford roadster. It must be spring if Bruce brings one of his beloved antiques out for a spin. Standing there in his corduroy jacket with the leather elbow patches and explaining something about the car, which is obviously a source of astonishment to the students. And no wonder! The model A looks like something from a storybook. It speaks of simpler times. Not better maybe, but simpler. In the sunlight its polished blue surface and yellow wire wheels fairly sparkle. As folks used to say, it's as cute as a bug's ear. Two summers ago Bruce took me for a drive in the little thing. I remember the hard seats and the thin clatter of the engine. As Jan passes, Bruce looks up and lifts a friendly hand.

In her parking space, Jan watches John Trimble make his way along the front walk with the aid of a cane. There's a pin holding something together in one of his legs. The story has it that it's there for the rest of his life. Watching poor John hobble along makes me realize how much I miss Liz around the school. She's now teaching in North York, where there's no one to share the jokes.

"No bezzazz. Everyone seems wiped out." Liz has lost weight and looks terrific. "And I ain't quitting now. You're the one who inspired me, you skinny bitch. Just wait till you see me this summer in a bikini."

On Sunday she's going to help me look at apartments. Maybe Max would like to come along too. Nothing would get by shrewd old Max. It's possible she will suggest we move in together, but I'm sure it wouldn't work. We both have our own lives to get on with. Besides, she couldn't stand it out here in the sticks. She'll go for a place downtown. Still, she can help me choose furniture. I want things to be jazzy. A little smart. Built-in bookshelves. No more pine boards and bricks. A new sofa. Some framed prints.

When she told her mother she was moving out on her own, Mrs. Harper looked vacant and dithery for a few moments. Beside her, Gordon stroked his smooth cheeks and rocked on his heels. He might have been inspecting a bogus ticket someone was trying to fob off on him. But in no time at all they got used to the idea and even, I suspect, find it an attractive one.

"If you think it's best, dear," as Mother said. And I do, I do. Now there's talk of selling the house and finding a large, comfortable apartment that's "handy to shopping." And for the winter months, a condominium in Florida is not out of the question. As Gordon put it, with a wink and a nod of his perfectly shaped little head, "We're not going to let the grass grow under our feet, are we, Lil?"

When Jan gets out of the car she sees Laura Keyes hurrying toward her. A plain, pale girl with an armful of books. Does she really study all those books or just cart them home for the sake of appearance? An uncharitable thought, Harper, but the poor kid just hasn't got it. Certainly she's failing English, and from what I hear most everything else. Under the long, pale lashes her eyes look worried. She offers Jan a thin smile. The sad, thin smile of the supplicant. "Good morning, Miss Harper. Have you marked the tests on *The Old Man and the Sea*?" Such an unhealthy-looking girl! She always looks so washed out. What does she live on, I wonder? White bread and rice pudding? Near Laura's temple a long blue vein throbs.

"Well, not yet, Laura. After all, you only wrote it yesterday last period. I'll try to get to them over the weekend." Fat chance of that. The girl nods.

"I really need a good mark on that test, Miss Harper. And I really studied for it. I think I should do really well."

Listening, Jan smiles. Every day and forever! These hopeless expectations that soon enough are crushed underfoot by brute reality. How right her father was! Life *is* a damn strange trip. But beside her Laura Keyes looks outraged. Angry enough for tears. "Well, I don't see what's so funny about it, Miss Harper. I really did study." She shifts her books about angrily while Jan puts her arm around the girl's shoulder.

"Oh Laura. I wasn't thinking of that. I was thinking of

something my poor father said shortly before he died. He said that he found life a damn strange trip." The girl looks at Jan. Casts a puzzled and suspicious eye on her teacher.

"Huh," says Laura Keyes.

RICHARD B. WRIGHT is the author of nine acclaimed novels, including *Clara Callan*, which won the Giller Prize, the Governor General's Award and the Trillium Book Award, *The Weekend Man*, and *The Age of Longing*, which was nominated for both the Giller Prize and the Governor General's Award. His work has been published in Canada, the US, and the UK to outstanding reviews. Richard B. Wright lives in St. Catharines, Ontario, with his wife, Phyllis.